QUIET WAR

ERIC SWAN THRILLER #5

DOM TESTA

Quiet War: Eric Swan thriller #5

By Dom Testa

This is a work of fiction, and a strange one at that. All organizations, events, and characters portrayed in this work are products of the author's imagination. Any similarity or resemblance to any person, living or dead — or reinvested — is not only purely coincidental, but downright remarkable.

Published by Profound Impact Group, LLC

PO Box 506

Alpharetta, GA 30009

Reach us at EricSwan.com

ISBN: 978-1-942151-58-6

Cover art by Damonza

More Eric Swan
from Dom Testa

Power Trip: Eric Swan Thriller #1

Swan takes on diabolical twins determined to bring down the power grid. If he fails, the country will slip into a dark age of chaos and anarchy.

Poison Control: Eric Swan Thriller #2

A treacherous madman is intent on poisoning the water supply. Swan must outsmart this rogue scholar before he can release his apocalyptic toxin.

God Maker: Eric Swan Thriller #3

Agent One has resurfaced, and he's kidnapped the mother of Q2's investment technology. Swan must not only battle this psychotic killer, but come to grips with his own fears.

Field Agent: Eric Swan Thriller #4

Swan's on the hunt for a tech billionaire who's out to control the world's food supply. But there's a sinister element to the plan with terrifying consequences.

Join the Swaniverse.
Get cool stuff.

With each new tale you'll learn a little more about Q2's super spy, Eric Swan.

You might also want to know how it all began. Join the Swaniverse and I'll send you Swan's ***Origin*** story as a thank you.

Plus, you'll be the first to learn of each new adventure *before* they're published. Just let me know where to find you.

Two ways to make it happen. Scan this QR code with your phone's camera and it'll take you to the Swaniverse page to sign up.

Or log on to EricSwan.com.

Thanks, and happy reading.
Dom Testa

CONTENTS

Chapter 1	1
Chapter 2	11
Chapter 3	19
Chapter 4	33
Chapter 5	43
Chapter 6	53
Chapter 7	65
Chapter 8	75
Chapter 9	85
Chapter 10	95
Chapter 11	107
Chapter 12	119
Chapter 13	129
Chapter 14	137
Chapter 15	147
Chapter 16	157
Chapter 17	169
Chapter 18	181
Chapter 19	189
Chapter 20	199
Chapter 21	209
Chapter 22	217
Chapter 23	225
Chapter 24	235
Chapter 25	245
Chapter 26	257
Chapter 27	273
Chapter 28	283
Chapter 29	291
Chapter 30	301

Chapter 31 311
Chapter 32 319

More Eric Swan adventures from Dom Testa 333

CHAPTER ONE

Compile a list of the most embarrassing things you can do in public, and vomiting in front of total strangers would earn a top-three ranking. Onlookers stare in shocked horror before averting their gaze, but then look back, torn between feelings of empathy and total revulsion. Nobody wants to be overly judgmental, though, because chances are they've either done it themselves, or they know at some point they will. If you've gone to college, I'm willing to bet you've done it more than once.

So far on the boat I'd tossed up my stomach's contents twice, both times in front of witnesses. I say *the boat*—it was actually a ship, one of those ridiculously long, strangely tall cruise vessels that convey thousands of excitable tourists from one island to another while plying them with food and booze and too much sun.

What made my nausea perplexing was the fact I'd never in my lives been seasick. That included multiple deployments with my special ops teams where they packed us into small water craft and bounced us across violent seas. Never so much as a tummy rumble. Until now.

The only viable explanation was that my latest body was a weenie when it came to water. I'd inhabited many of them through the years, and this one apparently had no stomach for the sailing life. Normally I wouldn't care—or wouldn't even know before it was time to invest into another donor body. This time, however, it was damned inconvenient.

My assignment began in Charleston, and from there took me south to Savannah for a day before a fresh tip brought me to Miami. One bad guy was down and out after I encountered him behind a Cuban restaurant. But two others, unaware of their associate's demise, had boarded the cruise ship for a rendezvous with some big-shot benefactor. My intel said this meeting would arrange the funding that ultimately would lead to a string of bombings in state capitol buildings.

Well, we can't have that.

The dead man behind the restaurant had killed one police officer and wounded two others during this rowdy ring's last operation. I'd stared down the barrel of his Sig 9mm and should've been his next victim. Until a bit of luck arrived in the form of a feral cat jumping out of a dumpster at just the right moment.

The killer didn't get a second chance.

Now, leaning over the cruise ship railing, astounded that anything else could be retched up, I almost wished the dumpster decoy had never happened. At this moment, death seemed preferable.

"Mr. Swan?"

The young woman from guest relations, smartly attired in her crisp cruise-line costume, stood beside me, one hand behind her back in what must've been her professional service position. The other hand held a small plastic cup containing two pills.

"Hi," I said, straightening up. "These will keep me from turning my stomach inside out?"

She gave a well-rehearsed smile. "You're not alone, I promise. We treat seasickness every day. Take one of these now and the other in four hours, and you should feel much better. You'll even be hungry for dinner tonight."

"Oh, god," I said, taking the cup from her. "Please, no mention of food."

She laughed. "It's good that you're out here getting some air. I'd also recommend drinking water. That may not sound appetizing now, but it often helps. And if you need anything else, please don't hesitate to call or come see us. We want you to enjoy the voyage."

As soon as she turned her back and marched away, I swallowed both pills. I might not be alive in four hours if things went sour with the deadly duo I'd been chasing.

It was almost five o'clock. I figured the meet-up would take place after dark.

The fact we were even on this ship was ludicrous. I would've been more than happy to slip down the corridor, tap on their respective cabin doors, and pop them without delay. The sneaky bastards in our Sanitation department could then swoop in and take care of cleaning up the scene. That's why they got paid.

But the identity of the bad guys' nefarious patron was of great value to the brain trust at Q2. I had to let the parties meet in order to make the ID.

It would be helpful if I didn't puke my way through it all.

I inhaled a few more lungfuls of salty sea air before heading back to my cabin, where I placed a call to Poole at Q2 headquarters.

"What's your status?" she asked.

"My status is that I'm trapped in a body unable to handle so much as a minor swell on the ocean surface without barfing. I'll bet this guy got queasy in a hot tub. But I've confirmed the two targets are aboard. I expect they'll connect with the money source when the sun goes down."

"If you're seasick, the ship's doctor can—"

"Yes, I know, and I have. Waiting for the pills to kick in."

"Okay," she said. "In the meantime, I'd recommend a progressive relaxation meditation session."

"A what?"

"It reduces tension, which relaxes the muscles constricting your midsection and makes you more comfortable. I use it to produce a gentle wave throughout my system before I go to bed."

"Don't say wave."

"Oh. Right."

I opened my balcony door, which brought a welcome return of the fresh air.

"I'm sure it's going down tonight," I said. "Have Sanitation standing by."

"They're two decks below you and ready."

We ended the call.

A HALF-MOON SPECKLED the surface of the sea. When full, I'm sure the glow produced an intoxicating backdrop, the kind that drives people to say things they regret in the harsh glare of a hungover day. Cruise lines sell this romantic image, safe in the knowledge that a third of the passengers will mean every word. Another third will wonder what got into them, while the remaining crowd was only there for the buffet and had no inkling of the shenanigans going on out there on the decks.

My stomach had agreed to a temporary truce, but I walked the upper promenade knowing damn well things could flare again without warning. The vomiting had stopped, but the cautionary sounds coming from my stomach inspired no confidence. The slow, methodical rise and fall of the ship on the sea didn't bode well, either.

Suspect One, a man named Fuller, stood a hundred feet from me, chatting up a woman who had to be twice his age. Both, however, seemed genuinely interested in the other. *Pretty ballsy of Fuller*, I thought. Hitting on another passenger during a high-dollar criminal transaction spoke to either a surplus of nerve or a shortage of brains. From the goofy smile he wore, I would've placed my bet on the latter.

He must've said the right thing, because the woman gave a hearty laugh, placing one hand on his arm and leaning in. It appeared Mr. Fuller was confident he could score twice in one night, assuming the financial meeting was still on.

If it wasn't, I was going to be one pissed off agent.

I checked my phone. Just after nine o'clock. It was possible this guy might try to conclude his personal business first, which astounded me. Then again, if the meeting with moneybags wasn't until eleven or twelve, where was the harm? He looked like the kind of guy who wouldn't need more than a few minutes, anyway.

A figure approached them from the far side of the deck, and I did my best to blend into the shadows. Could this be the man I was looking for, the one bankrolling the bombing operation?

No. It was Fuller's partner, the other suspect I'd followed onto the ship. Costillo. A little older, more experienced. His stroll was casual enough, but I sensed he was on edge. Anger that his buddy was on the prowl while they were on the clock?

Fuller noticed him and moved a step back from the woman. When Costillo got close, an awkward introduction took place. I almost wanted to laugh, and I definitely wished I had audio on the exchange. At any moment, I expected Costillo to take Fuller by the arm and lead him away from his date.

But the three of them continued to talk, and now Costillo seemed interested, too. *Holy shit*, I thought. Was I witnessing the larval stage of a threesome? Who *were* these guys? Maybe the horniest desperadoes I'd ever encountered.

I studied the woman. She was late 50s or early 60s, average height, and trim. She was dressed well, with her hair nicely done up for an evening on the make. I didn't know if she was the kind to take on two guys at once, but who the hell could tell? Would this new attention spook her, or would she go for it?

Any question evaporated when I watched her take both of them by an arm and guide them toward the back of the ship. With dinner still being served, there weren't many people around and it was difficult for me to keep out of sight and maintain contact. And, to be honest, I felt a little creepy. Voyeurism in the line of duty I could handle, but at the moment, I wasn't sure my stomach could manage this particular scene. I kept to the shadows and crept along behind them.

Once they were alone near the stern, the woman stopped and smiled. She said something to Fuller, who, after glancing around, pulled out a pistol with a silencer and fired a shot into the forehead of Costillo. He tipped over the railing and disappeared.

Ten thousand thoughts raced through my mind, all in the span of a few seconds. The first was purely reactionary: *Damn, Fuller apparently is not one to share.*

But the truth materialized just as quickly.

The bankroll, the source of funds, the moneyman . . . was not a *man*. I was looking at her.

Her happy chat with Fuller had nothing to do with a roll in the waves. Well, I mean, I supposed they could seal the deal later however they liked. But now her money-lending conditions had changed, and she preferred to worry about only one potential leak. Fuller, it would appear, was happy to oblige.

They chatted for another few moments, nonchalant. The fact that Costillo had swiftly disembarked didn't fluster them one bit.

After the surprise wore off, it was all I could do to keep from laughing. I hadn't wanted to take this case, preferring instead to stay home with a wife nearing the end of her pregnancy. But now I had to admit, it had turned into one of my more entertaining assignments, puking aside.

I eased back a little farther until I could turn and head toward the nearest stairwell. Fuller I could deal with later; he wasn't going anywhere, unless someone dumped his body overboard, too. The next order of business was trailing his new partner and discovering either her name, or at least the name she traveled under. After that, it would be up to Quanta, the head of Q2, to determine the next step.

They were four minutes behind me, descending the stairwell separately, as complete strangers. I watched through a crack in the curtain of a photo booth, sitting comfortably, willing my guts to behave. Fuller exited the stairwell, walked past me in the booth, and made his way toward the lounge. The woman kept going down the stairs, heading for a lower deck, likely her stateroom.

I followed her to the next level, drifting along behind her at a safe distance, pretending to scroll through my phone. The thick, gaudy carpet deadened my steps and she never once looked back. When she stopped and used a key card to enter a room, I slowed and used my peripheral vision to catch the room number.

Almost too easy.

Back in my cabin, I sat on the arm of a small sofa and called the ship's clinic. My stomach felt like shit again, and they promised someone would drop off another round of pills in just a few minutes.

After that I reached Poole, who, naturally, was working late. I gave her the number of the woman's stateroom so she could get to work on identification. Knowing Poole, it would take less than two minutes.

When I told her about the unfortunate outcome for Costillo, she paused before saying: "That shouldn't have happened."

"Well, yeah," I said, "especially from Costillo's point of view."

"No. I mean nothing about this arrangement predicted that move. Not with everything that we learned in Charleston."

I kicked off my shoes and stretched out on the sofa. "I can't worry about that right now. My stomach wants to sabotage this entire mission. Until I get a new body, this is my last voyage, Cap'n."

"Okay. Well, something gives me a bad feeling. You be careful."

"Poole, I'm going to take my pills, try to sleep, then dispatch Mr. Fuller at dawn before we get to port. By then you guys will have a plan in place for Ms. Moneybags."

Someone knocked on my door.

"In fact, my pills are here. I'll talk to you in the morning. Let Sanitation know."

I hung up, tossed my phone onto the sofa, and answered the door.

It was not a perky crew member.

It was Fuller. And the same gun he'd used on Costillo was now aimed right at my belly.

He used it to indicate I should back up into the room. When I did, he stepped inside and shut the door behind him.

After glancing between the gun and his eyes, I said, "If this is about me not leaving a gratuity at lunch, I swear I thought those were included."

"Let's start with your name," he said.

"Finch. Atticus Finch."

His eyes narrowed as he chewed on that. It must've sounded familiar, but the sap obviously couldn't place it. And honestly, that kinda pissed me off.

"What are you doing on this ship?" he asked. "And why are you following the lady?"

So he was an idiot, but not a *complete* idiot. He'd turned the tables on me and I'd either been too nauseated to notice, or too full of myself after a spy session that had been too easy. Much too easy, it now appeared.

"All right," I said. "If you must know, that lady is my mother."

"Your what?"

"You heard me. She's my mother. Dad's fed up with her gallivanting around on these solo vacations, and he asked me to watch and see if she's bringing anybody back to her cabin."

"Bullshit."

"That's what I told Dad. We all know Mom was a bit of a tramp in college, but that was a long time ago and, frankly, who wasn't? It's crazy talk."

He stood three feet in front of me, unsure of what to do next. My story *did* sound like total bullshit. But could Fuller take a chance on killing his benefactor's son? It was hilarious watching him work through the permutations, and it took all I had to keep a straight face.

All the while, as the ship plowed through the swells, my stomach lurched a little more, then a little more. It's bad enough having someone point a gun at you, but trying to remain cocky while simultaneously holding back vomit is the real trick. I considered it some of my finest work.

He squinted again, but had landed on a solution. "Let's go see *Mom*."

At that moment, a hard rap sounded on the door.

Out of reflex, Fuller glanced around, which was all I needed. It began with a kick to his gun hand, followed by a hard punch to his larynx. The heel to his jaw completed the unholy trinity. I caught him as he fell, lowered him onto the sofa, and added another vicious blow to make sure he was out. Perhaps that was overkill, but the asshole had threatened me with a gun.

Another spasm of nausea rushed over me, and before I could do anything about it, I puked all over the unconscious Mr. Fuller. God, I didn't envy the folks in Sanitation tonight.

From the corridor came another knock.

I grabbed a handful of tissues from the end table, dabbed my mouth, and opened the door. It was the same young woman from guest relations. She gave me a sympathetic smile as she handed over the new plastic cup of pills.

"Mr. Swan, I'm so sorry to hear you're still not feeling well. Is there anything else we can do to help?"

I offered an embarrassed smile.

"No, ma'am. But thank you very much." I held up the cup and shook it. "These are real lifesavers."

CHAPTER TWO

Corporate America is big on employee evaluations. Some companies call it a performance review. My wife said her first boss referred to them as an "opportunity check." But we all know the basic drill: A supervisor grades the employee's performance, makes an assessment of strengths and weaknesses, and then lays out expectations for the coming year.

My opportunity checks took place about once a month and consisted of my boss beating the hell out of me.

I fought back, of course, but no matter how long I trained or how much I learned, Quanta was—and always would be—vastly superior in the martial arts. In the office she might come across as soft-spoken, but the woman's genome was riddled with ass-kicking DNA. We held these workouts at her home in a suburb of Washington, DC, usually in the sprawling garden where at least the ground was soft enough to cushion my inevitable falls.

On this day I'd surprised her—and myself—with a couple of lucky strikes, the kind that gave me confidence. Just enough confidence, in fact, to leave myself open for a retaliatory blow that bloodied my lip and deposited me on my backside. When blood was drawn, it generally meant fun time was over. Without a word, Quanta stepped around me and went back into her house. After blinking up at the clouds a few times, I staggered to my feet and followed.

She'd left the usual ice pack for me on the kitchen counter and was off to meditate for ten minutes. I sat at the round table in her nook, nursing my wound and scrolling through sports scores. Apparently I'd missed some important games during the cruise ship assignment.

By the time Quanta returned, I'd transitioned from sports to celebrity gossip. My kryptonite.

She brought two glasses of water to the table and sat down.

"Before we talk business, how's Christina?"

Personal questions from the head of Q2 were rare and always caught me off guard. The fact that I'd violated company protocol by getting married in the first place used to put me in a defensive frame of mind. But over time, I'd realized that Quanta had genuine affection for Christina.

"She's good. Getting ready to evict her little tenant."

Quanta raised an eyebrow. "You refer to the unborn child as a *tenant*?"

"Well, yeah. The kid is just renting the space, right?"

She sighed. "Swan, only you could take the lovely act of being a surrogate and frame it in such a jaunty way."

I shrugged. "The whole thing fascinates me. But I do know this: The couple she's doing this for could never have found someone better, not in a million years."

"Am I being treated to the softer side of Eric Swan?"

"I'm a complex man."

"Hmm. Well, please give her my best."

"Sure. Listen, if it *was* our child, you would've been Aunt Quanta. Wouldn't that have been fun?"

I caught an equally rare smile that was gone before it grew

comfortable. She activated a tablet on the table and spun it between us.

"Poole will have this file to you by tonight. It contains the limited information we have on an individual who goes by the name Ceti."

"Setty?"

"C-E-T-I."

"Which means . . .?"

She shook her head. "As far as we know, it doesn't have any overt symbolism attached to it. Could be something personal. Not relevant at the moment, however. What *is* relevant is what this person might be planning."

I took a sip of water and studied her face. "That's twice you've been vague. No pronouns. I take it we don't know this detail?"

"Correct. In most of our early discussions, we referred to Ceti as *he*, but there's no confirmation yet."

"All right. And what exactly is the mysterious Ceti planning? If we're involved it must be something on a grand scale."

Quanta tapped on the screen. "Four weeks ago, an incident caught Homeland Security's interest. They shared the information with the FBI's cybersecurity division, and together they've connected with their counterparts in the UK and Germany."

"Cybersecurity," I said. "So it's a computer caper?"

Then something she'd said triggered a memory, and I sat back to look at her. "The UK. Would this be connected with the trip you made recently?"

"Yes. I've been back twice since then and I wouldn't rule out the possibility of you going over as well."

I snorted. "Then I was *way* off base. I thought you were inter-viewing for a job."

She looked surprised, then smiled. "What? And give up the joy of working with you?"

I returned the smile, but stayed silent.

Calling our relationship *complicated* seemed trite. Most of the time we got along in a conventional boss-employee manner; I think we at least respected each other. There were other times, however, when our professional link frayed to the point of snapping. She'd been furious enough with me to contemplate ending the arrangement altogether, and there was a time when I understood why my predecessor had taken a shot—as in firing a gun in her direction—before he skipped out.

I mean, I'd never do *that*. But I at least could see what drove him to the edge.

Look, the spy game isn't a nine-to-five grind, it isn't played by anything resembling standard office rules, and what you see in movies could never capture the real damage it inflicts on your soul.

Although after cycling through a significant number of bodies over the years, who's to say my soul was even intact? It was something I questioned every single day.

So now, sitting around her kitchen table and exchanging what, given our history, amounted to pleasantries, I privately acknowledged the *détente* and moved on.

"Who are these people?" I asked, tapping on two names on the tablet.

"Those are your primary contacts when you begin the assignment. You'll meet with them in Boston. I could sit here and fill you in on everything, but cybersecurity is what they do. They have a contract with both Homeland and FBI, top clearance, and they're good. They've been involved from the beginning of this case. In fact, they brought it to the attention of Homeland Security, so they have most of the details."

"Most," I said, scrolling down the screen. "I take it we don't tell them everything."

"We never tell *anyone* everything, do we?"

True enough. I studied the screen a bit more, then pushed it back to her.

"At least give me the bottom line before I get on a plane."

Quanta looked out her bay window into the garden. "If you think about it, we now trust our entire lives to digital devices. We encode every scrap of information and upload it to computers and databases. Personal, professional—" She turned back to me. "—and financial."

"And Ceti?"

"Ceti wants to bring it crashing down. All of it."

My flight the following morning was scheduled for 7 a.m., but Christina wouldn't be home from the restaurant until after 11. Plus, closing in on the eight-month mark of her pregnancy, she'd be exhausted from the long night on her feet. I expected her to be asleep before midnight. The nature of my job would once again prevent us from having much in the way of quality time.

She never complained. On the contrary, the circumstances were ideal for a woman who enjoyed having a relationship, but not *too* much of one. And that had nothing to do with her feelings for me; Christina was simply a loner by nature. Our little arrangement checked most of the marriage boxes for her while providing the quiet time she craved.

I was the one who wanted more. It was something I never verbalized, though; it would've come across as one part clingy and one part hypocritical. For as soon as I told her I wanted more time, I'd likely get an assignment that sent me off to Miami, or Phoenix, or Helena. Or, in this case, Boston. So I quietly savored every minute I could.

Rather than cooking a meal for one, I ordered takeout Chinese and timed the phone call so the food would arrive about ten minutes after I got home. Hopefully by then the bloody ache in my lip would've subsided.

After that call, I placed another, this time to Poole.

"You have some homework for me to read on the flight," I said.

"Just finishing up right now. I should have it to you in about an hour."

"And you put me in first class, right?"

"Yes."

I almost choked. "Holy shit, Poole, I was kidding. You didn't tell Quanta, I hope."

"Actually, she was the one who made the request. I thought you'd discussed it with her."

"Oh, right," I said. "I forgot."

I hadn't forgotten a damned thing. Quanta rarely paid for me to fly in business or first class, not so much for any budgetary restraint, but because I think she thought coach seating would keep me grounded. Well, not literally.

First the smile, then the pleasant comment. Now she'd okayed first class for a ninety-minute flight. Was I living in bizarro world? Or was my *ice-water-for-blood* spy boss getting soft?

I grunted the idea away. Whatever zone Quanta was in would be temporary; all the charming niceties would evaporate as soon as I bungled something on the case. Better enjoy the wide, cushy seats and free booze while I could.

"I have you booked into a four-star near Kendall Square," Poole said. "A courier will arrive with your gear at eleven."

"Fine. What about the meeting?"

"They requested a lunch meeting. The location and time will be in the data packet I send, along with the background files."

I thanked her and drove the rest of the way home in silence, thoughts of a curiously kind boss and a mysterious cybercriminal bouncing around my head.

. . .

CHRISTINA SURPRISED me by getting home early. At nine o'clock, the secret panel separating our two condos on the seventh floor of the Stadler Building slid aside and she walked in, smiling and holding a glass of water with a lemon slice.

Yes, we had separate condos, sharing a common wall. Originally the idea had been mine, my sneaky way of hiding the forbidden marriage from Quanta. We installed the panel so we could waltz back and forth without using the common hallway outside our front doors. We liked the privacy.

But as time went by, even after Quanta grew wise to the deceit, the concept of separate homes worked well for our unique situation. We could decorate our home turf however we liked, maintain our own fridge and pantry, and never have to share a bathroom—which more than one marriage expert has dubbed the secret to a harmonious and long-lasting union.

During the long stretches when I was away, my wife could bask in her own space and, should anyone need to drop by to see her, there would be no evidence in sight of her spy/assassin husband.

I stood up and met her halfway, wrapping my arms around her temporarily wider girth.

"How's the stowaway?" I asked.

"Kicking up a storm. She may not agree with the doctor's timetable."

"Well, she gets the last word. You know these fetuses; they're obstinate and will push you around whenever they want. What about work tonight? What did you love the most coming out of the kitchen?"

She lowered herself onto my couch. "A pretty killer linguine, if I do say so myself. With a clam sauce."

Christina Valdez had once reigned as head chef at one of New

York City's premier restaurants. That is, until I stumbled into her life and convinced her to move with me. I liked to believe she was happier running the show at her place in DC. If that wasn't true, she spared my feelings.

"Speaking of food," she said, glancing toward my kitchen. "Do I smell Szechuan?"

"I can't hide anything from you."

"Not with my senses on high alert these days. I could identify every dinner being served tonight on the seventh floor just walking down the corridor."

I slipped an arm around her shoulder, and for the next few minutes we sat in silence, gazing out the large window overlooking the park below. Scattered security lamps outlined a path winding through the grassy hills, while the glitter of city lights provided a postcard backdrop. Christina's natural scent worked its usual calming influence upon me.

My eyes had been closed for only a minute when she nudged me. "I'm sorry, I didn't ask about *your* day."

"Oh, just another banner day for America's greatest spy hero."

"So Quanta kicked your ass again."

I actually laughed out loud. "One lucky kick does not constitute an ass kicking, Ms. Valdez. Careful, or you'll bruise my delicate male ego."

I couldn't hear her laugh, but I felt it. It made me pull her even closer.

When she spoke again, her voice was soft. "Do you have another assignment?"

"Uh, yeah. Boston. Leaving before sunrise."

"Okay."

And that's all that was said about it. After years of living this existence together, it was all that *could* be said.

CHAPTER THREE

My plane touched down at Logan International in a relentless rain. It was still coming down when I arrived at the hotel and didn't let up until I'd finished a second review of the file Poole had sent.

Stretched out on the king-size bed, propped up on three pillows, I scrolled back until I found the notes on my upcoming lunch companions. Jared Hicks and Katrina Yu. He was 35, she a year older, and they were engaged. I frowned without understanding why; for no apparent reason, this arrangement didn't sit right with me.

I shook the thought from my head. As far as I knew, they were utterly charming and competent. I let it go.

The dossier sparkled with outstanding academic histories and stellar recommendations from former employers. In the six years they'd run their own cybersecurity consulting business, cutely named Kajartek, they'd recruited a small but impressive cluster of companies and, in a major coup, earned at least a portion of business from two of the country's prestigious law enforcement agencies, Homeland Security and the FBI.

To do *that* so quickly might've been the most impressive

accomplishment of all. The government was the ultimate good-ol'-boy network—well, if you didn't count the coaching ranks of professional sports.

I studied their headshots. Katrina Yu flashed the kind of megawatt smile that opened doors, while Hicks peered from behind rectangular glasses and the legal limit for facial hair. With a shave the guy would drop five pounds. He may have been smiling, too; it was just too hard to tell.

I moved on to the report they'd filed on Ceti. It had puzzled me during my first pass of the subject matter, mostly because it struck me as vague. But now, scanning the document again, it was clear that Hicks and Yu had intentionally chosen to be nebulous. It smacked of a corporate case of covering your ass, written up in true consulting language.

Either they were clueless about what Ceti was up to . . .

Or they knew damned well what was going on and were merely awaiting an audience with the right person before divulging it.

I looked back at their photos. Something told me it was (b).

A tap on the door at precisely 11 a.m. got me to my feet. A woman stood in the hallway, dressed in a Celtics hoodie and a Red Sox cap.

"Mr. Swan," she said. "You ordered a sandwich and chips?"

"And a cookie," I said.

With a nod, she handed over a rolled-up brown grocery bag. "Have a nice day." Then she turned and walked back toward the elevator.

The ridiculous code language was the only part of Q2's protocol I could never fully embrace. And yet, if I wanted my gear, I had to play along.

I dumped the bag's contents onto my bed. A small box contained the gun, my usual trusty Glock. Another small package held four 19-round magazines. And a laminated badge identified me as Eric Swan with the Department of Homeland Security.

Now, with all the tools and toys a spy might need, I put away my homework and grabbed a quick shower.

THE MEETING TOOK place at one of the seven million Irish pubs in the Boston area. That was fine by me. Shove a plate of shepherd's pie and a Guinness in front of me and I'm set for the rest of the day. The pub's ambiance was old-school dark and woody, and the same lunch crowd likely showed up four days a week. Your requisite shamrocks and sports memorabilia coated every wall. The place smelled of old leather and Old Spice.

My cybersecurity contacts sat side-by-side in a booth halfway back, both staring at their phones, not speaking. Half-empty pint glasses sat in front of them.

I stood beside the booth until they tore their gazes away and looked up.

"Hi. I'm Eric Swan."

Jared began the awkward climb out of the booth to greet me, but I held up a hand to spare him the trouble and slid onto the bench seat across from them. I returned Katrina's smile and knew immediately she'd be the one I would connect with. Jared seemed . . . reserved. He peered at me like I was a shark lingering just on the other side of his glasses. It didn't help the first impression that a tiny food particle clung to his thick beard. I turned my attention back to his fiancée.

"Katrina, please tell me the food here is the good kind of bad."

She laughed. "It's the best bad food on this side of town. Get the beef and Guinness stew."

"I'm famished and that sounds perfect."

"I've got chips coming," she said. "They make them here. Lots of salt."

"If I wasn't already married, Katrina, I would steal you away from this guy."

"Buy me chips, and I won't put up a fight."

It's an old trick: Dive right into a casual conversation with people you've just met in order to get a quick gauge on their personality. She was easygoing, fun, and had no trouble making friends. He, on the other hand, had yet to open his mouth, but his eyes wouldn't shut up. They scanned me, looking for flaws that would validate his reluctance to connect socially. He barely blinked, and his next smile would be his first. Jared Hicks didn't like me, and I had no idea why.

True, I'd just stated my desire to abscond with his bride-to-be, and if I did that, who would be around to tell him he still had breakfast in his beard?

I decided to force him to speak.

"Jared, before we talk about why I'm here, tell me a little bit about your company. You two have gone from zero to sixty in about two seconds. Lots of big contracts."

He started by clearing his throat, another sign he was uncomfortable.

"Well, a lot of that comes from the relationships we cultivated in college and at our first jobs out of school."

"Yeah," I said, "poaching clients is a great way to hit the ground running."

He stiffened. "No, we didn't poach clients. It was just a matter—"

Katrina leaned against him. "Babe, I think he was kidding."

I laughed. "She's right, Jared. I'm just giving you a hard time. I'm actually very impressed with what you've done. So why don't we back up and explain that to me. In layman's terms, what exactly do you do?"

He took a breath, and I got the feeling he relaxed a bit. Perhaps I'd judged him too quickly, but I tend to rely on my gut to interpret warning signals. In reality, Jared Hicks was still a young man, but a young man whose intelligence and creativity had funneled him into a field populated with some pretty nasty players. It was no wonder he chose to remain guarded, especially now that he had the attention of the most powerful organizations in the country—in the world, for that matter.

He started over. "When people celebrated the arrival of the internet, they saw all the good it could do for them, right? And don't get me wrong, I won't deny it does a lot of good. But it didn't take long for some people to find a way to use it in not so good ways. Everyone knows about spam email, and every so often you see a story about a computer virus.

"But the really bad stuff rarely makes the news. Ransomware usually goes unreported and companies that have major breaches don't want the press to find out about it. They're more concerned with protecting their reputation. The only way you find out is if it affects customers."

I glanced at Katrina, who only nodded. Looking back at Jared, I said, "How much money are the bad guys getting away with each year?"

He shrugged. "There's no way to know. Like I said, a huge portion of it goes unreported."

"But you're in the business of protecting people. What's your best guess?"

Jared and Katrina exchanged a look before he answered. "Globally? Katrina's estimate is north of six trillion dollars."

I blinked. "You said *trillion*?"

"And that number's only going up. Three years from now, it could be double that."

"How can any economy handle that kind of loss?"

Katrina spoke up. "For now, the damage is widespread, which

dilutes the impact to a certain extent. But as the numbers rise, it'll reach a point where companies won't survive."

Jared gave a low grunt. "Well, it'll start with the companies. But eventually *nations* won't survive."

"What do you mean?" I asked.

He spread his hands. "The world's economy is now married to the online business model, right? In order to compete as a country, you need to have your share of thriving industries and corporations, along with their millions of employees, to provide the tax platform everything is resting on. Once enough companies are crippled financially, it'll bring everything down." He paused, then said again: "Everything."

Our server interrupted to drop off Katrina's house-made chips, a basket overflowing with deep-fried potato slices. We ordered lunch, although my appetite had diminished over the last two minutes.

Now I understood Q2's involvement. If Ceti was the mastermind of a cyber crime beyond *these* numbers, the damage would be catastrophic. The bearded bro sitting across from me was right: Trillions of dollars spelled not just financial disaster, but also collapse. It was the kind of devastation that analysts within the government and the financial world perhaps whispered about, but only to each other. Better to let the googly-eyed public wander naively through their lives and hope the good guys kept the digital devils at bay, guaranteeing another day of freedom to scroll, swipe, and shop.

Not that I was perched on some pristine mountaintop, playing the role of Judgy McJudgeface over the great unwashed. I was elbow-to-elbow with the blissfully ignorant masses. I'd been as throughly indoctrinated as the next person when it came to gadget dependence, and that included the majority of my shopping and bill paying. Until Jared unloaded his prophecy of doom, I'd assumed the great green machine would run until an asteroid sent us the way of the dinosaurs. But now I was cast once again in the role of that good guy everyone counts on.

"Okay," I said. "Tell me about Ceti."

Katrina and Jared exchanged another quick glance, perhaps deciding who should take the lead on this part of the discussion. Jared sat back and took a drink of his beer while Katrina leaned forward and clasped her hands on the table.

"I became aware of the person who goes by the name Ceti when we were just starting our own business. They were already building up a mystique, I guess you'd call it. The hacker who played the Robin Hood card."

"Doing nasty things for the good of the common people," I said.

"Yeah. Whether that's bullshit or not, it's a tag the masses seem to embrace. The lovable troublemaker who only wants to bring down The Man."

"Do *you* think it's bullshit?"

She gave a shrug. "I don't know. When I was still a college student, I guess I wanted to buy into that mindset because young adults naturally gravitate toward a charismatic rebel. It's part of the adolescent manual, right? We're anti-this and anti-that before we even really know what this and that are all about. We think our ticket into adulthood is latching onto an ideology, and it'll likely be one that makes us believe we're good people. So I probably didn't think it was bullshit at first."

I smiled. "The bullshit detector doesn't engage until, what? Age 30?"

"Probably about right. I mean, not all the things we believe at 20 are suddenly crap at 30. We might hold on to several of them. But at least our filters have had more time to develop and we're not so wide-eyed."

"Oh, I'm all for the cynical screen," I said. "That way, an idea has to have merit and the force of truth to power through. It has to work for my support, not just sound pretty."

Jared's eyes narrowed as he listened to this and I wondered if he either disagreed with the sentiment or if he just didn't understand.

Katrina, however, nodded. "Anyway, I think Ceti's mission for the first few years was to play the part of hero while dishing out a little mayhem here and there. Nothing big, nothing that would cause widespread harm to the public. You know, hack an oil company or mess with a hedge fund, things like that. Go after targets they thought would paint them as anti-establishment while they practiced their craft."

I had to laugh. "Practiced."

"Well, yeah. There's no training ground for true corporate hackers. You learn by doing, and Ceti learned really quickly."

"Nobody wants to label them as he or she. So there hasn't been a single clue about their identity?"

Jared spoke up. "Nothing. And besides, there's no proof that Ceti is just one person."

I sat back and studied his Cro-Magnon face. It had never occurred to me that Ceti might be a syndicate of sorts, a cabal of crooks. But a glance back at Katrina told me she wasn't on board with the idea. So I asked her.

"I'm sure it's *possible*," she said, "and Jared has always thought that. But there are a few reasons why I'm skeptical. One, every move Ceti has made in the last several years has been narrowly targeted with simple messages. It doesn't strike me as group-think. Two, with more than one person, Ceti would be increasing the chances that someone slips up, something either gets intercepted or someone simply blabs. And three—" She paused. "Three, I think the world's greatest hackers hate sharing the limelight."

"It's not generally a team sport," I said.

"Right."

"Okay. Before we talk about the new stuff, give me some background. You said you've been aware of them for several years."

Katrina took her own sip of beer before answering. "I remember a group chat years ago where someone brought up this hack of a prominent Philadelphia law firm. They defended insurance companies against lawsuits. In the hack, most of their files were corrupted, others were copied and posted on Dark Web message boards. It was embarrassing for the firm, especially when dozens of their internal memos were published, saying all sorts of nasty things about not only the people filing the lawsuits, but a few nasty things about their actual clients, the insurance companies. I heard they lost at least a couple of those clients over it."

"Did they figure out how Ceti got in?"

Jared said, "Through a portal set up for one of their vendors. It's the way a lot of the big hacks you read about are pulled off. Rather than trying to get in directly, you find an easier entry point with one of the vendors, and you use *their* access point to invade the target. You remember that huge data breach that made the news just a couple of months ago? The hackers got into that system through one of the retailer's contractors—a heating and cooling company that had access because they remotely managed the temperature in all the various stores. All you gotta do is hack the contractor, then use *their* portal to get where you want to go. Happens all the time."

Katrina jumped in. "And it's especially frustrating for those big companies, because they spend untold millions of dollars safeguarding their systems, only to be tripped up by a client or contractor who isn't nearly as careful or doesn't take it as seriously."

"Okay," I said. "So Ceti made a mark by embarrassing some insurance muckety-mucks. Then what?"

"Then they disappeared for a bit," Katrina said, "before popping up again and hitting a different insurance company. This time they posted all the company's financials, with emphasis on the bloated compensation packages for current and former company officers and CEOs."

Jared said, "People thought Ceti might be someone who'd been wronged by an insurance company and was on some sort of vendetta against the industry."

"But then they branched out quickly," Katrina said. "They attacked an airline, an energy conglomerate, a major shipping company. Over two years they hacked into five fairly large players in a variety of industries, and each play got a little more intricate and almost flamboyant."

"They were starting to enjoy that limelight you mentioned," I said.

She nodded. "Jared and I began paying closer attention 10 months ago and compiled as much information as we could lay our hands on. But it's been the most difficult project we've ever worked on. Maybe that *anyone* has worked on. Ceti is a ghost."

I grunted. "Yeah. I've dealt with a ghost or two in my life."

Our food arrived. While the server set everything down, pushed drink refills on us, and made sure we had everything we needed, my mind briefly darted down the path I least enjoyed. A painful vision of my own ghost floated before me, taunting. Except I knew this man's face and his name. At least the name he used. He'd played hell with both my personal and professional lives for years. On one occasion I'd had him in my sights, had my chance to take him down, to even the score.

Well, that wasn't exactly true. This guy had way too many hash marks on his side of the ledger for me to ever even the score. Not even the satisfaction of putting a bullet in his brain could balance the books. That wouldn't stop me from trying as many times as it took. I'm not sure if everyone has their own personal white whale, but mine is a crafty son of a bitch named Beadle.

When the server shuffled off, I took a bite of my stew—Katrina was right; it was incredible—and shifted gears. "Tell me what happened that got me on a plane to Boston."

They exchanged another glance. This time, Jared took the lead.

"Since they first appeared, Ceti has struck at random and without warning. Often the targets didn't know they'd been compromised until a day had gone by. And in the digital crime world, a day might as well be a century. All the damage was done long before an alarm went off. It was the equivalent of a bank manager walking in on Monday morning and finding that the vault had been hit over the weekend."

"And what changed this time?"

"The randomness is still in play—we have no idea what their next target is—but for the first time, Ceti planted a warning."

I sat quietly, took another spoonful of stew, enjoyed a nice pull on my beer, and finally looked at Katrina. "Was this warning delivered to your company personally?"

She gave a short laugh. "You mean, did Ceti know we were stalking and reach out to tease us? No. That's not to say he or she isn't aware of our efforts. In fact, I'd be surprised if someone of this caliber *didn't* know a fox was sniffing around the coop."

I smiled at her. "I agree. I guess what I'm asking is—"

"He's asking if we're somehow in league with Ceti," Jared said. Through the forest of hair I detected a scowl. "He thinks we're partners with them."

Pushing my spoon around the bowl of stew, aimlessly stirring the mixture, I kept the smile on my face. But I also didn't deny the charge. Sometimes the best plan is to rush in and shove the interviewee out of their stasis, to make them confused and uncomfortable. People untrained in the arts of espionage are apt to reveal their true selves, especially if they're amateur criminals. And 95 percent of criminals are exactly that.

Jared continued to shoot fire at me with his eyes. Katrina, on the other hand, laughed. "If we were working with Ceti, why would we have alerted Homeland Security?"

"Well," I said, glancing around the bar in a disinterested manner. "Let's say you *are* working with Ceti. What better way to control the flow of information and know exactly what the government is doing? Sounds like a perfect setup to me."

I looked back at her, keeping the faint smile on my face, then locked eyes with Jared. "For that matter, who's to say *you're* not Ceti?"

Jared's eyes narrowed and the glare intensified. He snatched his beer, finished it in one long gulp, then got up from the booth. He spoke to his fiancée without taking his eyes off me. "I'll see you back at the office, Katrina." Then he strode toward the door, hitching up his pants as he walked.

"I've been known to make a lousy first impression," I said to Katrina, pushing my half-eaten bowl of stew to the middle of the table. "But that seemed a little overblown."

"Don't worry about him," she said. "He's always had a short fuse. And the entire thing has him worried, mostly because your people are placing a lot of responsibility on us to track this guy down."

"You're not bothered by my questions?"

"Not a bit. We've been so thoroughly background checked that it would be impossible for us to sneak anything past you guys."

"Well," I said in a slow drawl, "in my experience, anything is possible. And, as you've said, nobody knows the real identity of this Ceti character. Or characters. A comfy little team could be a nice disguise, don't you think? You know, husband and wife? A real family business."

Her eyes danced with laughter. "I like you, Mr. Swan. I'm not Ceti, and that's the best I can do for you right now." She scooted across the bench seat and got to her feet. "I'm really sorry, but I probably should go with him. He'll calm down soon and we can talk again. Cool?"

"Cool. How about I stop by your office around four? I'd like to see your operation."

"See you then." She walked off.

Interesting, I thought. Of course, it meant nothing, but Jared's behavior was an early red flag. He'd started out suspicious, he'd grown colder as the conversation progressed, and he'd stormed off in a huff.

And he'd stuck me with the check. Bastard.

CHAPTER FOUR

I had time to kill. For the first hour, I stayed in the booth, treated myself to one more pint, and again skimmed through the sparse file on the subject known only as Ceti. Jared's supposition that it could be a duo or even a team disturbed me. I preferred tracking down an individual; even if they oversaw a pack of pirates, it was much easier anticipating the actions of a lone boss. A troop of assholes, all hoping to call the shots, produced far too many permutations. And permutations can be deadly to a secret agent. We deal in probabilities.

As a Q2 agent, I'd had my share of surprises, several of which had cost me my life. Thanks to what we called our *investment program*, I was able to have my conscious mind, my personality, and my memories downloaded into a new body and then sent back into the field. The process required that I frequently upload, a form of backing up, to keep all those memories as current as possible. Anything that happened between an upload session and my body's death was lost, something I called the lights-out period. There's no telling how much critical information had been forfeited because I took a bullet before uploading. Hey, we do the best we can.

As for the bodies I inhabit? They're volunteers. Well, that's a loose definition. They're actually convicts who've been sentenced to life in prison with no chance of parole. Without telling them exactly what's at stake, they're offered a chance to donate their body to science in exchange for a tidy sum deposited in the bank for their spouse or family. Tidy as in $2 million, tax free. All the criminal knows is that they're essentially giving their lives to serve humankind, and their beneficiary will live a pretty sweet life.

Their own essence is uploaded and kept in digital storage—a life in complete limbo, not exactly dead, but not alive, either. No awareness, no worries, no pain. And out of an 8-by-10 cell.

It's the same type of space I occupy while I'm awaiting a new body. Christina once asked me if it was like sleep. It's not. With sleep, you have at least some semblance of awareness of time passing, even if it's distorted, and you dream. In my compact hard drive existence, there's . . . nothing. My mind goes immediately from the last millisecond of life in the old body to my eyes popping open in the next body. It's weirder than you can possibly imagine. The first few times it happened, I freaked the hell out. Now, I'm pretty seasoned.

Or damaged. That thought haunts me on a consistent basis. I've had numerous chats with Q2's resident shrink, Miller, on this subject. How much of my mind is being lost, chipped away, with each new download, each new investment? I describe it as a copy of a copy of a copy, ad infinitum. How can there not be degradation over time?

Yet I can't quit. Trust me, I've been close more than once and always keep coming back. And don't think it's entirely my steadfast sense of duty to my country—although that's certainly a factor. Let's just say I have my own agenda, a search for what lies beyond. I must *know*.

That search for ultimate knowledge is powerful enough for

me to risk turning into a monster, an outcome that's entirely possible. Nobody—not Quanta, not Miller, not anyone—knows for sure.

Now I glanced at the file on my phone. What kind of a monster was Ceti? What kind of person dedicated their life to destruction? You might think there's a world of difference between murder and a global financial meltdown, but there's not. The latter leads to the former, in numbers hard to compute. But don't kid yourself; the world's biggest financial villains *are* responsible for death. Lots of it. They may not physically pull the trigger, but they guarantee the guns get used.

Jared, before stomping out of the pub, claimed that Ceti had issued a warning. If so, it was a shift from the criminal's *modus operandi*. And yes, Ceti might be a he, a she, or any combination of genders. But, for the time being, I would go under the assumption that FBI profiles were accurate: The majority of felonious hackers were male. I could amend the pronoun if and when we caught the shithead.

So why would he issue a warning? What part of his game was changing? Was it part of a larger, complex plan or simply a way to keep those profilers guessing, to throw them off the scent?

I paid the check and left. The clouds were breaking up, a few patches of blue poking through, but the air still felt thick with moisture. I decided to take a walk toward the MIT campus and the Charles River. Maybe the proximity of so much brain power would produce a type of intellectual osmosis. Being around smart people has to make you smarter, doesn't it?

I pulled out my phone and called Quanta's number. To my surprise, she answered.

"So you're already alienating our partners on this case," she said without a greeting.

I snorted. "You're kidding. Hicks already called you and complained?"

"He doesn't know about me, remember? He called Homeland Security, which is where he thinks you work. *They* called me."

"What a turd."

"Swan, you haven't been in Boston for five hours and you've already alienated one of the people who could help us prevent a catastrophe. I shudder to think what you might accomplish by midnight."

"His girlfriend likes me."

Quanta sighed. "Stop being an ass and play nice with our partners. Did you get anything before tripping his switch?"

"He and Katrina Yu have spent the last year tracking Ceti, and they say for the first time he's actually giving a warning that he's about to piddle in the pool. I should know details in—" I glanced at the phone. "—in about two hours."

"Stay in touch. And make sure you upload as soon as possible after you get their report."

"In case I get hit by a bus?" Coincidentally, I said this as a large bus trundled past, kicking up dust and straw wrappers.

"That's always one possibility," Quanta said. "Or, at the rate you're going, Jared Hicks might shoot you himself."

"Putting aside his sensitive feelings for a moment, I'm calling to request a deeper background check on the gruff Mr. Hicks. I get a strange feeling from him that makes me think the FBI's standard checks may have missed something."

Quanta paused. "All right. I respect your instincts. I'll put the second floor on that right away."

We only referred to the real eggheads at Q2 by their location within the squatty, nondescript headquarters building in Washington, DC. They were the Einsteins who put together my online history every time I adopted a new identity. They also created any and all documents a good spy needs to go about his or her life of stealth. And, just as importantly, they scoured every nook and cranny of the web—both the light and dark varieties—to find every last scrap of information about any individual walking the Earth. Everything you've done since the start of the 21st century is in there somewhere, just waiting to be found. And that's not hyperbole; what they dig up is flat-out scary.

You think *you're* an exception? Please. Your digital fingerprints are smudged all over the place. Lucky for you, we're the good guys—but a lot of bad guys are just as industrious.

Sweet dreams.

I'd reached a rise not far from the river's edge and stared across at Beacon Hill. Between that tony neighborhood and the MIT campus on this side, an awful lot of wealth and knowledge was packed into a relatively small area. No wonder it was a breeding ground for ideas, entrepreneurs, and more than a few master criminals.

I started to ring off, then said, "Listen, while the jokers on the second floor are at it, couldn't hurt to probe Katrina Yu a bit more, too."

Quanta assured me she'd have both digitally strip-searched and closed by again telling me to play nice. I slipped the phone into my jacket, then shoved both hands into my pants pockets and watched a kayaker paddling toward the Harvard Bridge.

THERE WAS no sign on the building to indicate a high-level security team worked inside. Katrina and Jared kept a suite of offices on the fourth floor, *Kajartek* stenciled in dark letters on the glass door. The outer reception area was as boring as you'd expect. A young man behind a desk stared intently at a monitor and asked what I needed without tearing his eyes away.

"I've come for your liver," I said.

This got his attention. He looked up. "What?"

"I'm here to see Katrina and/or Jared. Both would be great,

either would be acceptable. If neither, then I'll definitely need your liver."

With that last line, I opened my eyes extra wide.

I'm an expert marksman, I can hold my own in most rounds of hand-to-hand combat—unless it's against Quanta—and I make a killer old fashioned. But I take much more pride in keeping a straight face when talking with clueless oafs. It's sort of a hobby. And riffing on old Monty Python bits is easy because few people under 40 know any of their stuff.

"Um," he said, and pushed his chair back. "Just a moment."

He could've made a call to either of them, but this was surely a conversation he'd want to relay in person.

He was back in 30 seconds. "If you'd like to have a seat, someone will be right out."

I shook my head. "I can't sit right now. I may need to run out of here as quickly as possible. And I may need you to come with me." I opened my eyes wide again.

The poor young man visibly started, then nodded and wandered out of sight again. He clearly did not want to wait in the same room.

A minute later, Katrina came down the hall and greeted me with a warm smile. She waved me toward her office in the back. It wasn't massive, but did have a sitting area with a small couch and two high-backed chairs. Jared sat in one of these, his arms crossed. He wore neither a smile nor a look of hostility. He was oddly flat and calm. Which was good; flat and calm I could work with.

"Now that we've had our time-out," I said, taking a seat on the couch, "let's get right to it. Jared, I certainly don't need you to like me, but let me make one thing clear. When you agreed to a security contract with the federal government, you basically assured yourselves of having to work with someone like me from time to time. We may be a bloated, wasteful bureaucracy in general, but we don't screw around when it comes to security threats. You could say we're overprotective. We have to be. Overlooking one little thing can have disastrous consequences. I don't need to point out lapses in our history that back that up. So, while you may bristle at some of my questions, you gave up your right to object and walk away the day you deposited your first check from the U.S. Treasury. Understood?"

"Yes," he said, still emotionless.

I glanced at Katrina, who busied herself with pouring glasses of water while her fiancé got chewed out.

"Good," I said. "Now tell me about the warning from Ceti."

Jared uncrossed his arms and picked up a tablet from the coffee table. He poked at it a couple of times, then handed it over. It was obvious from his demeanor that he was waiting for me to ask him to explain what I was looking for, his one puny attempt at regaining some power and dignity. The guy had probably been through enough for one day, so I gave him the satisfaction by asking.

"It's a report on data breaches and areas of vulnerability, sort of a security scorecard. Most large organizations—if they're smart, anyway—have their own. We created one that does more than examine individual companies or systems. It uses multiple nodes, ties them all together, and looks for patterns that can be assessed for threats."

"Nodes," I said.

"Yeah. Well, like Company A, no matter how complex their own individual system is, could be thought of as a node; Company B, with all of their data and security protocols, would still be distilled down to a node. While we always work to optimize each company's defensive system by itself, we think the modern way of dealing with cyber threats is to correlate data on a grander scale."

Katrina jumped in. "The idea is that if a cyber criminal,

including Ceti, finds a particular method that helps them infiltrate a company's shield, they'll be more likely to use that same protocol on their next victim. It's much quicker to just keep using what works, rather than devising an entirely new program for each company."

My eyes scanned the tablet's screen without really understanding what I was seeing. Jared knew this and I'm sure it brought him oodles of gratification. But what they were telling me was clear. "Hackers are lazy."

"No lazier than any other company that develops systems," Katrina said. "Systems are what make every business profitable. You don't reinvent your distribution system for every new product; you just plug it into the existing system, give it its own barcode, and keep everything humming along."

"Hackers often work the same way," Jared said. "They find a way to tunnel through security defenses and they see no reason to change it every time."

I set the tablet back on the table. "Okay. I understand. Now tell me how this applies to Ceti and his so-called warning."

Katrina handed me a glass of water. "There are potential hacks taking place all the time. And I mean *all the time*. Not just companies, but individuals. You're not even aware of all the attempts to breach your data. Your financial accounts. Your online shopping accounts. It can be as innocent as your automatic payments to a utility or a cell phone account. Someone figures out your lame password, or finds it actually written somewhere—yes, that's not uncommon—and it starts a chain reaction. They use that to get to your banking information, or your credit card.

"Well, we've learned over the years that hacks often leave a unique footprint. Probably because they come from an unusual IP address or they take a roundabout way to access data. With large corporations and their beefed-up security, those footprints can stand out like a beacon. In fact, that's how most amateurs are caught; it's tough to be subtle when you're trying to crack that kind of safe.

"So that takes us back to our system of studying patterns. We do it with all of our own clients, and we have partnerships with other security firms where we share the footprints they detect. A security engineer at one of those firms sent us a note that said we should look for specific patterns in strings of numbers. He was pretty sure he'd picked up on one string in particular. So we looked into that. The string he'd found turned out to not be important. But it at least made us start looking for similar strings."

"And you found one."

She nodded. "A distinct pattern that was . . ."

Her voice trailed off.

"Yes?" I prompted.

Katrina shrugged. "It was a pattern that we're pretty sure is Ceti's signature."

All I could do was stare, first at her, back to the beard, then back to her. "I assume you don't mean his or her actual name. You said these are numbers."

"It's mathematical," Jared said. "But simple enough for a middle-grade student to understand if they were looking for something."

"Ceti put together a variety of codes with every attack in the last few months," Katrina said. "Each incursion into a major company's defenses left either a fictitious IP address or just a string of numbers. But always the same numbers at the end. Here—"

She pointed to a line on the tablet: *92540081.*

"And here." She pointed to another spot, which featured the same string: *92540081.*

I grunted. "Okay, I believe you that it's simple mathematics. But explain it to me anyway."

Jared, for the first time, let a smug smile pierce the hair. "It's the squares of the numbers correlating to his code name. *C* is 3, squared 9. *E* is 5, squared 25. *T* ends up being 400 and *I* squared would be 81."

The scowl on my face must've relayed my skepticism.

Katrina gave a nervous laugh. "Well, we said it was simple."

I tapped a finger on the arm of my chair and looked at the eight digits that our high-priced security team insisted was a message from the world's most wanted hacker. I didn't want to appear too dismissive, though, because for all I knew it was indeed just that simple.

Finally I let out a long breath. "Okay, fine. So a bunch of incursions all leave the same digital signal. And using the decoder ring you got out of a box of Cracker Jack, you deciphered the name Ceti. So he's doing a computer version of writing his name in the snow." I looked up at Jared. "How is this a warning?"

He spun the tablet around and flipped to a spreadsheet, then turned it back to face me.

"Five hacks in the last six weeks that left the same eight-digit name signature, but that's not all. You'll also find another four digits on an adjoining line. The same four, each time. We think those digits are a date."

"Why?"

"Because why else would Ceti sign a name in the first place? It's a warning about what's coming. They're toying with us because they know they can. And they know there's nothing we can really do about it."

I scratched my head, still unconvinced, but moved by their insistence. I looked at the four digits. If they really were meant to represent a month and a day, then we wouldn't have to wait long.

It was tomorrow.

CHAPTER FIVE

You would think the beds in four-star hotels would all be spectacularly comfortable. This one was not. But I was stretched out for now, preparing to upload all of my experiences of the day. The process was perhaps the most sophisticated in history and involved science I still don't understand, even after having it explained to me many times. I suppose it wasn't critical for me to understand *how* it worked as long as I was a good boy and followed the steps on a regular basis.

Devya Nayar would've easily won the Nobel Prize for inventing the process we called *investing*—except the technology was the most intensely guarded secret in the world. While it's true that near-immortality of the mind would be desirable for the population at large, there was no practical way of rolling it out without creating more death and destruction than it could preserve. Not to mention the little problem of needing a new body to inhabit each time; there were only so many death-row inmates to provide the shells.

For now, the technology would remain the property of one small government agency in the U.S. Someday, perhaps, it could be used for the average Joe and Joanne. Until then, I was one of a select group used as guinea pigs for the process. And when I say select, I mean you could count the total number of agents who'd tried it on your fingers alone, with no need to use your toes. And of the fewer than ten, several had not ended well.

Let's call it a work in progress.

With total secrecy required, it meant no awards would be forthcoming for the Indian genius I called God Maker. That was fine by her. Nayar was more than happy to remain sequestered in her fortified mansion in Rhode Island. Well, significantly more fortified now than it was before she was kidnapped by a former rogue agent of Q2. That breach could never happen again.

The process of uploading all of my gray matter into something resembling a computer hard drive might've been the most compli-cated procedure ever, but the tools I used on the road looked ultra-simple. That was also by design; I could carry the gadgets in my carry-on bag without so much as a sniff of interest from security agents at airports or elsewhere. One looked like deodorant and the other like a small can of shaving cream. Combined with a good wifi connection and a sizable pill that works some minor miracle of its own on my brain's plasticity, that's all it takes. I simply lie down, read a magazine, and let the transfer begin. It used to take longer, but these days it's under 90 minutes and getting faster.

God Maker still hasn't figured out how to let me do this while sleeping—something about corrupting the data—but promised me that she's working on it.

Since my biggest fear lies within that whole corruption thing, I'm trying to be patient.

This is how I found myself horizontal in a Boston hotel room on a bed that should've been plush, based on the nightly room rate. Propped up on two large pillows, my distraction was a trusty Hollywood gossip mag, my guilty pleasure. I have to be the only secret agent in history who delights in trash magazines, but hey, we all have our peccadilloes.

I read about the B-list celebrity who found true love with a valet driver at her favorite restaurant, which was somewhat interesting. But nothing beat the national TV weatherman who was caught sending naughty photos to an unsuspecting makeup artist. The article was filled with the usual weather puns: *He was caught in a storm of bad publicity*; *the network now found themselves in a high pressure system*; and *the forecast for his future employment was cloudy.*

Personally, I preferred the one I came up with: *The makeup artist never asked to see his warm front.*

The only problem with the trash mags was that I always finished flipping through before the upload was complete. I tossed this edition onto the floor and stared up at the mottled ceiling. My thoughts turned to Christina, my favorite distraction from work. She was nearing the end of her surrogacy and I wondered—not for the first time—how it would affect her emotionally when she handed over the little human she'd nurtured for so many months. The psychology of it all fascinated me.

Plus, I couldn't ignore the obvious dichotomy between Christina's act of helping to create a new life and her husband's habit of terminating them. Hers was the most noble gesture I'd ever personally witnessed, and, knowing her as I did, didn't surprise me one bit. There were times when I allowed myself to ponder the possibility that she'd made this choice as a way of balancing the books with the universe. She wasn't disdainful of my career path and understood that I ultimately saved more lives than I took. But I liked to think she found the opportunity too perfect to pass up. She was cool that way.

I WAS STARVING once the upload finished. Packing away my tools, I decided to see if the hotel made up for their crappy beds with good room service. While I awaited a club sandwich and fries, my phone vibrated. It was Poole.

"You can't nag this time," I said. "I just finished uploading all my deepest, darkest thoughts."

"What?" she said. "Oh, no. I wasn't calling for that. But thank you for doing it anyway."

"All right. What's up?"

"A preliminary report from the second floor on the digital signatures that Katrina Yu and Jared Hicks found. We concur with their analysis. It more than likely is indeed a vanity tag, along with a date. In fact, our team gave it a probability rating of 87 percent."

"So there's only a 13 percent chance that a major attack *doesn't* go down tomorrow?"

"Correct."

I looked out the window at the sparkling lights of the city. "I'm guessing we didn't find any clues as to the target."

"Nothing." She fell silent. Poole's masterful efficiency wasn't confined to her job responsibilities; she was efficient with words, too.

In the silence, I thought about the case and all its frustrations. Very little information other than a threat, trillions of dollars and perhaps countless lives hanging in the balance, and at least one geek who wanted to stab me in the eye with a pencil. And he was supposed to be on *my* side.

"So," I finally said to Poole. "Any recommendations from anyone on how to proceed? Do we just let Ceti raise hell and then react?"

She didn't respond right away, and I imagined her processing my words. Then she said, "Unfortunately, I see no other option at the moment."

"Yeah." She couldn't see another option because there weren't any. I knew it as well as she did; I just wanted to hear it from another person.

Before hanging up, something else occurred to me. "Hey, Poole, are there any notes from Quanta's meetings in England that might help? They're not confidential, are they?"

"I can check. Whatever I can forward to you, I will."

I thanked her and hung up just as the sandwich arrived. Things were bleak, but I was still famished. And the hotel had indeed made up for the shitty mattress.

Just before ten o'clock, I got a text from Katrina Yu:

No new data. Remaining vigilant.

It struck me as an odd message. Had she been expecting Ceti to reveal something else before he attacked? What sort of data did she mean? For that matter, weren't we all remaining vigilant? It was all we had. We were relegated to sitting around, completely powerless, just waiting for damage reports to roll in. Does that count as vigilance?

I felt compelled to reply with something, so I sent back:

Sorry I freaked out your receptionist. It's how I entertain myself sometimes.

A minute went by before she sent back a smiley face.

Ah, modern communication. How did we manage to make so much technological progress while our language skills regressed to swapping crayon drawings?

What I needed was a long walk in the cool, late-night air. I threw on a windbreaker and fled the hotel. Sleep would've been the right prescription, but my mind would never cooperate. I needed to get outside, inhale some polluted big city air, and temporarily sweep this assignment to the side. Sometimes limited information is worse than no information at all. It causes us to extrapolate where we have no business extrapolating, and before you know it, you're making irrational assumptions simply because you feel like you have to be doing *something*.

Better to let the empty glass remain empty, rather than fill it with fantasy.

So I enjoyed the reprieve from thoughts of digital pirates and bearded boyfriends. Except the reprieve only lasted until eleven o'clock, just as I walked back into my room. That's when I got a call from Quanta.

Shit. She certainly wasn't calling to wish me sweet dreams. But we also were still an hour away from D-Day.

"What's happened?" I said.

"Ceti has pulled off another hack."

I paused in mid-stride. "Early? So the whole date thing was a smokescreen?"

"No. The date was correct. For this target, at least."

I let that rumble across my mind for a moment. "Europe," I said. Then, it hit me. "England."

"That's right. An hour ago, so about 3:00 a.m. in London."

"The target?"

"An academic pension fund, one of the largest in the world. Half a million members, overseeing billions of pounds."

"What's the damage?"

"We won't know the total for a few more hours. They're

scrambling right now to plug a handful of leaks. But we know Ceti siphoned about half a million pounds in that first hour. An extremely complicated arrangement. It had to take months to set up, and there's no way of knowing if the pension fund has fully slammed the door yet."

I nodded to myself. From the reading I'd done on the subject, I knew once an infiltrator snuck inside, just "slamming the door" didn't prevent more damage from being done. The most elaborate hacks could reprogram the defense mechanisms from the inside; the poor system had no way of knowing who was friend or foe and just followed directions. It could take weeks to go through every line of code to make sure the malicious worm had been scrubbed away.

I tried to look on the bright side. "At least the pension folks picked up on it fairly quickly."

"We were lucky," Quanta said. "The head of IT for this pension group decided to experiment with a sort of homemade trip alarm in case their system was ever breached. She was pulling an all-nighter, working on it from home. As it turned out, Ceti's hack basically happened right before this woman's eyes. In fact, at first she thought it was something *she'd* done."

"Do we find that suspicious?"

"We have no choice but to be suspicious of everyone and everything at this moment. And yes, she'll be fully debriefed and examined very closely after the mess gets cleaned up. We don't know how long that will be. But I have someone there in the U.K. who will take the point on this."

"You say that Ceti pulled out—" I did a quick conversion in my head. "—about $700,000. First of all, I'm surprised it's not more than that. But is there any way of finding out where the money went? I mean, it couldn't just disappear without a trace."

"In a sense, it could," Quanta said. "When you're dealing with transfers like this, it involves a series of digital ledgers. Large amounts are shuffled from one side to the other. Nobody sees real money; they see electronic spreadsheets. What Ceti did was adjust the spreadsheet. He—or she, or they—transferred the amount to one secret offshore account, and from there it was transferred at least one more time. The original offshore account was deleted. Trying to track the path is close to impossible, but several organizations are working on it, including ours."

I grunted. What Quanta had just described was one of the strongest arguments for the switch to cryptocurrency: a more transparent system, where there wasn't a single ledger, but hundreds, thousands, or more. This theft in England was not that different from Ferris Bueller hacking into his school's computer to change his grades. And that was decades ago; safe to say that Ceti employed a more complex set of skills.

My thoughts drifted back to my conversation with Poole, where I'd bemoaned the idea of just waiting and reacting. Well, we'd waited; what would the reaction be? I asked Quanta.

Usually when she sighed it was in response to something I'd said or done. Now it was clear the case had her completely flummoxed.

"The first step will be to do a digital autopsy on the hack," she said. "Most master criminals, including the cyber variety, can only stay in the shadows so long. Eventually their ego drives them to become more and more flashy, relishing the attention. I believe Ceti will be the same way."

I pondered this for a moment. "So our strategy is to hope he trips up?"

Now her voice took on the edge I'd heard so many times. "Unless you dazzle me, Swan, with a brilliant piece of spycraft. I find it hard to believe that someone, whether working alone or with a small group, could pull off attacks like this without leaving behind a digital fingerprint. I sent you to work closely with Hicks and Yu, which means I need you to roll up your sleeves and get deep into it. Follow any hunch either of them may have. Peel apart every piece of data they've uncovered on all of Ceti's previous attacks. Correlate anything you might find there with the information we get on the London job. There's something in all of that. Somewhere. You need to find it."

"Hold on a sec, my pen died. Can you repeat the list?"

"Don't toy with me right now, Swan. Not now. Just get to the bottom of this, and do it before Ceti has a chance to destroy the economy—which is the next move, in case you haven't done your homework. Find the hidden piece that will deliver us Ceti. Can you do that for me?"

"Have I ever let you down?" I asked, a smile playing across my face.

"We both know you have."

The smile faltered. She sounded genuinely pissed this time, an emotion Quanta usually repressed. I always admired her control, but I had to admit it sparked some juvenile need in me to poke at it, to try to pierce her steely armor. And yet, when I did, I often felt the sting of her fierce drive and intellect. You'd think I'd have learned by now.

"I'll be ready for the London data," I said. "And I'll be back with Katrina and Jared in the morning."

"Good. I'll be in touch." With that, she was gone.

I tossed my phone onto the bed, ran a hand through my hair—I still wasn't used to its curl—and knew that sleep would be a challenge tonight. My monkey mind would be roaring. But I brushed my teeth, got undressed, and climbed into the sheets to at least give it a try.

CHAPTER SIX

It was almost noon before we got the postmortem from London, and even then it was labeled *preliminary*. The breach had so far cost LeaCap Funds, the academic pension group, about $925,000. Again, I was perplexed at the amount. To go to that much trouble and then take only a fraction of the available funds? Was this Ceti's way of simply messing with us?

Sitting in Katrina's office, sipping on my third coffee of the morning, I heard Jared chuckle.

"Clue me in," I said. "What's so funny?"

He ignored me for a moment, locking eyes with his partner. "Do *you* get it?" he asked her.

It took about five seconds of her staring at the data before a slow smile spread across her face. Then she joined him in laughing.

"Listen," I said. "I'm all for inside jokes when the world economy *isn't* being threatened with total collapse. So tell me, please."

Jared finally turned to me. "Before I show you, let me point out that Ceti wasn't stopped by the good guys. Nobody turned off the flow of money coming out, correct?"

"That's right. As strange as it may seem, the siphon just stopped."

"And they stopped at, you said, about $925,000. I think in the final analysis you'll find that they took out $925,400—"

"And 81 cents," Katrina said.

I paused, looking at the screen on the table before me. "Oh, come on. You don't think—"

"Why not?" Jared said. "Ceti, whoever they may be, have shown us those digits over and over again." He tapped on the screen. "You think this is a coincidence? Really?"

No, I didn't. I just was stunned at the—the *audacity*. I was used to narcissistic villains; I'd encountered too many to count. You could say it was part of the super-criminal DNA. Crime experts would tell you that arrogance is almost necessary to pull off the most heinous plans.

Ceti, however, was in an entirely new league. This wasn't just a case of narcissism; Ceti was flaunting his superiority when it came to cybersecurity—or our lack thereof. He was taunting the high-level organizations that were now after him. He seemed to be treating this as a game. But the stakes in this game were much too high.

I ran my fingernails over my unshaved jaw, listening to the sandpaper scratch. It put me into a deep thought trance. Narcissism. Attention. Ceti had an agenda, one that could topple the world's financial stability. But he also got off on the attention. He wanted people to know who was behind the chaos. Which meant—

"Katrina," I said. "You said an engineer at another security firm suggested looking for strings that might not be part of the actual malware, but just as a sort of signature."

"Yeah. Um, Shawn Cook. He's at—" She gave a questioning look to Jared, who squinted as if trying to remember.

"He's at Bolinger Gomez," he said. "They're in Austin. Why?"

I leaned forward, my elbows on my knees. "It might be nothing at all. But I want to talk with him. I'll explain in a bit. Can you set up at least a video call?"

Katrina nodded. "I'll see what I can do." She got up and walked over to her desk, and I looked back at Jared.

"We need a win right now," I said. "Anything, no matter how small. Just a win."

He didn't respond, and instead went back to his tablet, fully engrossed. It was clear we were never going to be pals.

There was a sideboard along the far wall of the office, where coffee, water, and fruit were arranged. Just for something to do, I walked over to it and filled a mug from the hot water dispenser. After thumbing through the selection of teas, I unwrapped a serving of English breakfast tea and dunked it. None of the fruit looked appealing, so I picked up a generic energy bar that posed as a healthy snack. Everyone knew it really wasn't, but we all like kidding ourselves.

By the time my tea had steeped for three minutes, Katrina had joined me at the table.

"Well, this is horrible," she said.

"You don't like tea?"

"What? No, I'm talking about the engineer in Austin. He's dead."

I'd been just about to drop the spent tea bag into a trash can. Now I froze, the bag dangling in the air, and looked at Katrina. "How and when?"

"They were reluctant to give me specifics over the phone—"

Before she could finish the sentence, I'd dropped the tea bag and had my own phone out. "Text me his name and the name of his company. Please."

She suddenly looked worried but went back to her desk. A few seconds later I got her message.

"Excuse me," I said. "I hate to ask you to leave your own office, but could I have the room for a moment?"

Katrina and Jared exchanged glances, then each grabbed a tablet and walked out. By the time the door clicked shut, I'd called Poole. She picked up after one ring.

"Hey, I need a quick check on a dead guy. All the details: date, how it happened, anything you can find." I rattled off Shawn Cook's information from Katrina's text.

"I'll get right on it," Poole said.

"After that, sift through the earlier reports we have on Ceti hacks. What I'm looking for are the names and numbers of the people who alerted the authorities."

"Got it."

"Include whatever you can find on the director of IT for this London pension program."

She promised to have a file to me within two hours, but, knowing Poole, it would be sooner than that.

It was 75 minutes, to be exact. I'd left the office, telling Katrina and Jared I'd be back in a few hours, and walked four blocks in another light rain to a cafe. In the back, with a large booth to myself, I put a tablet, an old-fashioned legal pad, and my phone on the table and ordered a bowl of soup.

I opened the file from Poole on the tablet while enjoying my tomato bisque. She'd highlighted a couple of things in the police report on Shawn Cook, age 33. He was a software engineer for Bolinger Gomez, a digital security boutique shop in Austin. Employed less than a year. Prior to that, he'd worked at three other security firms, never for more than two years. Lots of down time between gigs. Now he had permanent down time.

The report from the Austin police department labeled it an accidental death. A long tumble down a flight of stairs in his townhome, resulting in a broken neck and massive head trauma. Toxicology said his blood-alcohol level was 0.29, which is creeping up on the zone where you sink into a coma. Neighbors saw no one entering or leaving. When found by a former partner who just happened to stop by to pick up some things, Cook had been dead for about two hours. Police said the former partner's alibi for that time frame was solid. They ruled that Cook got completely shit-faced and simply fell. Nothing suspicious in their investigation, the matter was quickly closed, and everybody but Shawn got on with their lives.

And chances were that it had gone down exactly like that. Dude in his early 30s, making pretty good bank in a town known for its tech and its parties. He'd recently become single again, got hammered—either to deal with the pain or to pretend there'd never been any—and didn't have the maturity or experience to call it quits. You're bulletproof in your 20s, and for some people that mentality lingers into the 30s, long enough to get you killed.

Except I'm trained to believe nothing at first glance. Even if he was a fragile thread to the case, Cook's death had sounded a klaxon horn in my brain the second Katrina mentioned it. To me, death is usually a pretty clear indicator I'm on to something.

What I needed was a pattern.

For a moment, I wondered about Cook's communication with Kajartek. He'd actually put them onto the idea of Ceti's digital signature. Why would he do that if he was on the inside?

As soon as the thought crossed my mind, I knew the answer. Ceti was indeed desperate for attention, hungry for attention. A supreme narcissist, he was probably irked that no one had caught the messages he thought would be blatant. A little nudge from one of his pigeons would garner him the attention he craved. To protect his helper, Ceti didn't let Cook ID the actual signature itself, but rather plant the idea in the minds of Katrina and Jared. Then he simply trusted that their curiosity would do the rest. It paid off.

I flipped to the next item in Poole's notes. Ceti's attacks on the airline and shipping industries had nothing that stood out. Those hacks weren't caught by an individual, but instead through the gross magnitude of the damages. Nothing that would set off the alarms like Shawn Cook's death.

But then I swiped back a page. The breach of a Canadian natural gas conglomerate a year ago resulted in a complete shutdown of their distribution system, as well as the leak of a few embarrassing corporate memos, similar to the insurance company pranks Ceti had played in the past. It was, as Katrina and Jared indicated, all good practice leading up to the devastating ideas Ceti harbored. And it also provided the hacker with some of the early love he seemed to require. For a week, posts could be found on social media trumpeting "the Green Angel," as one person labeled Ceti.

Of course, Ceti's motives behind the natural gas invasion had zilch to do with environmental issues, but that didn't stop some from latching on to the name and making him a minor celebrity—for those few days. It probably whetted his appetite for more.

Poole reported that the gas company's director of digital media—basically an IT person who doubled as a social media guru—dispatched two or three press releases that mentioned the Green Angel, and how the authorities would soon get to the bottom of it. The company was horrified by the releases, because they wanted to downplay the entire incident and certainly did *not* want to glorify the digital bandit. One day later, that digital media director, a woman named Ursula Fournier, "left to pursue other opportunities." Which meant she was fired.

And then, three days later, she disappeared. Literally. Poole included a copy of a missing persons report filed by Fournier's parents. A year later, there was still no sign of her.

I sat back, thinking, and took a sip of the thoroughly disappointing iced tea. Not a specialty of Boston, to be sure; they probably only brewed a new batch every few days. Then I swiped forward a page or two on my tablet, looking for the next report.

There. A prestigious accounting and tax firm in Kansas City, hacked seven weeks after the Canadian job. A slightly different ploy this time, whereby Ceti seemed bent on practicing his anarchist skills. He didn't steal anything and he didn't post embarrassing items relating to the company's management. Instead, he simply destroyed hundreds of valuable documents in a completely random fashion, sometimes altering them in a way that would take weeks to repair, or deleting certain files altogether. It was a disaster for the firm, however, and the report said it would likely cost them two million dollars by the time everything was addressed.

I flipped to another page. Of all the IT people questioned by the police and FBI, nobody came across as suspicious. But three days after the hack, one of the firm's mid-level IT specialists, a man named Tanner Leachman, went missing and was presumed dead. After not showing up for work and not answering his phone, his supervisor went by one evening and found the front door of his apartment ajar. Stepping inside, he immediately saw the room in disarray and a large puddle of blood on the floor in front of the couch.

The police report said it may have been a burglar caught in the act, but now, looking back with the hindsight of other similar crimes, we had to assume Leachman had been eliminated by Ceti.

So one dead IT employee, another missing, and a third missing and presumed buried somewhere. Did three constitute a pattern? The police might not think so, especially since they'd ruled Cook's death an accident, Fournier's case was still open, and Leachman was presumed to be in the wrong place at the wrong time. But it got my blood racing. These were the fragments of a case that could possibly give me something to grasp hold of. I felt worthless as an agent with nothing to chase down, no angles to work. I couldn't know for sure that all three IT people were connected to Ceti in any way, but it was *something*.

I realized I'd neglected my bisque for several minutes and quickly finished it before it got any colder. Then, as I re-read the two reports, it occurred to me: *This could happen again.*

Scrolling through the data, I landed on the bio of the IT director for the London pension. Samantha Das, 41 years old and single. Two and a half years at the company, excellent credentials. In other words, a profile not unlike that of Shawn Cook or Ursula Fournier.

I stared at the information for ten seconds before I called Quanta. There was no answer. It would have to be a text.

It's just a hunch, but I'd get surveillance and security on Samantha Das immediately. We can discuss when you get free.

It could be nothing. Probably *was* nothing. But it could also be something big. Really big. Any thread connecting all these cases was exactly what we needed. And even that would barely be a starting point.

Just a win, though. No matter how small.

Katrina and Jared were holed up in his office this time. It was smaller and austere, with nothing to suggest a personality of any kind. Perhaps because Jared didn't have one.

I took the only available chair, as uncomfortable as it looked, and asked for updates on the London hack.

"So far, nothing," Katrina said. "Their people aren't sharing anything with us. Well, with anyone, I'm sure. They're probably still in shock. But we've put in requests through the proper diplomatic channels, using our credentials with DHS and the FBI. Now we wait. I wouldn't expect anything for a few days, though."

Inwardly, I groaned. Lots could happen in a few days, and on a case like this it would be bad. But I kept my expression composed and turned to Jared. "Did either of you ever meet or talk with Shawn Cook? I mean, in person."

He shook his head. "When he called us about the code signature, he mentioned something about meeting me at a convention. But I've met hundreds of people at those things. I had no memory of it."

"Hmm," I said. "Does the name Ursula Fournier mean anything to you?"

He seemed to run the name through a sort of mental filter, then shook his head again. "Doesn't ring a bell."

"She's with that gas company in Canada, right?" Katrina said. "I recognize the name." She turned to Jared. "Remember? We exchanged some emails, then she stopped answering. You said she probably got sick of us."

He grunted an answer but clearly didn't feel like talking about Fournier. I stared at him for a moment, then turned back to Katrina. Before I could say anything, my phone vibrated. I looked at the caller ID, then excused myself and went down the hall to Katrina's office.

"Talk to me about your text," Quanta said.

"There are three people from Ceti's previous adventures who are no longer able to answer questions. I don't want the same thing to happen to Ms. Das."

There was silence for a moment. Then she said, "You're

implying that all of these cases might have an inside component to them?"

"Well, that certainly would make Ceti's job easier. But I'm not sure their involvement—if that's even the case—has anything to do with the hacks themselves. It could be as simple as a publicity campaign."

"Publicity."

"Yeah. In fact, I've nothing to do here except think, so that's what I've been doing. And if I had to make a wild guess, I'd say that missing $925,000 won't stay missing for long."

"Explain that."

"Well, up to this point, Ceti's playbook has pretty much involved a lot of digital chaos for some companies and a fair amount of embarrassment for their executives. He's loved the notoriety it brings him. Now, for the first time, he's flexing his hacking muscles to actually steal money. I don't think he'll keep it all for himself. He loves the association with Robin Hood." I paused. "It's just a thought."

Quanta sighed. "This has been a long day. Tomorrow will be longer. The British government is throwing their weight around, applying pressure. And since they're not exactly sure *where* that pressure should be directed, it's going out in equal measure to anyone and everyone involved in the case. That includes us."

"Not surprising," I said. "Ceti has scattered his attacks, certainly in terms of bravado. He's skipping between sectors, varying the kind of data taken, and leaving behind little codes because he knows we're chasing our tails. Now he's shown that he can siphon money away, too. Not much this time, but the potential is staggering. *Every* government should be concerned right now."

"Agreed," she said.

"What I'd like to request is a chance to interview Samantha Das."

"Granted. I'm going to get you on a plane over here right away."

"How about one of those private jets again?" I suggested. "That way I'd be well rested and ready to tackle anything."

Even though I couldn't see her, I heard the weary smile from 3,000 miles away. "That was a nice try. But no."

"Business class, at least?"

"Poole will be in touch." Before hanging up, she added, "Bring your A game, Swan."

CHAPTER SEVEN

The good people of British Airways whisked me from Boston to London in six and a half hours, and I was able to sleep for about two during the overnight flight. Once on the ground at Heathrow, I checked messages and found that my ride would be a woman named Ludo. There was a brief description of her and the car, and where I'd find her.

She was there, standing beside a Jaguar sedan, and opened the rear door as I walked up. I shook my head and pointed to the passenger door in the front. After throwing my bag into the back seat, I climbed in next to her and she floored it, merging into traffic and then quickly overtaking every car around us. She'd either been ordered to hurry or she just naturally had a heavy foot.

"You don't like sitting in the back?" she asked.

"Makes me feel like a pompous shithead. Plus, how else would I get to know you, Ludo, if we didn't sit together and chat like old chums?"

"Do you often feel like a pompous shithead?"

Well, this wasn't the usual chitchat I got from drivers. I turned and looked at her. She had a medium build, short-cropped hair that one could describe as sloppy, and a sleeve of tattoos that might've been an elaborate attempt to tell a life story. While I studied her, she reached for a pair of sunglasses and slid them on. Her face remained totally impassive, not caring one bit that I was sizing her up.

"Most people start a conversation like this by asking about the flight," I said.

Now she turned and trained her hidden eyes on me. "Oh, I'm sorry. How rude of me. You're probably dying to talk about all those hours spent sitting down."

I had to smile. "Where did they find you, Ludo? Or a better question: *Who* found you? Who exactly do you work for?"

"I like to think I don't work *for* anybody. You could say my services are requested by people who value my talents. Today I help people who claim they're the good guys. Tomorrow? We'll see. My calendar is pretty open."

She blew past another clot of cars and made a sharp right turn onto the M4. The trip from Heathrow to the SIS Building in Vauxhall usually took about half an hour, but Ludo seemed intent on doing it in 20 minutes.

"I shudder to think what all of your talents consist of," I said. "Do you count driving as one?"

"I'm getting better, that's for sure."

"Very reassuring."

"Well, you wanted to sit up here and get to know me. A front row seat."

After gunning it around a slow-moving bus, she glanced back at me. "So what's your story? Are you another spy?"

"*Another* spy? Do you mingle with many?"

"I try not to. They think being *daring* makes them *enchanting.* Most spies, though, are really rather boorish, wouldn't you say?"

I shrugged. "Most of the ones I've known are dead."

She gave a grunt. "Probably didn't alter their personality by much, though."

Her clipped accent was hard to place, but her attitude came straight from the street. Quanta may not have selected her to pick me up—we were on foreign soil, after all, and it likely wasn't her call—but she would've been keenly aware of who drew the assignment. It was hard to imagine my stern, generally humorless boss appreciating this. I liked it, but I also felt as if any minute Ludo could go too far.

And then she did. "How many of those dead spies did you kill?"

It took me a long time to get over the question. Finally, I said, "No more than you've killed with your driving. Should I have asked to see some sort of identification?"

"Well, perhaps you're not a spy after all. I wouldn't think they'd be so squirmy."

I forced my eyes off the road and back to my driver. She obviously wasn't just some flunky courier or office assistant, but it wasn't worth asking her; I didn't expect to get a straight answer about anything. Part of me was thoroughly entertained by her smart-ass routine, but another part of me was jet-lagged and my reservoir of patience was quickly draining away. Perhaps on another day I'd enjoy an extended round of verbal fencing with Ludo. At the moment, rather than engaging further, I turned toward the passenger window on my left and rubbed my forehead.

Ludo either took the hint or had run out of impudent comments. She matched my silence for the rest of the drive.

When we crossed the Thames and pulled up at SIS, a tall, young man stood waiting for us. But he wasn't there to escort me; as I climbed out and grabbed my bag, Ludo also stepped out and the young man took her spot behind the wheel. He drove off, leaving me there with my cheeky companion.

"Come on," she said and strode toward the secure entrance. After hesitating, I trudged behind her, wondering just what the story was. As we made our way through security—with Ludo somehow vouching for me—and toward a bank of elevators, I came to the conclusion that she must be with MI6 or one of the other British security divisions. Otherwise how would she have this clearance? So she was some sort of agent. Undercover. Street-wise. Irritating.

Out of the elevator, I followed her without paying much attention. Besides the fatigue, my head was spinning. When I finally looked up, I was in somebody's office, my boss perched lightly on a windowsill.

"Hello, Swan."

"Hello, Quanta." I set down my bag and looked at the well-dressed older man who stood nearby, clearly appraising me. "Hi."

He didn't offer a handshake but nodded a greeting. Quanta made the introductions.

"Swan, this is Sir William Johns. He's unofficially with GCHQ."

I raised an eyebrow. I'd correctly assumed that this specialty department, by necessity, would be involved in a major cyber crime such as this. The Government Communications Headquarters had been formed more than a century ago, primarily working in the cypher world. In fact, under a previous name they'd been the people who worked at Bletchley Park during World War II, cracking the famous Enigma codes. Now, based on what I'd read, their specialties spread a bit wider. But ultimately they were responsible for investigating and defending against the type of warfare Ceti waged.

Johns even had the look I associated with someone in that field. He was of average height, average build, slightly graying hair, and a manner that would make him the least likely person to stand out in a crowd. His clothing, although impeccable and obvi-ously damned expensive, was also as far from flashy as you could get. If there hadn't been but four of us in the room, I might not have even noticed he was there. Some people can blend in so naturally to a setting that they're practically invisible. I've seen it. Or . . . not. You know what I mean.

"*Unofficially?*" I said.

Johns finally spoke. His voice, like his bearing, was quiet and smooth. "Let's say my experience and my abilities make it preferable for me to work in the background."

I studied him for a moment. "NCSC?"

He casually looked over at Quanta, who said, "Sir William's credentials are not what's important here. What *is* important is that you respect his office and his directions. That includes anyone who might answer to him."

I nodded in the direction of my driver. "Like her?"

"She doesn't work directly for Sir William but is assisting his department on this case."

"Is it asking too much to know just who she *does* work for? It's certainly not Uber."

I couldn't be sure, but it seemed like the faint beginning of a smile touched the corners of Quanta's mouth. Maintaining her composure, however, she said, "At the moment, she works for me. She'll bring you up to speed on what we know. And together, the two of you will talk with Samantha Das this afternoon. There's a room for you nearby where you can stow your things. Take three or four hours to rest up and get some food in you, and then you can dive in. Any other questions?"

"About a hundred."

Quanta pushed away from the window, ignoring my comment. She walked over to Sir William and held a brief, hushed conversation. With a smile, he lightly touched her shoulder—a clear act of familiar affection—then gave me another curt nod, repeated it toward Ludo, and breezed out of the room.

"I've never heard anyone walk so quietly," I said.

Quanta turned back to me. "Get some rest. We'll talk before you meet with Das."

I crossed my arms. "I understand the need for discretion around Sir Cloud Walker. But before I rush off to nap time—" I glanced at Ludo. "—how about you clear up the mystery about Danica Patrick here. I think it's time we officially met."

"Oh, you *have* met," Quanta said. "But if you need me to introduce you again, fine. Swan, say hello to Parnell."

THE WALK to my temporary residence was done in silence. Parnell stayed a few feet ahead of me, leading the way. She understood I was still in shock and was willing to grant me the time it would take to process everything.

It made sense that it was her, of course. Her entry to the spy world had originally come through British Intelligence, but that relationship soured to the point where Parnell had resigned. Through a series of unfortunate choices, and in a phase of life where her moral compass may have drifted off true north, she did two things she later regretted: She married a man with a hard criminal background, and she accepted employment with a company—and with people—she'd not fully vetted. Both of *those* relationships soured as well, and both ended on the same day. Together, we took down the evil company.

Alone, I killed her husband.

In my defense, at that time I didn't know they were married. Although, honestly, it wouldn't have stopped me anyway. It was him or me, and in those situations I'm never charitable.

When that case had wrapped, something moved me to persuade Quanta into hiring the former British agent. To my surprise, she'd done just that. And then, not long after, I'd watched as Parnell was shot and killed during the most personal assignment I'd ever experienced. Her demise—ordered by a deranged former Q2 agent, someone obsessed with me, with tormenting and torturing me—was even more tragic because of the senselessness of it all. She was killed purely to antagonize me.

On the floor of a remote cabin, I actually watched the life force drain from her eyes. In all of my years of service, both in the military and with Q2, I'd never been shaken like I was that day. I'd not only roped Parnell back into the spy business, but had, in a way, led her straight to her death. A permanent death, I believed, under the impression that she'd never initiated the investment process.

It wasn't until I was recuperating at home from my own injuries that I discovered Parnell had indeed uploaded. She would live to fight again, with her same spirit encased in a new body.

That body now strolled a few paces in front of me. I shook my head. It was startling to think, after all these years and so many assignments, that I could be so taken by surprise. Especially since —now that I had a few moments to think back over everything— Quanta had practically given it away. When talking about the investigation in England, she'd said, *I have someone there in the U.K.*

Not *we,* as in the U.S. government, but *I.* And Quanta didn't have a squadron of agents at the moment. Unless she'd quietly taken on more spies and assassins, there was me and there was Parnell. I'd missed the clue.

Parnell stopped at a door, threw a quick glance at me, and then used a key card to gain entry. Inside was a small studio apartment with a kitchenette and tiny bathroom. I tossed my bag and jacket on the bed, had a quick look around, and then locked eyes with the reconstituted British secret agent.

"Well, you got me good," I said. "That must've been fun for you."

"Strangely, it was."

"Uh huh." I sat on the bed and indicated a chair for her. "I'm assuming there's a funny story behind the name Ludo, and you're probably dying to tell me about it."

"Latin for *prank*."

"Ah. Well, nothing like a good dose of intellectual hijinks when you're jet-lagged." When she only shrugged, I took a deep breath and said, "I haven't had a chance to visit with you since— since the cabin."

"Yes, well, I have no memory of the cabin or anything that happened there. I heard about it later."

"Right." It would've been during her lights-out period. Thankfully for her, she carried no memory of the bullet penetrating her heart. While I personally longed to discover what took place in that exact moment, I couldn't expect Parnell or anyone else to share my morbid dream.

"How long have you been back in London?" I asked, steering away from the awkwardness and back to business.

"Altogether? About two months. But only on this particular case for a couple of weeks."

"What do you know so far that I haven't read about?"

She gave a shrug. "Very little. From what your contacts in Boston said, Ceti gave something of a warning, then proceeded to drain nearly a million dollars from the retirement funds of teachers and professors. NCSC is attempting to trace it, but Ceti worked as hard on covering his trail as he did on the incursion itself. I'm not hopeful the money will ever turn up."

I chewed on that for a moment. The National Cyber Security Centre, which I suspected paid for Sir William Johns and his exquisite wardrobe, was the computer security branch of the GCHQ. Yes, the UK had the same love affair with acronyms as the U.S. There were times I desperately wished for a glossary.

Weariness was starting to take its toll on me. There would be time for more catching up with Parnell, but for now I could use that nap. She picked up on that and got to her feet. As she opened her mouth to say something, both of our phones vibrated at the same time.

I pulled mine out of my sport coat and stared at the words from Quanta. Looking back up at Parnell, it was obvious she'd received the same message:

Samantha Das is dead.

PARNELL and I both muttered *shit* at the same moment. All it took was one glance for us to acknowledge that the case had immediately elevated way beyond typical hacking. I could've been talked into believing the Cook death and Fournier disappearance were a coincidence; adding Das to the equation meant all three had been murdered.

The nap, which seemed critical just a minute earlier, was forgotten.

CHAPTER EIGHT

W e drove to the crime scene. En route, I put Quanta on speaker.

"How could this have happened?" I said. "I thought we were protecting her."

"To begin with," she answered, "we have no proof yet that she was murdered."

I turned and gave Parnell a look. She kept her eyes on the road but shook her head.

"There were two security personnel outside her door," Quanta continued. "Das was found inside, in her bathtub. Both wrists slit multiple times. Naturally, the preliminary call will be suicide."

"Bullshit," I said.

"And it will be thoroughly investigated. I'm not saying it *was* suicide, Swan; I'm saying that's what the coroner will suspect to begin with. She was alone in the house, with security stationed outside. She felt responsible for a data breach that could likely cost her not only this job but possibly her career. What else could they assume for now?"

I stayed silent.

Quanta gave a sigh. "Look, the three of us may believe Ceti is responsible for this, but it takes more than us stomping our feet to alter a police report. Find something at the scene and report back. And if you don't—well, we'll have to keep searching."

She was right. I didn't like it, but Quanta wasn't to blame. Without evidence, it would be difficult to cry murder. What had me worked up was *knowing* this was coming and yet still being powerless to prevent it. It wasn't the first time I'd dealt with that feeling on a case, and it certainly wasn't the first time being powerless had cost a life. I generally thought of them as *innocent lives*, but without more information, we couldn't know just how innocent Samantha Das had been. Her sudden death, and the manner of it, suggested some culpability.

"All right," I said. "We'll poke around at the scene, but I'll be stunned if we find anything."

Ten minutes later, we pulled up to a row of homes cordoned off by police tape. Parnell flashed the appropriate identification and we walked into a small but tidy flat that was tastefully decorated. A woman in civilian clothes approached and introduced herself as DCI Bagby. She'd obviously been ordered to cooperate with us, but the detective chief inspector's demeanor made it clear she considered us interlopers in her potential crime scene.

I was happy to see that Das's death was being fully investigated and not just automatically written off as a suicide. Bagby could be grumpy with me all day as long as she kept an open mind about what had happened.

She led us to the bedroom upstairs and then into the adjoining bathroom where the body had been discovered.

"Who found her?" I asked.

"I understand she was under some sort of security watch by your people. One of the agents went inside for a routine check."

By your people. Quick to let us know *we* had failed.

Parnell spoke up. "Is there a preliminary estimate on the time of death?"

"Likely around six this morning, give or take an hour."

I scowled. "Six a.m.? So she went to bed and set her alarm to get up early and cut her wrists?"

"I was asked for the time of the death, Mr. Swan. At this time, I can't speculate as to the motivations or the timetable of the deceased." With that, Bagby turned to speak with one of the other police officers on the scene.

I went back into the bedroom and glanced around, then returned to the main level. Parnell joined me a few minutes later and said, "See anything unusual?"

I nodded toward a sliding glass door. "There's a back entry to the unit. It's unlocked. And, from what I gather, no security was stationed there. Just the front."

Parnell gave a disgusted sigh. "All right. Anything else."

"No computers."

She looked around. "What do you mean? Nothing?"

"No desktops. No laptops. Not even a tablet that I can see. She's an IT specialist with no home access to the internet except her phone. Sound plausible to you?"

Parnell turned back to me. "What are you thinking?"

"Let's get out of here and talk. Take me to a quiet pub."

It was a short drive. I spent most of it with my head resting against the window, trying to ward off the fatigue. Coupled with the physical drain of the long flight and the funky jolt to my body clock, I now had a head buzzing with thoughts and questions. Rather than go to sleep, I wanted to vomit out everything in my brain, a mental purge that would hopefully clear up space for a fresh idea. Plus, doing a brain dump with Parnell might stimulate her own thinking process. Two heads, ya know.

She parked on a narrow side street and we walked around a corner into paradise. Well, paradise for a connoisseur of pubs, which I considered myself to be. You can have your traditional bars with blaring music and 75 television screens. I'll be tucked into a quiet, dimly lit joint that serves good beer and booze without mindless distractions. I want two things when I grab a pint: a quality bartender who knows exactly how much interaction to provide, and the freedom to have an intimate talk without shouting over classic rock or Ed Sheeran. No offense to Ed.

I passed up the high-top tables that required too much effort to remain perched and fell into a well-worn booth where I could slouch. Parnell caught up to me with a couple of pints in hand from the bar. I downed a quarter of mine in the first gulp.

"I'm not considering for a moment that this woman killed herself," I said, wiping my mouth. "Which leaves two possibilities, as I see it. One, Ceti used Samantha Das without her knowledge to gain access to the fund. He got what he wanted, which for now seems to be mostly a statement. Then he covered his tracks by snuffing Das, making it look like suicide, and removing all her equipment so we couldn't trace anything.

"Or two, Das was in on the whole thing and kept her gear in a separate location, just on the off chance that someone suspected her and raided her flat. The result was the same, though, with Ceti eliminating a loose end." I took another pull from the pint. "That seems to be his thing."

Parnell gave a nod. "Both make sense. But we do have to include the possibility that it *was* suicide. If she was in on it—"

"What? Guilt?" I said. "Over 900 grand? A lot of dough, but a drop in the bucket for this organization. Even if she was involved and got nailed for it, she'd probably be able to plea in order to help capture Ceti. It might not even mean prison time. And she'd kill herself over that? And so quickly? No, it doesn't figure."

"Well," Parnell said. "I guess the first place to start is finding out whether or not she was in on the hack."

"I'm hoping my new geeky friends in Boston can expedite that search. There must be some telltale sign that Das gave Ceti the combination to the vault. I don't know what the Boston team could find, whether it would be subtle or obvious. Maybe like the difference between using a spare key or kicking in the door. Whatever those digital clues would look like."

We sat quietly for a moment, watching a couple of older men flirt with the bartender while their wives engaged in their own chatter, ignoring the men making asses of themselves. Another man emerged from the loo, singing softly under his breath and wiping his hands on his pants. Outside, a tourist bus rumbled past, the sound of the PA system probably announcing that so-and-so lived on this street back in the day. Just look for the blue plaque.

Finally, Parnell tapped on the table. "You said something about Ceti only wanting to make a statement. What did you mean by that?"

I shrugged. "Couldn't be for the money. Not this time, at least. I mean, 900 grand is a lot of cheddar for you and me; but that pension fund had, what? Hundreds of millions, probably? And he only took out a million?" I shook my head. "If you're doing it for the loot, you take it all. Taking a specific amount means he's making some sort of statement. Other than his digital calling card, I mean."

She studied my face. "What do you think he plans to do with it?"

"I don't know. But this guy—and I still believe in my gut it's one solo shithead and not a team—will eventually show us he's not some crusader, out to do the world a favor. Although that will certainly be the narrative for the press to run with. No, sometimes it just takes these assholes a little bit of time for the public to see their horns."

Parnell got up to grab two more beers but paused beside the booth. "Digital footprints are a bitch to fully erase. I'll bet if we retrace everything from Samantha's last year or so, we'll find something that shines like cat piss in a black light."

"A disgusting analogy," I said. "But probably spot on."

She left to rescue the bartender from the two Don Juans.

My phone vibrated. I looked at the screen before answering. "Hey, Poole. What's up?"

"I have a report for you, but it's probably not what you were hoping for."

"Sounds about right for today."

"The second floor did a deep dive into both Jared Hicks and Katrina Yu. Mostly a cursory examination of their college years because of the time constraint, but a little more in-depth over the past five years. And they couldn't find anything that might tie either of them into Ceti or any other questionable contacts. No red flags." She paused. "But, um . . ."

"Yeah," I said. "How would we know what a red flag looks like in this situation? It could be completely innocuous on the surface. Just because we don't see something doesn't mean there's nothing there."

"Yes."

I closed my eyes and rubbed my forehead. The fatigue was starting to really drag me down. "Well, okay. Thank you, Poole."

"There is one other thing, though," she said.

"Tell me quickly, before I fall asleep."

She was silent for a moment. "I hesitate to mention it, because it's not evidence of anything. And it didn't show up when the second floor did their search because, at the time, our information was incomplete."

"Poole, you're killing me."

Parnell slid back into her seat, setting the fresh pint in front of me. She pretended to study the wood grains of the table while listening to my side of the conversation.

"Well," Poole said, "during the original background checks it wouldn't have stood out because it had no relevance at the time. But once we heard about the hack at LeaCap Funds, I went back and added *that* data to my search."

I had to smile. To think I'd once grumbled about someone as green and raw as Poole assuming the duties of Quanta's assistant. She was one of a kind, and now I couldn't imagine going on a job without her diligently toiling away in the background.

"Once the LeaCap data was factored in," she continued, "we got a hit. Katrina Yu co-authored a paper three years ago that got circulated throughout the security industry. It wasn't a landmark paper, and I don't know if the subject matter is germane to this case, but her co-author—"

"—was Samantha Das," I finished.

"Yes."

Parnell looked up from the table and I raised an eyebrow.

"Okay," I said to Poole. "Shoot me that file, too, please. And thank you. Great work."

I set down the phone and finished off the first beer in one gulp.

"What was that about Das?" Parnell asked.

I caught her up on Poole's findings. Then we were silent for a moment before I mumbled, "Could be nothing at all."

"Yeah," Parnell said. "The digital security community is a small group, comparatively speaking. It wouldn't be unusual for two people in the industry to intersect, especially if the paper's subject was something generic."

"And it was three years ago."

"And they're thousands of miles apart."

"Right," I said. "Two security experts collaborating on a paper is not unusual. I mean, it's what they do. Confer, share notes. Write papers. Forget Kevin Bacon; there's probably no more than two or three degrees of separation in the entire community. If we overreacted to every coincidence we'd never accomplish anything."

"Exactly."

We reached for our second beers at the same time and eyed

each other over the rims as we drank. The eclectic group at the bar all found something hilarious and the room filled with boisterous laughter for a few seconds.

"So," Parnell said. "Samantha Das was in on it."

"And Ceti had her murdered. Just like Shawn Cook and Ursula Fournier."

"Perhaps Ms. Yu wrote papers with them as well."

"God, I wish. But I'm sure Poole would've pounced on that right away. We couldn't be *that* lucky."

"When the news broke about LeaCap, did Katrina Yu share her connection to Das with you?"

"Never said a thing." I took another sip, then added, "And to think, this whole time I suspected her partner, Sasquatch."

"Sasquatch?"

"Never mind." I sighed. "Anyway, we're celebrating a connection that's beyond flimsy. Probably just desperate for even a reasonable clue. Plus, I'm exhausted. I don't know what your excuse is."

She smiled. "I could tell you, but you'll regret it the moment it comes out of my mouth."

"Well, now you *have* to tell me."

"All right." She laced her fingers together on the table and leaned across toward me. "This new body has cramps like I've never experienced in my life. I don't know how she could stand it."

I stared at her for a full five seconds. "You're right. I regret it. Who's gonna win the Premier League this year? Liverpool got a chance?"

Now she laughed. "These are the things you don't think about when you agree to join Q2. I'm sure you've had an equivalent experience."

"Equivalent to *that*?" I shook my head. "No. But I've had bodies with shitty taste buds, one had constant gas no matter what

I ate, another had lousy feet. This one had me puking my guts out on the high seas. It's never a picnic. Wait, I take that back; I had one that was like winning the body lottery. Damned near perfect."

"Well, that's good."

"And I was in it for a whopping 40 hours before getting whacked."

"The universe is so cruel."

CHAPTER NINE

When we're children, there's almost nothing worse than being forced to take a nap.

When we're adults, the idea of a nap can sometimes be more attractive than an offer of sex. Seriously, there are times I've had to think about it and make a tough choice. More than once the nap has won out.

Sorry ladies, I'm taken.

With our prime witness lying on a cold slab in the morgue, there wasn't much for me to do other than to grab a few hours of precious sleep. I crashed hard, pushing aside all thoughts of Samantha Das, Katrina Yu, Ceti, and any other digital monsters that might be lurking. There were likely dreams, but I remembered none of them. It was four and a half hours in a drool-inducing comatose state, what some call the sleep of the dead.

I'd love to speak on the distinction between sleep and actual death, but the truth is, I don't carry around much more data on it than you. I've been killed in the line of duty plenty of times, but no matter how badly I want to catalog that transition, it remains in my lights-out period. And that gnaws at me.

This peculiar facet of my psychiatric makeup has been a topic of conversation with Quanta or Christina a time or two, but more often with Miller. He's the shrink employed by Q2 to make sure I —and now Parnell—don't take the route traveled by the organization's first agent, a route that leads to becoming a psychopath.

During one recent session, Miller had casually steered the conversation back to my curiosity regarding the life/death bridge.

"At what point do you think you might accept the fact that you're never going to retain the memory of that transition?"

I'd leaned back in my chair and fully considered the question before answering. "Oh, I don't know. I guess I hold onto the hope that it's a matter of imprinting."

Miller squinted. "Imprinting. What do you mean by that?"

"Well, I'm constantly uploading my thoughts and memories. Those thoughts and memories are then being downloaded into a new host brain. Given enough times crossing that veil, how do we know that some tiny fragments won't begin to hold on?"

"Even without being uploaded?"

I shrugged. "Sure. Maybe they aren't being officially uploaded, but they're still leaving an imprint. A shadow."

"But the program hasn't been designed that way."

"True," I said. "And yet evolution has changed the basic human design countless ways over the years. Hell, we used to have a tail."

"You don't have millions of years for your little experiment."

"Please. You and I both know that technology has already altered the pace of human evolution. The investment program, by its very nature, is altering my own consciousness. I'm not the same person I was ten years ago."

"And yet you're no closer to finding the answer to your question."

I sat silently for a long while and Miller allowed me time to ponder this. Finally, I said, "I don't know that you're right about that. And, honestly, you don't know if you're right about it, either.

Besides, there's one thing we can agree on." I looked up at him. "It's not hurting anyone—or the program—if I keep trying."

He paused, and I could tell he wanted to say something but felt conflicted. Then he said, "It's not hurting anyone or the program—unless you've developed an unusual sort of death wish."

"You know better than that."

"Do I? We meet each time you download into a new host body, and you've sat in that chair an awful lot."

"Maybe I'm just a very clumsy secret agent."

A faint smile appeared on his face. "Or maybe you're just a little *too* curious when it comes to your quest."

I pointed at him. "If you'll recall, Miller, I'm the guy who raised hell that all these uploads and downloads are corrupting my files. Remember?"

"Yes, I remember. You're worried the investment program is turning you into a monster. But I notice you keep coming back, again and again. We all try to find a balance when it comes to risk and reward." He paused. "Let's put aside the idea of a death wish for a moment and let's assume you do manage to make an imprint, as you call it. For the sake of argument, let's say you somehow retain the memory of what death entails." He propped his chin on a fist and stared at me. "What will you do with that information?"

"Write a book and go on the lecture circuit. Make millions. Duh."

Miller laughed. "I'm serious, Swan. You get the answers you've wanted all this time. The search is over. Now what?"

I shifted in my chair and turned to look out the window at a gray sky. The room felt heavy in the silence, which stretched for nearly a minute. We both knew I had no answer. I'd *never* had the answer to this question.

It had plagued me before I'd even heard of Quanta or Q2. I'd agonized over it following the deaths of the three people closest to me, funneling my anguish into an obsession with the very nature of death and dying. Outwardly, I recovered from the trauma and concealed my grief behind a thin veneer of irreverent humor. Cynicism and sarcasm fueled me, allowing me to storm through life. But inwardly, I burned with an intolerable pain, an excruciating need to know what exactly they'd experienced and where their essence—their souls, if you prefer—existed now.

I'd convinced myself that if they'd succumbed to any form of natural death . . . well, that would've allowed me to grieve in a customary way and eventually move on. It was the manner of their passing that drove my compulsion.

The fact that a new employer had burst upon the scene with an opportunity—or, rather, *opportunities*—to explore that compulsion seemed, at times, like a definite sign from the universe that I was destined to learn the answer, no matter how long it took.

Or no matter how many lives it cost me in the pursuit.

When Miller spoke again, his voice was soft. "Here's my concern, Swan. Not that you're searching for the answer to the ultimate question, but rather that it's the search alone that's driving you. You tell me a lot, but not everything, which is normal. Very few people reveal *everything* behind the curtain. I don't know why you're so hell-bent on this personal mission of yours, but I can certainly guess. So let me ask you something, and I want you to really consider it: What happens if, after years of being driven by this one obsession, you eventually find your answer—but there's no real *application* to go along with the knowledge?"

He paused a moment before adding, "Especially if it turns out to be an answer you don't want to hear?"

I turned from the window back to Miller. For a moment, I simply held his gaze, processing his comments and questions. As much as I'd groaned the first time Quanta had instructed me to meet with Q2's head shrinker, over time I'd developed a fondness for Miller and his goddamned ability to weave his way through all the obstacles I laid down, through all the bullshit I tossed out, maneuvering like a pilot in World War II through the barrage of anti-aircraft flak launched by the enemy. I'd wanted to hate him. In a way, I loved the guy.

I cleared my throat and said, "Have you ever read a really long book, like one of those thousand-page doorstops? The author is taking you on a long, winding adventure. She might throw in a surprise here or there, she might even turn the story upside down at about the three-quarter mark. But you keep reading, because now you're invested, right? You've bought into the world she's created. The idea of *not* reading that last chapter is unthinkable. Even if you read it and it's so bad you want to scream, maybe throw the book across the room. You still have to know how it ends. Because it's not just an ending the author has decided on; it's an ending to your own thousand-page journey. And no matter how *she* ends it, in your mind you always craft an ending you think would've been superior."

He stared at me, his brow wrinkling. "What are you saying?" I didn't answer, so he added, "Christ, Swan. You think death is like one of those Choose Your Own Adventure books? That you get to write your own ending?"

I shrugged and turned back to the window.

"If that's true, then what's the point of your search in the first place?" he asked.

"Because," I said, "even knowing that we have a choice is more than we know right now."

He didn't respond, but, for the first time during that session, he picked up his notebook and scribbled something. It drove me crazy when he did that.

"Since you're suddenly taking notes," I said, "here's an answer to your original concern: No, I don't have a death wish, and I'm not actively sacrificing myself for some grand search for knowledge. It's too much of a pain losing the data that I acquire in the lights-out period."

I grunted, then added, "Besides, it's a bitch getting used to every new body."

I WOKE up from the nap with a pain in my neck. Not an annoyance; a literal pain in my neck. I'd left two pillows under my head and the weird angle must've created a nasty-ass crick. I sat on the side of the bed and tried rubbing it, which didn't help a bit.

Checking my phone, I saw a missed call from Parnell and a text from Katrina Yu. This last one made me raise an eyebrow. Since I wanted to speak with her, too, it was convenient that she'd reached out, even if it was just a simple *'anything new?'* But in my earlier sleep-deprived state, I hadn't trusted a conversation with her until I could put together a cohesive plan of attack. Now, with at least a modicum of rest, I began outlining how that phone call would go.

But I'd also been in the same clothes for thousands of miles and far too many hours. A quick shower and change of wardrobe did wonders, nearly as refreshing as the nap. After pulling an energy drink out of the apartment's fridge, I fell into a stuffed chair and returned Parnell's call, putting it on speaker.

"Preliminary results from the coroner," she said. "No surprise, death was indeed from loss of blood. Three slashes on each arm."

"Seems excessive," I said. "Wouldn't one do it?"

"Of course. But either Ms. Das was being helped along by someone who wanted to make sure it was fatal, or she was in a hurry to depart. There's also the possibility that she wasn't exactly in her right mind at the time. A toxicology report is being worked up to see what she might've had in her system. We're assuming it'll show depression medication. The not-so-cooperative DCI Bagby at least shared some of the evidence in the home, and that included two different prescriptions normally associated with treating depression. A call to her doctor confirmed she's been on those medications, or something similar, for several years."

I closed my eyes and rolled the chilled energy drink can across my forehead. "So we're still left with the same possibilities. Either she was murdered and they set it up to look like suicide, or the weight of what she'd done finally caught up to her and, coupled with an ongoing battle with depression, it was too much. She checks out before we can talk to her."

"I spoke briefly with the president of LeaCap Funds. He was, naturally, reluctant to say much until the investigation is further along."

"Covering his ass for now," I said, my eyes still closed, leaning back in my chair. "Did he give you anything?"

"Said he and the entire organization were, quote, '*devastated by the death of Ms. Das, a loyal employee and energetic personality who will be missed*,' blah blah blah."

"Yeah, right. But did he *give* you anything?"

"Said when Das called him about the incursion, her first words were, '*Well, he did it. He got in.*'"

I opened my eyes and sat up. "She said '*He did it*?' Not '*We've been hacked*,' but *he* did it?" I set the can on the floor. Parnell remained silent, but I felt her smiling through the connection. "And you weren't going to tell me this right away?"

"Just reporting the conversation in the order it took place," she said.

"Of course."

"When the LeaCap president asked her what she meant, she recovered and said that *someone* had broken through the security seal."

"And there was no obvious Ceti signature in this hack, right?

Nothing that Das could've noticed in those first moments that would identify him. Or anyone else for that matter."

"I'm sure we'll find the usual Ceti signature during the digital autopsy. But Das wouldn't have seen it at first, no."

I got to my feet and began pacing, letting this new information simmer. LeaCap's head of IT just happened to be working in the middle of the night when a hacker breaks in. When she alerts her boss, she either makes an educated guess that it was Ceti—or she *knew* it was Ceti.

And less than 24 hours later, she's dead.

"Look," I said, still moving about the room. "Neither of us doubts that Das was in on this. For now, let's put aside the specifics of her death—which at this point are irrelevant—and see if we can find the trail leading from Das back to Ceti."

"My guess is there will be no direct connection," Parnell said. "More than likely we'll have to be content with finding a link to an intermediary."

"Well, that would be a good start." I stopped pacing and rubbed my forehead. I hated to think the intermediary could be Katrina Yu. I'd much rather it be her crabby boyfriend. Had she really suckered me so easily with that brilliant smile and infectious laugh? And all the while, I'd naturally suspected the asshole she was engaged to. Which, upon reflection, seemed like the perfect cover for her: Play nice, be refreshingly open and engaging, and secretly giggle every time Jared Hicks goes into his Sulky Sam act.

All of this was simply taking up brain space, though. We had no real evidence that Yu or Hicks were involved, we had no real evidence that Samantha Das had been involved, and we had no real evidence that she'd been murdered.

The truth is, needing real evidence is a royal pain in the ass.

My phone vibrated and I walked back over to check it out. It was Quanta, requesting an immediate video conference with her two spies. At least the two I knew of.

Parnell and I ended our phone call and a minute later the three of us were on the screen.

"Ceti has taken another step," Quanta said.

"Another hack?" I asked.

"No. Well, in a way, perhaps. But he has apparently converted the million dollars from this pension hack into cryptocurrency and is distributing it randomly."

"Randomly. You mean just handing out currency?"

"That's right. Using a sort of Dark Web money transferring account, he's sending about a thousand dollars each to a thousand different accounts. And people are making quite a fuss about it, too."

Parnell spoke up. "Swan, your comment to me about Ceti making a statement. This must be it."

"Or part of it," I said.

"Yeah. He really is playing Robin Hood now."

Quanta scowled. "Robin Hood? No, I can't believe his ultimate goal is to rob from the rich and give to the poor. It has to be more than that."

"I agree," I said. "I don't think this is the end game he's working toward. But I do think it's a calculated part of his plan. We've managed to keep the name Ceti mostly under wraps. I mean, people in the industry have heard of him—or *them*, according to Jared Hicks. But the average person on the street doesn't know who Ceti is."

"But they will now," Parnell offered.

I nodded. "That's right. You don't just hand out a million bucks to strangers, even on the Dark Web, without the word getting out. And that'll mean Ceti starts out on the high ground. He'll be a certified hero with the public long before we can paint him as some sort of villain. It's actually quite brilliant."

"A great PR move, at the very least."

"And there's more," Quanta said. "Swan, I'll need you to fly back to Boston right away."

"Sure. Why let my body clock adjust to anything at this point? I take it this has to do with the *more* you referenced"

"It does. The team working for Sir William confirmed the usual Ceti signature left behind from the hack. But he left one other message, too. The letters USAURNXT."

I scribbled them on a notepad, then grunted. "Not too subtle. *USA, you're next.*"

CHAPTER TEN

We decided to leave Parnell working in London for the time being. Her job would be to stay on the LeaCap theft, attempt to find out to what degree Samantha Das had been responsible for the breach, and to track down Das's tech gear, if possible.

My time in England had been brief and almost useless. Of course, we had no way of knowing before I arrived that our key witness/suspect would end up bleeding out in a bathtub, or that the shadowy villain we were pursuing would loft a clear threat at a US institution. No matter how sexy Hollywood makes it seem, the truth is that the bulk of a secret agent's job is commuting and waiting.

On my way back to Heathrow, I sent a text message to Katrina Yu.

Heading back to the States. Anything important you need to report, or were you just checking in?

I STILL WASN'T ready to talk with her, and this would buy me time. At the moment, she didn't exactly inspire trust. But I couldn't string her along indefinitely without her getting suspicious that *I* was suspicious.

Sometimes it's a silly game we play.

She instantly wrote back:

No, just curious what you'd found.

I'LL BET. I imagined her wringing her hands.

The plane was delayed for an hour. I used that time to call Christina, but got her voicemail. She was likely at the restaurant, no doubt elbows deep in a sauce. I left my usual syrupy message and apologized in advance for not bringing her anything cool from London. We both knew she wouldn't care. I missed her.

Once aboard, I was able to get some food in me, then hunkered down with the help of a sleeping pill and dozed on and off for three hours. I didn't want to think about the case and instead granted my brain the peacefulness of a reboot.

But once I touched down at Logan, it seemed those three hours might be all I'd get for a while. I'd barely made it through customs when I got a call from Quanta.

"Ceti has struck again."

"Shit," I muttered. "That didn't take long. Where?"

"Multiple targets. At least four that we know of right now, covering healthcare, pensions, a major union account, and banking. The FBI's cyber crime unit has every single agent working on it right now, but it's—it's bad."

It wasn't often that Quanta's voice took on a tone of despair. But I knew it wasn't just the scope of the British attack combined with at least four in the States; she was contemplating the magnitude of chaos these incursions only hinted at. And based on what I'd witnessed in the past few days, her concern was warranted.

"What's the damage?" I asked.

"Still too early to tell for sure. But my source at the FBI says it definitely will top 500 million."

I moved to the side of the concourse to let the bustling foot traffic pass me. "Wait. Are you saying half a billion dollars?"

"That's on the low end of the estimate. There are whispers it could be significantly more. And it doesn't stop there. We have an unconfirmed report of a banking breach in Australia. Not as massive as the ones in the US, but troubling nonetheless."

"We think *all* of these are the work of Ceti? His message warned us about the American attacks, but he never said anything about other countries."

"Which means nothing. In one of our meetings this week, Sir William suggested that we might see a smattering of diversionary attacks. It looks like he was right. Those not only create confusion, but they're sure to spread our resources thin by assigning teams to investigate all of them."

I paused to let a particularly loud group of high school volleyball players—adorned in their matching travel gear—stroll past, laughing and chattering, their roller bags bumping into one another. Once they'd moved off, I said, "I tend to agree with Sir Billy. I would go so far as to suggest that of these four attacks here, only one or two are probably serious. The others are smoke screens, like the breach down under. Getting us to chase specters." I let out a long breath. "The timing suggests all of these have been in the works for a while, too. He just waited for the right moment to spring everything all at once. It's like a digital version of shock and awe."

Quanta agreed. We spoke for another minute, and I shared my concern about Katrina Yu's connection with Samantha Das.

"Well," Quanta said, sounding unconvinced, "it's certainly worth exploring. But it's probably a coincidence. Let's not create drama simply because we're desperate. That, too, will waste time by sending us barreling down a wrong path. Right now we can't afford to waste time. Look into it, but don't make it the crux of your investigation."

I ended the call, a frown on my face. The tenuous connection between Yu and Das could very well be a wrong path. But at the moment it was the only path I could see.

It was late afternoon when I got back to my hotel. We'd held the room while I was in London, so I didn't need to check back in. I went straight upstairs, checked the room safe to make sure the Glock and spare magazines were still where I'd left them, then ordered a sandwich and beer to be sent up. While I waited, I called Katrina Yu.

"You're back," she said. "And back just in time for another big mess."

"So I hear. How late will you be in the office? I need to eat something and change clothes, but I'd like to stop by if you're around."

She gave a wry laugh. "I may not go home tonight. Way too much going on. I keep a change of clothes here in case this happens."

"Great. Give me about two hours."

"Sure," she said. "We need to talk anyway. While you were gone, I found out who the IT person was at the London pension fund. And get a load of this: I know her. That's why I called you earlier."

I pulled the phone away and looked at it in comic disbelief. It was the last thing I'd expected her to say, and that sent my brain racing in different directions. Was she completely innocent after all, as Quanta had suggested? Or was this a clever ploy to make me *think* she was innocent? Really, what could it hurt for me to know she'd had some sort of relationship with Samantha Das? She'd probably realized that I'd eventually find out, and then it would look suspicious if she *hadn't* said a word about it.

I played along. "No shit. How do you know her?"

"Met her at a conference. Discovered that we shared a similar interest in certain security algorithms. Pretty nerdy, right? Anyway, we decided to co-write a paper on it. Nothing major, but I'm completely weirded out that she's the one who found the Ceti hack."

I hesitated before answering. Katrina had expressed surprise at finding out that Das worked for LeaCap—but hadn't uttered a word about her death. Did she not know? Was that not common knowledge yet? I didn't dare say something I shouldn't.

"Well," I said, "I could say something about it being a small world, but I guess in your business it's always a rather small set of people. When's the last time you spoke to her?"

"Oh, two years ago? Maybe a little longer. She's wicked smart, but not the easiest person to talk with. You know what I mean?"

I started to say, *Like your boyfriend?* but kept that to myself.

"All right," I said. "We'll talk more about it when I get there. Like you said, a lot's going on. See you in a bit."

Lunch arrived and I relished the cold beer and sandwich. Fries were not an option, so I picked at the flavorless house-made potato chips while thinking about the semi-awkward chat with Katrina. I often prided myself on being able to sniff out a fraud, but with her it was difficult. She was so damned disarming with that buoyant personality. I hated to think I'd been so easily fooled.

I sent a quick message to Poole, asking if there were any updates. I also asked if the police had officially released the news about Samantha Das, or if that was still being kept under wraps.

Poole's response was that it was not being withheld from the public, but maybe the news hadn't spread through the community yet. That much was obvious.

She added that more details on the latest hacks were forthcoming. In the meantime, based on the limited data we had, it was beginning to look like I'd guessed right. The pension fund reported more than $200 million had been siphoned away from their holdings. But that was nothing compared to the bank. They'd quietly informed the FBI that they'd been hacked to the tune of $600 million, despite pouring significant resources—time, technology, and money—into cybersecurity.

For Ceti, though, it was like they left the money sitting in a bag on their front porch.

Now the question was: Would the digital thief start handing out this money, too? Parnell had said he was playing Robin Hood, and while I didn't think there was one generous bone in the shithead's body, I knew the love he'd garner from the tactic would be a narcotic for him.

But what was the *real* goal? After shaming dozens of public figures, stealing millions of dollars, and generally wreaking havoc on the world's cybersecurity systems, what exactly was the driving force? Ceti had built a small cult following that fawned over him, and now he seemed to be pandering to a global audience. Granted, narcissism is a remarkably powerful trait, and it has impelled plenty of assholes through the years. It just didn't ring true in this case. There had to be something else behind the mayhem.

I shook my head. I never understood why this element of the job would so often hijack my thoughts. The government of the United States paid me to hunt down the baddest of the bad guys, the *knaves*, as Quanta referred to them. They paid me to use my intelligence and my training to find them and—often—eliminate them before they killed more people.

The government did *not* pay me to play junior psychologist with the super criminals we chased. And yet, no matter how determined I might be to simply follow the standard procedures and kill without too much analysis, it had become common for me to insist on getting inside the heads of my villains. Maybe after taking so many lives and giving so many of my own, I needed to know what drove our species to sink to the lowest levels. Instead of the ever-increasing body count making me numb to killing, it was making me desperate to understand the *why.*

More than once, my incessant need to crawl around inside the head of a target had backfired. But seeing how I had access to real-life do-overs, I considered it not only an acceptable risk, but also critical intel on a larger scale. Critical not in terms of actually pulling the trigger, but in helping to tamp down the sometimes raucous battle raging inside my *own* head.

I GRABBED A LONG, hot shower before leaving the hotel. At a coffee shop, I picked up a caffeine boost that I could nurse on the walk. The wind had picked up, but for now it was at my back. I'd experienced my share of dreary weather in Boston over the years; a stiff breeze I could handle.

The same nervous young man sat at the front desk in Kajartek's lobby. He recognized me the moment I walked in. The look of terror was quickly replaced with a forced smile, although his voice cracked when he spoke.

"Here to see Ms. Yu? Let me get her for you."

"Please hurry," I said, then threw an anxious glance out the window. "I need to get back home soon. If they find me here, it won't end well." I turned back to him and opened my eyes wide. "For any of us."

He practically pulled a hamstring hustling out of sight. I allowed myself a grin.

I heard Katrina's laugh before I saw her. When she poked her head around the corner, she shook her head at me and then waved me back. During the walk down the hall, she said, "You really need to stop terrorizing Aaron."

"Who's Aaron?"

"Our receptionist. You've gotta stop scaring him."

"I have no idea what you're talking about. Is your betrothed not in today?"

"He's battling a wicked sore throat, so we thought it was best that he go home."

"I'm sure he'll be sad he missed me."

We got to her office and she offered me a bottled water, which I accepted. Once seated, we got down to business.

"First," I said, "have you or the FBI uncovered the way Ceti wormed his way into these new systems. Did he use an outside vendor again? Did he have inside help? Any clues?"

Katrina let out a long breath, the sound of exasperation. "I haven't heard any updates from the Feds yet. Did you learn anything in London?"

She'd quickly shifted from providing information—of which she had none—to requesting information. Was there a reason she was so anxious to find out how much we knew?

"My time in London was shorter than Britney Spears' first marriage. The police and some of England's finest James Bond types are digging through everything."

I didn't want to offer anything else until I was sure the person on the other side of the desk was actually an ally. It was time to address the item that really gnawed at me.

"So tell me about your association with Samantha Das. You say you wrote a paper together?"

"Yeah. It was based on a cybersecurity issue we're both inter-ested in, so we agreed to collaborate on it. She did the bulk of the research and the initial draft. I cleaned up a few things and added more of a real-world element, based on some of the work Jared and I had done since we left school. I'd credit her about 70-30 on the content, but I think she liked the idea of having me and my qualifications to add some credibility." She gave a small laugh. "In the end, it didn't matter. The paper didn't make much of a splash."

"And you never collaborated again?"

"No. The last time I spoke to her was right after the paper was published. I'm sure if it had been a hit we would've teamed up again. I didn't know she worked with this pension fund. When we wrote the paper she was doing mostly freelance work. I'll have to reach out and connect with her. Maybe there's something she can tell us that'll ring a bell."

"No, you won't be able to talk with her."

Katrina raised an eyebrow. "Is she being isolated by the police?"

"No. She's being cremated."

There was no sound in the room for a few moments. I kept my eyes on Katrina, even when I took a slow sip of my water. I watched for any sign that might give something away. All I saw was a slow realization of what I'd said. Then her face clouded.

"Samantha is dead?"

"Suicide."

Again, silence. I set down the bottled water and leaned forward, my elbows on my knees, waiting her out.

She got up and walked over to the window, where she stood quietly for nearly a minute before turning back to face me. "So people naturally think she was in on this, right?"

I shrugged. "I'm not sure anybody knows *what* to think. But it doesn't take Scotland Yard to float the theory that, yeah, she was involved somehow. Either that or she'd been fighting her own demons for a while and this failure was just the final straw. We never know what another person is battling and what will push them over the edge." I sat back. "But yes. There will be some who believe she was involved."

"Some. Like you?"

Now I stood up so we faced each other. "Katrina, with your icy tone you've succeeded in conveying your disgust that guys like me automatically default to thinking the worst of people. Well, not to sound all Peter Patriot or anything, but if it wasn't for guys like me assuming the worst, then you might find yourself facing a lot more nightmares than you do. We don't convict people without evidence, and we don't make anyone's life hell while we search for that evidence. But to catch a bad guy, you have to start with a very large pool of suspects and filter your way down to the messy bottom. So while I'll never be crowned Mr. Congeniality, I will do the dirty work that'll get me the shithead I'm after. And that means suspecting anyone who has a tie to the case. Feelings be damned."

She hadn't expected the lecture. After processing it all, she crossed her arms in the classic defensive posture. "Which means you suspect me, right? Because I wrote a goddamned paper with the woman who found the LeaCap breach and then offed herself."

"Suspect you? No. Curious about what you may have gleaned from your association with Ms. Das? Sure. Would you say that's a smart move on my part?"

After a few moments, she visibly relaxed. Her arms went back to her side, and she let out another long breath. "Yes. All right. I'm sorry I got upset. I'm—I'm not used to things turning this nasty."

"At the risk of sounding condescending, it's a big, bad, and very nasty world. And I hope you don't ever have to get used to things like this. It's a common occurrence for me; let's hope it's a unique chapter in *your* life."

I'd mentally shoved her backward, hoping to crack the brittle defenses of an amateur. It was always a risk; you might rattle them enough until they give something away, or you could drive them further behind a defensive wall. I had to trust that Katrina Yu's genial personality wasn't entirely a front and that she'd show me a sign if she was involved.

The jury was out. It had been worth the attempt, but I'd really learned nothing.

After a few moments to reset, we changed the subject.

"How do you think Ceti was able to pull off four hacks in one day?" I asked, sitting back down. "Is this a sign that he's a prodigy, or does he have a team working with him?"

She went back to her chair. "I'd say he's for sure a prodigy. Anyone can learn to code, you know? But some people speak it like their mother language. They take in everything at a glance, they see paths and loops and backdoors that the rest of us need to concentrate on in order to see. I don't want to oversimplify it, but they—well, they *speak* code, if that makes sense. It's their language of choice. I'd almost call it scary how fluent they are. And that's what makes my job so tough; I can work for weeks or months to find a solution to one of their hacks, and in a matter of hours—or less—they see another path that I haven't factored in.

"And I'll be blunt: I'm really good at this game." She shook her head. "But people like Ceti? They're uncanny. I'd go so far as to say they're savants. I mean, honestly, I wouldn't be surprised if Ceti was classified with high-functioning autism. Very high on the spectrum, but certainly laser-focused on routine, with selective habits of order that you and I might find out of the ordinary. But to him, it's beyond a gift. And in a digital world, he might be the most highly-adaptable form of life. A sort of—"

She paused, then finished.

"Well, as our species continues to evolve into a hybrid of human and machine, he might be on the highest rung, if that makes sense."

I sat back and steepled my fingers against my chin. Not only did it make total sense, it was perhaps the best explanation anyone had ever given regarding the divide between pre-digital humans and those who were coming of age in the coded world. Someone who connected naturally with machines would of course be best suited to win. The rest of us could never keep up in a world that evolved and morphed daily. We relied on the machines to help us learn; people like Ceti were essentially *melded* with the machines. How could we compete?

The meeting had been brief, but suddenly I had lots to think about. We needed more information on the day's hacks or a breakthrough on the London front. In the meantime, I wanted an old fashioned made with rye and an extra cherry. I wasn't hungry, but the cocktail just sounded right.

I told Katrina I'd be back in touch and stood up. She merely nodded at me, then turned to her laptop. The front desk was vacant—no sign of the nervous receptionist—so I let myself out and grabbed the elevator. I could either have that drink now and think about everything, or do a quick upload first before popping into the hotel bar. It had been far too long since my last link to the Q2 computers, and the walk back was long enough for my sense of duty and responsibility to override my desire for booze. The old fashioned would have to wait. I waltzed past the lobby bar and went up to my room.

It took a couple of times for the electronic key card to work on the door. I pushed inside the dark room and began to slip out of my jacket before turning on the light.

I felt an insect sting on my neck. It hurt like a bitch. I threw a hand up, hoping to slap it away, when someone with a ridiculously strong grip took hold of my wrist and twisted me onto the floor.

"Relax," a rough voice breathed into my ear. "You'll be going to sleep now."

CHAPTER ELEVEN

W hen the average civilian thinks about training exercises for elite military soldiers, they imagine it involves a ton of weapons practice and some badass hand-to-hand combat lessons. That's all true, and I went through countless hours of it. Came in handy more than once, too. It's the kind of stuff that becomes lodged in your muscle memory—which, fortunately for me, is transferred right along with my other memories.

There's another component of the elite training, though, that isn't as glamorous as the action hero shit, but will more often than not be the element that saves your life:

Thinking and reacting with lightning reflexes.

Within seconds of hitting the floor, I realized two things. One, that wasn't an insect I'd felt; it was a needle. And two, if the asshole on top of me managed to put me to sleep, as he'd promised, I wouldn't be waking up.

Well, I would—but it would be in an all-new body in the Q2 basement in Washington, D.C. And dammit, I hadn't uploaded yet. There would be a shit ton of stuff I lost. And that was just not acceptable right now.

Anyway, that took four seconds. At the five second mark, all of the ass whoopings I'd suffered at the hands of Quanta paid off. I did as the asshole said and relaxed, but just long enough for him to think I'd become compliant. There was a tiny letup in his pressure, and that was enough. With a quick jerk, I freed my left hand and fired that elbow up hard, smashing into his jaw. The jolt wasn't enough to force him off me, but it stunned him, allowing me to roll slightly. Another vicious crack with my elbow to his forehead sent him arching backward. I freed my left leg and launched a heel into his jaw. I heard a sharp crack, a pretty sure signal I'd fractured his face. He slumped back.

But there was a problem. I was slumping, too. I felt a wave of fatigue rush over me, and the already dim room grew a shade darker. Whatever rat poison he'd injected was taking effect.

I heard a moan from my attacker. He was barely hanging on himself, but if I passed out, he would most certainly recover enough to kill me. I fumbled through my pants pocket, struggling to stay conscious and retrieve my phone. I managed to hit the button that connected me with Poole.

"Swan?" I heard her say.

"Code . . ." I was starting to fade out. "Code three. Hotel . . . hotel room."

The phone slipped out of my hand, clattering onto the fake wood floor beside me. There was another groan from the hulk. He was pushing himself up onto his knees. Summoning every ounce of strength I could find, I pulled my foot back and, before passing out, fired a solid kick straight into his chin. He flew back, his head slamming into the lower cabinet, producing another satisfying crack. Well, probably not that satisfying to him.

He lay still, and I stared up at the ceiling as my own world went black.

To my surprise, I did not wake up in Q2's basement.

I was on my hotel bed. Someone was pressing something cold against my forehead, and I could hear a muffled voice somewhere.

Before investigating, I took an immediate reading of my physical status. My stomach felt like it needed to purge itself while my head was in complete and utter turmoil. There was pain that didn't seem to settle into any one spot but preferred to sprint around the perimeter of my brain. My ears were ringing, which might've contributed to the difficulty picking out the voice.

With two deep breaths, my stomach settled just a touch. I squinted through the headache until my eyes fell upon a woman sitting beside me on the edge of the bed. She was the one pressing the cool towel against my head.

I blinked a couple of times to center myself before croaking out a single word. "Sanitation?"

The woman gave one curt nod.

"How long did . . . did it take you . . . to get here?"

She pulled the towel back. "Seven minutes."

The people in Q2's Sanitation department would never be accused of being wordy. They were absolute technicians when it came to cleaning up any mess caused by a field agent, even to the point of setting things straight with local law enforcement. When there was an emergency situation, especially those involving blood and bodies, they were your best friends.

But they didn't talk much to agents. Someone, perhaps Quanta, had deemed it unnecessary, maybe even risky, for the two departments to mingle. They showed up, worked their magic, and were gone. In all my years with the agency and all my encounters with Sanitation, I'd never so much as learned a first name. Now I knew better than to pry.

There was information I did need, however. Taking another centering breath, I was finally able to talk without a struggle.

"What about the piece of shit who injected me? Did he get away?"

"No. He's being held in another room down the hall."

I nodded thankfully. "I'm assuming a doctor is here?"

She didn't say anything, but stood up and dropped the towel on the nightstand. She walked away and a minute later a new face swam into view, another woman. This one, however, smiled.

"Welcome back," she said. "You probably feel like crap."

"That I do, ma'am." I swallowed hard, pushing back some of the pain. "What did he shoot in me?"

"We'll do a thorough test of the hypodermic needle we found, but it appears to be a form of a party drug. Causes either deep relaxation or, in some cases, unconsciousness in about a minute or so."

"Sounds about right," I said, then grimaced. "Can I get something to drink? My mouth tastes like a compost heap."

She smiled and handed me a bottled water from the table. I took a small sip, then another. My head still screamed with pain, but I needed that to simmer down pretty damned quick. There were answers I needed.

As if reading my mind, the doctor stood up to leave and handed me my phone. "There's someone who wanted to talk with you as soon as you came to. I'm told you would know who that was."

"Oh, I know," I said. When she walked out, the woman from Sanitation followed her, leaving me alone in the room. I was connected with Quanta seconds later.

"How do you feel?" she asked.

"Like I've been eaten by a bear and shit off a cliff."

"You're lucky to be alive. The doctor says you'll feel better in a couple of hours. We're assuming there wasn't enough juice in the shot to kill you."

"No. Going by the fate of previous Ceti problems, I'd either have been the victim of some terrible accident or I'd have killed myself. Hell, they might've done the bathtub move again. I'll be having a chat with the goon who jabbed me."

"Do it soon. I'm going to have him taken to a nearby FBI office," she said.

"Fine. Then there's the matter of who put the finger on me."

"Yes. I know you're suspicious of Hicks and Yu. But it might have been someone who tailed you back from London, too."

"Sure. I haven't exactly been hiding in the shadows on this case, but I also didn't think I'd done anything worthy of taking me out of the picture. In fact, we really haven't learned squat. So why was I suddenly a threat?"

"You must have stumbled onto something without knowing it."

I grunted. "Right. But *they* know it, and Ceti wanted me removed before I got smart enough to figure it out."

I took another drink of water. The pain receded to a dull ache and a second-class annoyance, but the nausea refused to settle down. Nothing I couldn't deal with, especially with the shithead responsible for the discomfort waiting down the hall. But I still had questions for the boss. "Any updates from Parnell on the Samantha Das case?"

"She's operating under the assumption that Das kept another base of operations for her shadow life. And, if so, it won't be too difficult to track it down. There may be some answers there."

"Unless Ceti beats you to it."

"There is always that possibility, yes. That would leave your assailant as the closest link to Ceti that we have at the moment. As soon as you're up for it—"

"I'm ready," I said, swinging my legs over the side of the bed. A sudden wave of dizziness forced me to steady myself with one hand. "Well, almost ready. Don't let the Feds take him away until I get down there."

We ended the call and I pushed myself to my feet. After a moment, I staggered toward the bathroom and threw up.

HE WAS BIG, in both height and width. His eyes were open to mere slits, but they tracked me from the door to the side of his bed. The same doctor who'd treated me was finishing up some minor work on the brute's face, but her bedside manner was decidedly different now. There was no smile, no gentle voice, and I got the immediate impression the good doctor wasn't overly concerned with whether or not her ministrations caused the killer any pain. I watched her finish a quick stitch to his face. It had to hurt, but he didn't flinch one bit as she tied it off.

After putting away her tools, the doctor gave me a nod and moved to the side. Two stout FBI agents, a man and a woman, hovered a few feet away, never taking their eyes off the beast, even though one of his wrists was handcuffed to the bed frame. One agent held her service weapon at waist level, ready to act. I moved over and stood next to the bed.

"How's your face?" I asked. "I mean, besides the hideous features you had when you walked into the hotel."

He kept a flat gaze leveled at me but remained silent.

"He's got a fractured cheek and a busted nose," the doctor said from behind me. "When he leaves here, we'll take him to a hospital before he goes to a cell."

"Oh, no. Where does it hurt?" I leaned over and touched the side of his face. "You mean here?"

The guy finally showed a reaction to the pain. He yanked his head away from my hand and his eyes burned above the grimace.

"What about here?" I asked, probing his face again. He jerked backward, and this time a small grunt escaped his mouth. From the corner of my eye I saw the female agent take a step closer. The other agent worked hard to keep the smirk off his face.

I shook my head. "I don't feel so hot either. I should probably warn you that I've puked twice in the last few minutes and I'm liable to yack all over your broken face. Something about my body trying to cope with that shit you pumped into me. That's on top of the fact that I've been puking a lot lately, anyway. It's disgusting, I know, but probably just the way I'm built. It sucks, and that little concoction you gave me didn't help things at all. But the bottom line is, if you get vomit on your face, you only have yourself to blame."

I pulled a chair over and sat down beside the bed. "Well, yourself and your boss. The guy who sent you over here to kill me. Believe me, I wouldn't mind barfing on him. Sort of a fetish."

A ghost of a smile appeared at the corners of his mouth.

The doctor touched my shoulder. "If you need anything, ask the kind agents here to give me a call. I can be back in just a few minutes."

"Thank you. What about Big Boy here? He's able to form words with that fracture, right?"

"It'll hurt like hell, but he can talk if he wants to." She breezed out of the room. For the brief moment the door was open, I saw two other officers parked outside.

"Did you hear that?" I said to the cuffed man on the bed. "She said you can talk. So I'm hoping we can cut through the usual shit you see in the movies. You know, where the bad guy plays tough and refuses to talk. Then we have to go through the whole song and dance of offering you a deal, because you're not the big fish, blah blah blah. You've seen it before. You and I both know that eventually you'll talk with me, so how about we cut out all that stupid stuff at the beginning and just have a nice chat. Well, nice for me, painful for you. But that's your fault, too. What's your name?"

He opened his mouth a fraction of an inch and his words came out in a croak. "Piss off."

I shrugged. "Must've been hard going through school with a name like that. Good thing you're big enough to take care of yourself. Unless you get kicked in the mouth. Help a guy out, will ya? What's your name?"

"Kiss my ass." Yet even as he said it, there was almost a twinkle in his eye. It was as if the big galoot was enjoying himself.

I leaned forward and he instinctively pulled back. "No," I said with a small laugh. "Relax. I'm not throwing up. Yet. But here's the thing: You and I are not that different. We basically do the same job, just for different people. It's like—like you're Netflix and I'm HBO, right? Come on, give me something besides '*piss off*' and '*kiss my ass*.' Those aren't even creative."

He studied me for a moment, then gave the best smile he could manufacture, given the pain it must've caused. "How about go pound gravel up your ass?"

I nodded. "Okay, we're making progress. At least you're trying something new."

At that moment, my phone vibrated with a message from Poole. I sat back and scrolled through her findings. Apparently even with the job I'd done with my elbow and foot, facial recognition software was still able to identify the hulk lying before me. Arlo Benn, aged 41, with an impressive rap sheet spanning North America, Europe, and Australia. He'd served time for assault and armed robbery, and had been in a French prison for attempted murder when he managed to escape with two other nasty types. That had been six years ago, and in those years he'd become wanted for murder investigations in Amsterdam and Germany. I'd been seconds away from becoming the latest entry on his resumé.

The rest of the file filled me in on his background, which I found fascinating.

I held the phone up to the female agent. "What do you think? Same guy? Without the damage, of course. Cute, right?"

She squinted at me, unsure how to answer. Her partner grinned.

I put the phone back in my pocket. "Okay, look. It's Arlo, right? Well, Arlo, I think you should talk with me. Our technical wizards have taken your phone, so it's only a matter of time before they unlock all the treats inside."

After a brief flash of surprise, he gave another slight smile and warbled, "What's *your* name?"

"Eric. "

"You're not with the FBI."

"No. I'm with Pampered Chef. I'm here to sell you a badass potato peeler that doubles as a wine bottle opener and comes in a variety of bold colors. But now that we're friends, I'll just *give* you the potato peeler and we can talk about who hired you."

He gave a subtle shake of his large head. "Eric, I can't talk to you about any of that. And you know it."

"If you say so. You wanna talk about the lieutenant you punched a few years ago?"

This brought a disgusted grunt. "He was an asshole."

"Of course he was. Every country's military is filled with lieutenants who need a proper ass kicking. The number of captains who need the same treatment is a little less, and the list gets even smaller when you move up to major and colonel. But lieutenants? Hundreds of them who should get their teeth knocked out. Hell, I punched one myself when I served."

He raised an eyebrow. "No shit."

"No shit. In a South American jungle. Lucky for me, he got bit by a poisonous snake before we got back to civilization and croaked right there in the bush before he could write me up. Damnedest thing."

After staring at me for a few seconds, he said, "Bullshit."

I grinned. "Total bullshit, Arlo. Just trying to bond with you.

Although I did *want* to punch one guy, but he was a full-bird colonel. That wouldn't have ended well for me."

Arlo turned his head and sized up the two agents in the room with us, then looked back at me. "So you've got my record. But there's only one assault of an officer on there. The other one never got reported."

"You're quite the badass rebel, aren't you?"

He shrugged. "Actually, I like to think I'm easy to get along with."

"Except when you're murdering people."

"It's a job, Eric. Doesn't mean I can't be courteous."

I laughed. "Arlo, you are officially the oddest thug I've ever questioned."

"I'm complex."

"Fair enough."

"And I should tell you right now, I'm gonna have to wait for an official notice—"

"Hold on a second," I said. I stood up, walked to the bathroom, and heaved into the toilet. It was almost like I was back on the ship in the Caribbean. Embarrassing, sure, but Arlo was at least talking now, and I didn't really want to puke on his newly busted face. After rinsing my mouth out in the sink, I walked back into the room. Both FBI agents stared at me, wondering what the hell was going on. Even the grinning one now looked confused. I sat down again.

"Now, you were saying?"

He seemed to prepare for the pain involved in a long speech. "I was saying that you seem like a decent guy, Eric, and I'm sorry I tried to kill you. But I'm gonna need an official notice of immunity before I offer you anything. And I'll tell you up front that even what I have probably won't help you at all."

"Well, Arlo, from one mercenary to another, I can tell *you* that right now I'll take any scrap I can get. Let's start with this: Did you kill Samantha Das?"

"I don't have that official immunity offer, Eric. So, for the record, I'll say, '*Who is Samantha Das?*'"

I tapped a finger on the arm of my chair. "You're really gonna make me wait for some penguin to come in here and draw up a government offer?"

"I really am."

"Shit," I muttered, and kept tapping, trying to think of a way to expedite the information that Arlo sat on, no matter how thin it might be.

"Look," I finally said. "I'll make sure somebody talks with the DA. All I can do is give my word, which I know doesn't mean shit to you. But that's all I've got. How about you give me a nibble, just to make up for trying to kill me. That's fair, right?"

He studied my face while I searched his, which was battered and bruised. I'd done a good job doling out the kind of damage that would leave him in significant pain for a few weeks. I didn't really expect him to help me at all, the *Band-of-Brothers* connection notwithstanding.

Then, through his fractured face, he spoke. "He hangs out around a node of the Dark Web called ZigbyNet. Uses a string of numbers to identify himself."

I tried to not look shocked. Instead, I spelled ZigbyNet back to him and he nodded. Then he said, "Now get out of here, Eric. We're square."

CHAPTER TWELVE

I went back to my room to tough out the nausea while Arlo Benn was hustled off to a hospital under the watchful eyes of four armed escorts. For the most part, I was happy to have squeezed anything out of the guy; it was more than I really had any right to expect. Although, in reality, hired meat like Arlo weren't necessarily reluctant to spill their guts. Fictionalized bad guys always seem to live by some ridiculous code, and the cinematic hero is stonewalled by the perp who refuses to rat out anyone.

Real life? It's nothing like that. They'd give up their grandmother to shave two years off a sentence. They might even trample the old gal making a break for it. Don't be fooled by Hollywood's portraits of loyal goons. It's every man, woman, and asshole for themselves.

But as much as I appreciated the tip, this new snippet of intel left me in the same awkward position. The best people to help me track down Ceti on the Dark Web were the people I suddenly distrusted the most: Hicks and Yu. What was the point of having them on our team if I couldn't tell them anything? They'd suddenly become the appendix of our investigation.

After puking one more time, I began to feel a little better. Which was a relative term for me lately, given the circumstances. I decided the cocktail Arlo had jabbed into my neck was partly responsible, but the bulk of the blame lay squarely on the fact that I currently inhabited a wimpy body. It happens. The investment process is far from perfect.

I called Quanta and told her my reluctance to share the new information with our cyber security experts.

"Tell them," she said without hesitation.

"But they—"

"*Tell* them," she repeated. "We have no real evidence of collusion between them and Ceti, and if we start working around them it'll only bog down the entire investigation. Plus, they're good enough that they'll figure it out sooner or later if we're withholding information. No, we've hired them to help us; until you can prove they're compromised, let them help."

I kept my mouth shut and let the silence drag on between us. It was my immature way of announcing that I disagreed.

Quanta sighed. "Listen, Swan. Under ordinary circumstances I might be willing to put things on hold while we find another team to work with. But we're on the precipice of a full-scale global digital catastrophe, and we're getting pressure from all sides: *our* government, the UK, Europe, Central Asia, South America, and now Australia. We can't wait around while we vet another group and then get them up to speed, simply based on a hunch. I appreciate your concern, and I'm not saying you're dead wrong on this. I'm saying Ceti has backed us into a corner. We have to fight our way out of it and hope we get in a lucky punch or two."

She paused, then added, "Okay?"

It was my turn to sigh. I often got worked up when I felt like my advice was being ignored, especially since that advice was seasoned by years of experience on the job and countless cases, some successful, some not. This particular assignment, however, was unusual in that it involved cooperation with foreign governments. That wasn't Q2's style. I was spoiled by having to answer only to Quanta and the nameless/faceless group *she* answered to. This time, Sir Softy Pants and a collection of other allies were exerting pressure on my boss, which meant . . .

Which meant, as tough as it was, I needed to back off and let her have this win.

"Okay," I said. "I'll share what I know. But if I end up being right, you know I'm going to be hell to work with for a long time."

"You're already hell to work with. Let me know when you get something."

I tossed the phone onto the bed and contemplated the condition of my stomach. It made a few disgusting sounds, but for now the urge to barf had dissipated. With a little bit of down time, I stretched out on the bed and uploaded.

THE NEXT MORNING, I was in Katrina's office. She and Hicks, apparently recovered from his sore throat, were both quiet. It could have simply been that the impact of Das's death had finally sunk in. While I'd grown numb to body counts, I had to remember it was shocking for the average civilian. And, since Das had been one of them, it brought home the realization that overnight they'd made the move from Triple-A to the Major Leagues. It was now serious in a way they'd never contemplated.

I sat down with them and shared the information I'd received from Arlo Benn.

"My first question," I said, "is why didn't you stumble across Ceti's signature on the Dark Web?"

They exchanged a look, something I'd grown accustomed to in working with them. They seemed to constantly require mutual approval before commenting. I began to wonder if I'd be better off talking with them individually.

"Well?" I prompted.

Jared shifted in his seat. "It's not that simple. We did as much of a search as we could for the full string of his signature. But you probably just don't understand exactly how the Dark Web works."

"That's why I'm here, Jared. For you to explain all of this to me."

He shifted again. "You're wanting the equivalent of a bachelor's degree of information within a single paragraph. It's way more complicated than explaining how to right click on a photo. In a nutshell, though, this portion of the internet is generally encrypted and basically impervious to web crawlers."

I studied him. "Web crawlers. Like the bots used by search engines."

"Exactly. It's dark for a reason, Mr. Swan. If it was just another browser, it would be accessible to everyone. It's not. There are large portions of it that can't be indexed. And that's why it works as a home base for people or groups that are either selling something illegal or planning an incursion like—well, like the ones we've seen from Ceti."

"All right," I said. "What can you tell me about ZigbyNet. And please—" I looked at Katrina. "Please stop checking in with each other on every question. Just answer them."

She shrugged. "ZigbyNet is not unlike the old bulletin board systems from the early days of the Arpanet."

"Launched by the Department of Defense," I said. "One of the foundations of the modern internet."

"Correct. The people who started ZigbyNet were essentially creating an homage to the old time bulletin boards where academics used to communicate. Same type of system, but without the academics. A chance for people to trade information, complain, flirt. The usual stuff."

"And anyone can jump on?"

"No," Hicks said. "It's encrypted."

I turned back to him and stared for a moment. "So not just anyone can log in." I leaned forward. "But *you* can. Am I right?"

He glanced at Katrina then quickly must've remembered my lecture. He faced me again. "Yes. Well, we used to. Unless things have changed."

"And why were you able to access a site used by criminals?"

"It's not just criminals," Katrina said with an edge to her voice. "Okay, a lot of criminals use it, but there are some legit people and enterprises on there, too. Remember, Mr. Swan, there are criminals running amok on every social media site. And all over Wall Street, throughout many local political organizations. Everywhere. But that doesn't make everyone in those groups a criminal by association."

I gave a half smile. "Sure. But my Aunt Edna ain't posting pictures from her quilting club on the Dark Web. So climb off the soapbox and jump down here in the mud." I looked back at Jared. "Why did you have access?"

He didn't answer for a long moment, just peered out from behind his bush of facial hair. The same hatred sizzled in his eyes, and I knew it was painful for him to cooperate with me.

"Were you ever a college student?" he finally asked. When I nodded, he continued. "Well, I was once a college student, too. So I did things I wouldn't do today. Just like you probably did. And I raised a little hell, just like you, too. That doesn't make me a bad guy; it makes me pretty normal, actually. So yes, I found a path to ZigbyNet and felt emboldened to say some things. I felt superior, which is what those sites mainly do: make otherwise foolish or insecure people feel superior. The traditional internet is filled with people who grow remarkably brave behind the anonymity they get online. Wouldn't you agree, Agent Swan?"

I'd never heard him string so many words together. "Well, you got me there, Jared. But about the worst thing I did in college was make out with my roommate's girlfriend after he'd passed out at a party. A shitty thing to do, but it doesn't quite measure up to murder and global financial terrorism."

He opened his mouth to reply, but I held up a hand. "Hold on. You made your point. So let's agree there are good people and bad people, and the rest of us who maybe have a little bit of both. I'm only interested in one of the really bad eggs. Now that you know where to look, can you poke around and see what you can find?"

After blistering me with another look, he stood up with his tablet and walked out of the room toward his office. I looked back at Katrina.

"While he's sifting through the dark side," I said, "why don't you school me on what's happened in the light of day. Ceti has wormed his way inside some of the most secure networks in the world. At least they were supposed to be. Now, he accomplished these break-ins either with a little help or entirely on his own; seems like it's a little of both."

"I agree," she said. "He doesn't often repeat his techniques, at least not back-to-back."

"So what's the commonality in these cases?"

She looked puzzled. "You mean, what do they all have in common?"

"Sorta. Only instead of the obvious answers, I'm wondering if our little hacker doesn't have another agenda that might show up in his trail of misery. Something that will tip us off to either his identity or his location. Both would be great, but I'd be thrilled with either one. And I think clues to this scavenger hunt might show up in his style or—" I thought about it for a moment. "Or maybe there are clues hiding in older cases. Pre-Ceti cases."

Katrina shook her head. "I still don't know exactly what you're saying. You think—"

"I think, when you get right down to it, Ceti is not that different from the guy who robs a bank or embezzles a shitload of money from his company. They all have stories. They didn't wake up one morning and just suddenly decide they needed to rob people. I mean, sure, you'll always have your morons who just think they can walk in with a gun, grab the cash, and run. But the big players—they have an agenda. They almost always do."

She studied my face, and it looked like it was dawning on her. "Motivation."

"Well, yeah. Sounds cheesy, but most of the big-time creeps I track down have some kind of story that drives them. It's usually a derivative of revenge, a way of striking back at some perceived injustice. And sometimes it's not just *perceived*, but an actual injustice. More than one super criminal was a perfectly normal, law-abiding citizen until some other asshole crossed them and sent them off on a new course. So the rest of us have to suffer because one jerk pissed off the wrong guy, and he goes on a spree."

Katrina nodded. "So you think one of Ceti's early strikes may have been aimed at someone who wronged him?"

"Maybe. Or maybe he's smarter than I think and he knows we'd look for that." I rubbed my forehead. "I've been told to use your talents to solve this case. And I think this is one way you could best put those talents to work. You study cyber criminals; find me a list of people who've either done time for digital crime or been humiliated by their peers."

She gave a laughing grunt. "God, you're talking about hundreds of people. Maybe thousands."

I shook my head. "I don't think so. You know enough to weed out the small timers; you've been tracking these freaks for years. I'm trusting that only a few of them will set off your radar."

"Okay." She started to get up, then stopped and looked back at me. "I guess I've always thought Ceti was just an anarchist. I never thought he might just be someone who got pissed off and is lashing out from an old wound."

I laughed. "You'd be surprised how many big heists are a case of punching back. And if you relieve your enemy of a few million bucks, well, that goes a long way to putting some salve on old wounds."

AN HOUR LATER, I was eating a sandwich we'd ordered from the deli down the street. Food still didn't sound terrific, but I hadn't eaten in almost 18 hours. If I could manage even half of the sandwich, it would at least be fuel for my drained reserves.

I'd left a message for Christina, the usual sappy stuff about how much I missed her—but it was always true.

Sitting in the conference room, I studied all the general details of the crimes we'd so far registered as a Ceti attack. To my left I put individual pages for each incursion, and to my right I placed the one-sheets on each of the victims who'd either died or disappeared. I turned my attention to those four people.

Shawn Cook, Austin, Texas: dead, assumed to be drunk when he fell down a flight of stairs.

Ursula Fournier, working for the Canadian gas conglomerate: disappeared within two weeks of the crime, and no trace since.

Tanner Leachman, IT specialist at a Kansas City accounting firm: missing just three days after the hack, presumed dead because of the copious amounts of blood found on his apartment floor.

Samantha Das, the London pension fund: dead by what was made to look like suicide.

There could be no doubt, really. Some master criminals might pay their help, probably on the odd chance that they'd use them again sometime. Ceti took no chances at all; he used his moles and then, just like the game says, had them whacked. As one particularly vicious knave had once sneered to me: "You're an idiot if you don't tie up loose ends. Loose ends talk; they *always* talk. So you kill them before they can ever open their goddamned mouths. That's how it's done."

Yeah. That was certainly how Ceti had it done. He was cold-blooded on multiple levels and wasn't afraid to murder as many people as needed.

I took another small bite of the sandwich and was grateful it went down without incident. I looked at the photos of each of the dead and missing, chewing slowly and wondering how they could've gotten tangled up with someone like Ceti. And did they even know *who* they were dealing with?

Glancing at the time on my phone, I picked it up and called Quanta. She answered after one ring.

"Anything?" she asked.

"Not a damned thing. Jared Hicks is trying to chase down Ceti's history on this ZigbyNet site. Katrina Yu is going further back, looking at cases pre-Ceti. And I'm making love to an Italian grinder on wheat with a spicy olive oil dressing that I hope I don't regret later."

"I'm assuming you didn't call to dictate a Yelp review. What is Katrina looking for in the older cases?"

I explained my theory of an instigating moment, something that may have spurred our antihero to lash out. Granted, it was a long shot, but certainly worth investigating.

Then I transferred the phone to my other hand and pulled the victim sheets closer. "We might be doing this all wrong. So far, we've assumed there's no connection between any of the victims, other than an association with Ceti. But what if we tunneled back into the history of all of them? Something that would inspire them to want to work with Ceti. What if maybe, just maybe, we were able to find a link between even two of them? The collateral data might offer up a hint to how they hooked up with our boy."

Quanta grunted her approval. What else could she do, really, when we had nowhere else to go? I asked her about Parnell's investigation in London.

"She's as frustrated as you," Quanta said. "The two of you should connect tomorrow and compare notes, no matter how thin. I'll have her call you. In the meantime, I'm on my way back to Washington within the hour."

She hung up just as Jared and Katrina appeared in the conference room doorway.

Hicks shook his head. "It's no use. Everything is so encrypted that it would take days, maybe weeks, to crack into ZigbyNet. And the way it's designed, the admins would probably know about it. As for the signature string, I haven't been able to dig it up anywhere else."

I cursed under my breath, wadded up my dinner remains in the sandwich wrapper, and tossed the ball into the trash. Hicks picked up on my irritation and walked away.

Katrina Yu leaned against the door, crossing her arms. "Before you ask," she said, "I haven't had time to find anything yet. But I'll keep looking."

"Fine," I said.

"I'm exhausted," she added. "But I also think it's time you and I had a one-on-one meeting."

"Oh?"

"Yeah. Let's go to the bar. I need to tell you a few things."

I rubbed a hand through my hair. I was still getting over a distressed stomach that I'd just taunted with a sandwich, and alcohol didn't exactly sound appealing. Part of me wanted to tell Katrina it could wait until later. But I asked, "Anything in particular we need to discuss?"

"Yeah. I think it's time I scared the hell out of you."

CHAPTER THIRTEEN

We were back in the Irish pub where we'd first met, sitting in the same booth, in the same positions. Without the company of Cousin It, Katrina seemed a tad more relaxed, although it was obvious something heavy weighed on her mind.

Once we'd settled in—she with a beer and me a total lightweight, sipping a glass of water with lemon—she began.

"I know you're still not sure about me, and that's fine. I get that you're in the business of suspecting everyone and trusting no one. Seems like a shitty way to live, but I understand why you have to be that way. But whether or not you trust me, you still need to know exactly what you're up against, and I'm not sure you do."

I sipped my water and let her continue.

"Up until now, I think you've looked at Ceti as some kind of one-off freak, a computer geek who went off the rails and is now killing people who get in his way. And he is, for sure. But there's much more at risk here, so much that I don't want you to go on thinking this is an isolated problem you can just stamp out and the world will go back to spinning peacefully around the sun."

She gripped her pint glass and leaned forward. "Unless we get dramatically lucky, there will be no more peaceful days. Not like we were used to. Ceti is simply the most well-known of the master hackers and cyber criminals—and he's still relatively obscure, at least for the moment."

"All right," I said. "Tell me the part I don't get."

Katrina downed some of her beer and sat back. "Everyone knows about hackers. They've been around since about five minutes after the first code was written. There's something innate in us as a species, that we love puzzles and we love the challenge of breaking a code. For a certain group of people, cracking a security code is about the highest high you can achieve. Better than drugs, better than booze, better than sex. To sit in front of a monitor and study someone else's code, then find a way to bypass it and sneak inside? It's gotta be the same thrill that old-time safe-crackers felt when they spun that dial and opened the door.

"And then you have ransomware. Most people have heard of that, too, but, like Jared told you that first day sitting right here, the bulk of those attacks are never reported. Companies don't want people to know they're vulnerable, and they certainly don't want to wave a flag in front of other hackers that says, '*These guys got us, why don't you take a shot?*'

"For years, companies have hired people like us to help safeguard their systems. But it's not just good guys hiring good guys to keep the bad guys out; a lot of times the bad guys figure out a way to get in, and then sell that information back to the company they just hacked."

I squinted at her. "What do you mean?"

"Happens all the time. Let's say another hacker like Ceti—we'll call her Zeta—finds a way into Bank ABC's system. Zeta has found what we call a Zero Day vulnerability."

"Which is?"

"Zero Day means nobody with Bank ABC or their programmers knew anything about the bug in their code when they woke up that morning; they've had zero days to find a patch for it. Zeta makes her living by finding Zero Day vulnerabilities. She then tells the bank, '*I'll show you what I found and how to patch it for one million dollars. If you don't pay me immediately, I'll sell what I've found to someone who won't play nice with you and could take you for multiple millions.* '"

"Blackmail," I said.

"Of course it is. But most businesses pay immediately. They know the cost of paying Zeta will be less than what they stand to lose. And the deadline issued by Zeta doesn't give them time to sift through and find it before someone else can exploit it. So she takes the payoff, usually in some type of cryptocurrency, she shares the vulnerability with the bank, then moves on to her next victim. Or, the bank might hire Zeta to continually use her skills to spot any problems."

"They can't just pay their own people to do that?" I asked.

Katrina shrugged. "Sure they can. But they're not paying their people a million bucks to find problems. Their own software people aren't as motivated working for $50k a year. And there are plenty of people who take jobs with companies like that, secretly insert their own bug into the works somewhere, then let an outside friend know about it. The friend can then hold the business hostage. The friend gets paid the big ransom, and then quietly splits it with the employee."

"Holy shit," I muttered. "It's a nightmare."

"No. I haven't gotten to the nightmare yet. I'm just letting you know how Zero Day vulnerabilities are exploited. The reason few people know about them is because neither side wants it to get out. The hackers keep it relatively quiet because it's a big payday for them, and companies and governments don't want to take a chance of their customers or citizens losing faith in them. The government part is where I'm steering this conversation."

She had my attention, that was for sure. Our server stopped by and I ordered a beer. Any concerns about my stomach had receded to the background.

"Governments, especially some of the more volatile, smaller nation-states, are using hackers to help monitor their own citizens. They're taking otherwise innocent software or apps and finding ways to basically spy on their people. Think of some of the citizen-sponsored uprisings we've seen through the years; well, there are plenty of governments that believe their best shot at quelling those revolts is to find out about them in advance and eliminate the people stirring up trouble. They use some of the most skilled hackers in the world to help them."

I grunted. "And probably not just the smaller-nation states, either."

"No. We've seen hard evidence of major powers controlling their people and their economy. But what frightens me the most, Eric, and the thing I wanted to really talk with you about involves more than just controlling a population. I'm talking about war."

My beer appeared, along with another for Katrina. I clinked my glass against hers and we took a long drink.

"We're concerned about things like banking and pensions, and for good reason," Katrina said. "The stuff Ceti has been doing over the last couple of years is dangerous and a serious threat, no question. But the area where this stuff is going to really impact everyone on the planet is the war machine."

She leaned forward. "Think about it. Countries have now figured out how to hack into an enemy's infrastructure: power, communications, fuel. And we're all so reliant on the grid today that one cyber attack in the right place at the right time can cripple not just an economy, but destroy a country's chance to defend itself militarily. We used to feel safe because we had missiles and tanks and fighter jets and warships. And sure, those are still important to a country's defense today.

"But they're also vulnerable to a cyber attack. What if you

can't get a message to your attack force? What happens if the electronic system that controls the oil pipelines is taken out? A nation's army still runs on oil, and when the tap is shut off, all hell breaks loose. We've already seen something similar to that on a smaller scale. But what happens when it's massive? What if we can't make a simple phone call? This is not just idle speculation, Eric; it's a very real possibility. I'll even go further than that; I think it's likely. The next major war will be won or lost based on cyber security. Who will control that? Whose cyber specialists will be clever enough to defend against the other guy while obliterating the other guy's entire ecosystem and war machine?"

I took another drink and kept my eyes on hers. What she was talking about was chilling. But it also wasn't news. Governments around the globe were aware of the consequences of falling behind in the cyber race. I'd been briefed a few times, even sat through a torturous conference on the subject.

Plus, I'd had some experience with it, to an extent. I'd helped take down a group of people who were determined to crash the power grid in the US. And they weren't relying entirely on computers to do it. Throw in the digital component and things did indeed get scarier, because the attack could come from anywhere in the world. A guy sitting in a hut on a small island off the coast of New Guinea could strike as serious a blow as a warlord in a vast country.

No one, however, had explained all of this the way Katrina Yu did. And I knew the part she said was the most frightening was still to come.

"All right," I said. "I understand what you're saying. And yeah, it's frightening to think about. How exactly does this involve Ceti?"

"It may *not* involve him," she said. "But I've been thinking about all of the incursions he's done, all of the damage he's responsible for. And I've wondered what all of it's leading up to.

One really big score? Billions of dollars? Is that really what someone of Ceti's talents is after? A shitload of money?"

I inhaled and let it out slowly. "No."

She shook her head. "No. I mean, it's *possible*. And if that's the case, I'm actually relieved. I would be happy if we got off the hook with just a few numbers exchanged on a big spreadsheet somewhere and a few stockholders left holding the bag. But why would somebody like Ceti explore all of these different vulnerabilities and start stacking them, like he's done?"

I tapped a finger on the table, thinking back. "When we first met, you told me that Ceti was *practicing*. That was the word you used. So I take it you weren't necessarily thinking that he was practicing for bigger versions of what he's already been doing."

Katrina gave a humorless smile. "I don't know. How can anyone know what he's really aiming for? But no. I don't believe he'll stay in this lane. I mean, why would he? He'll already—"

"He'll already have done everything he needs to do to be the greatest hacker in history," I said. "If he's not there already."

She nodded. "And this is what I think is the most frightening thing about Ceti. It's bad enough that we can't seem to catch him or anticipate his next move. But I worry about what his *ultimate* move will be. If he's already reached the top of the mountain in one area, he strikes me as the kind of person who would want to reach even higher."

"And that means toppling at least one government. Maybe more."

"Yeah."

The server wandered past again and asked if we needed more. Katrina declined; I asked for two fingers of bourbon.

"Ceti can't do the war part himself," I said. "He'll need some sort of connection. Or connections, plural. How do you see that happening?"

She made a face like I'd asked the dumbest question of the

year. "Are you kidding? One or two more big scores like he's racking up and he'll be swamped with offers of partnership. Shit, he probably already has more invitations to dance than he can handle. You think I'm the only one thinking about this stuff? I guarantee there are countries who are scrambling, trying to be the first to lock up a deal with Ceti. He's like a number one draft choice coming out of college, you know?"

"How do they reach him? We can't find him."

"They don't have to reach him. All they have to do is get the word out. Believe me, he'll hear about it and contact them."

Of course she was right. Every nation on Earth, regardless of their basic moral fiber, maneuvered to improve their leverage or operating strength. Ceti was a wild card, but the kind that could tip the balance in the favor of whatever country hired him. Which brought up another question.

"If we agree that he's not entirely in this for the money, then what's the bait some warbird could dangle in front of him? What would get him to choose a side?"

The server returned and placed my bourbon on the table, then walked away.

"God, I don't know," Katrina said. "I've thought about that the last day or two. It would have to be someone who he thought could perhaps win a conflict anyway, and his help would simply improve the odds. Ceti wants to be associated with winners."

I nodded. "And he's giving the impression that he likes the idea of being a type of Robin Hood. So perhaps a country that has issues with the West and could be perceived as a David fighting Goliath. That strikes me as his kind of thing."

"I agree," she said. "It narrows down the field somewhat, but there's no way of knowing who he'd throw in with." She sat back and let out a sigh. "And remember, I don't know for sure if this is what he has in mind. But given his track record, we'd be foolish to not plan for the possibility. Because if Ceti collects enough experience and data to really disrupt the US or Britain or some other NATO country, let's say, then he becomes a potent weapon in the next war. And I'm telling you right now it will be ugly."

I picked up the drink and knocked it back. The burn actually felt good. My stomach could piss right off.

"Let's hope your boyfriend comes up with something on the Dark Web. We're falling further behind by the hour. We need something. Now."

Katrina responded with a cold stare, then reached for her beer. And accidentally knocked it over.

CHAPTER FOURTEEN

The sun was setting through a break in the clouds. I took another stroll toward the river, hoping to digest everything Katrina had brought up and trying not to get depressed. It wasn't a matter of me failing that tore at me; it was the fact that I was fighting a foe I couldn't understand. And not just his motivations, which were still clouded. My training as a Q2 agent allowed me to win a match against Arlo Benn, but I'd probably never face Ceti in hand-to-hand combat. His was a world of ones and zeroes, bits and bytes. While I'd become quite proficient at ordering food and shampoo online, battling an enemy who'd basically become a cyborg was not just out of my league, but out of my world.

That was the thought that stuck with me as I turned along the path fronting the river. In a strange, twisted way, Ceti and I *did* have one thing in common: Our minds were fundamentally digital. For him—I still thought of our target as male—it was the only part of his life where he felt at home, maybe the only place where he felt at peace. I could imagine him as a social outcast, perhaps revered by gamers and hackers-in-training when he was young, but a complete loser in the field of common, everyday life. It likely was self-perpetuating, driving him further underground, twisting him into a virtual double helix, where he represented one strand while computer code made up the other. I've heard futurists predict the eventual assimilation of human consciousness into a machine; Ceti could indeed be the Adam of that new species.

And what did that have to do with me?

For several years, I'd jostled my way down a similar path. The Q2 investment procedure kept my own consciousness housed for a time within a computer hard drive while I awaited a new body to call home. The constant uploading and downloading, a process I'd completed more times than I care to think about, had made my sense of self portable. At no time in human history had we ever done anything like that, unless you count the concept of meditation and other spiritual constructs.

But for me it was portable in a literal sense. Computer algorithms supposedly kept the real me intact as I swung from one host body to another—but could I swear they'd been entirely successful? Would I ever know how much of the original Eric Swan remained? Perhaps dozens of transfers had rewritten part of my own code, and, if that were true, how *could* I know? My new self would naturally think it was the same as the previous version. My mind only had its current edition with which to process anything, leaving me to assume all was well and in tip-top shape.

I'd recently learned that there existed an original copy of my personality, the file from my first ever upload, saved in its own special hard drive. Freaky, if you ask me, to know that the essence of young Eric Swan was on call, available to be downloaded into a new body at any time. How different would he be? I mean, we all change and evolve as time passes, hopefully for the better. But what if the best part of me was that younger, slightly naive and ideological Swan?

The idea haunted me daily. It's nightmarish to know you can never *really* know for sure that your identity is secure. Not only could my face be different from one day to the next, but perhaps my mind was a chameleon, too. The only thing giving me hope was that Christina and Quanta reported no extreme changes. At least nothing on the order of the first Q2 agent, a project that failed spectacularly.

All of this left me curious about my prey. If and when we met, would I sense a kindred spirit? Nobody likes to think they're simpatico with an asshole.

I swept the thought and the case out of the spotlight for a moment and instead focused on Christina. During a recent assignment, I'd wondered if I was being fair to her. She'd agreed to a relationship that, on the surface, seemed unlikely to work. One person who stayed close to home, holding down a successful career and having a heart so big she could agree to become a surrogate parent for friends unable to conceive. And her partner, the guy who crisscrossed the country—and sometimes even *left* the country—in pursuit of the scuzziest criminals alive. And rather than sharing the beautiful gift of life with friends, this partner *took* lives on a regular basis.

For the millionth time, I acknowledged the fact that I didn't deserve Christina, and she certainly could do better than me. And yet somehow—

As I stood on a high point, looking out at the river and contemplating these thoughts, my phone vibrated with a message. I wanted to ignore it, to devote just one more minute to the one good, solid thing in my life.

Ignoring anything during a case was not an option.

It was from Katrina, regarding Jared's search through the Dark Web. I found it curious that he hadn't sent the note, but left it for his fiancée to communicate with me. What a d-bag.

Jared says nothing turned up on his next search. He'll try some other ideas regarding ZigbyNet tomorrow.

Swell. Another dead end. Then an immediate follow-up from Katrina appeared.

I may have found something. I know things are critical right now, but I can't stay awake another five minutes. Can we meet first thing in the morning? And it may be nothing.

With the mood I was slipping into, it was easy for me to take a jaundiced view of this. Part of me wanted to reply with something flippant, maybe *No rush, get some sleep. This lead won't pan out anyway.*

Instead, I sent back an okay and left it at that. Right now, information was information, and, with the paltry amount we had, it would be stupid to ignore any scrap that came along. Plus, Katrina had been working just as many hours on this case as I had; she had to be absolutely fatigued. We all had to sleep sometime. Even with the world on the brink.

That included me. I looked up to gather one more glimpse of the sunset.

The clouds had returned, obscuring the show.

Another alert from my phone jolted me awake at 5:19 a.m. I'd managed the night before to at least get my clothes off and pull down the blanket before crashing hard. Now someone was torturing me with a call.

I thumbed the phone and muttered something unintelligible.

"Swan, are you really sleeping? Now? With a crisis on our hands?"

I let out the groan of the newly awakened and rubbed my eyes. "Parnell, I'm not on London time."

"I would've thought America's greatest spy hero would be up by 4, doing calisthenics of some sort."

"I haven't done a sit-up in years. Why don't you call me back in 15 minutes. Let me splash some water on my face and get some coffee. Get yourself a scone or whatever you eat in the morning."

"Splash fast. I'll give you a video call in 10." She hung up.

Stumbling to the bathroom, I flipped on the light and took stock of the grizzled face in the mirror, which brought another groan. I shut the light back off.

Five minutes later, I'd ordered room service coffee and whatever food they thought might revive me, and had put on a clean T-shirt and jeans. At exactly the 10-minute mark, my tablet announced the call.

Parnell looked awake and ready for action. It was 10:30 a.m. in the UK, but she probably would've looked exactly the same at 7.

"Didn't Quanta tell you we were conferencing this morning?" she asked.

"She said *today*. She never said anything about an obnoxious call before sunrise. I hope you've solved the case."

"As a matter of fact . . ."

I stifled a yawn that had just begun and leaned forward. "What? Are you serious?"

"No, of course I'm not serious. Just giving you an adrenaline jolt to help you wake up."

I held the classic solitary finger up to the tablet's camera. "Cute. All right, Miss Marple, tell me what you've found. It's gotta be more than I have."

She looked down, probably at notes. "Samantha Das kept another apartment, rented under her mum's name. I was there until two o'clock this morning. As you suggested, it's where she kept her digital life. We had an IT specialist with us so we wouldn't have to waste time taking everything back to the shop. Our guy did two years for a bit of hacking himself, so he knows his stuff, yet it still took him nearly three hours to break into her files. Well, some of them."

"And?"

"And Ms. Das led quite the double life."

"So she was an IT specialist by day and someone with a sense of humor by night?"

Parnell shook her head. "You better hope the people on the second floor aren't monitoring your video chats."

"I can say that. Some of my best friends are IT specialists. Give me the details."

"We found all the usual files we expected from her work at LeaCap Funds. And there were some strange clumps of data for another pension fund, this one in Scotland. It was pretty clear, according to my guy here, that she'd done a little hacking in her time, too. Almost as if she were—"

"Practicing," I said.

"Yeah. Not anything that would show up on the Scottish fund's radar; more exploratory, you could say. Poking her nose in."

I sat back. It made sense. If Ceti needed inside help on his jobs, it stood to reason he'd want his helpers at least somewhat proficient at breaking into high security sites. Not much different than superstar rock bands who want an up-and-coming opening act that won't steal the show, but at least has good chops and can warm up the crowd. It wasn't hard to imagine that Samantha Das —and Shawn Cook, Ursula Fournier, and Tanner Leachman—had essentially auditioned for their cyber boss before he took them under his wing, used them, and then killed them.

"Okay," I said. "I know the answer to this before I even ask, but I'll ask it anyway. Anything that might point to Ceti? Email, DM, text? Maybe they're in the same show tunes group on social media?"

"No. However, there was an email from Ursula Fournier."

I leaned in toward the screen. "Don't screw with me right now, Parnell. It's too early and I haven't had a drop of caffeine."

She gave a sly grin into the camera. "You know how I like to save the good stuff for last."

"Yes. It's one of your more loathsome traits."

There was a quick double tap on my door. My thoughts had obviously summoned the coffee. I told Parnell to hold on and greeted the perky hotel employee who wheeled in a small cart. He began to fuss with setting everything up, exclaiming how beautiful the day was going to be after so much rain. I slipped him a $10 bill and escorted him out before he could gush about the Celtics game the night before.

Grabbing the coffee and two pieces of bacon from the plate, I sat back down in front of the tablet. "Okay, go."

"One email, saved in a folder labeled '*Stuff*.' Funny, I used to keep a folder with that same name. Anyway, only four messages inside, one of them from an email address that was all numbers and letters, a string of about fifteen of them. Overkill if you're trying to simply camouflage your name.

"But we confirmed it came from Fournier's IP address, although it was an account we had no record of. A secret account. And it was signed with just the letter U."

I washed down the strips of bacon with a gulp of the hot coffee, then wiped my hands on my jeans. "Quit leaving me in suspense. What did it say?"

Parnell looked back at her notes. "It said, *You were right. F this.*"

I stared back at her with a slow blink. "That's it?"

"That's it. *You were right. F this.*"

"Well, hell. She could've been talking about relationship advice. She could've been talking about some normal shit at work." I got up and went back to the cart for a coffee refill, but kept talking. "She could've been talking about the last season of *Game of Thrones*. Most of us who watched that said 'F this.'"

I heard Parnell's voice from across the room. "For the moment, it doesn't matter *what* they're communicating about. It's the first direct connection between two dead people who worked with Ceti."

Poking around the tray on the cart, I found some butter to spread on the toast. "*One* dead person and one missing person."

"Oh, don't be dense," Parnell said. "Ursula is dead and you know it."

Half the piece of toast went into my mouth and I brought the rest back to the table, along with the coffee. "Fine, if you want to chalk her up as dead. But really, this doesn't surprise me. I figured there had to be some sort of connection with all of them, even if it wasn't direct. Like they all attended the same IT conference, or they all belonged to the same online group. And even if the four of them didn't know each other before, they probably came from the same pool of available minions. Somehow Ceti managed to convince four high-level cyber security people to dance with him. And maybe more that we haven't uncovered yet."

"You know there's more," Parnell said. "They're like mice. If you see one or two, it means there are ten."

I took another bite of toast, thinking about that. Something else occurred to me. "There's hardly any trail to speak of, with *any* of the people involved. It's as if they got all their marching orders in face-to-face meetings out on a country road. So why this one email? We've combed through the records of everyone and nothing shows up. Ceti apparently has them all trained to avoid anything that can be digitally traced. And yet Ursula sent this note, and Samantha kept it. Why? What's so special about this?"

Parnell fell silent, taking a sip of what looked like juice. She finally said, "Maybe she kept it because it's so random. It doesn't say much of anything and certainly nothing that would seem suspicious. As you pointed out, the subject matter could've been anything. So maybe Fournier assumed it wouldn't raise any red flags when she sent it, and Das saw no problem with keeping it. Obviously neither of them counted on being assassinated, which is the only reason we found anything."

I ran a finger around the top of my coffee cup. What Parnell said could very well be the reason, but it just didn't sound right.

"No, they weren't reaching out across the ocean to bitch about relationships or family. This is a message about the incursion Ursula helped with." Then something struck me. "No, wait. What's the date on this email?"

"Um . . ." She glanced down. "July 9th, two years ago."

"That's about a week after Ceti broke in. Remember the press releases Ursula sent out? The ones that climbed on the band-wagon calling Ceti—what the hell was that? Something angel."

"Green Angel."

"Right, Green Angel. This email would be about the time of those releases. I'll bet anything that Fournier was disgusted by that nickname. Especially if she was working with the little asshole. He probably fanned the flames, loving the attention and glamorous tag people had applied to him. The timetable is right, and '*F this*' probably sums up how she felt about the whole charade."

Parnell gave a slow nod. "All right. Does it help us?"

"It tells us that Ceti spent a long time setting up his attacks. The Canadian job was a year before the London hack. Das had only been with LeaCap for a few months before this email. We can assume she was a plant. Someone Ceti already had on the team."

"And she wasn't scared off by the first three deaths and disappearances?"

I opened my mouth to answer, then paused. "It's possible the only other person she knew was Fournier. And Ceti could've told her that Ursula was safe with him, out of sight. And hell, she may be. Her body was never found."

"So Ceti either keeps you on his private island—or wherever he's hiding—or kills you?" She shook her head. "He's not staying up at night worrying over his death toll. She's buried somewhere or at the bottom of a Canadian lake."

I enjoyed the mental exercises with Parnell, but it was essentially getting us nowhere. I asked what her next move was.

"If nothing else pops up here, I'm sure Quanta will send me back to the States. You're obviously helpless without me."

"Okay, good. It'll be a nice change to work with someone I trust. Katrina and Jared may be perfectly innocent, but I'm having a hard time with them in the faith department."

We exchanged one or two more glib comments before signing off. I checked the time and saw it was still a few minutes before six. Going back to bed was out of the question, so I threw on a pair of shorts and running shoes and headed out into the rain-scrubbed city, determined to blast myself out of the foul mood descending upon me. With a complete lack of answers, my attitude was rapidly aligning with that of the late Ursula Fournier.

F this.

CHAPTER FIFTEEN

Once again, Jared Hicks had a remnant of breakfast lodged in his beard. It danced and shifted each time he barked at me.

Yes, the hairy cyber security dude actually raised his voice and even punctuated his points by stabbing a finger toward my face. I came pretty damned close to grabbing it and twisting until it snapped, but Quanta had insisted I play nice with the clown. Of course, she was hundreds of miles away, likely meditating in her atrium with a nice hot mug of oolong tea beside her, and wasn't putting up with this shit at 8:45 in the morning.

Granted, within the first five minutes of our chat, I'd intentionally prodded Hicks by questioning his technical abilities. I'd even suggested he might farm out some of his efforts to see if they could deliver better results. My purpose wasn't to piss him off—although I knew that would be one of the outcomes—but rather to keep both personal and professional pressure on him. I fully expected him to blurt out something in his rage that might tip me to his true allegiance. To me, Jared Hicks always seemed to be one good shove away from breaking.

Plus, I simply didn't like the guy.

Not that I trusted his fiancée much more. But at least Katrina Yu was pleasant. She might be a villain in disguise, but she was a villain I didn't mind sharing a few pints with. I've always been torn when it comes to fun, fictional villains; maybe we were supposed to detest Vizzini from *The Princess Bride*, but I thought he'd be a hoot to socialize with. And before his character became conflicted, Loki was a barrel of monkeys, too, in an interesting way.

Hicks? He was neither fun nor interesting. I let him blow off steam for about 20 seconds before cutting him off.

"News flash, Jared. You're selling your talents to the US government, which means you can't just talk big and make promises; you actually have to deliver. And for Christ's sake, comb that Pop-Tart crumb out of your beard. It makes it hard for me to concentrate on what you're saying."

He kept his glare on high beam, but Katrina reached over and picked out the flake. It was now official: This guy would never cooperate with me. If it was possible to have a complete nerd as your mortal enemy, this was it. And I just didn't care anymore. He'd provided nothing of real value after adopting a defensive stance from the beginning. He'd carried a massive chip on his shoulder from the moment I sat down in that pub booth and started flirting with his partner. I considered him worthless.

Which also potentially made him dangerous.

This latest tiff had been set off when he'd announced there was no sign of Ceti on ZigbyNet or anywhere else he could find. I found that to be unlikely at best and suspicious at worst. So I said so. I'm a spy, not a diplomat.

Katrina made another attempt to build a bridge. "The good news is that we're ahead of where we were a few days ago, before we knew about the Fournier connection with Das. The more data we compile, the sooner we'll find the one fragment that will put us on Ceti's trail. That's the way it always works in cases like this. One small piece, maybe something we don't even recognize as important right now, could wind up being critical. I'm still confident we'll uncover it. Let's not blow up now."

I got up and limped over to the sideboard. Like an idiot, I'd landed awkwardly during my morning run and now my right ankle was protesting. The three minutes it would take to prepare my hot tea would allow the caveman to cool off a bit and allow me a chance to plot another approach to our problem.

When Jared stepped out to use the men's room, Katrina sidled up next to me. "What is with you two? You could cut the testosterone in here with a knife."

I dunked a tea bag a few times in a mug of hot water and smiled. "I have a juvenile habit of goading any guy who I know doesn't like me. Most people try to patch things up; I'm inclined to poke at them. Gotta be a personality flaw because I usually enjoy it. Especially if the guy has a short fuse. Your boyfriend's fuse is the length of a pencil eraser."

She laughed and began peeling an orange. "Well, for the record, I've never seen him like this. He's always been a serious guy, but this case has him on edge." She elbowed me. "Or maybe it's just you. Maybe your pheromones and his can't coexist in the same room."

"For the last few days I've been trying to figure out how *your* pheromones can get along. Katrina, you could not have picked a more polar opposite to hitch your wagon to. So allow me to be nosy as hell and ask you: What the hell are you doing with this guy?"

"Are you married?" she asked.

"I am."

"And you're telling me she's just like you? I would find that just as hard to believe."

"No. She's got oodles of patience with people like Jared. But to your point, we may not be mirror images, but she also doesn't want to smother me with a pillow as soon as I fall asleep. Couples don't have to be identical, but they at least have to be civil."

We took our tea and orange back to the chairs. "Listen, I know Jared is not a cuddly toy to most people," she said. "But I see him outside of work. I get to hear his ideas and his dreams and—well, I get to peek behind his tough-guy image and see a really nice guy. When he first started asking me out, I turned him down twice. Then I walked into the library on campus and saw him peering up at some books on a shelf. And it was the romance section."

I'd started to lift the tea to my mouth and stopped. "Shut up. Jared Hicks does not read romance novels."

"As soon as he saw me, he shoved one back on the shelf and started walking the other direction. I followed him to the table where he was doing some research work and gave him a hard time. Embarrassed the hell out of him. So then I felt like I owed him a coffee date since I'd seen his vulnerable side. And, well, I've enjoyed seeing more."

"Fine. He gets off on Nicholas Sparks. He's still a tool."

"He can be, yeah." She laughed and raised an eyebrow. "But he's *my* tool."

"Gross," I said, just as the subject of our discussion walked back into the room. The break had indeed lowered his stress level, it seemed. He helped himself to his own beverage and joined us.

"I have another option I can look into," he said, avoiding eye contact with me and talking directly to Katrina. "Remember the article we talked about earlier in the year? The one about back-door encryption?"

Katrina smiled. "You told me it was garbage."

"It's mostly garbage. But I know a guy who's been messing around with it for the last year. I'm going to call him in a few minutes."

"The information we have is classified," I said. "Your friend can't know who you're looking for."

"He won't. I just want him to share his code-breaking notes. It might help."

I nodded. "All right. Good."

My phone shook with an incoming call. I put it on speaker.

"Hello, Poole. I'm here with Katrina Yu and Jared Hicks."

"Good morning. I have some information. Australian Security Intelligence reports that they have the people who hacked into the banking system. There's still a lot of work to be done, but so far they're pretty sure it's a copycat crime."

"Someone who wanted to ride the Ceti wave."

"It would seem so. The agent I spoke with referred to it as 'sloppy work.'"

Katrina nodded. "Probably won't be the last. With more and more people starting to rally behind Ceti, I won't be surprised if intelligence organizations around the world have their workloads doubled in the next few months."

"I wonder," I said, "if Ceti will be irritated that someone is trying to steal his thunder, or if he'll be more like a proud papa."

"Seems like it would play into his hands for global disruption," Katrina said. "So maybe he's thrilled to have it steamroll, even if they're not as talented, which gets them caught right away. Like the Australian gang."

I considered that, but shook my head. "He's a narcissist. Until he truly makes his mark, I don't think he'll want to share any headlines. It's becoming intoxicating for him."

"Along those lines, I have more," Poole said. "Quanta reports that her British contacts found another distribution of cryptocurrency, this time spread across Europe. One thousand people, each getting the equivalent of $1,000. The message attached says, *Save this for a rainy year.*"

Katrina frowned. "*Rainy year*? Isn't it supposed to be for a rainy day?"

Jared spoke up. "I think what he's trying to say is that the coming financial meltdown will take at least a year to repair. If at all."

We fell quiet. After a moment, I thanked Poole for the information and hung up. Turning to Katrina, I said, "Now that he's released more funds to the public, do another search. See if the bandwidth on Ceti love has increased."

She already had her laptop open and made some quick keystrokes. "Yeah. That didn't take long."

She flipped the screen around and showed me the results on her search. Headline after headline about Ceti, all within the last hour, and all referring to him either as a modern-day Robin Hood or picking up on his earlier attribution, the Green Angel. Both tags made me sick.

"So he's now officially getting the love he wanted," I said, then turned to Jared. "I know cryptocurrency accounts are, by their nature, difficult to identify. But with a thousand different transactions, is it possible to swim up the stream to the source?"

He shook his head. "One gift or one million gifts, it wouldn't matter. He can stay shrouded as long as he wants. No one is going to betray the confidentiality of this system. It's what attracts some people in the first place."

I knew he was right. After one more gulp, I set the tea mug on the table and stood up.

"We're stuck in the mud while the race goes on around us. I need to get outside for a while and figure out another angle of attack on this thing. If you guys think of anything else we can try, let me know."

Katrina nodded. Jared ignored me and began scrolling through his phone.

· · ·

MY AUDITION for the job at Q2 had taken less than a day and involved a captured American scientist, a Russian spy network, and the future of the US space program. Another mission near San Francisco ended with me facing down two former demolition experts who'd gone off the rails and were moments away from blowing up the Golden Gate Bridge in order to make some bizarre statement about oil dependency. And a failed magician-turned-movie stuntman actually came within a minute of gassing everyone inside the Academy Awards before I brought him down with a perfectly thrown knife. Not my preferred method, but sometimes you're in a pinch.

The point is, each of these escapades—and a plethora of other missions—usually kept me on the go from the beginning. Sure, downtime is part of the job, and I have my trusty music playlist to keep me entertained during long drives or flights. But it's rare that a case left me with absolutely nothing to do. I don't handle stagnation well. It's a personality thing, and that's one trait that hasn't morphed throughout my tour of bodies.

But the Ceti case, despite all the data points we'd acquired, was basically going nowhere. I knew it, Quanta knew it, and I'm pretty sure Parnell knew it but refused to acknowledge it. We had hints and vague clues. We believed Ceti was relying on inside help with each job, then murdering the hapless helpers before they could unwittingly spill anything that might help us track him down.

We were pretty sure he danced in and out of the Dark Web, taunting us with his digital signature. And yet, even with the best cybersecurity people on two continents, we were flummoxed. I had but one hope for a break in the case, and it was a slim hope at that.

I had to trust that Ceti's lust for love and attention would finally be his downfall.

Around 11 a.m. I wandered into one of those bakeries that

also sells soup and sandwiches. I peered through the glass display at rows of various delights and cracked a smile. With the investment program, I never worried about calories or cholesterol; I wouldn't inhabit a body long enough for excess weight or hardened arteries to matter. I sometimes felt like Bill Murray's character in *Groundhog Day*, sitting in the diner and stuffing his face with every unhealthy morsel he could get his hands on. As he famously says, "What if there is no tomorrow?"

My tomorrows were as mysterious as yours, times ten.

"I see you eyeing the Nut Buddy," said a cheerful woman behind the counter. Her name tag proclaimed she was Wanda. "Want me to wrap up two of those for you?"

"Does it pair well with the BLT?" I asked.

"Honey, it pairs well with everything. One of each?"

"One sandwich, one side of pasta salad, and yes, one . . . of those." I couldn't bring myself to say the name.

I sat near the front window and tried to enjoy my lunch as I corralled my thoughts. Quanta called as I started on the chocolate.

"What are you doing?"

"I'm taking out my frustrations with a Nut Buddy. For the record, Wanda was right; they do indeed pair well with bacon."

She paused, then must've decided to let that go. "The team on the second floor may have found something."

I set the remains of the bakery treat on the table. "Tell me."

"They were able to dig through Arlo Benn's phone. The gentleman who accosted you in your hotel room?"

"Oh, I remember Arlo. And? What'd they find?"

"As we expected, it was purely a burner phone; no social media, no browser history to speak of, no email. There were a couple of coded text messages, but they'd been sent through an encrypted network, not a traditional carrier, and probably bounced through multiple sites. Useless. Arlo was careful."

"And yet you're calling me. What's the good stuff?"

"A photo."

I sat there and stared at the half-eaten Nut Buddy, processing. "A photo? Arlo kept photos on a burner phone?"

"He kept *one* photo. I'm sending it to you right now."

I pulled my phone back, opened the messages, and touched the image file that arrived.

"Huh," I said, looking at the photo of a sign. It read: *Level 3-D*.

"That's . . . from a parking garage?"

"That's what we think," Quanta said. "The time stamp is the day he attacked you, so it might be somewhere near your hotel."

I laughed. "We all do that, don't we? Park in an unfamiliar garage, and take a picture to help you remember where you left the car. Have you identified the specific garage?"

"Not yet, but we have the Boston FBI office working on it. They'll let me know when they have it nailed down. Then it's a matter of using the garage records and security cameras to identify the car. I need you to be ready to check it out."

"We don't really expect to find anything in the car, though, do we?"

"No. But we didn't expect to find the photo, either." She paused. "This case is frustrating for all of us, Swan. But we're accumulating tiny scraps here and there, like uncovering Ceti's digital signature, you capturing Arlo Benn, this photo. I know it doesn't seem like much, but with so much at stake, I'm happy with even small gains for the time being. If it all adds up to a win, the painfully slow progress will be worth it."

She couldn't see the slow smile spreading across my face, but she'd undoubtedly hear it in my voice. "Quanta, did you just give me a pep talk?"

I couldn't be sure, but it sounded like a faint chuckle on her end. "Swan, I would never waste my time on a pep talk for you. I know you well enough to know what motivates you, and it's not a speech from the boss. Either I or Poole will be back in touch with the information on Arlo's car. Be ready to go. Who knows, something in the car might make something click. In the meantime, hopefully you, Katrina, and Jared can figure out what all these cases and their victims have in common."

I know she heard my groan. "That's all I've done the last few days. I'm starting to wonder . . ." My voice trailed away as a new thought emerged.

Quanta said, "Starting to wonder about what?"

I didn't answer for a few moments. Then I sat up straight and pushed my tray away. "You know what? I may have just stumbled onto something. Let me do some digging and get back with you."

Without waiting for her response, I hung up and got to my feet. After depositing my trash and tray near the door, I hurried outside and turned toward my hotel. It had started to rain again.

CHAPTER SIXTEEN

I'm not a detective. Technically, my title is agent/operative for a clandestine US government agency that works as a last resort against some of the nation's worst threats. We don't suffer much in the way of oversight, congressional or otherwise, and we thankfully get to live out of the spotlight. That's simply another way of saying we fly under the radar and don't get pestered by loudmouth politicians who don't know shit about real national security. They're professional moochers who generally have never worked a day in their lives and somehow take pride in that. It astounds me.

Since I'm not a detective, you might think I rely primarily on brute force to accomplish my missions. And you would be right. Sometimes.

But even the toughest, most badass fullback in the NFL, the one who uses his 250 pounds to bulldoze over the opposition, still has to learn the plays, study his opponents for weaknesses, and devise a game plan to use his physical skills to his advantage. In other words, brawn without brains might land you a role in a *Magic Mike* movie, but it won't help you defeat the world's nastiest terrorists.

Take my associate, Parnell. With her Krav Maga training, she could crush most bad dudes in a fight to the death. I made the mistake of thinking I could use my size advantage to subdue her, and she cured me of that notion in about two seconds. But Parnell also employs one of the most astute minds for working out problems that I've ever seen.

So at some point, a specialist in espionage must rely on the little grey cells. It helped that I grew up reading mystery novels, starting with *The Hardy Boys*, *Nancy Drew*, and *The Three Investigators*. I worked my way up to Agatha Christie, Raymond Chandler, Dorothy Sayers, Chester Himes, and any others I could get my grubby hands on. And while I rarely beat the fictional detective to the answer, I learned a lot about the *process* of solving a crime.

Mainly, look where they don't expect you to look.

Back in my hotel room, I pulled out the file containing the Ceti breaches we knew about to this point. In particular, I separated the pages we had on the insiders who'd been murdered following each incursion.

I laid out the individual sheets, and stared at the faces of the dead.

Shawn Cook. Ursula Fournier. Tanner Leachman. Samantha Das.

I knew these four people—four insiders who paid the price for their naive greed—held the key to finding the mastermind. Proof? Well, I had no proof. But years in the trade developed a mental muscle that every real or fictional detective thrived on: intuition. I felt something, and after so much time spent chasing my own tail, the feeling now imbued me with the charge I needed.

I texted Parnell across the pond, asking if she was free for a quick consultation. Four minutes later we were on a video hookup.

"How's Boston?" she asked. "Still teeming with zealots and traitors to the throne?"

"It's been centuries, Parnell. Will you ever get over the revolution?"

"You say revolution, I say insurrection. What's on your mind?"

I held up each one-page on the victims, shuffling one at a time in front of the camera. "You know how I've been hung up on these insiders, right? While everyone else is focusing on the breaches and the technical details, I keep coming back to the people. I guess it's easier for me to work a case that way."

"Aw, look at Swan, suddenly a people person."

"Nobody can withstand my dashing personality, it's true. But to me, if we were going to break this case, I've always thought it would be through these names. Because it's a weak point for Ceti."

Parnell frowned. "How so?"

I set down the sheets and laced my fingers on the table. "Do we really believe he needed to turn these people in order to break in? I mean, he's the greatest hacker of all time, or so we're told. He's spent years tunneling into some of the tightest security systems in the world, and now he's in a phase where he hires help? It doesn't fit with his style. And it's a weak point simply by its nature; with every person he brings in, it's another vulnerability to his plan."

"Well, sure. But he eliminates that vulnerable point by killing them."

"I disagree. He kills them, sure; but that doesn't eliminate the vulnerable point itself. It still leaves a connection to Ceti. When he worked alone, there were no outside connections and nothing to clean up. Made it that much harder to get a handle on him. So the question is: Why is he recruiting helpers *now*, people inside the businesses he wants to attack, and then killing them?"

Parnell sat quietly for a moment, simply staring at the screen. Then she shrugged and said, "All right. Tell me."

I cracked open a diet soda I'd pulled from the minibar and took a sip. I'd been trying to kick the habit, but the fizzy drinks always managed to suck me back in.

"What finally got to me was the fact that I've been racking my brain, trying to figure out what these people have in common. I mean, they're all tech nerds, they each have training in cyber security, and they're all fairly young. But it wasn't until today that something struck me. Instead of what they have in common, the key might be what they *don't* have in common."

I held up two of the sheets. "Shawn Cook and Samantha Das. They were killed, and their bodies left for us to find. Cook's death was made to look like an accident, and with Das we were supposed to believe she'd committed suicide. Regardless, their bodies were right there."

Then I held up the other two. "Tanner Leachman and Ursula Fournier. No bodies."

Parnell sat back and clasped one wrist over her head, looking at the sheets. "Uh . . . okay. And you think this is important?"

I grunted a laugh. "It makes no sense, and therefore it has to be important somehow. Why murder two of the accomplices in such a visible way, and yet two others are—what? Taken off somewhere and either buried or—what was that you said about Fournier? Dumped into a Canadian lake? You're a professional; tell me why Ceti would do that."

A slow smile broke across her face. "No, Swan, this is your hypothesis. You tell *me* why Ceti would do it. You know you're dying to."

To milk the suspense, I took another sip of the soda and quietly let out a low-key belch. "Because," I said, "they're not dead."

Parnell squinted into the camera. "You think they work with

Ceti? They're not just insiders he recruited, but they're actual partners?"

"Partners, employees, relatives, lovers. I don't know. But if he didn't leave their bodies out for us to find, there's a reason. And I can't think of a better one right now."

"Okay. I'll play along. So what now?"

"Well, now we throw a lot more time and effort into the life and times of Ursula Fournier and Tanner Leachman. When you're under the assumption that someone is dead, you don't look for them among the living. I'm going to get the ghouls on the second floor to track these two."

She nodded. "I take it you haven't shared your theory with Quanta."

"I wanted to try it out on you first and see how you reacted."

"And, by speaking it, you wanted to see if you believed it yourself."

"Parnell, the philosopher."

"No," she said, "just Parnell, the observer of human nature. Besides, I may not have worked with Quanta as long as you have, but I probably went through a harsher baptism with her than you did."

"Well, yes, but you were a criminal, while I was a military hero. Naturally, she would put you through a finer filter. But let's get back to the theory. You're on board, no?"

She looked away for a few moments, then turned back. "Sure. Now that you mention it, I'm surprised none of us thought of it before."

"Good," I said. "To me, this is a classic case of a criminal who's smart enough to get away with a crime, but too stupid to use the advantage. Ceti could've pulled off these incursions for years without us tracking him down, but two things will burn him: The open cases with Fournier and Leachman, and his sudden addiction to fame."

"You should call the boss and walk through this with her. I'll book a flight back and we can go looking for the two missing computer nerds." She gave a sigh. "It'll be good to actually *do* something again."

Quanta listened as I presented the possibility that Fournier or Leachman—or both—were alive and still on Team Ceti. It was the second time in an hour I'd laid out the idea, and it sounded more plausible this time around.

Either that, or I was just hungry for anything that even faintly smelled like progress.

As a way of stamping it with her approval, Quanta suggested that Parnell fly directly from London to Toronto and look into Fournier's disappearance. I would fly to Kansas City and dive into the case of Tanner Leachman and his bloody carpet. I was happy with the division of labor; although Toronto was one of my favorite cities in the world, I was a sucker for KC's barbecue. And, if I was being honest, I just wanted to get the hell out of Boston for a while. I'd been stymied in Beantown by the lack of headway and nearly murdered, to boot. A change of scenery sounded good.

Three hours later, I was on a plane out of Logan, and three hours after that I was on the ground at Kansas City International. Poole had a car waiting for me, a boring but reliable sedan, along with a hotel confirmation number. Her digital info packet also included the name of the police detective I'd meet in the morning. I spent a quiet evening in my room, reading through the Leachman file and sampling the takeout brisket from a cafe across the street.

Just another thrilling chapter in the life of a secret agent.

The following morning, I presented myself at the Overland Park Police Station and, while waiting for Detective Krup, glanced at a collection of flyers posted on a community bulletin board. One invited the public to have '*Coffee With a Cop*' at a nearby healthcare facility for seniors. Another featured surveillance photos of an idiot who'd shoplifted a handful of electronics equipment and was thoughtful enough to stare directly into the camera in order to provide a crystal clear image of his face. I was confident the fine officers toiling for the OPPD would have their man within a matter of days.

"Mr. Swan?"

At the greeting, I turned to find a woman studying me with a curious gaze. As a federal agent, I got that look a lot. She offered her hand. I shook it and sized her up, as well. Detective Alison Krup—one L—was tall, at least five-ten, and fit, dressed in dark pants with a plum-colored jacket. Her handshake was the perfect pressure. She made a great first impression.

"Hello, Detective. Thanks for meeting with me."

"Sure. Come on back." She led the way to a conference room where she'd already deposited one large file folder and had a bottled water on my side of the table.

"You're here to find out about the disappearance of Tanner Leachman," she said.

"Yes."

"Then I'd like to ask the first question. Why the interest from the feds?"

"Mr. Leachman was sharing his streaming passwords. Netflix told us they'd had enough of it and asked us to get rough. Someone beat us to it."

There was no reaction for the first few seconds. Then Krup gave me a smile. "Good thing we've got you on our side."

I matched her smile. My first impression had been spot on. I would easily be able to work with this Midwestern homicide detective.

"Okay, here's the deal," I said, leaning forward, crossing my arms on the table. "As you know, the security breach at Leachman's tax firm was carried out by a hacker—or hackers—going by the name Ceti."

"Yes," she said. "And the security experts think Tanner Leachman may have helped Ceti break in. Then he was killed before he could talk."

"Well . . . probably."

Krup raised an eyebrow. "Probably what? He *probably* helped Ceti?"

"No. He definitely was on the inside of the caper. I'm saying he probably was killed."

She hesitated, then laughed and pushed the file across the table. "This contains some pretty gruesome photos of the crime scene, Mr. Swan. Leachman didn't cut himself shaving."

"First of all, it's Eric. And second, I'd be happy to look at the photos, but I'd also like to go over everything you've dug up on Leachman's past."

She sat back and stared at me for a moment, then stood up. "All right. It's been a couple of years. Give me a few minutes to retrieve the other file. Just hang tight here. Do you need anything besides the water?"

I told her I was fine and proceeded to hang tight. I flipped through the manilla folder, which began with standard police paperwork. It didn't really tell me anything I hadn't already seen in the file I got from Poole. A little farther down, however, were the photos, which delivered on Krup's promise. They were indeed gruesome. An overturned barstool with a spattering of blood on and around it. From there, a bloody trail serpentined into the small living room, where it expanded into a swampy mess. It was presumed that Leachman had first been attacked in the kitchen, then staggered toward his couch, where the killer finished him off. Then his body was hauled out and disposed of.

Other photos showed similar chaos—minus the blood—

throughout the apartment. The bedroom had all the earmarks of being ransacked, and a smaller bedroom that Leachman used as an office was practically destroyed. Every desk drawer had been dumped out, books were strewn about the space, and even the window blinds had been mutilated. I gazed at the carnage, not expecting to find anything. But after a minute, I realized the cumulative damage on display told me plenty.

Krup returned with another folder and sat down. "See anything?" she asked.

I tossed a few of the photos on the table, facing her. "What's your gut reaction when you see these?"

She didn't hesitate. "Overkill. That's what I've thought from the beginning."

I nodded. "You ever really see anything like this?"

"Only in movies. This has all the hallmarks of someone tossing an apartment the way they *think* criminals do it. Pulling out drawers, ripping the sofa cushions, dragging pictures off the wall."

I pointed at one photo in particular. "I didn't think much about it until I saw this. I mean, I hate mini-blinds as much as the next person, but I've never physically abused them. Besides, how would something be hidden in a blind?"

"I've been going under the assumption that Tanner Leachman was killed because of his connection to the security breach," Krup said. "Then the killer or killers wanted us to think he walked in on a burglary. But they were clumsy. It doesn't wash." She paused. "So now you're walking in here and telling me you don't even think he's dead. The problem, Eric, is the blood. It matches the DNA sample we have on Leachman."

"Yeah, I get that."

"And it's not like he just pricked his finger and let it drip on the carpet. We're talking a significant amount, and *all* of it belongs to him."

"Yeah," I said again.

A smile curled up at the corners of her mouth. "Yeah, what? What's your hypothesis, professor?"

I chuckled and helped myself to the bottled water. Then, screwing the lid back on, I said, "Let's assume the goal was to make us believe Mr. Leachman, who spent his days working to protect the digital firewall of his accounting firm, got tangled up with the wrong crowd. In this case, a crowd that has probably killed in the past. Suppose they wanted you—the trusty Overland Park Police—to be convinced he'd been slain in his apartment. You'd need the blood to actually be his. And you'd need, as you said, a significant amount."

"And?"

"And in order to do that, you—" I stopped and looked back down at the photos taken from the living room. Then I blurted out my thought. "To do that, you gradually draw Tanner Leachman's blood, perhaps over a month or two, and store it until the time comes to splash it around his apartment."

Before I'd even finished the sentence, the detective was laughing. "I see. So they keep their own personal blood bank, purely to set up a scene and make us *think* he's dead."

"Yeah."

She laughed again. "Well, I'll give you this much. It's unique. But isn't that going to an awful lot of trouble? Why not have the so-called victim just run away? Wouldn't that be easier?"

"Oodles easier," I said. "But if he really is dead, the part that has no logical explanation is the bad guys gutting him and then hauling away his body. Why do that? It would be a gory, disgusting mess."

"I can't argue with that. But there *is* a shower curtain missing from the guest bathroom, which could've been used to wrap up the body before they carried it out."

"Still doesn't address the '*why*' part of the equation."

She coolly tapped a finger on the table, looked down at a photo, then back up at me. "Look, the missing body has bugged me, too. It doesn't make sense unless there was something about it that would point to the killer. Or maybe—"

"Detective Krup, these guys have killed before and in at least two instances they've had no qualms about leaving behind a corpse."

"I read the files," she said. "The difference is that they made those look like either an accident or a suicide. This couldn't have been staged as anything other than a homicide."

I raised an eyebrow. "So, even after two years, you're still keeping up with all the details on the other cases. Impressive."

"I don't like open cases, Eric. They piss me off. I get shit from above and below, especially with the public now keeping a score-card on how many we close. Or *don't* close. So yeah, I keep up with it."

My phone vibrated with a call from Katrina Yu. I hadn't bothered telling her about my quick trip. I sent it to voicemail, then turned back to Alison Krup and pointed to the new file she'd brought in.

"If you don't mind, I'd like to spread out the contents of that and see if something stands out. The water is nice, but could I get some coffee? The hotel's was putrid."

"Not sure you'll like ours any better, but I'll get two. You get started and I'll come back and sit in with you for about an hour."

"Oh, and wait," I said as she reached the door. "Could you also check to see if the blood samples from Leachman can still be tested?"

"Sure, I can ask. What are you looking for?"

"I did a little digging and came up with an additive solution called SAG. And if they could also check to see if a substance called mannitol is mixed in." I shrugged. "They'll probably know what I'm talking about when you say SAG."

"What is this stuff?"

"Little cocktails they add to blood to keep it fresh during storage. Blood banks use it. I want to know if our so-called victim was using it, too."

She shook her head. "You really think this guy is still alive, don't you?"

I let out a long, slow breath. "Detective, it's called desperation. This is my half-court heave at the buzzer."

She turned and left, and I began spreading out the contents of the new file. "I'll even take a bank shot off the glass," I muttered to myself.

CHAPTER SEVENTEEN

By the time the hour was up, we'd pretty much gone through the life and times of Tanner Leachman, along with an additional cup of coffee each. Krup deciphered some of the handwritten scrawls I'd seen on a few pages, quick but sloppy notes taken during the department's routine investigation into the alleged victim.

Leachman was 34 at the time of the crime, an employee at Barhardt-Billings for only nine months, but lauded by his supervisors as "one of the best hires in years." They'd granted him a lot of freedom to experiment with cutting-edge security designs, his specialty.

Hey, how could they know what was about to happen?

A graduate of the University of Washington, he'd done post-graduate work at UC-Berkeley, but left before finishing to join a small start-up. That had gone well, providing him with enough of a nest egg to explore other opportunities.

But that's where the story got interesting. Tanner Leachman *hadn't* explored other opportunities. As far as I could tell from the file, he hadn't done anything. He was the poster child for dropping out; there was no record of him anywhere for nearly six years, until he showed up to apply with Barhardt-Billings. When questioned after his disappearance, a sister who was his only surviving relative told OPPD that she thought he took the money he'd made and went to Europe. When asked why she hadn't stayed in touch with him, her response to the inquiring officer was, quote, "He's an asshole."

I showed this to Krup. "We never heard that from his employer or any of his co-workers," she said. "They all described him as a somewhat reserved guy, but friendly. Maybe the sister's the asshole."

"I might give her a call. Maybe two years has been enough time for her to develop sentimental feelings for her brother." I sat back in my chair and laced my fingers together on top of my head. "How could there be no record of this guy for six years? People can't really fall completely off the grid, can they?"

"Sure they can. It's not easy, but if you have money and know computer science as well as Leachman did, it's not impossible. I don't blame him for checking out. Don't you ever wish you could?"

"I actually do check out from time to time," I said. "It's not as romantic as it sounds."

Krup grunted a reply, but I left it at that. I couldn't tell her that when I checked out, it wasn't some idyllic life on a beach with endless umbrella drinks and no phone access. It happened when my consciousness drifted in a dark, mindless void within a sophisticated hard drive buried in a concrete bunker. I mean, when I checked out, I *really* checked out. And it only happened when I'd been killed.

But the thought of Leachman skipping around Europe—or wherever he'd been—for that long intrigued me. It essentially meant he'd disappeared twice.

I flipped through the papers until I found the one with the sister's information. Kimberly Leachman was now Kimberly

O'Dell, last known to be living in Arizona. I made a call that went quickly to voicemail, so I left a brief message, identifying myself as a federal agent who wanted to ask a couple of questions about her brother. She called back in less than three minutes. I answered it on speaker.

"Thanks for getting back to me so quickly, Ms. O'Dell."

"Sure. What do you need? Did you find my shitty brother's body yet?"

I quickly muted the call and muttered to Krup, "So much for developing sentimental feelings." Going back to O'Dell, I said, "No, unfortunately there are still no signs. I'm sorry if this is going back over ground you've already covered with the Overland Park Police, but I'm just getting up to speed and wanted to ask you a few questions about Tanner's past."

"Yeah, okay. I'll bottom-line it for you. He'd always be the smartest guy in every room he walked into, but he was a dick. And that's the Tanner Leachman story."

I muffled a laugh. "All right. Uh, I'm looking for a little more than the headline. Anything from his early years you can share that might relate to his work as an adult?"

"Yeah. He got arrested for some computer shit."

I shot a look at Krup, who scowled. She didn't know about this either.

"He was arrested? When? I don't see that in his records."

"He was a juvenile. They made him do some community service, gave him a stern talking to, and all that other shit that doesn't add up to squat. He thought it was funny. And when he turned 18, they wiped his record. What's it called? Expunging?"

"Yeah," I said. "Do you remember what the crime was?"

She paused and I thought I heard the sound of her drinking something. I hoped to God it was a beer—out of a can—because that's exactly how I pictured her.

"Oh, hell," she said. "I don't remember exactly. Some kind of hacking. He was always hacking into whatever he could. It was his hobby. Other kids just played with computers as their hobby; Tanner wasn't satisfied with that. If there was a lock on a door, he'd wanna pick it. Computers just gave him a chance to do that without leaving his smelly bedroom and the 12 pack of Mountain Dew."

I'd talked to Kimberly O'Dell for a whopping 90 seconds and I already loved her.

"Are we talking serious hacking or just farting around stuff that kids do?"

"Both. I mean, at first he just did stupid shit like hacking into the nearby bank's sign—you know those digital signs that show the time and temperature and say stupid things like '*Have a beautiful day*?' He got in there and changed the message to something like, '*The end is near, we're all about to die.*' Dumb stuff like that. Then he worked his way up to where he got inside some company's accounting and sent out a check to himself. Not for much, like a hundred bucks or something. I don't know, I tried to ignore the goofy bastard as much as I could."

I laughed. "All right. After he did his time with juvie, he straightened himself out?"

"Said he had. Said he'd seen all the ways you could get inside the software, so he could sell his talents—that was his term—sell his '*talents*' to companies who wanted to keep assholes like him out. Went to school for a while, then dropped out and used the meager savings he had to drive around the country. Went to the upper peninsula of Michigan for a while, said he might chuck the computer stuff and be a lumberjack or something. That was a hoot.

"Spent some time in Canada, I think. Drove through New England, gushed about Vermont and how our grandfather had done okay for himself there and why didn't the family ever stay there. Oh, and he talked about driving down to the Florida Keys and maybe getting work on a fishing boat, one of those touristy things. All of it was total horse shit, of course. He was a hacker and coder and that was all he was ever going to do. So instead of working on a fishing boat, he went to work for some new computer company in California somewhere. When I saw him at Thanksgiving right after that, he said he was the youngest guy on the staff but the only one who knew what was what. Which sounded just like him."

"Okay, great. Do you know any of the details about why he quit the start-up?"

We heard a grunt of laughter through the speaker. "Quit? He didn't quit. They threw his ass out."

Krup and I locked eyes again. The life story of Tanner Leachman was much more interesting than I'd been led to believe. Before I could say anything, O'Dell kept going.

"Before you ask me exactly what happened, I don't know. He and one other programmer apparently were responsible for some accidental hole in their firewall code and I guess it cost the company a major account. Tanner said it was totally the other guy's mistake, but of course he would say that. I don't know, maybe it was. But the point is, it was ugly, and when the other guy killed himself over it, that left Tanner as the only person they could really punish."

"Wait, hold on a sec," I said. "You said this co-worker killed himself?"

"Yeah. I think so. Look, you should talk to the company, because this was at the point where I wasn't really communi-cating with my brother too much. Our parents were gone, he was a dick, and then he screwed up something at this new company and left to go drift around Europe and the Far East for a long time. One of the last times we talked, he said his eyes were finally wide open."

"What did he mean by that?"

She sighed. "Oh, who knows? I took it to mean he was never going to find success working in a traditional environment. Once or twice he casually mentioned something about finding people who thought the same way he did, about a lot of things. Real counterculture stuff, you know? Almost like a 21st century version of 1960s hippies."

Krup spoke up. "Ms. O'Dell, this is Detective Krup with the Overland Park Police. Did your brother share any names with you? Give you any details of who his counterculture friends were?"

"No. He just sounded like someone who felt mistreated by their employer and took comfort in talking to other sad, miserable souls. I didn't take it that seriously. If you look around, you'll find people who'll bitch about anything."

I sat quietly for a moment, digesting this news. Tanner Leachman had fallen into a funk; was it Ceti who'd found him languishing in despair and offered him a way out? It wasn't the craziest idea.

Regardless, Kimberly O'Dell was right; a call to the start-up company was very much in order, especially now.

"Okay, thank you," I said. "You've been extremely helpful."

"No prob," she said. "Let me know when his body turns up, and I'll see that he gets a decent burial somewhere."

I assured her we'd do that and ended the call. Then I looked at Krup. "That was . . . enlightening."

"Incredible. How about I grab us some lunch and then let's call California?"

"I could stand to walk around a bit. Tell me where to go that's nearby and lunch is on me."

She gave me directions to a deli I could walk to in ten minutes. I got back an hour later with two bags stuffed with some of the best-smelling takeout I'd sniffed in a long time. Krup finished some paperwork then joined me back in the conference room. I hadn't waited and was a third of the way through a ridiculously sized sandwich and macaroni salad. We were both famished and deep in thought, so there wasn't much said while we tackled lunch.

As I finished the sandwich and balled up the wrapping, I said, "How do you guys around this joint stay in shape with that place so close?"

She pushed her Cobb salad away then pointed at it. "I try to choose these most of the time."

I reached into the second bag and tossed her a small dark cube bulging through plastic wrap. "Oh, really? You specifically requested this."

She caught the fudge with one hand and laughed. "I order the salad so I *can* have this. I would offer you a bite, but I won't share. Not this." She took a healthy bite and just nodded. "Let's not wait any longer. I'm dying to know what this company says about Tanner Leachman."

After wiping my hands on a napkin, I spun my phone around, dialed the number on the West Coast, and again punched the speaker. It took a couple of minutes of introductions and explanations before we were finally connected to the company president. Just dropping the words 'Homeland Security' will usually get you through, and I didn't even work for them.

"Jaladi Shamar."

"Hi, Mr. Shamar. My name is Eric Swan, and I'm here with Detective Alison Krup of the Overland Park Police Department. Thank you for your time."

"This is about Tanner Leachman, I'm assuming. I understand he went missing a year or so ago."

"Yeah, two years," I said. "If you have a couple of minutes, we'd like to ask you about the work he did for you. Can you tell us what his role was with the company?"

"We develop high-level security systems for online business

transactions. Tanner was one of our lead developers. Remarkably skilled for such a young guy. A real natural. Got in early with our team, worked with us for almost three years. I didn't stay in touch after he left, but I heard the news about him going missing. Word spreads in a community like this."

"That's what I've discovered," I said. "Was he a good employee?"

"Well, that depends on what you mean by '*good employee.*' He was very talented at the technical aspect of the job. So no complaints there. There were a few personal habits that irked some people, but . . ." His voice trailed off for a second. "I'll just say that this field has been known to attract, um, unique individuals. A lot of independent thinkers, which is good, but only to a certain extent. Tanner wasn't always open to collaboration, and he made that very clear."

"But he had a partner on one particular project, I understand."

Shamar fell quiet for a moment. "Uh, yes. He worked with a guy named Abel Suman. Suman had created a new program that showed a lot of progress. We put Tanner on it, too, so we could speed it along to market. They didn't mesh very well, but it wasn't horrible. I'd say they tolerated each other."

Krup spoke up. "We understand things did not end well."

Shamar let out a long breath. "Yeah, you could say that. We thought the program was ready and we offered it to three of our biggest clients who snapped it up and used it as their primary online defense. If everything had gone well, it would've essentially catapulted us to the top of the industry. But somebody was able to worm their way inside the files of one of those clients, a hedge fund. They placed some ransomware on critical files. It cost the company nearly $50 million dollars and cost us our two biggest clients. It was a nightmare, really. It shoved us back a couple of years, competitively speaking, but we were fortunate to survive it. For a while it didn't look like we would."

"But Suman did *not* survive it," I said.

Again, silence for a few seconds. "Uh, no. He did not. Abel was devastated and . . . well, he'd battled some personal demons for a while. We'd offered mental health counseling even before this breach, which he declined. I remember pleading with him to get some help, but he always waved it off. Then, after the blowup with the hedge fund, he killed himself in his car in our parking lot. Gunshot."

"I'm sorry," I said. "That had to be traumatic for everyone in your company."

"That's an understatement."

"So what happened with Leachman?"

"We, uh . . . we were under a lot of pressure. Word doesn't always get out about breaches of this magnitude; a lot of companies do everything they can to hide it. But somehow this particular incursion got around. We felt we had to do something to show we were contrite for the disaster, and so we, uh, we let Tanner go."

"You needed a fall guy, and the creator was dead."

"Hey, they were both creators," Shamar said, an edge to his voice. "Abel had the original idea and code, but Tanner put a lot of work into it. He was just as culpable as his team partner for what happened. He didn't spot the backdoor breach, either. And, honestly, sometimes you just know when it's time for someone to move on."

Krup leaned toward the phone. "Would it be safe to say that Tanner Leachman felt like a scapegoat for the whole thing?"

Another pause. "I don't like that term. We don't have scapegoats, Detective; we simply hold people accountable in a very high-pressure world of digital security. There's a lot more than $50 million on the line, you know. We're talking trillions of dollars at stake. For our company to have a solid reputation, we need to show clients that we take every transaction seriously. I don't think we did anything out of line. Any other company in our field would've done the same thing. And like I said, it was just time."

I tapped a finger on the table, glancing down at Leachman's file. "You didn't actually fire him, though. Instead, you bought him out. Isn't that correct?"

"It's complicated. We brought him in, had a long talk, and told him the score. Honestly, I thought he would understand and just take his severance and move on to another shop. Even with the breach, he would've been a valuable asset for someone. So I was astonished when he threatened legal action if we didn't do the right thing by him. Said he would bankrupt the company."

"He threatened you," I said.

"I mean, in a way, yes. Nothing in writing. But the implications of what he said were pretty obvious. And you know, we already had a PR issue bubbling under; we certainly didn't need all the negative media attention of a court case on top of it."

"So you paid him off to kick him out."

"I don't like that terminology, either."

I chuckled. "We're not a newspaper, Mr. Shamar, and this is not going on any record. We're just trying to piece together the complicated life of a guy who may have met with a violent ending. Let's not get caught up in the vernacular, okay?"

He paused, then said, "Yeah, okay. Yes, we paid him off to go quietly. I'll put it that way. It was a gut punch for us, but ultimately cheaper than a trial and the resulting fallout."

"Fair enough," I said. "One last thing. You said you didn't keep up with Tanner after he left the company. Did you ever hear anything about what he was doing or who he might be associating with?"

"Associating with? No. Well, wait a second. Maybe. One of our coders said she got a text after he'd been gone for a while, asking if she'd be interested in getting together to talk about . . . .

what did he call it? Something about people who had *a 'new way of looking at things.'* Something like that. I was under the impression he'd tried to find solace in talking to other tech people who'd been through a tough time in the industry. This business can be ferocious, really, especially here on the West Coast. I've seen it chew up a lot of people and spit them right out."

"Did she go? The coder, I mean. Did she go with him to meet these people?"

"Not that I know of. I told you, Tanner wasn't the most loved person on the staff. It would've been difficult for him to recruit anyone for anything. I'd be surprised if he even stuck it out with this new group for more than a week or two."

I looked at Krup and raised an eyebrow to see if she had any other questions, but she shook her head. So I said, "Thank you for your time, Mr. Shamar. If Detective Krup or I have other questions, we'd appreciate you being available to talk again."

He agreed and hung up. I looked across the table at Krup. "Thoughts?"

She held out a hand, palm up. "It's all fascinating stuff. But I don't see how any of these details add up to Leachman getting killed, unless it was this new group he fell in with. But even that's vague, and who even knows if it's true? The bottom line is, when you look at the whole picture, from his sister to his former boss, he doesn't sound like the nicest guy. But enough of a jerk to get murdered? I don't see it."

"No. I don't either." I stood up and stretched. "But it's a lot to think about. Might help with some of the other cases attached to this. I think I need to get back to Boston and start putting the pieces together."

I took my trash over to the waste can and dumped it in, but not before extracting another plastic-wrapped treat from the bag. I held up the duplicate fudge square to Krup and smiled. "I knew you wouldn't share."

CHAPTER EIGHTEEN

Somehow I managed to get into a car at Logan Airport with the most cautious rideshare driver of all time. He tapped his brakes approaching every green light, refused to even sniff the speed limit, and kept nervously checking his mirrors and whipping his head around to see if anyone lurked in a blind spot. It became a game for me to see if a yellow light would prompt him to actually come to a complete stop in the middle of an intersection and then back up to wait at the red. I didn't dare make conversation for fear it would plunge him over the edge. Instead, I checked headlines and sports scores on my phone. By the time we reached my hotel, I'd aged two years.

During the trip, I hadn't returned any of Katrina Yu's messages, partly out of frustration and partly out of simple distrust. I felt like the person in a relationship who claims they need space, which, of course, is code for *'I'm breaking up with you but we're going to do this gradually to lessen my feelings of guilt.'*

Now, back in my room, I texted her and asked if there'd been any progress. It took nearly an hour before she replied with a thumbs-up emoji and asked if I could stop by. I inwardly groaned;

I was tired of that office and too tired to think of a new way to terrorize the jumpy receptionist. I suggested she meet me at the pub in an hour, either alone or with Jared.

I'd barely set my phone down when it buzzed with another message. This time it was Quanta, asking me to check in.

I spent the first few minutes catching her up on my chats with Leachman's sister and his former boss.

"Interesting," she said. "Do you have any thoughts on these new associates that his sister referred to?"

"Well, it would help tie everything together if it was Ceti. There's just no proof yet."

Quanta said, "What about your theory that he wasn't murdered? Did Detective Krup have an idea when the blood test would be back?"

"Could be anytime. She put a rush on it, and I get the impression people jump when she speaks."

"Very good. I'll be curious to see if Parnell turns up anything in Toronto. She's there now, meeting with the police and Ursula Fournier's company in about an hour. Also, I wanted to let you know I heard back from the FBI team in Boston checking out that photo we got from Arlo Benn's phone."

"And?"

"As we thought, it's from a parking garage. Those same signs are used in garages all over the Northeast, but this one was damaged a bit. They found a sign with identical damage about a quarter mile from your hotel. They confiscated security footage and isolated Arlo getting out of a blue Toyota. After tracing it to a rental company, they got inside and scoured it."

"Tell me they found something," I said.

"An empty disposable coffee cup and a large bag of M&Ms."

I laughed. "I like his taste. What else?"

"The rental agreement, under a fake name. We used that to track down his flight from London. Your flight, actually."

"So he *was* with me the whole way, just biding his time."

"But that was it. Other than his prints and his snacks, the car was clean."

"Yeah," I said. "He wasn't the most skilled assassin I've come across, but he was good enough to keep us in the dark. Have the geeks on the second floor been able to find any kind of digital background on him, like email?"

"First of all, I disapprove of the term '*geeks*.' Second, the answer is no; somebody did a good job of scrubbing his digital footprint, assuming he did anything under his real name."

"Yeah, well, Arlo worked for someone who'd be really good at scrubbing. It was worth a shot."

I told her about my upcoming meeting with Katrina and Jared, and we agreed to touch base again in the evening.

KATRINA SHOWED UP ALONE. Our usual booth was occupied, so we moved to one farther back and ordered pints.

"You've been hard to reach," she said. "Did something come up?"

"Out of town. Looking into some of the other Ceti cases."

"Oh. Well, I've got good news. We're pretty sure we found some traces of Ceti on ZigbyNet."

I gave a wry smile. "*We*? Or was it you? Your boyfriend hasn't seemed too intent on finding anything."

She frowned across the table at me. "We stayed late last night and worked on it together. You've got to get over this stupid feud with—"

"So tell me what you found," I said, cutting off her lecture before it could pick up steam.

She seemed to gather herself for a moment. "If someone doesn't want to be found, and if they're smart enough—and I'd say diligent enough—it's difficult to track them down. I just want you to recognize that. It's not like doing a Google search."

"Got it. So what cracked the case for you?"

"It didn't have anything to do with the actual incursions. Ceti is much too careful in that area, and we'll probably never get lucky enough to find that. But twice now he's done that Robin Hood act, using the Dark Web and cryptocurrency. The person who must've set that up for him laid down some preliminary groundwork for distributing the coins, and one of those messages referenced a transaction from—and these were their words —*Codename Green Angel.*"

It was my turn to frown. "The stupid nickname has gotten around lately. Couldn't anyone have dropped that term?"

"Yes. Except this person's thread was nine hours before the latest crypto gifts, and it labeled the file *Rainy Year.*"

It took me a moment before I placed those words. "Ceti's message to the people he gifted the money to: *Save this for a rainy year.*"

Katrina smiled and took a draw from her beer.

"Okay," I said. "So now what? Are you able to trace this helper who left the messages? And how do you know it's not Ceti himself?"

She shrugged. "I don't. But he seems bright enough to insulate himself. I don't buy into Jared's theory about Ceti being an organization rather than a single person; but I do believe he or she has a team doing some of the dirty work. Pawns, in a way."

My mind jumped to the conversations I'd had with Tanner Leachman's sister and former boss. If Tanner was still alive, I was convinced he was one of those teammates. Or maybe the lone teammate. Could he have been the one who dropped the *Rainy Year* clue?

Katrina continued. "As for what to do now? We're trying to infiltrate the thread, acting like someone who just wants to be in on the next payday. So far we haven't heard anything back. Of course, thousands of people are buzzing about the Green Angel. And each time he does this Robin Hood trick, the number will go up exponentially."

For the next minute, we just sipped our beers in silence. As much as I tried to talk myself into distrusting her, Katrina gave off the wrong kind of vibe for a villain, even the low-level variety. I'd felt a connection with her from our first meeting, which probably explained why my later suspicions chafed me so much. I hated to think my instincts could be blunted by a friendly smile and a sarcastic wit.

I decided to take a chance.

"My trip was to Kansas City," I said. "I wanted to dig into Tanner Leachman and the role he might've played in everything."

She studied my face. "He went missing, right? But they think he's dead?"

"Yes and yes. But he has an impressive background in cyber-security, on both sides of the law. And he had an incident a few years ago that may have shoved him back over to the dark side, so to speak. I'm wondering if he's this helper you mentioned a few minutes ago."

"So you don't think he's dead?"

I hesitated, then said, "I think he staged his disappearance to look like he was killed. And—" I took a deep breath, wondering why I was suddenly so chatty about the details of the case. *Screw it*, I decided; I *wanted* Katrina Yu to be one of the good guys. "And I'm not so sure that Ursula Fournier is dead, either."

Her eyes stayed locked on mine, and I could see her processing the possibilities. After a few moments, she slowly nodded her head. "I guess it would make sense. He probably doesn't want to kill all of his connections. Maybe after using some of them, he recalls them or something like that."

"In old time spy lingo, he's bringing them in from the cold.

So, if we base our strategy on that premise, it's not so much a case of tracking down Ceti, but rather tracking down his team. As you've pointed out, for one very skilled person it might be easy to disappear. I'm banking on the fact that each new person added to the team increases the chance of someone slipping up and sending us a beacon. It's not that different from a boxing match; one minor mistake, one tiny opening, could be enough for us to land a knockout punch."

Katrina grinned. "Look at you, busting out the sports metaphors to inspire the team."

"Yeah, I'm a veritable Knute Rockne."

"Who?"

"Never mind."

My phone rumbled in my pocket. Fishing it out, I saw a text from Parnell who, according to Quanta, was in Canada.

I read the message twice before slamming the phone down on the table and uttering a few choice words under my breath.

Katrina set down her glass. "What is it?"

I ignored her and lifted my own beer to my mouth, gazing out across the pub but not really seeing anything. Years of training and a wealth of experience had taught me to hold my temper. For one thing, it serves no purpose but to vent, which a professional shouldn't need to do. But it also has a cumulative effect on overall performance; getting pissed off shifts your thinking patterns to the point where you begin looking at your case through a prism of failure. That leads to faulty conclusions based not on solid work and evidence, but on making up for the setback you encountered earlier. It's sloppy.

But I was pissed. I'd just built a case based on what I thought would be our best bet for finding the shithead orchestrating a global financial disaster. And one text from Parnell brought it toppling down.

"Can you tell me?" Katrina said.

After taking another healthy gulp of beer, I set down the pint and dragged the back of my hand across my mouth. "That was one of my partners. She's in Canada, working on that breach of the gas company. Chasing down Ursula Fournier, actually, who went missing right after Ceti got in and made a mess of things."

"Yeah? And?"

I looked back at Katrina. "And they just pulled Fournier's body out of a shallow grave in Toronto."

CHAPTER NINETEEN

Memories of my family are not something I dredge up often. Miller, our Q2 shrink, has a pretty clear understanding of the peculiar motivation I derive from my parents and sister. Or rather, from their deaths. He's respectful enough to talk *around* the provocation and how it drives me to continually push the boundaries of my career as a government agent and killer, particularly in regard to the investment process. Or maybe he just understands that I wouldn't really know how to put it into words myself.

But one memory that played across my mind as I walked from the pub to my hotel room involved my dad and video games.

Like any typical eight-year-old, I could easily become absorbed in the screen while trying to reach the final level or save the princess or whatever the cheesy endgame might be. And while I was not ordinarily prone to temper tantrums, something about these graphically-created storylines turned me into a monster when I lost. My game system was put away more than once until I "learned to control my temper."

Which, as a third grader, I thought was the stupidest directive ever. They only said that because they hadn't felt the indignity and shame of having an animated ghost in Hyrule beat them.

The funny thing was, I was competitive as hell in sports all the way through high school, but never lost my temper. It was only during video games or board games. You could kick my ass at basketball and I'd just try harder the next time. Whip me in a game of Risk or Catan, and my blood would boil. The day came when my dad had had enough. I'd sustained another casualty in some ridiculous video game, and I made sure the universe heard my cry about the injustice I'd suffered.

He shut off the television, quietly took me by the arm, and led me outside where we had about a 30-minute chat. What I gleaned from his scolding—which, by the way, featured no shouting, no raised voice—was that my particular flavor of competitive spirit had nothing to do with a physical desire to win. What he'd observed was the fact that his son could not tolerate someone *outthinking* him when it came to strategy and tactics. I methodically plotted every step in the animated worlds of Nintendo and other systems, and to have a cold, inanimate machine humiliate me touched off my fireworks.

That explained why football, baseball, and basketball didn't generate the same outbursts. Those involved thinking, sure, but they also involved physical exploits. Games, on the other hand, were primarily about your head.

I never outgrew that characteristic. My mind was arranged to maneuver through problems and mysteries by applying logic and systems. That mind may have gone through an astounding number of uploads and downloads, but the edge has—I don't think, anyway—never been sanded down.

Ursula Fournier should be alive. I'd worked out the details of how Ceti was operating, how he killed the temporary help while nurturing his A players. Ursula's body wasn't found at her home, the victim of some clumsy accident; she'd disappeared, which meant she had a backstage pass to Ceti's show.

But now she didn't. She'd been murdered and her remains quickly hidden in a wooded part of a nearby park. And it wasn't just the fact that Ursula Fournier was dead when she should be alive. It was the fact that if she'd been killed, Tanner Leachman was likely decomposing somewhere, too.

I do not like to lose.

My hotel came into sight, and I decided the last place I wanted to be was cooped up in a room. I detoured to my right and decided to take advantage of clearing skies and mild temperatures to walk and let my fiery emotions burn off. I hadn't gone even a block before Parnell called.

"Who found the body?" I asked.

"The usual. Someone on a morning run with her dog. She says she stopped to let the dog pee and that's when she saw something sticking up out of the ground. Turned out to be a horribly decomposed hand."

I didn't respond. Parnell added, "I know you well enough to tell when you're angry."

"Yeah. I'm pissed. Ursula Fournier should not be dead."

"I'm sure she's not thrilled about it either."

It was the perfect thing to say, and it had the desired effect. I started laughing, which lifted about 300 pounds off my shoulders. "Okay, well played. I know it's ridiculous, but this entire *assignment* is ridiculous. I'm scrambling for anything that might even hint at a trail back to Ceti, and I counted on Fournier and Leachman to provide that hint."

"You still have Leachman."

"Do I? Just when I thought I'd deciphered the patterns in these cases, my decoder ring gets mangled. Why wouldn't his body be the next one to turn up? Somebody could be tripping over it right now in Swope Park."

"In what?"

"Never mind. Did you find out anything else about Fournier that we didn't already know?"

"Her best friend was also a co-worker. Name's Jada Orren. She said Ursula got weird—that was her friend's word—about a month before the breach. Started missing a lot of work, calling in sick. And when she *was* there, her work went to shit. When I asked if she could think of anything that might've caused this erratic behavior, Jada said, '*I think she was bothered by something her mentor was doing.*'"

I'd reached a cafe on a corner and took the liberty of plopping down at one of their outdoor tables. "Her mentor at work?"

"No. Jada didn't know who it was, but apparently Ursula was like a child prodigy at coding and hacking, and she studied in her spare time with some computer guru. Underground sort of stuff. But I guess things had turned sour with this person."

"And we're thinking this is Ceti?"

"Well," Parnell said, "it *could* be Ceti. Maybe things turning sour was a reference to what was about to happen with Ursula's company. But listen, just a week before shit went down with the oil and gas company, Ursula went away for a long weekend. Wasn't a vacation, though; she told Jada it was more like a digital security retreat. Which sounds to me like a final tune-up with Ceti for the big takedown coming up."

"Interesting. Have you tracked her movements for that weekend?"

"You'll love this: She went to Boston."

A server at the cafe stopped by my table and reacted to *my* reaction to Parnell's bombshell, which was a loud, "No shit!" I pulled the phone away from my mouth, apologized to the startled woman, and ordered an old fashioned.

"Bourbon?" Parnell said. "Aw, it has been a tough day for America's super spy, hasn't it?"

"It's getting better. So Fournier flew to Boston to meet with her mentor—who could be anybody, but possibly Ceti. And she did this during a time of stress. Went back to Toronto, helped Ceti do his damage, then got whacked."

"That's essentially it."

I chewed on this for a minute. "Well, my first thought was that we might have narrowed down Ceti's location. But obviously that's wrong."

"Why? Make it obvious to me."

"Because he or she is smart enough to know that by killing Fournier, her movements would be analyzed, and we'd know about the trip to Boston. So he wouldn't bring her to his home base; he would've met her here."

"Makes sense."

"What about credit card or bank debit records? Do we know where she stayed or places she may have gone?"

"Working on that right now," Parnell said. "So far nothing. She may have paid cash for everything. Plus, even if Ceti flew in to meet her, they'd want to be discreet, so we may not get lucky with security cameras."

"Agreed. But we *can* check the security cameras at Logan. Let me get with the FBI and have them check out the footage from when she left the terminal."

"I've already made the request," she said.

"Excellent. We may be able to at least catch a cab number or Uber license plate or something." Then something else occurred to me. "Of course, once she got dropped off in town, Ceti could've picked her up and driven to Worcester or Providence or anywhere else. No reason they'd have to stay in Boston."

We sat quietly for a few moments, 500 miles apart, each trying desperately to think of a way to make this latest nugget work for us. My old fashioned arrived. It might not have helped me come up with a brilliant idea, but it tasted magnificent.

It was a ping on both our phones that broke the silence. I imagined Parnell checking her screen at the same time I did, both of us absorbing the latest missive from Quanta.

Another breach. A phone carrier. It's bad. Check in when you can.

"I'LL CONFERENCE US," Parnell said, and a minute later the boss was on the line with us.

"This should've been one of the hardest systems to hack into," Quanta said. "Betcher Telecom. Over 23 million accounts accessed, service shut down for many of them, and, worst of all, data wiped on a large scale."

"They have backups?" Parnell asked.

"They do, but it's a mess. More than anything, it's a true act of terrorism; it's caused terror and panic among a lot of people. And that's all in-house. When the news leaks out—which it will soon —it could disrupt not only Betcher itself, but the stock market altogether. Make that markets, plural. Because the message to the world is that nobody is safe."

My mind was already racing ahead. "I'm guessing we've started an investigation into the company's IT department. There could very well be another Ursula Fournier or Shawn Cook tinkering in the background."

"It was one of the first things we did. There are no fewer than a dozen federal agents already at the company headquarters, locking down the facility and looking into employee records. Or trying to, at least. I understand the CEO is pushing back, citing privacy issues."

Parnell grunted. "Privacy? They'll be lucky to survive the

fallout of this, and they're worried about giving out someone's work history?"

"They'll give it out," I said. "They have to make noise like this at first, just to look good. Show that they're protective of their people. But I hope the charade is short-lived. As we've discovered, a Betcher employee could be dead any day now."

"We'll lean on them," Quanta said. "I think if they know about the personal danger involved, they'll open up. In the meantime, Parnell, I'm sending you to their offices in Philadelphia. Swan, with this news about Fournier's trip to Boston, you'll obviously stay there. I'm hoping to have security footage from Logan Airport any minute now."

We ended the call and I sipped my drink. In a matter of minutes, I'd gone from depressed to hopeful. In my experience, the more times a bad guy sticks his neck out, the more opportunities there are for mistakes. Another incursion, this time in Philadelphia, basically meant another data point for us. And if Ursula Fournier had really flown to Boston to meet with Ceti, one tiny crumb on the trail could blow up everything.

My funk was over. It was time to catch a knave.

A QUICK TRIP across the Mystic took me to the FBI offices in Chelsea. Grabbing a coffee, I sat down with a burly agent named Ricci, who was friendly enough but still eyed me with suspicion.

The video he played from Logan was remarkably clear and provided a wealth of information. Ursula Fournier had traveled light, with one small carry-on bag. After getting off the plane, she'd made the requisite stop in a restroom before hopping into a cab. The number was easy to pick out, and within minutes we knew the destination. Fournier had been dropped not too far from my hotel, actually, but not at a specific location. Apparently she'd simply jumped out and finished her trek on foot.

That meant Ricci could apply facial recognition software for the street surveillance cameras in that area, input the date and time, and hopefully track her movements. The agent was nimble on the keyboard for having such meaty fingers. They danced across the keys before finishing with a dramatic punch of '*return.*' I appreciated the massive screen on which we could witness the hustle of Bostonians in slightly exaggerated speed.

It made me once again contemplate just how much of our lives we offer up for free. Not just all the data we voluntarily surrender to web sites and apps—which is a staggering amount—but also the implicit permission we give to track our movements around the streets of a city. Not long ago, it was rare to find metropolitan areas that had more than a rudimentary network of surveillance devices; today, it's the opposite. It's more difficult than you think to stroll around unobserved. And with the tech Ricci applied to the imposing amount of petabytes available to law enforcement, unless you were damned good at disguising your look, the AI employed by these systems could easily read your facial design and tell us '*You are here.*'

Is this a good thing? Is it not? I'll leave that for the ethicists to debate and for each individual to decide for themselves. For the time being, it was helping me track down some really, really bad people.

While the databases at his fingertips were left to do their work, Ricci stepped out for a few minutes. I made a quick call to Katrina Yu, to see if she had anything substantial on the Betcher Telecom breach.

"This one may not have involved an insider," she said.

"Explain that."

"It'll take time for the full postmortem, but from what we can tell right now, this was more brute force. The others had a finesse to them. I know that doesn't make sense when we're talking about digital crime; those are just ways I have of classifying them."

"Honestly, Katrina, I'll leave the finer details to you. Bigger picture: Why do you think he did it this way this time?"

She paused. "Well, it could be this one was put together more quickly. We know that some of his other incursions were set up over a matter of months, maybe as much as a year. I think he's just making sure he's still on everyone's mind."

"So he doesn't want too much time to pass between jobs. Top of mind."

"That's a possibility, for sure. What are you working on?"

"Believe it or not, Ursula Fournier made a trip here to Boston about a week before the Canadian job. I'm trying to track down her movements to see if it was related to Ceti." For now, I left out the news of her body being found.

Katrina sounded shocked. "She was right *here*?"

"Yeah. Anyway, let me know if something helpful turns up with the telecom case. How long until you get a more extensive report?"

"Probably by tomorrow, maybe late afternoon. Well, if their people are good."

We ended the call as Ricci strolled back into the room. He sat down at the oversized monitor and pointed to a late afternoon shot he'd retrieved from a street camera. "We got her. This is two minutes after getting out of the cab. She's going into a bakery and coffee shop."

It was indeed Fournier, and one thing about her jumped out at me. A friend of mine had once described someone by saying, '*They walk with purpose.*' If that meant what I thought it meant, Fournier had the same gait. Even when played back at normal speed, it was brisk, swiftly maneuvering between clumps of pedestrians, a woman on a mission. She even pulled the bakery's door open with gusto. All of her movements, taken together, struck me as nervous, worked up.

"No video from inside the shop," Ricci said. "But here, 40 minutes later, she leaves."

This time, her demeanor was totally different. She paused just outside, seemed to contemplate going back in, then moved off, first in one direction, then abruptly turning and heading the other direction. Rattled.

Scared.

Ricci began tapping in commands. "We can pick her up on other nearby cameras."

"No, wait a minute," I said, putting a hand on his shoulder. "Leave it here for a bit."

"You want to see someone else coming out." It was a statement, not a question.

"Yeah."

"Expecting someone in particular?"

"Nope. I'd just like to get pictures of anyone who walks out that door in the next 30 minutes. Hell, the next hour."

He grunted but said nothing.

It didn't take an hour. It didn't take 30 minutes. Exactly six minutes after Ursula Fournier walked out of the bakery, looking flustered and completely discombobulated, a familiar face exited.

"Son of a bitch," I muttered under my breath as I watched the man wiping what might have been muffin crumbs from his comically large beard.

CHAPTER TWENTY

It was hard to not mentally kick myself as I sat in the back seat of an FBI vehicle, darting through traffic, making our way to Katrina and Jared's office. The drive would take 25 minutes, which allowed plenty of time for me to berate myself.

From the first moment, I'd been suspicious of Jared Hicks, and at one point I became leery of *both* cybersecurity experts. Now, with video evidence, I cursed the very essence of good nature and how the world's lowest life forms took advantage of that weakness in our makeup.

Of course, that was an overreaction, and I'm sure the human element of good nature does more to help our species than harm it. But for the time being, I still cursed it.

I considered calling ahead to ask Katrina and Jared if they'd like to go out and grab a beer, or sit down and brainstorm, or a dozen other bullshit ideas to keep them from leaving the office. But it wasn't worth taking a chance of spooking either of them; better to just roll in with the two FBI agents and corner them.

I did, however, make a call to Quanta, which went to voice-mail. Next, I reached out to Poole, who would be available even if the Yellowstone volcano exploded and began coating all of North

America with a toxic, pyroclastic flow. With a brief description, I conveyed the news that we'd been duped by the people who were supposed to be helping us. After perhaps two seconds of silence, Poole fell into her typically thorough, efficient behavior. She would track down Quanta, and she'd also alert Parnell, who was en route to Philadelphia.

Casually patting the right side of my jacket, I felt the Glock neatly tucked into a holster provided by my temporary partners. It was doubtful I'd need it, but the leather rig provided a better and more reassuring home than simply stowing the gun in a pocket. I glanced at the team sitting in the front seat. Coincidentally, they were the same two who'd been assigned to watch over Arlo Benn in the hospital. The man, named Gant, drove; his partner, a woman named Greenberg, sat in front of me. I made eye contact with Gant in the rearview mirror and noted the same wariness I'd encountered with Ricci. It wasn't a case of territorialism; I think it was purely curiosity and doubt. And who could blame them?

We pulled up outside the office building and Gant stayed with the car, idling in a no-parking zone. Greenberg and I jumped out and made our way inside. Walking through the lobby, we approached the elevators just as one of them opened and Katrina Yu stepped out, a bag over one shoulder. She stopped short when she saw me, a look of surprise on her face.

"Mr. Swan," she said, then gave an anxious look at Agent Greenberg. "What, um, what's going on?"

"Where are you headed?" I asked.

"Just going to pick up a prescription. We've been going nonstop and I want to get there before they close."

"What about Jared? Is he back in the office?"

"No, he left a little while ago. Said he had some errands to run, some things we needed at the townhome." She nodded at my companion. "Who's this?"

"This is Agent Greenberg, of the friendly neighborhood FBI.

Do you mind if we all go back up to your office for a minute, just to see if Jared maybe snuck back in while you weren't looking?"

She pressed her lips together hard and shifted her bag to the other shoulder. "What is this, Eric?"

"Let's go upstairs and then we can have a nice talk. Okay?"

After a moment's hesitation and another unhappy glance at Greenberg, she spun around and marched back toward the elevator. A minute later, we pushed through the outer doors, into the Kajartek lobby. The receptionist's eyes immediately grew wide when he saw me.

"Hello, Aaron," I said. "Listen, if I get any calls, I'm not here, okay? In fact, you've never heard of me."

He opened his mouth to speak, then saw the look on Katrina's face and remained silent.

I turned to her. "You and Agent Greenberg can have a seat here. I'll be back in a flash." I looked at Greenberg, who nodded.

It took less than four minutes to scour the suite of offices. There were a few people milling around, but it was the end of the work day and most had probably gone home. Once I was sure Hicks was gone, I went back to the lobby and signaled for Katrina to follow me. Greenberg would stay in the lobby, just in case Hicks returned.

We settled into the comfy chairs in her office. Before she could speak, I put up a hand. "Let me start with a direct question, and I need an honest answer. Believe me, your life will become a living hell if you lie to me. Where did Jared go?"

She leveled an angry gaze at me and punctuated each word with a period. "I. Don't. Know."

"Rushed out to run some errands? Really?"

"Yes."

"And he didn't tell you where he was going?"

"No."

I sighed and rubbed a hand across my tired eyes. "All right.

So if we just sit here, he'll be back within the next half hour or so?"

"However long it takes him. We didn't know he had a curfew. So now why don't you tell me what's going on?"

I continued to rub my eyes for another few seconds, then leaned forward. "I'll tell you what's going on, Katrina. Jared isn't coming back. Not this evening, not ever. In fact, unless you've got me completely bamboozled—and God, I hope you don't—I wouldn't be surprised if you never saw Jared Hicks again."

It took her a moment, then she let out a grunt of laughter. "What a bunch of horse shit. Why?"

If she was playing me, she was really good. But that instinct I rely on told me it was no act. I didn't think Katrina Yu was on the wrong side. I decided, right there in her office, with her eyes blazing and her body language telegraphing that her insides were tied in knots, that she was partly furious and partly terrified. I decided to trust her yet again.

"One week before the Canadian breach, Ursula Fournier came to Boston."

"Yes, you told me that."

"And while she was here, she met with Jared."

Katrina remained motionless, her gaze dancing from my right eye to my left and back again before locking in. She opened her mouth to speak, closed it, then slowly leaned back in her chair. I gave her credit for not automatically insisting this was bullshit, too.

After a long silence, her chin dropped and she spoke in a half whisper. "Son of a bitch."

"You know, that's exactly what I said."

I let the bad news dissolve for a bit longer. Then I said, "I'm guessing you told Jared that I knew Ursula had come to Boston."

She nodded. "I just mentioned it because I thought it was such an interesting coincidence. You know, that she was right here. I didn't know he'd—"

"I know." I let out a long breath. "Well, he's smarter than he looks. He probably figured out we'd catch him on surveillance video somewhere. I'm guessing he bolted not long after that."

Another soundless nod as everything began to sink in. Her shock was normal, but I had to be the bad guy and cut short the grief session.

"All the hard work you've done, Katrina, over the last five years—all the effort you've put in, and all the time you've spent essentially growing up studying the workings of some pretty bad people—this is where you have to condense everything you've studied and everything you've invested into your career and put it all to work. Do you understand?"

She wouldn't look at me for the longest time. When she finally raised her head, her eyes were filled with tears and two of them escaped down her cheeks. Again to her credit, she let them lie there.

"No," she said. "I don't understand. I don't understand any of this."

I wanted to be gentle, but there was way too much riding on this. Taking a deep breath, I plowed ahead. "Yeah, you do. You understand everything I've said. You've spent the last decade or more of your life working for this moment: to catch Ceti. Your motivation in the past may have been some noble goal of serving your fellow humans. Well, I'm here to tell you the noble shit is out the window. Your training and your skills now have one purpose: Catch the rats who are perhaps days away from unleashing a global financial meltdown."

More tears spilled down her face, but I kept going. "Your fiancé is one of the rats. He betrayed you at the same time he betrayed his country and his calling. I think it's pretty clear he used you and your partnership to help a true villain escape detection for a long time. Jared basically lived a double life, and you provided the perfect cover. Now, if all of that's not enough motivation for you, then I'll let Agent Greenberg escort you back to FBI headquarters for a full debrief. Or—" I paused. "Or you can help me stop these assholes."

She finally reached up with a hand and wiped her face dry. Then she gave a short, mirthless laugh. "What a shitty speech. Was that really supposed to motivate me?"

"Was it that bad?"

"Straight out of a Liam Neeson movie or something. Jesus, is that the best you've got?"

I shrugged. "I'm kinda pressed for time. It's what came to me. Sorry. Usually I'm much better at ad libbing, and my motivational skills are off the charts."

She leaned forward and pulled a tissue from a table dispenser. After blowing her nose, she got up and went to the sideboard. Even with her back to me, I could tell she wasn't getting a glass of water. She returned, sipping from a tumbler of whiskey.

"All right, coach," she said. "What can we do?"

By 11 o'clock that night, it was clear Jared Hicks had officially fled. He never came back to the office, he returned none of Katrina's calls or texts, and the FBI reported that he never showed up at their home. His phone was shut off and he'd made no calls or texts since vanishing. Police and the feds were on the lookout, but my guess was the Ceti Machine had whisked him out of town, perhaps with him lying out of sight on the back floorboard of a car as it raced out of Boston, and likely out of Massachusetts.

What I didn't verbalize in front of Katrina was the question of whether Jared would survive the next 48 hours. Ceti had a nasty habit of dealing with loose ends in the most discourteous ways. Perhaps the bearded wonder was already bleeding out in some scuzzy motel room, or feeding the fishes in Quincy Bay, or buried somewhere in World's End.

I also realized I didn't *need* to say these things; Katrina had probably already considered the possibilities.

Even so, she toughed it out. For three hours, we pored over data and potential connections. She'd started by reviewing many of the reports from her earlier work on the assignment, but we quickly ditched that and concentrated on the casework Jared had supposedly focused on. As Ceti's inside help, there was no telling how much shit he'd buried.

We were both exhausted when a call came in from Parnell in Philadelphia. I put her on speaker.

"I'm here with Katrina Yu. But you go first; what've you found out?"

"I've discovered that Betcher Telecom was an easy target for Ceti. Too easy. Some of the worst security measures imaginable for a company this size. And in case you haven't looked at any social media, the word not only got out, it's gone viral in the last couple of hours. Half the people outraged and demanding some sort of compensation, and the other half singing the praises of the Green Angel."

"God, that's *such* a stupid name," I muttered. "It doesn't even fit."

"Well, to be honest," Parnell said, "I think a lot of people just aren't sure how to pronounce Ceti when they see it. Although easily a third of the comments can't spell angel, either. So in many cases he's the Green Angle."

"What's the actual damage so far?"

"A lot of personal data has been stolen, including bank and credit card accounts. A lot more was simply wiped, and I do mean wiped. Hundreds of thousands of phone accounts were deleted, along with the service, so there's pandemonium with people around the country foaming at the mouth. Their IT people are fairly astonished at the scope of the attack. And if you ask me, they're in over their heads. It took them hours to lock everything down before they could even begin assessing the damage."

"Do they have any help?"

"Two other IT specialists just arrived, one from a local cyber-security company and the other from New York. As they say, heads will roll over this. Oh, and after-hours trading of Betcher is down almost 20 percent. It'll be a bloodbath when the markets open tomorrow."

I leaned forward. "And the consensus is that Ceti didn't have inside help this time? How could they know that?"

"Well, they don't, not for sure. But I'm telling you, even before the cybersecurity big guns arrived, the FBI's cyber team said a college kid could've pulled some of this off."

For the first time, Katrina spoke up. "What about a digital signature? Did Ceti leave his usual calling card?"

"He did. It's actually scattered throughout. Like, people's account numbers were changed to *92540081*."

"I almost can't be mad at that," I said. "The guy is Public Enemy Number One right now, but I do love his style."

"Yeah, well, that style is going to put this major telecom player into a grave. I just got handed a note that said nearly two million people have already initiated canceling their service. It's crashing the system."

Katrina looked up at me. "This was always the way he intended to provoke anarchy. A million cuts, some more catastrophic than others, but all of them geared to break down the economy. Like she said, this one hack is enough to maybe destroy a big player. He could do a dozen more before the end of the year."

I got up and paced around. "Parnell, what else besides the signature? Have they found anything else that could be a clue?"

"Nothing. Maybe by tomorrow or the next day. But I'm not hopeful."

Neither was I. We ended the call with an agreement to touch base again in the morning.

I checked the time on my phone. It was sneaking up on midnight and I was exhausted. Katrina was clearly dragging, too. We wouldn't be able to accomplish much if our brains didn't unplug for a few hours, at least.

"Okay, let's get out of here for now," I said. "The two agents will escort you to your house where you can pick up a few things and pack a small bag. You'll be staying under FBI care for a while."

She frowned. "Why? Why can't I stay at my house?"

"Because your boyfriend works for a guy who kills anyone who can stop him. You happen to be someone who can do just that. I wouldn't be surprised if they tried to do something in the next 12 hours. So you'll be under protective custody until we get things tidied up."

I could tell from the look on her face that she hadn't considered that her own life was at risk. I didn't have the heart to tell her that she'd been at risk since the moment Jared Hicks hooked up with Ceti. She was already crushed; no reason to point out that her pseudo fiancé had marked her for death years ago.

"Come on," I said. "Let's go. We can pick up again tomor—"

Her phone rang. We'd made sure it wasn't silenced just in case Hicks decided to at least say goodbye. She held it up to show me that it was a blocked ID. I pointed to it and nodded.

Three seconds after answering, her face drained of color. She mouthed to me: *It's Jared.*

CHAPTER TWENTY-ONE

My gut reaction was to jump out of my seat and start coaching Katrina on what to say in order for us to track her now-ex-boyfriend. But I shut down that instinct, sat quietly, and just stared and listened.

She wasn't saying much. In fact, after the initial hello, she hadn't said a word. It would seem that Jared Hicks, asshole extraordinaire, had plenty to say. He likely also wanted to blurt out everything as quickly as he could out of a fear of being traced. Naturally, we were trying to do just that. Poole had set that up as soon as we knew he was gone.

Finally, Katrina got in a few words. "If this call is just to make you feel better, I'm not sure why you bothered. If you want to make *me* feel better, you could at least have the decency to tell me to my face."

I nodded. That's exactly what we wanted: a face-to-face meeting between the two. I also mimed that she should put the call on speaker; she shook her head no, which only made me scowl.

"Look," she said, but was apparently cut off. After he spewed a few more syllables, she tried again. "Jared, you owe me a meeting." Pause. "Yes, I'll come alone. Swan left nearly an hour ago. In case you're at all concerned about how I'm doing, I'm not really in the mood to be around anyone."

I doubt he bought that. We could only hope.

"Fine," she said and hung up.

"Well?" I said.

She set the phone on the coffee table and covered her face with her hands, slowly shaking her head back and forth. I waited patiently for her to recover.

When she spoke, it started from behind her hands. "I hate him right now."

I wanted to console her, but I knew it would only come across as phony. After my failed pep talk, any lame attempt to show compassion would probably be thrown back in my face. So I just sat there, crossing one leg over a knee, tapping a finger on the back of the couch.

She lowered her hands and reached for her drink. After a large gulp, she looked at me. "I didn't put it on speaker because the very first thing he said was, '*If you put this on speaker, I'm hanging up.*'"

"All right. What was the gist of the call?"

"He said he wanted to explain and to let me know he was sorry for running out. Something about how scared he was and how I just don't know how deep this whole thing goes."

"Yes, I'm sure we're all broken up over how scared he is. That was the extent of his explanation?"

"He said he's not a bad person—he said that a couple of times, actually. That he's not a bad person, he's just seen the light." She took another sip. "Those were his words. Seen the light. Something about a lot of other people who were tired of the way things were. I don't know. He was rambling, like he was in a big hurry to get off the phone."

"He knew we'd trace the call. What about your offer to meet? Did he shoot that down?"

She let out a tortured breath. "Yes. Well, no. He said that would be highly unlikely, but he'd think about it and call me again if there was a chance to meet for just a few minutes." She paused. "I'm not expecting that."

My phone vibrated. It was Quanta.

"We saw the call to Katrina Yu," she said. "Techs were able to narrow it down to a tower in the Portsmouth area."

I pulled the phone away and addressed Katrina. "Does Portsmouth, New Hampshire, ring any bells? Anything Jared may have said at any time? Any trips he may have taken there?"

She seemed to think on it, then shook her head no. I went back to the call.

"Doesn't mean anything to her. We've been going over data here, but still a blank."

Quanta was silent for a moment, then said, "You seem to have changed your tune about Ms. Yu. A few hours ago you were convinced she was on Ceti's team, as I recall."

I looked at Katrina, who'd walked back over to either refresh her drink or switch to water. I lowered my voice. "I'm pretty sure we're okay there. Could be wrong, but I don't think so."

"All right." She didn't sound convinced.

"I need to crash pretty soon," I said. "I'll be back on it first thing tomorrow."

"Upload tonight," Quanta said.

My groan was supposed to stay inward, but enough seeped out for Quanta to add, "I mean it. Too much has happened."

"Roger that, boss." We ended the call.

The truth was, I was in that weird state where I was probably too exhausted to sleep. It would be tough getting my brain to calm down for a while, so uploading would be no problem.

I pushed myself off the couch and walked over to where Katrina stood. I was glad to see a glass of water in her hand.

"Go home and get some things," I said, as gently as I could. "You don't even have to worry about locking it up before you leave. I'm sure a handful of agents will be keeping an eye on it. I'll see you in the morning."

She turned to face me and I saw that a few more tears had leaked out. And then, without any warning, she set the glass down and wrapped her arms around me, burying her face into my shoulder.

Her sobs were the silent kind. The most heartbreaking kind.

I DECLINED Agent Gant's offer for a ride back to my hotel in favor of walking. It was midnight, and a warm breeze kept the night's chill at bay. I soaked in the sound of the city, the smells, the vibe. I'd always found Boston to be a fascinating intersection of tough, blue-collar workers and elite, snobby brainiacs. Southie wasn't all that far from Harvard and MIT—but then, Southie had been changing culturally for years. Boston's longtime residents had seen a lot of changes, and not just the happy dismissal of the Curse of the Bambino. Everything was morphing, to the delight of young professionals and to the dismay of old-timers. I was merely an observer.

Pulling out my phone, I took a chance and called Christina. She answered on the first ring.

"Late night for America's superspy," she said.

"Villains never sleep, so how can I?"

"True. Sorry I've missed some of your calls. I've either been swamped at the restaurant or napping. I've been doing that a lot lately."

"Is that normal? I have no idea."

"Not this late in the pregnancy. Most women say sleep gets

more difficult the further along they get. But I took a two-hour nap today. I haven't done that in years."

"You deserve it. So what looked good coming out of the kitchen tonight?"

She laughed. "Nothing. It was one of those nights where everything seemed to go south. Oh, except the risotto. That rocked."

I matched her laugh. For Christina, one of the premiere chefs on the East Coast, nothing *ever* went south. For her, a kitchen fail probably meant one bowl of soup had too much salt by an eighth of a teaspoon. We made idle chitchat for a few more minutes, before her tone turned serious.

"Honestly, you sound beat. I take it things are not going well?"

I turned a corner and walked around two people embroiled in a loud argument of some sort. Neither seemed to be listening to the other's rant. Both were well past the point of intoxication. I heard Christina chuckle.

"I'm doing better than those guys," I said. "But not by much. I'm pretty close to using the same language, at least."

"That bad, huh?"

I sighed. "Bad guys always leave clues. I mean, really, they're not that hard to track down. Criminals are usually tough guys, but not the smartest guys. It's the firepower you've got to worry about. But this time, the bad guy is a ghost. I can't get close enough to even draw a bullet from him because I don't know who he is."

"This is the hacker, right? Someone in the kitchen tonight said something about him giving away cryptocurrency. Is that the same guy?"

"Yeah. He fancies himself a modern-era Robin Hood. People might love him now, but they won't be that adoring when their phones and streaming devices stop working."

"Well," Christina said, "I just discovered a cool new show about the British monarchy, so don't let him shut down anything until I at least finish season one."

"I'll make a special request."

"Hey, did I ever tell you my college roommate was studying cybersecurity?"

"What? No. Who was this?"

"Her name was Tish and she used to talk for hours about the stuff. Normally a really fun roommate, but if you pulled her string about online security, she could lecture until you ran out of the room screaming. Super smart about it all, but that stuff was just too scary. Nobody wants to hear doom and gloom in their sophomore year."

"Of course not," I said. "But imagine how much scarier it is now, all these years later. Like, a *lot* of years."

"Hey Buster, careful with the age jokes. You're older than I am. I think. Or are you?" She laughed again. "That's funny; age doesn't even apply to you anymore. Except mentally, I guess. What would you say your emotional age is these days, Swan? Maybe around 12?"

"I need to stop calling you so late at night. Or maybe stop calling altogether."

"You miss me too much to stop."

I smiled, a fool strolling along a mostly deserted early morning street with a grin plastered on his face. In a quiet voice, I said, "I really do. More so tonight than ever."

She purred a sweet response and we let ourselves swim in the moment for a while before I steered us back to the conversation. "Tell me about this roomie again. Tish or Trish?"

"Tish. She wasn't always grim. I remember her getting a big kick out of the fact that one of the first uses of the old ARPANET—back when it was mostly just a playground for college faculty and students, along with defense department folks—anyway, she said one of the first times it was used for a transaction was when Stanford students used it to order marijuana. Tish always thought that was the funniest thing ever, the fact that the very first online order may have been a bag of weed."

"These days there's a lot more than pot being bought and sold," I said. "Now you have the Dark Web, and it's even scarier."

"No, Tish said the pot purchase *was* part of the Dark Web."

"No shit."

"Yeah. She told me about the Dark Web, how it went way back to the beginning of the early web and ARPANET. So it's not new. Neither is how people line up on one side or the other."

I frowned. "What do you mean? Lining up on the good side or the bad? Even back then?"

"Yeah. I guess that's where someone first came up with the idea of using former bad guys to help the good guys. I don't remember everything she talked about, but I do remember that. She talked about hackers being recruited. And it sounded like both sides seemed to have their own little societies. Almost like unions."

I walked in silence for a moment. Something was rattling around my brain. Somewhere nearby a car alarm went off briefly before being silenced, and from behind me I thought I could still make out the drunks fighting. But my mind was busy sifting through recent files, with something bubbling just beyond my reach. *Little societies, almost like unions.*

Yes. Little societies.

"Are you there?" Christina said.

"Yeah. You just triggered something and I'm trying to figure out what it—" I came to a stop with my mouth still open. "Oh."

"Figure something out?"

I started walking again, slower this time. "You know, babe, I think I did. Thanks to you."

"Well, don't explain it to me now. I'm too tired. You go catch some bad guys and tell me about it when you get home."

We ended the call and my pace picked up. I made a hard left turn at the next intersection and began working my way back toward the hotel. This new thought required that I upload immediately—which I'd promised Quanta anyway—and then I'd force myself to sleep. The idea seemed important; whether it actually helped us bag Ceti was TBD.

But at least now I had a notion of what club the asshole belonged to.

CHAPTER TWENTY-TWO

Nobody quite understands—or will probably *ever* understand—exactly how something goes viral. Until the 21st century, the word itself was associated almost entirely with bad things. Generations of people grew up hearing the word viral and immediately thought of the plague or the flu or some other deadly contagion. Sometimes the term was even spotlighted in specific diseases, like '*viral meningitis.*'

It wasn't until the world found itself connected by ears and eyeballs that the term shifted from being feared and shunned to being something desired. Make a video, pray it goes viral. Write a song and hope it goes viral. Choreograph a dance and go so far as to even strategize ways to blast it into becoming a viral sensation.

And yet nobody could actually tell you the secret sauce that made *this* video explode around the globe while *that* video languished in obscurity. It was some mystical cosmic alignment of factors stacked in such a way that tickled one app or network into pushing the content before more and more eyes. Some things, it seems, are simply "shareable," while others are not, and success today won't necessarily ensure success tomorrow. Fame is a fickle bastard.

When I awoke just before 7 a.m., I discovered that Ceti had tripped the magic algorithm and become the latest viral hit. While before there'd been some buzz around the Green Angel, his attack on the telecom folks had launched him into the stratosphere of worldwide celebrity. One news outlet estimated there were thousands of chat threads about Ceti; the outlet even made sure to pimp their own thread, inviting breathless readers to log on and *"Tell us what you think!"*

I mean, when Christina—who cares not one iota for pop culture—has heard of you, you're officially viral.

Scanning the major news sites, I took note of the divide between Ceti's fans and his critics. The usual, automatic fawning over anyone who pees in the face of the social or political status quo appeared curiously balanced against the automatic fear and loathing of anyone who dared rock the boat. In my mind, both sides made valid points, but both sides also had no bloody idea what was actually at stake.

In the meantime, it occurred to me that Katrina might very well have been right when she hypothesized that Ceti had quickly knocked out this job to remain relevant. As she'd told me, *"He's just making sure he's still on everyone's mind."*

Mission accomplished. Now I had to hope the attention became his downfall.

My phone buzzed with a text. It was Detective Alison Krup from Overland Park.

You were right. Blood test from Tanner Leachman's townhome shows elements of SAG and mannitol, along with some citrate and phosphate. Color me impressed.

MY SPIRITS LIFTED. Ceti wouldn't have bothered with such a complicated charade if Leachman was merely going to wind up with his throat slashed for real a day or two later. Leachman apparently was one helper who'd earned an all-access pass to the shit show being staged. I sent back a quick thank you to Krup.

The next message arrived from Poole. Things were obviously heating up and Quanta wanted a video conference with me, Parnell, Poole, and Sir William Johns. Yes, the Cuddly Knight was being looped in. The connection would begin in one hour. That gave me time to grab a shower, down a gallon of coffee, and scribble a few notes from my brainstorm the night before. The conference would be my first chance to talk through it and see if it had any legs at all.

The lead-up time also gave me a chance to check in with FBI agent Greenberg, who'd been tasked with overseeing the protection detail on Katrina Yu.

"I was just about to call you," Greenberg said, sounding flushed.

I grew tense, the normal reaction to impending bad news. "What's wrong? Is Katrina okay?"

"She's fine. I just talked with her. I mean, she's obviously depressed over the situation with—"

"Agent, what's the problem?"

"I just got a call that the guy who assaulted you in your hotel room has escaped."

I shot out of my chair. "*What?* When?"

"About an hour ago. They were transferring him from the hospital to jail and three men intercepted the van two blocks from the hospital. One driver, two gunmen. Nobody killed, but a police officer is being treated for a pretty ugly head wound. The two other cops say it happened so fast they barely had time to react at all."

"Shit," I muttered. "All right. Even though you've got her in a safe house, let's double up the security around Katrina Yu. If Arlo is back in circulation, she might be his next assignment."

After hanging up, I paced, letting the news sink in, thinking about the sheer audacity of Ceti ordering the ambush of an armed patrol. Up to this point, I'd convinced myself that he was dangerous with a keyboard, while the physical attacks from his hired help had been nothing but gutless murders of fellow techies. But if he was brazen enough to strike a team of police officers, it meant his hubris had grown in proportion to his ego. We were witnessing the evolution of a true monster.

The news regarding Arlo Benn was the first thing discussed when the video conference got underway. Quanta, at her home outside Washington, had a few more details that she shared, but the particulars didn't really matter as far as I was concerned. It was the scope that bothered me. Ceti's top assassin could now go back to what he did best, and that could only spell trouble for us down the line. In fact, if we ever managed to track down our cyber terrorist, I'd probably have to go through Arlo to get to him. Which meant my job would likely involve killing the killer. And while Arlo may have tried to off me, I kinda liked the guy. That should give you an idea of just how screwy things are in the world of hired killers.

Quanta handed things off to Sir William. He greeted us in his polished, proper, and utterly charismatic voice, relaxed tones like a hypnotist. Using a remarkable economy of words, he updated the investigation of the LeaCap Funds case. Surprisingly, they had more than I expected. Cybersecurity investigators with GCHQ found a link between Das and another woman, Serena Appleton, within the company. In Sir William's words, it "seemed to be more than professional." They brought Appleton in, and after an hour she broke down and told them she and Das had started as friends before acknowledging there was more to be explored. Romantically.

"Any indication she was involved in the breach?" Quanta asked.

"None," Sir William said. "She worked in the communications department, putting out press releases, that sort of thing. They kept their relationship quiet because it violated company policy. No fraternization among employees, you know—something I must say I find a bit *archaic*," he added, attaching a flourish to the last word to showcase his disgust.

I opened my mouth to make a snarky comment, then shut it just as quickly. I realized I might have to start thinking of the old guy as Sir Hugs-A-Lot, what with this new sensitive side on display. I caught the warning look from Parnell, who must've read my mind. I sat quietly and just listened.

"Ms. Appleton was naturally reluctant to share much with us, out of fear of getting sacked. When assured that we'd keep the matter in the strictest confidence, she broke down."

He paused, out of what struck me as some respectful sense of decorum. Then he said, "We were fairly certain early in our conversation with Ms. Appleton that she had no knowledge whatsoever of the incursion. But what we hoped to glean from her was perhaps something about Ms. Das's behavior that could shed some light on her partner in crime."

I sat forward, expecting the bombshell, until he said, "Unfortunately, there's been nothing, yet."

I leaned back again, trying to keep the disappointment off my face. Sir William, bless his heart, desperately wanted to help crack this case, either to impress Quanta or simply to uphold the British end. I couldn't fault him, though; our investigations hadn't turned up much more than his disclosure about the Das/Appleton affair. Nobody spoke for a few seconds.

"Parnell," Quanta said. "Anything new from Philadelphia?"

"Nothing beyond what I reported yesterday. The security team is almost 95 percent sure this was not an inside job. Just a case of shoddy defensive measures. There's an emergency meeting of their board this morning. I expect some turnover in the cybersecurity department. Not a happy place at the moment."

Quanta nodded. "Swan? I've briefed everyone on your exposure of Jared Hicks as a member of Ceti's team. Any other thoughts?"

I cleared my throat. "Actually, yes."

Here was my chance to present the idea that had occurred to me while walking the streets. Laying it out there for Quanta, Parnell, and Poole was no problem; in fact, I relished their observations and feedback. It was the new guy who made me somewhat nervous, which was dumb. I didn't work for the mellow mushroom, and it's not like he'd set the meeting on fire with his own revelations. But for some reason, I felt an enormous amount of pressure to shine. Perhaps it was more out of concern for Quanta than for me. My performance on this case would be a reflection on her and her ability to produce the world's best secret agents.

For a moment, I wondered if I should've waited to share my thoughts with her in private.

Then I mentally shook myself. Screw that; why should I be afraid to speak in front of the class just because the principal was sitting in? Besides, my confidence was high.

"With almost every case we work," I began, "we're looking for a motive. As we all know, sometimes it's nothing more than a petty grievance. But sometimes it's a *life-changing* grievance. And although there's not always a correlation between the depth of the perceived slight and the magnitude of the crime, we tend to find that really pissed off people put in the extra work to make their assault particularly heinous. Like what we're seeing with Ceti. The guy wants to shatter the world order."

"And he's eating up all the attention he's getting," Parnell said. "That could be behind a lot of this, too."

"Sure. But that's almost like some added fuel injection; it's not the driving force. Besides, when he started his escapades, nobody knew who he was and yet he still escalated his attacks."

"All right," Quanta said. "So far this isn't an Earth-shaking observation, Swan, but I'm sure you're getting to that."

I studied the four faces staring back at me and plunged on.

"Something has come up a few times that I don't believe is a coincidence. It started with the sister of Tanner Leachman, Kimberly O'Dell. She made it clear she's no great fan of her brother, but lucky for us she remembers just about everything he told her. In this case, she said Leachman, after getting axed by the start-up company, found some kindred spirits. A group of people she described as 'counterculture.' I believe she even used the word 'hippies,' which was cute. But these kindred spirits apparently had one thing in common: They felt wronged. They bonded as a sort of mutual victim society. This was interesting to hear, but it didn't really demand top billing in my brain.

"Then I had a chat with Leachman's boss at the start-up, Jaladi Shamar. He said that Leachman told one of his former co-workers that he'd started talking with people who had '*a new way of looking at things*.' Those were his words."

I saw the puzzled looks. "Yeah, it still didn't fully register with me, even though it was sticky enough to stay in my subconscious. Until late last night."

I didn't want to mention that I'd been talking with my wife; instead, I alluded to a vague earlier conversation. "Someone once explained to me that the Dark Web isn't a new invention; it's been around practically as long as the actual web itself. It's like no matter what our civilization creates, we need to have a light side and a dark side, a yin and a yang. Anyway, this person happened to mention that even in the early days of the web, people lined up on one side or the other, and they settled into—well, I guess you could call them silos. The term she used, though, was '*little societies*.'"

For the first time, I saw a glimmer of recognition in Quanta's face. She pursed her lips, a look she often reserved for times when she fell into an internal debate. Poole intently stared at the screen, as if trying to discern my meaning through digital precognition. Parnell and Sir William were clearly interested, but their blank faces told me they didn't understand the reference.

So I said it.

"I don't yet know how this impacts the case, but I'm pretty sure Tanner Leachman hooked up with the group known as the Arcetri."

CHAPTER TWENTY-THREE

Since our puny species first climbed down from the trees—or, more likely, got shoved off the branches—we've naturally congregated. Often it was for safety reasons; a large group huddled together was better prepared to ward off the roving bands of predators that quickly developed a taste for human flesh. Groups also provided an advantage when it came to hunting, especially when armed with primitive weapons. Plus, teaming up came in handy when it was time to trash political opponents.

But an advantage in numbers could also be thoroughly exploited by another particular group: the aggrieved. This deeply personal motivation, as it turns out, works extremely well as a bonding agent.

Round up an assortment of misfits and outcasts, especially those who'd been ostracized for proposing ideas and solutions that went against the popular grain, and they'll coalesce into a quiet but powerful force, thrumming with an energy that can be focused like a laser. Refine that group down even further, into a network of fiery scientific minds capable of actually building and firing that laser, and you had the group known as the Arcetri. Spelled without the '*h*,' but pronounced Ar-Chet-Tree.

When I'd first become aware of them, I'd been skeptical. The idea of a ragtag collection of pissed off scientists wasn't so much frightening as it was just plain funny. My snarky brain immediately envisioned a handful of guys in lab coats firing paper clips out of rubber bands or aggressively cracking all the microscope cover slips, then running out of the room, giggling.

It wasn't until I found myself chasing down an award-winning scientist to stop him from poisoning an entire city's water supply that I grasped the magnitude of the Arcetri. Or, more appropriately, grasped the magnitude of their animosity. When accountants get angry, they might sabotage your tax return. But get on the bad side of a Nobel-winning chemist and you might wind up with cyanide in your sweet tea.

It wasn't just their seething resentment at being ignored or mocked through the years; they were probably just sick and tired of all the damned nerd jokes. In other words, the bullies had picked on the wrong Poindexter.

Now, staring into the faces of my spy network compadres, I wanted to make clear the fact that computer scientists could just as easily get miffed and could just as easily produce a terror attack. Instead of poisoning the water or fouling the food supply —as I'd encountered in another recent case—Ceti used computer code. Different plan of attack, but just as ominous.

It was Quanta who spoke first. "This actually makes sense. And Ceti's MO does seem to parallel the behavior of some of the other Arcetri cases we've seen. His need for attention sounds like the actions of someone who not only wants to punish his detractors, but also show the world how wrong it was to misjudge them."

Sir William cleared his throat. "Well, yes, I suppose that's true. Not having had any firsthand dealings with the Arcetri myself, much of this is new to me. I've read briefings on the organization—if one can truly call it an organization. Do we know just how structured and organized they might be?"

"No," I said. "And I'm only *suggesting* that Leachman could be involved. However, if he's Ceti's right hand, it stands to reason this would be a point of overlap."

"If I understand correctly," Parnell said, "it's a very loosely organized group. It's not like they have conventions or monthly meetings. In fact, other than some people Swan has knocked off, we've haven't identified anyone else who belongs. And we've really only been able to interrogate *one* Arcetri member, isn't that right?"

I nodded. "Steffan Parks. He recently negotiated better prison conditions in exchange for information on the group."

"All right," Quanta said. "Now it's a question of whether this *suggestion*, as you put it, can help us find any of these suspects: Benn, Leachman, Hicks, and Ceti. We seem to have accumulated a roster of our villains. But I want them captured. Swan, Parnell, I want them tracked down before they can wreck the economy or kill anyone else."

I sighed. "I'm going to sit down with Katrina Yu again. All of these scraps might jar something loose."

Parnell said, "I've done about all I can here in Philadelphia. I can rendezvous with Swan in a day or two, unless we find another clue elsewhere."

Quanta agreed and we ended the video call. Sir Laffy Taffy hadn't offered much input, and Poole hadn't uttered a word. It struck me as a meeting for the sake of having a meeting, which only underscored the desperation.

When teams are losing a game, they always call time-out to talk.

. . .

THE FBI's safe house was in exactly the neighborhood I would've expected. Upper middle class, nondescript, a Toyota parked out front. The lawn could stand some work but wasn't in bad enough shape to require a nasty letter from the homeowners' association. Although, to be real, HOAs aren't above crucifying homeowners over one solitary weed.

Katrina Yu was in a foul mood, and who could blame her? Dumped by her boyfriend who'd turned out to be working for the other team, then forced into leaving her home and staying in what amounted to a sterile Airbnb guarded by a team of federal agents. It certainly was not the best week of her life. Even the half-gallon of ice cream I'd brought with me failed to generate a smile, and ice cream should make anyone happy.

"What do you want, Eric?" she asked, curled up in an over-sized chair in the living room, one foot twisted beneath her. The television was on but muted. I got the feeling it had been muted the whole time.

I popped the lid to the peanut butter/chocolate combo and held up a spoon to her. She shook her head.

"Well," I said, shrugging and digging into the sugary treat myself. "There's no sense in you just sitting here, being miserable, without us using the time to crack this case. I work better when I can distract myself with something like this." I held up a spoonful of ice cream. "And honestly, Katrina? I'm not leaving here tonight until we come up with something that will point us to Ceti. So settle in, my friend, and get ready for a deep dive."

She scoffed. "We've been over everything. This is pointless."

"No. Sitting around crying is pointless." When her face contorted into a sort of rage and she opened her mouth to curse me out, I held up the now-naked spoon. "Uh uh, hold on. Before you fight back, just sit there and listen. You'll have plenty of time to lob foul words my way when we're finished. For now, we're going to talk and then talk some more. We're going to find something that Jared said or did that will give us something."

With a disgusted sigh, she sat back and crossed her arms. "That sounds so productive. But it's shit. Jared never said anything that could possibly be a clue. Wishing it won't make it come true."

I dragged another scoop out of the container. "You'd have been stunned if I'd showed up in your office knowing everything about cybersecurity."

She narrowed her eyes. "What does that mean?"

"If I'd waltzed in off the street and started spouting off formulas and code and whatever else you guys operate with, you'd have probably gaped at me."

"Yeah. So?"

"So why in the world do you think you know the first thing about tracking down criminal assholes like your fiancé and his boss? That's my line of work, Katrina. I don't wish things; I make shit happen. And I do that by talking about stuff you would never think important. I take some tidbit that doesn't seem to fit and I use it to nail the bastards. I've done it a lot. I'm pretty good at it. Sure you don't want a scoop of this before I finish the whole thing?"

She waved an irritated hand and turned a vacant stare at the silent nonsense flashing across the TV screen. After a moment she said, "All right. How do you want to do this?"

We spent nearly an hour going over conversations, trips they'd been on together, fights they'd had. I felt strongly that their arguments could've been an opportunity for something to accidentally spill out; people, especially hotheads like Jared Hicks, tend to lose any sense of filter when they're angry and just spewing out words, trying to win. But no matter how much we deconstructed the sometimes volatile relationship between the two cybersecurity geniuses, nothing seemed to hint at Jared's shadow life. Either he was way better than I thought at cloaking his alter ego, or these particular fights just never pushed the right buttons.

We took a pee break and I checked to see if there'd been any word from Quanta, Poole, or Parnell. Poole had shared a file with each of us, a clip from a major social media influencer who laid out a case for the Green Angel to be anointed the '*Disrupter of The Year.*'

I didn't know that was even a thing. But somewhere, Ceti had to be grinning.

"Keep smiling, asshat," I muttered.

Five minutes later, Katrina and I moved to the kitchen and sat down at a small, round table. I was itching for a beer, but settled for the off-brand diet soda found in the fridge. I made a mental note to request the FBI stock a higher quality of beverages in their safe houses.

"All right," I said. "Let's try another angle. Instead of trying to think of things that were suspicious, how about anything that was just odd. Did Jared ever get mail or a package that seemed out of the ordinary? Did he ever take a strange call late at night and then say it was family or something? What about travel? Did he ever leave suddenly on a trip and not take you?"

"Well, yeah, we both went on small trips without each other. It's part of our job. Conventions. Seminars. That kind of stuff."

"Okay. Did anything ever strike you as odd? Anything, no matter how small and insignificant it may have seemed on the surface?"

"No. I'm telling you, he never—" She paused.

I moved my diet soda can to the side and leaned forward. "Say it. Don't try to rationalize it. Just say it."

She let out a long breath. "The only thing I can think of is a trip he took to see his father."

"Great. Tell me about the trip to see dad."

"About eight months ago. Maybe seven. Anyway, he left for a long weekend to spend time with his dad. His mom died when he was a teenager and he tries to see his dad a couple times a year. Anyway, he was gone for—what was it? Like a Wednesday through Sunday. When he got back, he was in one of his bad moods, and he said his father had been extremely difficult. I've met his dad, and I know he can be tough on Jared. So I just pampered him a bit more and he got over it.

"Then a couple days later, I was doing the laundry while he was working late. I was about to throw one of his hoodies in the wash when I decided to check the front pocket. He's always leaving napkins or Kleenex or something in there. This time it was a receipt from a gas station. I started to just throw it away, but then out of curiosity checked to see where he'd filled up. And it was a station in Barre. That's a town in Vermont."

"Okay. Is that important?"

"His dad lives in Bethlehem. In Pennsylvania. Barre is nowhere near the route to Bethlehem."

I felt a small charge build at the base of my spine. But I kept my voice even. "So you asked him about it?"

"Yeah. The next day, I just said, *'Hey, I found a receipt in your hoodie, but it was from Vermont. Did you drive up there instead of going to see your dad?'* At first he was surprised, and it seemed like he took a while to think of what to say. I just assumed he was pissed that I'd gone through his pockets. But it was innocent; I was just doing the laundry."

"Yeah, that's fine. So what did he say?"

"He said that he'd *told* me was going to Vermont. That his dad had been up there for a week or so, visiting an old friend, and wanted Jared to meet him. So he met him in Montpelier and they stayed there, with the friend. He kept saying, *'I told you that before I left. You didn't listen to me.'*" She paused and offered a feeble smile. "That was totally believable, because his dad did get around after retiring. And it's also true that sometimes I would tune out when he was droning on and on about his family. So I just let it go and it never came up again."

I sat still, staring down at the table, trying to access a memory. Vermont. Something about Vermont. That's a state that—no offense, Vermonters—doesn't pop up too often in casual conversation, and they pretty much prefer it that way. But I'd heard it recently.

Kimberly O'Dell. Tanner Leachman's sister. She'd mentioned that Leachman had spoken highly of Vermont, something about a family member. Could be a total coincidence; the guy had driven all over the place.

"Hold on a sec," I said to Katrina and walked out of the room. Outside, I nodded to one of the FBI agents who sat parked in a car across the street and pulled out my phone. This time, Kimberly O'Dell answered after two rings.

"Yeah, I remember you, Mr. Swan," she said after I'd reintroduced myself. "Did you find the sumbitch?"

"Working on it, Ms. O'Dell. Listen, you said something about Tanner driving through New England. Do you recall that?"

"Yeah. It was before we drifted completely apart. He'd check in once a week or so, I think just to have a human connection. He was a loner for the most part, so I'm sure he didn't make a lot of new friends on his little excursion. As aloof as he liked to think of himself, I think he got lonely."

"Right. Tell me about Vermont. You said something about a family member. An uncle?"

"Grandfather. Our dad's dad. Batshit crazy. Lived on a spread just outside—oh, what's the name of that town. The big one. Well, big for Vermont."

"Burlington?"

"Yeah, that's it. I was only there once, when we were kids. Place creeped me out. The house, not the town. I mean, I like trees, but there were too many of them around this house. It stayed in the shadows all the time, even in the middle of the day in the middle of summer. I hated it."

"Is your grandfather still alive?"

"No, he died years ago. I didn't go to the funeral. Didn't know the guy that well."

"What happened to the creepy house?" I asked. "Do you know?"

"Sold, I think. Nobody in our family could afford to fix it up. It was pretty run down. I think it got auctioned off."

"Okay, great. What was his name?"

"Grandpa."

I laughed. "No, seriously."

"Um, his first name was, uh, well, shit, hold on. What *was* his name?" She chuckled. "That's kinda pathetic, ain't it? I honestly don't remember. I can look it up."

"Don't worry about it. I can find out. He was a Leachman, though, right?"

"Yeah. So why are you asking about this? What does Vermont have to do with anything? Tanner was killed in Kansas City, wasn't he?"

"Probably nothing. Just running down everything we can think of."

I thanked her for her time and the information and hung up. My next call was to Quanta.

"What do you have?" she asked.

I spent two minutes recapping all of the tangled stories. Then I added, "And I'd like it on the record that I suspected Jared Hicks from the very first meeting and a certain somebody told me to go ahead and trust him. I won't name names, but her initials are Quanta."

"Yes," she said. "You're remarkably prescient. I'll put a gold star in your file."

"That's all I ever really need, you know? A good pat on the head." Then I added, "So I'm on my way to Burlington first thing in the morning."

"Seems like quite the long shot," Quanta said. "But I suppose it's a lead you should follow. Do you want Parnell to meet you there?"

"Probably not yet. Let's call this a scouting trip. But have her standing by."

Back inside, Katrina stood in the living room. "You're going to Vermont," she said. "I can tell."

"It's probably nothing. But it's a lead, no matter how flimsy. So you—"

"I'm going with you."

I chuckled. "Not a chance, Katrina."

She crossed her arms. "And that's exactly what you'll have trying to talk with Jared, *if* you find him. No chance. He won't tell you shit. In case you forgot, he doesn't really care for you, Eric."

"Yeah, but—"

"He'll talk to me," she said. We just stared at each other for a moment, then she added, "Even if the whole thing with me was a fake—the relationship, the engagement, everything—he still has feelings for me. I know he does. And if we find him, I'm the only chance you've got of him spilling anything."

I gave an exasperated sigh, mainly because she was right.

She uncrossed her arms and her tone softened. "He may do it just out of guilt."

Hands on my hips, I looked down at the wood floor, running everything through my mind. "All right," I said. "Grab a jacket and let's go."

CHAPTER TWENTY-FOUR

The perfect road trip is not something that happens accidentally, but it can't be meticulously planned, either. You should invest a minor amount of preparation, just enough to produce the elements necessary for a satisfactory experience; too *much* prep work, on the other hand, invariably leads to an atmosphere of artificial enthusiasm, raising the bar on expectations and injecting pressure into an environment that, by its very nature, should be the epitome of laid back and chill.

I'm a road trip expert, an appellation earned through a lifetime —in my case, multiple lifetimes—behind the wheel, not to mention thousands of miles logged in the back seat during family vacations growing up. I know the benefits and the responsibilities of the driver, as well as passenger etiquette and expectations. If you're not steering the ship, it's your job to help with navigation and to watch for potential food and/or pee stops, to keep an eye out for speed traps, and to dole out any and all snacks while the car is in motion.

And during a road trip, one rule is sacrosanct, above and beyond dispute: The driver chooses the tunes. Period. End of discussion. If you disagree, get out and hitch a ride with the next loser to come along who doesn't know the rule and will let you sit there in the passenger seat and subject innocent people to Florida Georgia Line. Not in my car, friend. If I'm driving, I command the playlist, too.

My relationship with Katrina was already strained, thanks to her association with one of the country's worst traitors of the last decade and to her detainment in a safe house drowning in taupe paint and Pier One accessories. I could understand her frustration over that last item.

But when she wrinkled her nose at my music and asked if she could "put on something else," I slowly turned and gave her my best *you-must-be-out-of-your-mind* look. I knew there was no saving her soul when she followed that up with "Do you at least have any Coldplay?"

"We've still got more than three hours to go," I said, turning down a song by Toy Matinee, but just a touch. "Let's try to make it as pleasant as possible. Why don't you forget about the music and tell me something about you that I don't know yet."

"Like what?"

"Like something from your childhood, or your secret side-hustle wish."

This produced a genuine laugh. "Side hustle. You mean like something on Pinterest or Etsy?"

"Sure. Everyone has a hobby or passion they think could sustain them if they walked away from their job."

She opened a bag of chips, offered it to me, then put two in her mouth. "I'll make you go first. What's a spy like you dream about doing when he hangs up his gun and witty repartee?"

I didn't answer for about two-tenths of a mile. "You wanna hear something sad? I don't really have any hobbies."

"Oh, please," she said. "Everyone has a hobby. What's the

deal? You're just too embarrassed? What is it, ballroom dancing or something?"

"Tried it once. No rhythm. But seriously, I don't have a hobby. I don't watch a lot of movies. I don't do anything crafty. I used to wonder if that's what made me a good candidate for what I do. I don't get distracted by much. Very focused."

"You say that like it's something to be proud of. You're right, it's kinda sad. Everyone needs a hobby."

"All right," I said. "Now that we've established that I'm a freak, what's yours?"

She crunched on two more chips. "I like escape rooms. I like reading really old, really stodgy classic literature. And I like baking. Not cooking; baking."

Without drawing attention to it, I noted that she was slipping back into her friendly persona. I got the feeling Katrina Yu's personality wouldn't allow her to stay down for long. Or maybe it was just the junk food spiking her blood sugar.

"Why does the literature have to be old?" I asked.

"I guess the same reason some people prefer old movies. For one, it just seems like a different world without having to be some fantasyland. I'm not into dragons or wizards or stuff like that."

"You long for a simpler time. Is that it?"

She shook her head. "No. I don't think anything about the early 20th century was simpler. It was hard. *People* were hard. They lived hard lives and worked twice as hard as we do. Anytime someone says it was a simpler time, I think it's a cop-out. In our culture today, life is pretty much as hard as we make it. People schedule themselves to death, they schedule their kids beyond belief, then cry about how hard everything is." She gave a grunt of laughter. "We're basically soft, so we label all our self-inflicted drama as so damned *hard*."

I smiled. "You sound pretty cynical about it all."

She turned to look at me, her face screwed up into disbelief. "You think that attitude is cynical? God, I think it's about the most realistic observation you could make. We have every creature comfort you can imagine, we have gadgets that do most of our thinking for us, and we think life is tough? That's just stupid."

A moment later she added, "And that's really at the heart of what I do for a living, if you think about it. People do everything they can to simplify their lives as much as possible—or at least they *think* it's simplifying them—and that usually means turning things over to devices and apps. They divulge all their damned personal data, and they end up not just using the apps, but relying on them. And that's what people like Ceti count on. The more we rely on the digital side of life, the more access he gets, and the more we almost—well, the more we almost expect to get hacked."

I nodded but just let her keep talking.

"Hell, Swan, remember what I told you about the next great war? It's really already here. We're engaged in a war with some of the most dangerous people on Earth right now, and no one really pays attention. It's a quiet war."

She studied the passing scenery for a minute, then turned back to me. "You know what makes it even harder? I'm fighting against the people I'm trying to protect as much as I'm fighting against Ceti."

"What do you mean?"

"Well, when people have to change a password again, who do they curse? It's not Ceti or other hackers; they curse the people trying to protect them. If they have to do two-factor authorization, they grumble. Then Ceti hacks into systems, steals millions of dollars, destroys files, and what happens? A bunch of idiots proclaim him the Green Angel and fawn over him. They don't even stop to think that it's just making things more challenging for us and for them to protect their data and their money."

"It's a thankless job, Katrina."

She looked out the passenger window. "I guess you know all about thankless jobs. I shouldn't whine." A moment later she turned back to me, smiling. "I thought we were talking about old books. I don't know how I got sidetracked into all that. Sorry."

It was my turn to shrug. "Hey, it's what this road trip is all about. Chasing down arrogant assholes is pretty much what I do on a weekly basis. I enjoy hearing your perspective on it. It's educational. No apology necessary."

The next half hour was spent in quiet introspection, with nice background music I loved and Katrina tolerated.

WE ROLLED into Burlington just before three o'clock. While cloudy conditions had continued to blanket Boston, the charming Vermont town sat bathed in sunshine that may not have warmed it much given the time of year but helped to buoy spirits. We grabbed a quick bite to eat before driving to the police station on North Avenue. Poole had paved the way and we were greeted by the Deputy Chief.

Wayne Garritson more than filled out his dark uniform, with bulging biceps and a chest that looked thick enough to never even require a protective vest. After quick introductions, he led us back to his office.

I started by showing him a photo on my tablet. "His name is Tanner Leachman. Does the name mean anything to you, or does he look familiar?"

Like any good cop, he took his time. "No on both counts," he finally said, pushing the tablet back. "What's his story?"

"He's a person of interest in a cybersecurity case that Ms. Yu is helping us with. We thought he might be in the area." I flipped to a new photo and turned the tablet back to face him. "This man is named Jared Hicks. Same questions."

This time he took a little longer. "Well, not to sound snotty, but we have a lot of men around here with this look. The beard, I mean. I'm trying to look through that to his face. But no, I don't think I've seen him. I take it he's a person of interest, too?"

"Correct. I'm going to send you both of these photos. I'd appreciate it if you could circulate them among your patrol force and have them contact you if they see either of them. Under no circumstances should your officers approach them or try to apprehend them; report only, and let me know right away."

I could see this request didn't go over well. It never does. Police officers aren't crazy about simply being spotters. They're trained to act. Garritson pursed his lips. "All right. Anything else?"

I shook my head. "Not at the moment. Honestly, Deputy Chief, this was a courtesy call. I like to make sure local law enforcement's aware when I'm poking around. I'm sure you don't care for surprises. But for now, if you could just quietly have your people keep an eye out for either of these men."

"All right," he said again. We shook hands and Katrina and I went back to the car.

"That wasn't at all what I expected," she said. "We weren't in there even five minutes."

"I meant what I told him. I just wanted them to be aware I'm working in the area. Professional courtesy. Besides, I didn't really expect him to be any help at the moment."

"So what now?"

The 'what now' was a visit to the local building inspector. Unlike Deputy Chief Garritson, Kyle Henshaw was rail thin and decidedly unfriendly. He made us wait nearly 15 minutes before allowing us into his office, then spent our entire meeting showing extreme displeasure at being bothered.

"Why do you want to know about construction permits?" he asked with a sniff.

I gave him a friendly smile. "Might help me catch a really bad guy, Mr. Henshaw."

"Catch a bad guy," he repeated with the same irritated tone. "Yeah, gonna catch yourself a bad guy. Crack down on someone who put in an extra bathroom without a permit."

My smiles were wasted, but I persevered. "Not exactly, although I'm all in favor of throwing the book at people who don't keep their toilets up to code. No, I was wondering if you just happened to recall anyone either building a substantial new estate or refurbishing a rather large piece of property, say within the last three or four years."

He rocked back in his chair. "Lots of 'em. Too many to name. A lot of money come into Burlington in the last few years."

"Bully for Burlington," I said. "The place I'm talking about would be a little different, though. Perhaps set up for a lot of high-tech equipment. I'd think the power requirements might be a little more substantial than normal."

This didn't register with the blunt Mr. Henshaw at all. He just ran his tongue around his teeth and shook his head. "Nope, doesn't sound familiar. I think everyone's putting in game rooms and such these days. Got a nice home theater myself. You don't think I'm a bad guy, do ya?"

I could feel more than see Katrina grinning next to me. She was enjoying the show. I stayed calm.

"Gosh, Mr. Henshaw, I hope you're not a bad guy. But I'm sure the good ol' boys at revenue service back in DC will let me know if they find anything. Routine, but in a full investigation like this we gotta cover everything. You understand, I'm sure."

This caused him to sit back up. "What's that? Revenue what?'

I ignored his question. "Listen, someone else from the feds might reach out to follow up. If you think of anything that might interest us, I'm sure you'll let us know, right?"

He stared at me, the IRS threat likely still bouncing around his head. I stood up and curtly thanked him for his time, then gave a polite nod and left. Katrina didn't say a word until we got outside, where she let out a laugh.

"You can be a real bully when you want to, can't you?"

I got behind the wheel and started the car. "Oh, that wasn't bullying. Sometimes you just gotta give the Kyle Henshaws of the world a nudge to play along. The threat of an audit is about the most effective stick I can wield. Works every time, too."

"I'm sure. Do you ever actually sic the IRS on anyone?"

"Nah. That'd be cruel."

I'd just put the car into gear when I noticed a woman walking from the building straight for us. I shifted back into park and rolled down my window as she approached my side of the car. She looked to be in her 50s, with short hair and no obvious jewelry. A faded tattoo peeked out from the top button of her shirt. It might've been a bee. Her manner gave every indication that she was nervous.

"Hi," I said.

She glanced back at the door she'd come through, then knelt down so her head was even with mine. It also put her out of sight of anyone inside the building.

"I work outside Kyle's office, and I couldn't help but overhear your conversation with him."

I felt a small jolt of adrenaline, as if something important was coming. "What's your name?"

After another glance through my car's windshield toward her office, she looked back at me. "I'd rather not tell you my name. Is that okay? I just work here."

"Sure, that's fine. But you have something that might help me?"

"Maybe. I heard what you said about power requirements for a remodel."

"Yeah."

"Well, my brother does freelance electrical work. Sort of like a handyman, but he specializes in electrical."

I flashed a pleasant smile. "Well, isn't it convenient that you work for the town's building inspector. You must be able to steer some work his way."

"Oh, no. I don't—I mean, sometimes I hear about jobs, but I don't—"

"It's okay, I was kidding," I said, the hundred-watt smile still on my face. "But you know something?"

She bit her lip, looked past me at Katrina, then back at me. "Rob—that's my brother—said he did some work about 15 or 20 miles out of town. Said it was a really freaky place. Like a museum or something. He put in a couple of extra utility boxes and things like that. He said it was like something being built for NASA."

I nodded my approval at the information. "That's excellent. You said about 20 miles out of town? Do you know where?"

She shook her head. "No. I think he said it was around Arrow-head Mountain Lake, but I could check."

"That would be great. Let me give you a number to reach me, okay?" I tore off a piece of the bag that held Katrina's snacks and scribbled my cell number on it. Classy, I know, but also less likely than a professional business card to intimidate someone. Handing it to her, I made solid eye contact. "Would you at least share your first name with me? I promise, I won't tell anyone we've spoken."

After another furtive glance through my windshield, she said in a low voice, "Annette."

"Well, Annette, I really appreciate this. Please let Rob know I'd like to chat with him. Again, it'll stay private, but I can tell you that finding this house is vital. Okay? Clear it with him first, but let him know I'd like to give him a call or stop by and see him."

This seemed to really frighten Annette, but she nodded and

stood up. Without another word, she walked around the car and wound her way back toward the building.

I turned to look at Katrina, who said, "*A freaky place*. Sounds promising."

CHAPTER TWENTY-FIVE

Rather than sit and wait for the call from Annette, I located Arrowhead Mountain Lake on my phone and got us moving that direction. On the outskirts of Burlington, I pulled over at a convenience store. Katrina went inside to grab some waters for us while I strolled to the edge of the parking lot to call Poole with an update.

"See if you can find anything on your end about a home renovation near the lake. The sale of the property will be in the public record, too."

"I'll go back over the last ten years," she said. "I can dig through the permit records, too, for everything around that area."

"Good. Screw Kyle."

"I'm sorry?"

"Nothing. Anything for me?"

"Yes. Another blast of coins from Ceti, another million dollars. And each came with another message attached."

"Oh, wonderful," I said. "Let me guess: *The end is near.*"

"Close. They said, *Spend it now before the world transitions.*"

"Transitions. He's a cryptic bastard, isn't he?" I turned to see Katrina walking back to the car. "I'll let you know when I get an address, unless you beat me to it. Tell Quanta I feel good about this."

We'd just pulled back onto the road when I got a call from an unknown number. It was Annette, coming through like a champ.

"You did not get this information from me," she said, her voice subdued. Probably at her desk.

"It's our secret," I said. "What've you got?"

She gave me an address, which I repeated aloud. Katrina plugged it into her phone.

"Any chance I could talk with Rob?" I asked.

"He said no way. He still has to work around here, and it's technically confidential information. I've got to go."

"Okay. Listen, Annette, thank you for your help. You've done a really good thing. I mean that."

She disconnected without saying anything else. I turned to Katrina. "Got it?"

"Yeah. It's 19 miles. Says 29 minutes."

I subconsciously patted the Glock tucked beneath my jacket, slipped my sunglasses on, and shifted into game mode.

WE ACTUALLY DROVE past the rutted dirt trail without realizing it. It was barely visible from the main road, which wasn't that *main* to begin with. Whipping around, I approached the turnoff slowly, glancing through the trees, but no structure was visible. I nosed us off the asphalt and onto parallel tire trails with weeds thrusting up between. The path snaked away into a dense patch of trees, quickly growing dim beneath the canopy.

It was the perfect place to hunker down. Well off the beaten path, miles from civilization. And Vermont, to begin with, wasn't exactly a place one normally associated with a master criminal hideout. And yet it was within a few hours of Boston and a mere

80 miles to Montreal. If this was indeed Ceti's playhouse, he'd planned it well.

There were enough ruts and the occasional large rock on the trail that I barely crept along, keeping an eye out for a house, a car, any sign of life. Katrina and I didn't say a word as we jostled along. I could feel her anxiety, and wondered if this had been a horrible idea to bring her. I honestly hadn't expected to get a good tip so quickly. But if she indeed could help if Jared was on site, then it would be worth it.

After we'd worked our way a quarter of a mile, the trail turned abruptly to the right and went over a small rise. On the other side sat a cabin. I stopped at the peak of the rise and examined the area. There was no vehicle in sight. With my window down, I listened but heard nothing.

In a voice barely above a whisper, Katrina said, "Could this really be it? It's . . . not much."

It wasn't. In fact, it was much less than not much. I found it hard to believe this was the freaky place Rob had described. It looked deserted.

Then again, if Ceti really wanted to stay hidden, what better way than to make the exterior as decrepit as possible? Maybe his lair was underground or beyond the ramshackle cabin in another building.

I grabbed my small backpack from the rear floorboard and climbed out, then leaned my head back inside. "Wait here. I'm gonna do a quick search."

Katrina nodded, her eyes wide and her fists balled in her lap. In the same soft voice, she said, "I just checked. I don't have cell service here."

I patted the backpack. "No worries. The phone I'm carrying works everywhere." I didn't mention the other toys tucked inside, the ones I used to upload my consciousness to Q2.

Softly pushing the car door closed, I walked down the hill. A startled critter scurried through the brush nearby, and a crow screamed irritation at my intrusion. A soft breeze blew woodsy smells into my face, mixed with either the scent of garbage or a dead animal. It was a combination of the delightful and the disgusting.

At the bottom of the rise, I turned and looked back up at the car. Katrina gave a child's wave. I nodded back to her and offered a smile I didn't believe in.

The cabin's door was open about a foot. One peek inside told me the place hadn't been inhabited for many years. Either Rob was completely full of shit, or Ceti had things well hidden behind this front. I pulled out the Glock and used it to nudge the door open a bit more. All was crypt quiet. Taking one step in, then another, I let my eyes adjust to the gloom. The dead smell intensified; whatever had croaked had done so in one of the rooms.

The place had to be investigated, just in case there was a lower level. I doubted it, though. This struck me as nothing more than how it appeared: a dead end. Literally, based on the stink. A minute later I discovered its origin. A large raccoon was mostly disemboweled, covered in flies and a variety of other grazers. My stomach, which had proven itself to be the biggest punk I'd ever dealt with, twisted a bit.

I hated this body and couldn't wait to trade.

After finishing a tour of the layout, I knew there was no cellar, no hidden rooms, no secret passage to Ceti Land. This was bullshit. And the first tremor of an alarm began to trill in my mind.

Plus, I'd left Katrina alone in the car.

Before leaving, I rubbed grime off one of the windows and looked out the back of the cabin. It was pure woods, and no indication of another building, not even a trail. The property began and ended with this shitty cabin. I'd been intentionally diverted here.

Hurrying outside, I double-timed it up the hill to the car.

Which was empty.

I spun around, a full 360. There was nothing.

"Katrina," I called out. "Katrina!"

Then, I heard her. "O-over here."

I peered through the trees. A moment later she stumbled out. With a large man behind her. A large man with a large gun pressed against her head.

"Shit," I muttered.

"Oh, it's worse than that," I heard someone say behind me. Slowly turning around and lowering my gun to my side, I looked into a familiar face.

Arlo Benn, grinning from ear to ear, and pointing his own gun straight at my face.

THE RIDE back to Burlington was uncomfortable, both physically and mentally.

I was in the back seat of an SUV, my hands zip-tied behind me, and the business end of a Sig Sauer jammed into my ribs by the guy who'd escorted Katrina from the woods. She was in the vehicle trailing us, probably equally uncomfortable and terrified beyond belief.

My mind was racing. I'd succeeded and failed at the same time, and that pissed me off. Ceti had been damned hard to find for the longest time, and then, when it looked like I'd finally located him, he'd actually lured me into his little web and easily clamped down on me. It was a totally amateur move on my part. I'd believed the song and dance put on by Annette, who no doubt was employed by the cyber criminal. I'd galloped right to the coordinates she suggested, and I'd done it without any backup. Making matters worse, I'd relayed the cabin's address with Poole, so now any search would be centered there, miles from where we were now being taken. Both my cell phone and

Katrina's had been left in our car, so there was no way to track us.

I had been brilliantly played. Ceti was probably laughing his ass off, emboldened by how easy it had been to capture the big, bad government agent chasing him. The only thing I could be grateful for was the fact Arlo hadn't put two rounds into my head and left me rotting next to the raccoon.

I would've loved to have chatted up Arlo, but he rode in the vehicle with Katrina. I had the tough guy next to me and two clowns up front, and nobody seemed open to chitchat. We traveled in grim silence.

Back in Burlington, the SUV made random turns before cruising down a street that shifted from business to residential. Eventually we ended up in an area where the houses were spaced farther apart and had increased in both size and opulence. Well, Burlington opulence wasn't exactly Hyannis Port, but still.

After one more turn, we rolled up to a large home set off the road. I made a quick mental note of the address and repeated it a few times in my head. The fact that they hadn't bothered to throw a hood over my head meant only one thing: I'd be leaving in the trunk of a car, probably rolled up in a sheet or body bag. It didn't concern them one bit if I memorized the address.

There was no gate, nothing to give the house the feeling of a compound. That made sense. Ceti was all about blending in, sailing under the radar, and a fortified lot would've had everyone curious. This way he was just another quiet fat cat, keeping to himself in the Vermont way.

The driver took us up a curved driveway until we were beside the impressive house, where trees shielded us from the road. Tough Guy pressed the gun harder into my ribs, indicating I should climb out. But instead of walking into the house, I was shoved toward a smaller structure behind the main residence. Apparently I didn't rate an invitation inside.

But this was no cheap guest house. It was well lit, well designed, and sported the kind of touches one associates with the *nouveau riche*. Not quite ostentatious, just this side of tacky. Ceti had the money but hadn't yet learned how to properly wield it.

Passing through a kitchen, I was hustled down a staircase into the basement. Arlo walked ahead and unlocked a door, then opened it and stood back, gesturing for me to enter. Katrina, who'd been brought in right behind us, followed me in. Her face was tear-streaked and two shades too pale. I wanted to console her and let her know everything was going to be okay, but in my heart I knew it would be nothing of the sort.

Tough Guy snipped off the zip ties and I massaged my wrists, watching Arlo as he rummaged through my backpack. He grunted a smile as he removed a small folding knife, but left my toiletries and a light hoodie. After patting the backpack on all sides, he tossed it onto the floor, waved his gun at me in a mock salute, and walked out, slamming the door shut. I heard a deadbolt turn. Katrina stumbled ahead and collapsed into a large chair, clearly petrified. I knelt down before her and took one of her hands.

"Hey. Listen to me." All I got in return was a nearly vacant stare. I squeezed her hand. "Katrina."

Her eyes finally focused on me. "I'm scared," was all she could say.

For some reason, this struck me harder than almost anything else she could've said. Two simple words that pretty much sized up how any normal person would feel in this situation. Again, I'd become numb to the whole secret agent game, the constant danger and death. But for Katrina Yu, a normal, suburban-raised, college-educated, hard-working citizen who expected to move through life without worrying about goons abducting her—and probably killing her—it could only produce a crippling fear.

"I'm gonna get us out of here," I said, injecting as much confidence as I could into my voice. I wasn't sure she even heard me. "Or maybe *you'll* get us out of here," I said. "You're the one who's good at escape rooms. Help a brother out."

No response.

I left her, glazed eyes and all, sitting there while I quickly scouted our prison. The room was about 10 by 15, no windows, two small vents in the ceiling, and sparsely furnished with only a couch and the oversized chair that held my traumatized companion. The door to the outside world was solid as hell, but even if it had been flimsy, I was sure at least one or two armed thugs waited on the other side. I walked to the only other door and found it housed a small bathroom, toilet and sink only. A thin, mostly decorative window near the ceiling was far too small for even Katrina to wiggle through. There was nothing I could see that might come in handy as a weapon, which was no surprise.

I began to wonder why they hadn't killed us already.

Until we got a chance to talk with someone, there was no sense pacing the room like a caged lion. I moved over to the couch and stretched out, draping an arm across my eyes. I never fully drifted off to sleep, but after a while I sank into a deep resting state, my own personal version of meditation. My heart rate slowed and I cleared my mind.

An hour or so later, the lock turned and the door flew open. I pulled my arm away from my face and propped myself up. Arlo walked in, followed by the same shithead who'd pressed his gun into my ribs during the ride. This one stood near the door, his gun held casually at his side. I pulled myself up into a sitting position on the couch and stole a glance at Katrina. She was alert, staring at the two new arrivals in the room.

"Eric," Benn said, barely moving his injured jaw.

"Hey, Arlo," I answered. "How's your face? Still no hard feelings?"

He smiled. "Getting better. And no, no hard feelings. I know it brings you a lot of joy to rub it in, but you won't get a chance to do any more damage. And anyway, I'm sure I'll have the last laugh."

"I'm sure, too. In the meantime, what's with keeping us here in the green room?"

"Someone wants to talk with you. But he had work to do first."

"Work. Like hacking into some other companies and stealing more money? That kinda work?"

Arlo shrugged. "Oh, hell, Eric. I really don't care what he does to pay the bills as long as he's paying mine."

He. Arlo had said it twice. So Ceti was indeed a man.

"When do I get to meet your lord and master?" I asked.

A voice from the open doorway said, "How about now?"

I turned to see another familiar face. He'd breezed quietly into the room and stood, arms crossed, beside the other goon. I immediately recognized him from the police file I'd stared at for days.

Tanner Leachman. Not only alive and well, but alive and quite smug.

Nobody said a word for a moment. Arlo Benn kept a shit-eating grin on his face. Tanner Leachman awkwardly relished his power over the situation, while I sat there, trying to comprehend this new bombshell.

Leachman didn't work for Ceti; Leachman *was* Ceti.

Finally, I let out a soft chuckle. "Well, don't I feel like a big idiot."

His grin was somewhat crooked, one side of his mouth higher than the other in a most unattractive way. "You're all idiots, Mr. Swan."

"And by *all* you mean . . .?"

He spread his hands. "You. Your fellow government stooges. The idiots who oversee all of the companies I've had my way with. The public. Everyone. All idiots."

I nodded. "Well, this might normally be where the good guy

stands up and objects. But the fact that you haven't been captured or even identified, the fact that you've gotten away with every incursion, combined with the fact that I'm sitting here at gunpoint —yeah, I'd say you're right. We've all been complete idiots. Congratulations. You've won."

With a small, theatrical bow, he said, "I do appreciate a gracious loser. How are you able to stay so upbeat at a time like this?"

I flashed a grin. "I've found that no matter how badly I get my ass kicked—and believe me, I've had my ass *royally* kicked over the years—I always come back and win the rematch."

His smile shifted into a confused frown. "I don't even understand what that means. You think you'll get a *rematch*? Really?"

"Sure. It's the ace I keep up my sleeve. But enough about me; unless you're planning on destroying the world economy tonight, how about satisfying my curiosity with a lengthy talk?"

The smile returned. "Lengthy? Probably not. But I'm about to have a quick dinner. You've been working so hard, Mr. Swan— even flying back and forth to the UK—that I feel a sort of pity for you. You and the lovely Katrina Yu are cordially invited to dine with me." He turned his attention to her. "Is that acceptable with you?"

She answered him with a glare, which I didn't understand until I looked past Leachman, out to the hallway. Standing there, peering in at the conversation, was Jared Hicks.

"You're not inviting Wolfman Jack, are you?" I asked, nodding toward Hicks.

Leachman looked over his shoulder, then gave a laugh. "You're funny, Mr. Swan. Your company will be really appreciated. You have no idea how boring it is to eat dinner with the help, night after night."

He communicated his wishes to Arlo with a look, then spun around and left the room.

Arlo nodded once at his gunman partner, then looked at Katrina. Tough Guy walked over and roughly pulled her up out of the chair, propelling her out of the room.

I stood up and faced Arlo. "Is it necessary to treat the woman so poorly? You're better than that, aren't you?"

He walked over, his significant bulk looming over me. He pointed his gun squarely at my heart.

"Better? Not really, no. Oh, and before you go to dinner, there's something I need to give you."

I wasn't prepared at all when the gun came crashing across the side of my face. Dazed, I fell to one knee, putting a hand up where he'd cut me open, feeling the blood seep out. It felt like at least one tooth had been rattled loose. For a moment, I knelt in agony, a small, animal-like groan escaping my lips. It hurt like bloody hell.

"Okay, there," Arlo said. "We're not even, but that at least helps." He pointed the gun at my face this time. "All right, Mr. Spy. Let's take you to dinner."

I staggered to my feet and began an awkward march toward the door.

He added, "Gee, I hope for your sake they're serving soup."

CHAPTER TWENTY-SIX

All of us who were raised on classic spy movies were suckers. We fell for the glamorous image portrayed by the actors who starred as James Bond and we totally bought into the dazzling world inhabited by the world's most brilliant master criminals. When Bond was treated to dinner by the nefarious Dr. No, they sat at a table which wouldn't have been out of place in a luxurious restaurant. The finest china, perfect linens, a multi-course meal served by an impeccably dressed staff, and food that rivaled any restaurant with three Michelin stars. I watched that scene as a kid and imagined being a spy eating dinner with the bad guy must be the coolest experience in the world.

Now, I sat in a chair that had one leg a little shorter than the others, in a kitchen nook area of the guest house, with an excruciating gash on the left side of my face. An older woman, her hair in a severe bun and a neutral, practically robotic look on her face, finished laying out plates of what looked like fish and rice atop a round, Oak Express dining room table.

I needed a director to yell *'Cut!'* and reset the scene.

Katrina sat to my right, with Leachman across from me, looking at something on his phone, ignoring me and his cook/server for the moment. Tough Guy stood just behind and to the side of Leachman, one hand grasping the other wrist in front of him, his eyes never leaving his boss. Another goon stood to the other side of the hacker, his frigid gaze locked on me.

I used the time to run my tongue around the loose tooth and study the nemesis I'd chased back and forth across the Atlantic. Thin, almost emaciated, with short, curly dark hair and a habit of subtly moving his lips while he read. It wasn't the first time I marveled at how the nefarious assholes who caused the most chaos so often resembled anything but an intimidating monster. Tanner Leachman reminded me of the classic 98-pound weakling, getting sand kicked in his face.

This weakling's revenge would be to crush the world's economic machine.

He set down his phone and gave a quick glance to the woman who'd served us. "Thank you, Jan." After she nodded and left the room, Leachman picked up a fork. "You like haddock? I have this at least twice a week."

"One of my faves," I said. "You'll forgive me if I don't dig in right away. My mouth hurts."

Leachman flashed his lopsided grin. "Mr. Benn told me that he owed you for putting him in the hospital." He took a bite then added, "You gentlemen live such violent lives. Even though you seem to actually like each other, you inflict such damage. It's a macho thing with you, isn't it?"

I shrugged. "It's a violent world. Some people use their fists, some use guns. Some use keyboards."

He gave a thoughtful nod. "This is true. I much prefer my way."

After throwing a glance at Katrina, who also refrained from eating, I said, "Before we talk about anything else, satisfy some of my curiosity. You've got a lot of people in your pocket; I'm guessing that includes the local building inspector, Kyle Henshaw."

Leachman took another bite. "Kyle is a turd at heart and has about as much charisma as this fork. But what he *does* have is enough influence with all the local government departments to keep everything off the books for me. This property is listed under a rather bland LLC, and none of the improvements I've made will show up on any licensing or code documents."

"Improvements? Do I get to see the main house, or am I confined to the servants' quarters?"

"Oh, no need for you to see anything, Eric—do you mind if I call you Eric, by the way?"

"That's fine."

He gave a sort of giggle. "Oh, this is really quite fun. I almost feel like I know you, after having watched you so closely."

"Yeah, that's terrific. Tell me about your setup here. What kind of improvements did you make? Other than the tech upgrades, which I'm sure are marvelous. Did you put in a jungle room? Maybe an indoor water slide?"

He smiled. "Let's just say I got to fulfill some of my childhood fantasies about what a really fun house would have. More than anything, it's completely self-sufficient. Power, water, and food for at least 18 months. It's taken almost two years to get all of it quietly finished. But enough about that. I'm sure you've got way more important concerns than my decorating touches."

I pushed the plate of fish forward and rested my arms on the table. "Talk to me about the Arcetri."

The effect was dramatic. Another helping of fish froze halfway to his mouth and he locked eyes with me, clearly startled. Then, setting the fork back on his plate, he dabbed at his mouth with a napkin and chuckled. "Oh, my. Of all the things you could've said, Eric, that is the last one I expected. I will admit to being very impressed. Why don't you tell *me* what you know about the Arcetri."

"A bunch of whiny-ass science types who instead of getting mad, get even. That pretty much sums it up, wouldn't you say?"

He pursed his lips. "Well, I wouldn't agree with the '*whiny-ass*' characterization, but otherwise, yes, that's pretty succinct. We do have our axes to grind."

I shrugged again. "If you say so. Most people use a setback as motivation to strive harder. You shitheads take setbacks personally, to the point where you end up destroying society and killing people. All for a slight. That's pretty whiny-ass in my book."

Again, the crooked smile. "I can tell you're really trying to push my buttons. I suppose it's all you've got left. But those buttons have been disconnected, my friend. There's nothing you can say that will raise my blood pressure."

"Oh, I'm sure you've got more than a few buttons disconnected."

"See? You're trying so hard to be incorrigible. It's cute. But I'd love for you to explain how you know about the Arcetri."

There was nothing to lose by sharing this information with him. It wasn't like I was betraying state secrets. "I was part of the effort to bring down Steffan Parks."

This must've impressed him. He gave a slow nod. "I see. Yes, I heard Steffan got careless down in—where was it, New Mexico?"

"New Mexico and Arizona. Honestly, Tanner, I'm just disgusted that it took me so long to realize that scrawny computer scientists could be a part of that murderous little club. I mean, it makes sense; I just didn't connect it. Who else in this scheme of yours belongs? What about the bearded wonder, Jared? Does he know the Arcetri secret handshake?"

At the mention of her ex-fiancé's name, Katrina stirred. She wouldn't know about the Arcetri, but she looked at Leachman for an answer, nonetheless. Her head must've been swimming.

Leachman grunted. "Jared doesn't need to bother with all that. Like the majority of my helpers, he's been useful in his own way."

"But unlike the others, he's still alive. Why is that?"

"Oh, they're not *all* dead. Only the ones who crossed over from helpful to harmful."

I raised an eyebrow. "In other words, once you'd squeezed everything out of them you could get, and before they could say something to the authorities. Jared's not at that point, I guess. Not yet, anyway."

He smiled and reached for his fork. "Mr. Hicks might stick around longer than most."

That apparently was too much for Katrina. Breaking out of her stupor, she lunged from the chair, hands outstretched, going for Leachman's throat. Tough Guy stepped between them and caught her forearms in his hands. I shoved my chair back, but before I could get to my feet, the other hired muscle had his gun pointed straight at my nose. Katrina, whimpering in pain from the steel grip around her wrists, was guided back down into her chair and I slowly sank back into mine.

Leachman never stopped the motion of taking a bite. "Well, that was exciting," he said. Then, reaching over to pat Katrina on the shoulder, he added, "I'm sorry. I should've known there would be some residual feelings still tucked inside. You can't get over him in a day, right?"

She shrugged away his hand and refused to look at him.

"Actually," Leachman said, turning back to me, "I thought my little network was pretty ingenious."

The secondary goon had returned to his original position, so I sat back. "Ingenious how?"

He took another bite. "Are you sure you're not hungry?"

When I shook my head, he went on. "Well, I got busted as a kid doing some hacking."

"So I heard."

He scrunched up his face. "I thought that was off my record when I turned 18."

"It is. Your sister told me."

Another smile spread across his face. "Ah, sweet Kimberly. Does she miss me?"

"She said you were a complete dick. But what does your teenage hacking have to do with this?"

"I got busted, did some community service, the usual chores they pawn off on naughty adolescents. Stuff they're sure will humiliate us into going straight." He leaned forward and gave me a conspiratorial look, lowering his voice. "Truthfully, all it does is teach you to not get caught the next time." He sat back. "Then the local sheriff's office asked if I would take what I'd learned about hacking and help them set up systems to keep the bad people like me out. They gave me the whole *'use-your-powers-for-good'* speech."

"Yeah," I said. "Happens all the time. The FBI hires hackers, too. So what?"

"So I just took that approach and flipped it around. I found people working on the protection side and hired them to work for me, helping me figure out the newest cybersecurity tactics and then reverse engineering them to find ways to crack 'em. Works both ways. My way pays better."

"Until you kill them."

He flashed a wry version of his crooked smile, because he was right and knew it; the tactic was pretty damned ingenious. But I wasn't going to give the little shit the satisfaction.

"And you recruited these people how? I'm guessing the Dark Web. Like ZigbyNet, perhaps?"

He speared another bite. "Mostly. That's where I found Ursula and Samantha, for sure. They had an interesting presence on that site. Who else did I find there? Oh, right—Jared. He was rather outspoken, so I tracked him down."

"Besides him, Shawn Cook, Ursula Fournier, and Samantha Das, how many others have you lured to the dark side and then offed?"

He took a last bite, then wiped his mouth and pushed his plate aside. "I don't think I'll answer that question. Let's just say they're not the only ones. And it really was the only way I could maintain the secrecy and privacy I need."

"To stay in the shadows, you have to kill anyone who could shine a light."

His face lit up. "Yes, exactly! Oh, Eric, what a wonderful way to phrase it. You're practically a poet." Then he leaned toward me. "Don't get the wrong idea. It's not like I've killed dozens of people or anything like that. It's a modest number. But if you think about it, they were all criminals, too. I mean, I'm not a sociopath."

"No, you're a goddamned psychopath. There's a difference, you know. But neither one has any empathy for others."

"Remember, Eric, you can't push my buttons."

"See what I mean? A true psychopath."

He actually laughed out loud.

"So let's talk about your ultimate plan," I said. "You do have an ultimate plan, don't you? Please don't tell me you're just randomly taking down companies and pension plans without some grand design all laid out in your mind. I'll be so disappointed in you."

With this, the smile faded and his eyes narrowed. "The plan? The *plan*? You think there's some grandiose plan, laid out in steps and strategies, complete with a Gantt chart? You think I'm working toward some glorious utopia? Are you *insane*?"

As far as I was concerned, only one person at the table was

certifiable and it wasn't me or Katrina. But our host was on a roll, so I kept quiet and simply maintained eye contact.

"Let me tell you something, Mr. Big Shot Government Agent. I've been on the side that people call the good guys, and I've been on the other side, too. So take it from someone who's walked in both worlds and is intimate with the inner workings of both— there's very little difference."

When I allowed myself a painful smile, it seemed to inflame him even more.

"Oh, that's funny? You think that's a stretch? You don't know shit about what goes on in the banking world, the oil and gas industry, the great insurance scam, and a lot of others. There are people in those fancy corner offices who are a lot slimier than I am, my friend. At least I don't hide behind some phony business front."

"No," I said. "You hide behind a phony name. Ceti. Even your death was a fake. So let's not pretend that the *Green Angel* is really some sort of avenging angel. Like everyone else I've met inside the Arcetri, you claim to be fighting the insidious evil within 'the system.' But you're really just a sad, pathetic weasel who got picked on one too many times, so you're using your superior intellect to stick it to everyone. Not just the handful of assholes who peed in your Wheaties. *Everyone.*"

He leaned toward me, his voice rising. "It's all bullshit, Eric. There's not a company I targeted that hasn't screwed over hundreds—if not thousands—of people. Yes, even the pension funds. Go look at the big shots managing those funds and tell me they're not living large off of Grandma's decades of hard work. And please, don't insult my intelligence by insinuating they've never killed to get what they're after. They may not kill directly, but the result is the same. You're either naive or simply a fool if you think their hands are clean."

He paused, then turned a palm up. "And I tried doing what

you might call *the right thing*. I invested time and a lot of brain power, and what did I get in return? Blamed for someone else's mistake, then left to shoulder all the responsibility when the coward killed himself. Cast aside. Blackballed. Belittled. So don't lecture me, Eric. Yes, I hide behind an alias. If you were smart, you would, too. Anyone who ties all their money, all their assets —hell, their entire personal life—to some legal identity the government stamps with its own registration number? You're nothing but a commodity. Bought and sold. Traded. Like I told you: idiots."

I raised my eyebrows. "Good thing I can't push your buttons."

He stared at me for a long time, then slowly sat back. The bent smile returned.

"Oh, God, I really do miss stimulating conversation. That's been the loneliest thing about this life."

"Yeah, I'm sure. So back to having no plan. I don't believe a smart guy like you doesn't have some goal in mind. It can't just be utter chaos you're after. Come on, Tanner, level with me. You owe it to me. I mean, I even went to *Kansas* looking for you, for Christ's sake. That's gotta be worth a scrap of information."

He picked up the glass of water in front of him and watched me as he drank. Which was sorta creepy. But he seemed to be considering my request. Finally, he said, "I'm clearly not going to take the time to fill you in on everything. As much as I love your company, I've too much to do and all sorts of deadlines crashing down.

"But I'll tell you this. You think I'm trying to take down dozens or hundreds of corporations. I know the intelligence services in Europe are talking about how my goal is to systematically cripple all of their biggest companies. That's what happens when you show them how easy it is to bust into almost anyone's back channels. But here's a news flash: I don't need to crash dozens of big corporations. I just have to select a handful of key conglomerates and they'll start taking each *other* down."

It was my turn to stare at him. "What does that mean?"

He waved a hand. "It's really simple. Throughout history, countries were their own separate domains. They had lands they protected, armies to make sure no invaders got in. The Great Wall of China stretches for thousands of miles and it was built for one purpose: to keep out the raiding, nomadic tribes to the north. Hell, civilization has always relied upon easily defined borders to keep the other guys out.

"But today? The digital revolution has erased all the borders. We wanted an interconnected world? Well, we got it. A woman in Western Australia is essentially right next door to a man in Montreal, Canada. We can carry on conversations globally, with no delays. And—" His eyes grew wide. "And the world economy has linked up digitally, too. I can sell a box of buttons in Mumbai and deposit the money into a bank in Fargo, North Dakota."

"Yeah," I said. "So what are you saying?"

"I'm saying, Eric, that this great, worldwide connectedness, the dream that so many idealists have prayed for, is going to come right back and bite everyone in the ass."

I tapped a finger on the table, thinking. "You only need to cripple a few key players—"

"And they topple like dominoes, my friend. I've spent the last two years keeping everyone guessing, picking off a few shitty companies here and there that deserved a good slap. And the whole time I've been dishing out these misdirections, I've actually been worming around, setting up a bunch of little landmines that will all pop at the same time."

I felt a chill. *Setting up a bunch of little landmines.*

We'd had it all wrong. Ceti wasn't going to drop the equivalent of a digital atomic bomb; he was going to strategically blitz a variety of critical organizations around the globe.

"Right," I managed to say. "And when *they* go down—"

"Global breakdowns happen because of one thing," he said. "Mistrust. Banks, even currencies themselves, only work through trust. You give me a dollar and I know that dollar is good in every store in the country. I trust it. But once the global connections are blown up, no country will trust another. And that will cause internal hemorrhaging on a scale no one ever imagined. All because the world rushed into a digital economy at breakneck speed, before they even knew what kind of power they were dealing with. The internet was a fun toy that quickly became just about the *only* way people do business anymore. Everyone just came bounding in, without setting up proper protocols and without ever considering how they'd just tied their entire livelihood to every other idiot around the planet. And not only to idiots; they often have tied their hands to some of the most evil bastards alive. They just don't know it, because the evil bastards are conniving behind an innocent-looking web presence."

He leaned toward me. "You've done business online. Are you telling me you know everything about the places that have access to your personal information? They've got a bunch of five-star reviews, so they must be good guys, right? Well, once those dominoes start to fall, you won't be able to protect yourself fast enough. The global economy will stutter just long enough to induce panic. And we all know what happens when happy-go-lucky citizens begin to panic, right? How many recent examples do I need to cite?"

It was one of the most cold-blooded examples of foretelling armageddon I'd ever heard, simple in its detail and brutal in its apathy.

And I couldn't disagree with a word he said. We had willingly chucked all of our data and financial lives into the shiny new cart rolling by, and we had no idea where the cart was going or who was even driving it. Plus, anyone could climb in at any time when we weren't looking. For years, security experts warned that we were too free with our personal information. People who expressed concern over digital commerce were tagged with the label "luddite" or called dinosaurs.

The dinosaurs would get the last laugh—assuming anyone was able to muster a laugh. Ceti was on the brink of pulling off the unthinkable: toppling the global economy like a giant game of Jenga, and he would do it through strategic attacks on individual sites.

I kept coming back to his line about how we so desperately wanted this interconnected world. We did. We just didn't know how vulnerable it made us.

Well, *some* people knew. We casually ignored them in our haste to buy toilet paper online.

The worst part of all was that Jared Hicks had pretty much said all of this during our very first meeting in the pub. He'd looked right at me with his ZZ Top beard and told me, "*Once enough companies are crippled financially, it'll bring everything down.*"

Perhaps I hadn't totally believed him at the time. Because I hadn't liked him from the get-go, maybe I failed to give Jared any credibility. And yet he'd begun our relationship by laying out exactly what was going to happen.

All of this shot through my head in about three seconds while I contemplated my next move. The problem was I *had* no next move. I was being held at gunpoint with no way to disrupt Leachman's plan and no way to contact Quanta or Poole. It was unlikely Q2 would be able to find me, given that my last report would basically send them dozens of miles in the wrong direction. There was no official record anywhere of Tanner Leachman owning property in the region. It was a disaster. And the clock was ticking.

Leachman must've seen the hesitation, and I'm sure he basked in it. In a nonchalant voice, he said, "You know, I'm tempted to offer you a spot on my team."

I actually laughed out loud. "What? So first you send Arlo to kill me and now you offer me a job?"

"Why not? You obviously get along with Arlo, and neither of you seems to hold a grudge about what happened before. The two of you would make a great team. I've watched your work for the last few weeks and, other than you stumbling right into my trap, I've been quite impressed. As a bonus, you and I could have friendly debates long into the night about the hypocrisy of modern commerce. What do you think? You can't really like what you do now, chasing around after people who are just gonna come out on top anyway. There are too many of us."

"Yes, you're like never-ending cockroaches," I said. "Listen, Tanner, deep down you're probably an okay guy. In fact, it wasn't long ago that I actually wondered if you and I might be kindred spirits. Well, I was obviously way off the mark. And it's not just that you're a little warped; I mean, my own sliding screen door is a little off the track, too, so I can't talk. If you were still just hacking into digital signs and punking their message boards, we could probably have some beers and laugh about it."

Now I stared hard at him. "But you're trying to cripple the world economy simply because you can. Because it gets you off in some non-sexual way. Or maybe it's sexual; I don't know. No judgment there. Oh, and you murder people. So I'm gonna take a hard pass on the job offer and instead just take you and your clown posse down. Like, all the way down. Fair enough?"

Now the crooked smile evaporated. Leachman took one more quick drink of water, pushed back his chair, and stood up. "Take them back to their room," he said. "And tell Jared I want to see him."

Katrina and I were led back to our unusual cell without another word. Once inside, they slammed the door and locked it.

We stood there, trying to absorb everything we'd just heard. My frustration built to a boil and I scanned the room again, looking for anything that might help us to break out. There was nothing.

"This is unreal," Katrina said. "It sounds like the plot of some B movie. This can't really happen."

"Except it *is* happening," I said. "And I can't find anything in his plan that isn't completely believable."

I could tell by the look on her face that she reluctantly agreed. And she was the expert. That made it even more frightening.

We took turns using the bathroom, then found ourselves again standing in the middle of the room, feeling helpless and too keyed up to sit down. I didn't expect to see the door open again until the next day, which is why I was stunned to hear the lock turn a minute later.

Two of the nameless thugs entered, guns drawn, playing their tough-guy parts. But right behind them walked Jared Hicks. Katrina crossed her arms and avoided eye contact with him.

"Are you now relegated to the role of messenger boy?" I said.

"Shut up, Swan," he said. "I'm here to tell you that you're going to die of starvation and dehydration in this room. We're shutting off the water to the bathroom, and you'll pass out in a few days after the toilet water runs out. No one is coming for you. Do you understand? You can just continue to make your smart-ass comments as you wither and die."

"You know, Jared, other than the actual delivery, which was lame, you have the dialogue of a real villain down pat. Maybe Tanner wrote that for you. But I'm not exactly quivering in fear. So unless you've got some important message to pass along from your lord and master, why don't you just scram. Your ex-girl-friend and I have things to discuss."

His face flushed red enough to show through the outrageous growth of facial hair. I thought he was going to rush across the room and try to claw my eyes out. It gave me immense pleasure.

"And what about me, Jared?" Katrina said, surprising me. She took a step forward and looked up into his face "Are you going to just let me wither and die, too? Is that what I meant to you through all these years?"

Her voice, usually so strong and full of purpose, was the gentlest I'd ever heard from her. As angry as she was, as stunned as she had been by his betrayal, I felt anguish pouring from her broken heart. Damn, she really did love the brute. I'd never understand, but there it was.

He shifted his gaze to the floor and took a couple of calming breaths. I tried reading the emotion in his eyes but it was hard with his face lowered, his shoulders hunched. Was this true sorrow? Regret? Were the softly spoken words from his fiancée melting the ice block around his heart?

I felt a flicker of hope. Katrina could be the key to getting out. Even if Leachman condemned *me* to death, he probably never counted on this particular wild card. Love, no matter how bruised, how battered, sometimes found a way.

Jared looked up and I noticed a definite redness to his eyes. The hulk with a heart? My flicker of hope grew into a small flame.

He slowly shook his head. "No, Kat. I would never let Ceti torture you like that. We've been through too much together."

Katrina let out a small sigh. She, too, saw the chance.

Jared held out a hand and one of the thugs gave him a gun.

"So," Jared said, "I'm going to spare you that pain."

And he shot her.

CHAPTER TWENTY-SEVEN

I let out a primordial scream as the roar of the gun blast died away, but I don't know if it was in the form of an actual word. More of a guttural expression of shock and rage. My natural instinct was to grab Katrina as she plummeted backward, bracing her against a fall and trying to gently lower her to the ground. At the same time, I caught a glimpse of all three assholes backing out of the room, Jared lingering for a few additional seconds—long enough for me to look up and stare into his hideous animal face. He stared at the bloody mess he'd made of his ex-fiancée, and I recognized the confused look of sadness mixed with shame. And surprise at what he'd done.

As I turned back to examine her wound, I heard the door click shut and the lock engaged.

Katrina's eyes were opened wide, absolute shock registering on her face. Her lower lip was quivering, and her breath came in fits. Both of her hands were pressed against the wound in her abdomen, but the flow of blood was extreme.

Leaning close to her, I somehow coaxed a gentle voice out of my own shock. "Let me see, Katrina. Relax, I won't do anything right now. Just let me see."

She let me pull her hands away. It only took a quick glance to know that this was a mortal wound. Even if I could somehow staunch the blood rushing out, her insides were probably scrambled. She had to be in agony.

"Hold on, I'll be right back," I said, and lowered her head to the wood floor. I rushed into the bathroom, grabbed the lone towel on the rack and the entire roll of toilet paper, and hurried back to her side. "Let me stop the bleeding. No, don't push me away. Let me stop the bleeding."

She finally relented and clenched her eyes tight against the pain as I pressed the towel against the wound. From behind her, I saw the pool of blood expanding. The exit wound would have to be addressed somehow, too.

Yet while I automatically went through the steps I was trained to take and uttered the words to Katrina that seemed to be right, one thought kept forcing its way across my mind:

I've got to stop these monsters. No matter what it takes, they have to be obliterated.

I could detach emotionally from most cases because that's an absolute requirement for the job. I've seen people die, and lord knows I've been responsible for countless more. But something about this casualty sickened me. It was not only unnecessary, it was purely retaliatory. We were both going to die, but Ceti was determined to make me suffer mentally long before the food and water ran out. I'd called him psychotic to mainly get under his skin, but the tag was earned.

So much for the harmless reputation of keyboard pirates.

And as for Jared Hicks? I would personally send him to hell.

I had to shove all of that out of my mind for now. Katrina was about to bleed to death, unless her internal injuries killed her sooner. Pushing to my feet, I took a chance that someone outside the locked door might have at least an ounce of integrity. I walked over and banged on it with both fists, as hard as I could.

"Hey," I shouted. "Don't leave her in here like this. Get some medical help, now." I waited a moment, then tried again. "Hello! If any one of you has any decency at all, even a *scrap* of decency, get this woman out of here and to a hospital right now."

I waited another 30 seconds, but no one answered. The door would not open again while Katrina and I were still alive. I lowered my hands, placed them on my hips, and stared down at the floor, breathing slow and deep. I'd been in more than a few shitty situations, but this was one of the cruelest. I turned around and walked back over to the computer scientist lying on the floor. The circle of blood around her had expanded.

Sitting down beside her, I did the most natural thing at the moment: I took her hand. She instantly squeezed it and looked up at me, tears in her eyes. They had to be caused by both the physical pain and the emotional betrayal. Her goddamned fiancé had fired a slug right into her gut.

"Hey," I said softly, then pulled a strand of hair out of her face. "I'm so sorry, Katrina. I should never have let you come with me."

She swallowed hard. "No. I wouldn't have let you go without . . . without taking me. You didn't . . . you didn't do anything wrong." She took another hard breath. "Not this time, anyway."

I chuckled. "Yeah. This time. Listen, do you want me to try to make you more comfortable on the couch? I'm just a little worried about moving you."

"No . . . don't move me. Please don't move me." She clinched her eyes shut tight for a moment, then focused on me again. "God, it hurts so bad. I . . . never had any idea."

I nodded. "I've been there. I've been shot more times than you would believe."

"Really?"

"Really. Look, I am going to move you just a touch. I want to patch up your other side, okay?"

She didn't answer, which I took as permission. I scooted over to where my backpack had been discarded by Arlo, then unzipped the large compartment. At the bottom, I found a rolled-up, light hoodie. Bringing it back over, I leaned down toward her face. "This won't feel great. But I'll make it real quick. Here we go."

I pulled her toward me, rolling her onto her right side just enough to get a view of the ugly exit wound. Somehow it didn't seem to be bleeding as much, but that could've simply been an illusion. I took a large wad of toilet paper and cleaned around the wound as much as possible, while Katrina let out a yell. Then, I wrapped the hoodie around her, keeping the thickest part up against the hole in her back, and tied the arms around her front. It was the lousiest body tourniquet I'd ever seen, but I had nothing else to work with.

I eased her back so she wasn't lying directly on the wound, sort of angled to her right side. I sat back against the couch and pulled her head into my lap.

"There," I said. "All comfy now, right?"

She couldn't speak at first, but at last the pain subsided enough for her to say, "Yeah. You're a regular Florence Nightingale."

We stayed like that for a few moments, me stroking her hair while she took labored breaths, fighting back the burning pain. I calculated she might have 10 minutes before it was over, perhaps even less time conscious. She had to realistically know she was dying. How the hell do you pass the time in that situation?

Which is why it surprised me when she said in a voice barely above a whisper, "Swan, what do you think happens when we die?"

I couldn't let her see how this struck me like a seismic wave. The very question I'd pursued for years, the nagging thought tantalizing me. I'd discussed it with Miller during several of my sessions with the shrink, so it wasn't like I didn't have my answer ready. I just didn't know how to talk about it with someone who didn't know my—well, my unique situation.

But I had nothing to lose at the moment.

"Well," I said. "Believe it or not, Katrina, that question has driven me for years. You could almost say it has become my purpose in life."

She tried to angle her head around to look at me. "No shit."

I laughed. "No shit."

"But . . . why?"

It was my turn to let out a long breath. "Before I answer that, tell me what you think."

Her face clouded. "Honestly? I don't think—" She had a spasm of pain and let out a small grunt and tried to shift her position. My heart hurt for what she was going through, and I longed to bust through the door, find the bearded bastard, and beat him to a bloody pulp with my fists.

A moment later, Katrina recovered. "I don't think there's anything."

"Nothing? Nothing at all?"

"Nothing at all. Darkness. No sense of being."

"That's grim," I said.

"It's no different than what you remember from before you were born. There was just . . . nothing."

She wasn't alone in this thought. One of the things that had always fascinated me was the vast array of hypotheses regarding the afterlife—or at least what came after life. Religious followers subscribed to one idea, others who might lean simply toward the mystical had their own notions. There was a group of people, like Katrina, who held that this was it; there was nothing before or after.

"Now you," Katrina said, closing her eyes, perhaps as a method of dealing with the agony. "I really want to hear this."

I hesitated for a moment. That little prick Leachman could

very well be recording this whole scene. He was sick enough to do that. But I didn't think so. He probably never expected to have company like this. Regardless, I decided to spill.

"I lost my parents when I was in college. That's always tragic, and it's not like I have a monopoly on grief. But . . . it was senseless. To me, the pain you feel with the loss of someone close to you is amplified when it's a stupid, senseless loss. Makes it worse somehow." I paused. "I don't know. Hard to explain. Maybe you know what I'm talking about."

"I do," Katrina said, her voice sounding weaker.

"A year later—I'd joined the military by that point—my sister died. She was killed. I guess that's senseless, too, but in a different way. With a senseless accident, you feel unlucky, like the universe just called their number. But when someone you love dies through violence?"

I trailed off for a moment, unsure if I wanted to keep talking about this. We were discussing the kind of stuff I didn't even really open up about with Christina. But then, maybe we don't always share those types of feelings with the ones we love the most because we want our time with them to be light and easy. Somehow dishing all of this with my wife felt . . . wrong. Like our time was reserved for escaping from all the shit the world dispensed. I know, the relationship experts who dole out advice if you buy their books or their online courses will tell you that you should share everything with your partner.

I don't subscribe to that thinking. I could be wrong. I've never sold a book on relationships, and it's entirely possible I'm botching everything by keeping these thoughts from the person I've bonded with. It could also be a consequence of not spending much time together. For the precious moments we got, I'd rather not dredge up the darkest chapters of my life.

It was a life I left behind long, long ago, but I still heard the echoes.

I'd been silent for an uncomfortable length of time. I cleared my throat and said, "Well, when you lose someone to violence, it can either drive you into reclusion or it can push you into action. Any kind of action, which is just a way of running."

Katrina looked up at me. "Running?"

"Yeah. Running. Either running away from the reality of what happened, just avoiding the truth and hoping it'll help you avoid the pain. It won't, by the way. Or running *toward* something. I—" Again, I came to a stop. This time, though, I soldiered on. "The death of my parents created a lot of emotional kindling, you could say. My sister's murder was the match that lit everything. Made me apply for special ops training in the military, then made me take a job with the government. A job where I come face-to-face with death all the time. Because I need to."

Katrina remained quiet. Her lip began quivering again, and I knew she was using every bit of strength she had left to repress the pain that had to be excruciating. But she also was listening to everything I said.

"People have always been strangely curious about death. Specifically, what happens after. You said you think there's nothing. Just darkness. Well, I have to know. I have to know what the people closest to me experienced. And I don't want to wait until I finally die to know the answer. I want to know it now."

She trained her eyes on me again. They were filling with tears. "How can you do that?"

It wasn't lost on me that I was talking about death with a woman who would cross the threshold within a few minutes. In a way, it was cruel. But it had been her idea. It was, in reality, her last request.

"Katrina, I can't tell you exactly how I do that. Not because I'm worried about any stupid confidentiality at this point, but because it's complicated as shit—and you'd think I was pulling your leg. But I'll boil it down to this. My work puts me in a position to see both sides in ways no one in the world has ever seen. And my personal mission for the last several years has been to answer your question. I want to know what's over there. I have to believe . . ."

I let my voice soften. "Katrina, I have to believe it's not the dark void you think it is. I don't personally believe there will be pearly gates or choirs or Clarence from *It's a Wonderful Life*. Although how cool would *that* be?"

A painful smile spread across her face. She looked almost thankful for the levity.

With my voice still gentle, I leaned down to her. "Katrina, my soul tells me that it will be exactly what I want it to be, and I think exactly what you'd want it to be, too. When we cross over for good, I think our spirits will mingle with the power of not just this universe, but all of them. And we'll have the answers to every question we've ever had, and answers to the ones we haven't even thought of yet."

Her eyes fluttered, and a trickle of blood seeped from her mouth. I dabbed it away with a wad of toilet paper.

Then she fixed her gaze on me and smiled again. "That will be glorious."

I felt her shudder with her final breath.

Completely out of my control, a tear rolled down my face and landed on her forehead. I bent down and kissed it away.

I DON'T KNOW how long I sat there, cradling her body. But if a door had somehow miraculously opened in the wall, granting me escape from the room, I wouldn't have moved. I wasn't going to leave Katrina Yu for a little while. She deserved someone to be there with her while she transitioned to that glorious next realm.

God, I hoped I was right about that.

At least an hour went by before I finally moved.

.   .   .

I POSITIONED her on the couch, her arms at her side. I made her last repose as peaceful as I could, given the staggering amount of blood enveloping her. I whispered one last thing into her ear. But that was just between us. Sorry.

I bent over to pick up the backpack and carried it into the bathroom. My shaving kit was unzipped, having been examined and left behind. I withdrew the small replicas of shaving cream and deodorant, and fished around in one of the pockets until I found the large pill I'd need.

These were my tools for uploading. They required an internet connection, but that was the least of my concerns. Ceti's compound would have loads of it, but it would also be the most highly-protected wifi on the planet. It was easy for me to sneak into someone's account, but he was just the kind of computer nerd who'd spot it.

The neighbors, however . . .

I took a minute to let the device hidden inside the deodorant track down a signal that was accessible. Q2's brain trust on the second floor had designed it to attach and siphon the wireless juice I needed. Given the strength at this distance, it wouldn't be nearly as fast. But I wanted the extra time. There was a lot I had to consider in the next couple of hours.

Once it was locked in, I hooked up the rest, popped my pill, and stretched out on the floor beside the couch and Katrina. I took off my shirt, wadded it up, and used it under my head. Then I lay back, placed an arm over my face, and let myself wander out of my right mind.

What must've been two hours later, I was finished. And also drained. Physically, to an extent, but emotionally to the max. I'd fought off tears about halfway through, thinking of Katrina, my parents, my sister, Christina. Wondering, for the one millionth time, just what the hell I was doing. But also clearly memorizing what I was about to do. Sealing it into my memory.

I packed away the shaving kit, leaving no trace that I'd done anything other than sit with a corpse. Then I went back into the bathroom, leaned on the sink, and stared into the eyes of the convict whose body I'd used for the past few months. I tried to see if there was anything in the reflection of the eyes, anything that distinguished Eric Swan from the criminal who'd previously owned the shell. I don't know if it's true that the eyes are a window to the soul—but, if so, the shades were drawn for now.

I stood up tall, took a deep breath, then slammed the back of my hand into that mirror. It cracked. When I struck it again, even harder, a couple of large pieces tumbled into the sink.

With one more deep breath, I picked up the largest sliver, sat cross-legged on the floor, and sliced ugly, deep, cavernous grooves into both of my wrists.

CHAPTER TWENTY-EIGHT

The face before me was blurry, the sounds muffled, and the pain in my head was doing its best to pound me into oblivion. It caused me to squint, which actually helped with the blurred vision. The face swam into focus.

I tried to say "Hello, Sherilyn," but it came out—at least to my ears—as "*Ho Sharon.*"

It must've sounded funny to her, as well, because she smiled and raised her eyebrows. "Creating a new language again, Swan?"

Sherilyn was my favorite of all the techs working in the basement lab of Q2. While not in charge of the overall science behind the procedure, she nonetheless had become the point person when my lights turned on. I imagined she did the same for Parnell. If there were other agents now working for Quanta, I didn't know about them. And really, I didn't *want* to know.

In my peripheral vision, I watched a fuzzy form that had to be Sherilyn inject something into my IV. It was undoubtedly pain medication, along with a science cocktail I'd never understand. As long as it eased the pain, it could be grape Kool-Aid, for all I cared.

I drifted back into a dream-like state for a few moments, which was normal. You don't just suddenly inhabit a new body and have it fit like the comfy sweatshirt you've worn on weekends for the last ten years. The adjustment process can often be gnarly, accompanied by a headache—like the one I suffered at the moment—and a rotating menu of other miseries. Some worse than others. Some downright disgusting.

There's been only one time I took to a new body with barely a break-in period. Since then, I'd put in a request for God Maker and her minions to prioritize this element of the investment program, but I don't think they stay up at night concerned about my comfort. The last I heard, they were working on accelerating the upload procedure again. Poole had even suggested that a day would come when my uploads went to a satellite orbiting the planet instead of into a hard drive in the bowels of the Q2 building. I'd started to say, "You're joking," until I remembered who I was talking with.

There was even hope that the day would come when I uploaded continually, without the need for the spy toys. It would just be automatic, like a document updating and saving every few seconds.

But who could complain, really? The fact that *any* of this was possible blew my mind when I stopped to think about it.

Eventually, I opened my eyes again. The pain had subsided to bearable and I could see much better. I cleared my throat, then did it again. I spoke a few words. The voice was baritone and quite pleasant. For now, I didn't notice any quirks that would cause a problem. I've had bodies with tinnitus, bodies with awful taste buds, and bodies with shitty lung capacity. Or, like the one I'd recently departed, a wimpy stomach. But there were times when I got rock star bodies, strong and finely tuned.

I was beginning to think I had one of those for this go-around.

The thought of my previous body made me pensive. My last

memory was of lying on the floor to upload, with the dead body of Katrina Yu on the couch above me. Everything after that had fallen into the lights-out period, so I couldn't envision what had happened. But I clearly recalled making up my mind to terminate the body, so that meant it was lying there in that same room, or possibly in the bathroom, just waiting for someone to discover it. I knew that Tanner Leachman would be in no hurry to do so.

Which is what I'd counted on. I couldn't wait to surprise the son of a bitch.

Sherilyn wandered back around. "How long since I checked out?" I asked. It was the common way of asking when my last body had ceased operating, which automatically sent an electronic code to this basement lab at Q2 headquarters. I once had joked to Christina that my death was like an airline: always announcing its departure.

"Um," she said, checking a page on her old-fashioned clipboard. "Six hours, maybe? This was a quick turnaround. Quanta had your replacement body ready to go." She smiled down at me. "She must've known you'd fall out of a tree or something."

I smiled, and it was at that point I noticed a couple of teeth were missing in the back of my mouth. Hey, convicts often live violent lives; this guy, although quite fit, must've been on the losing end of at least one fight.

"You ready to sit up?" Sherilyn asked.

In response, I took her offered hand and pulled myself, slowly, into a sitting position with my feet dangling off the table. The pain in my head flared again, then just as quickly subsided. As much as I'd love to speed things along, the entire initiation process was a slow grind. Sort of like a first date, where my new body and I got to know each other. Once I'd stabilized, I took a moment to check out the goods. As I'd surmised, the frame was fit and toned. Both arms were covered in a colorful patchwork of tattoos. I picked out the name Lola amidst a montage of ocean-themed designs.

It was little things like that—a tattoo—that always shocked me into remembering I was renting space originally occupied by someone who'd had their own life, their own successes and failures, their own highs and lows. There were people they'd loved and who'd loved them. They'd had good days, horrific days, but *thousands* of days. It always grounded me, even momentarily. We each take our life for granted, and the days blur from one to another. But those days end, and for the average person, those days will never be documented. They're but fragile electrical impulses stored in our heads, and they're erased when the power is shut off.

Depressing, in some ways, but uplifting in others. A nice reminder of how precious each of those days could be. *Should* be.

Sherilyn went off to attend to something or other, leaving me to acclimate. We'd both been through the drill so many times that few words were necessary. At this point in the process, she was there to assist in case I ran into trouble. It was rare but had certainly happened. The time I fell off the table and died right there was something she and I still laughed about from time to time. Of course, I had no memory of it at all, but Sherilyn liked to point out that at least I'd still been under warranty.

The woman had my sense of humor.

Another hour passed while I got up to speed. After giving Sherilyn a hug and promising to write—another of our ongoing shticks—I reported to one of the pods where I'd sleep again for a couple of hours. It helped, for some reason. Who would ever know why?

When I awoke, I enjoyed a long shower, got dressed, and rode the elevator upstairs, where Quanta waited for my debriefing. She sat in a small conference room with Poole and Parnell.

"Ladies," I said, walking in and nodding at each one in turn. "The all new and improved Eric Swan, reporting for duty."

While Quanta and Poole made only a perfunctory greeting, Parnell's eyes roved up and down, taking in my new body. I would expect nothing less of her, someone who'd now experienced the investment procedure for herself.

"Is it everything you dreamed of?" she asked. "Able to leap buildings in a single bound?"

I sat down at the head of the table. "Never been partial to leaping. But I do feel like I could bench press a piano."

"Enough small talk," Quanta said. "Tell us what you know."

"Fortunately, quite a bit. I uploaded just before killing myself."

There were glances around the table. They, of course, wouldn't know how I'd bought it at the end, and an agent committing suicide was rare. Rare and certainly frowned upon. Procuring bodies was tough enough; it was hoped that we'd protect them at all costs.

So I quickly explained. "Katrina Yu is dead. She was shot by Jared Hicks, right in front of me. Then I was locked into a room with no chance of escaping. And Ceti is about to launch the real deal; everything else has been preliminary. I needed to get out and get back right away if we're going to have any chance of stopping him. Is that acceptable?"

Quanta would expect a more detailed report later, but we were up against the clock. She was quick to nod. "I'm sorry to hear about Katrina. You made the right decision, of course. I take it this did not happen near Arrowhead Mountain Lake, as you first reported."

"No. That was a decoy. Ceti has paid off people to help him, even though they have no idea what he's doing. That includes an asshole in the building permits office, name of Kyle Henshaw, and at least one woman in his office. She told me her name was

Annette, but that's probably bogus. They directed me north and Arlo Benn was there, waiting. But that's not the biggest bombshell in this case."

Quanta merely raised an eyebrow.

"Ceti is none other than Tanner Leachman."

It was Parnell who responded first. "Leachman? The dead guy in Missouri?"

"Kansas, it turns out. And reports of his death were grossly exaggerated. The best I can figure out, he borrowed an old trick from Agatha Christie and lumped his own alleged death into a group of others. One death or disappearance would stand out; a string of them provides cover. Would've worked, too, if he hadn't pissed off his sister as much as he did. Anyway, we know he has Hicks working for him and, from what he said to me in our brief chat, there may be a few others. Other than Hicks, a handful of hired guns, and a cook, I didn't see anyone else. They may be in the main house."

"All right," Quanta said. "Now tell us about this '*real deal.*'"

I spent a few minutes sharing everything Leachman had told me about his '*little landmines,*' as he called them. I expressed my concern about the domino effect his plan relied on, and how he'd use the world's interconnectedness to accelerate the devastation.

Repeating what I'd heard from the madman only underscored just how dire it was. I could see on the faces of all three women that I wasn't alone in my distress.

"We have to hustle back up there," I said. "And we can't ask the police to rush in. For all we know, Leachman has bought his way into that department, too. The last thing we want is for him to get a warning we're on our way. Even a large attack squad of FBI agents could cause him to set everything in motion. This is one of those cases where we have to clean it up ourselves. Quietly. He thinks I'm still cooling my heels in his guest room. So I'm ready to go crash his party and give him the surprise of his life."

"And I assume cutting all the power would be pointless?" Parnell said.

"He's covered all of that. Power, water, and who knows what else. He's quite proud of how self-sufficient everything is. And again, if we try to cut power, he'll know we've found him and he might launch his attacks. I need to slip in before he can do that."

"I'll go with you," Parnell said.

"Yes," Quanta said. "Both of you. And we'll have a team of FBI with you. They can hang back until you need them."

I stood up and made eye contact with Parnell. "Just remember one thing," I said to her. "I don't care who takes down Leachman. But Jared Hicks is mine."

THE SMALL JET carried us from Washington to Burlington in no time. The flight was cataloged as carrying tourists, and the word around the airport was that we were a bored, wealthy couple looking for something new to do. A spontaneous trip to Vermont was just the ticket.

A car awaited us, and we drove a few miles before pulling over to double-check our gear.

"So," Parnell said, holstering her gun, then running a hand through her short hair. "*Jared Hicks is mine?* Got a bit of a vendetta going there, Swan? Not exactly professional."

I didn't answer for a moment, focused on my own prep work. Then I said, "Well, I've never been accused of being the consummate professional." I looked at her. "Neither have you. Why do you think we work for Quanta? I doubt the woman has ever hired a *professional*."

"I like to think I used to be professional."

"And it got you kicked out of British Intelligence."

She smiled. "That was a marriage doomed from the start."

"How's your current relationship?"

"Oh. I'm still in the honeymoon phase. Ask me again after I've been killed a few more times. So what's our plan?"

I glanced out the car window. "It'll be dark soon. We know the property will be saturated with security devices. Maybe a goon or two patrolling."

"Nothing we can't handle."

"Once we're inside, we move fast. No prolonged engagements. Every minute we give this shithead is another minute he has to blow up the world."

CHAPTER TWENTY-NINE

It was a new moon. We'd let the purplish colors of sunset dissipate into the dark of night and now had the cover we wanted to make our preliminary sweep. From there, we would decide whether or not to pop in. Of course, that was standard operating procedure, at least according to the government manual: scan, analyze, regroup, attack. But my natural proclivity was to splice out the middle sections and jump from scan to attack; I didn't understand leaving and coming back. I figured I was there anyway, so why not give 'em hell before overthinking everything? Countless military campaigns had suffered from analysis paralysis. I would never be accused of that. Get in, kick ass, get out. Or limp out. Whatever. Better than just talking about it.

Parnell parked three blocks from Leachman's property. We climbed out just as an older woman shuffled past, tugging the world's slowest dog behind her on what appeared to be a home-made rope leash. Under the street light, the woman looked into my face with a gaze labeling me an unwelcome stranger. I returned the glare with a wink and a smile.

I called the leader of the FBI team to let him know we'd be taking a quick look around. They were in two cars, parked down the street from us. He acknowledged they'd be standing by. Bypassing Deputy Chief Garritson and the rest of the Burlington police would undoubtedly create a big, maple-flavored fuss between the state politicians and the FBI. Between me, Parnell, and the eight federal agents tucked into the shadows behind us, we hoped to have enough to get the job done.

As for the quick look around, some of it would be done with our eyes while some would take place from the air. Parnell popped the trunk, then leaned in and snapped open a protective case. A moment later, she retrieved a drone and we carried it to the empty lot across the street. I was a pretty fair hand with these gadgets, but Parnell was a much bigger tech freak than I. She'd spent hours training with drones and the surveillance gear they carried. I was happy to let her flex her geek muscle.

When the systems checks were finished, Parnell glanced around, but between the trees and the darkness, we were pretty well hidden. With a deft touch, she had the whisper-quiet rotors spinning and the drone lifted off the ground. I moved back into the passenger seat of the car and opened a laptop. The split screen shared diagnostic info on the left and an infrared camera view on the right. For now, the little spy machine hovered above the park. Parnell slid back into the driver's seat, holding the control unit.

"How we look?" she asked.

"All good. Take it up over the tree line. I'd like to get a neighborhood view."

You may be really proud of the image quality on your phone and puff your chest at the photos captured by your fancy DSLR camera. I'm not trying to diminish your pixel joy, but here's the deal: While the government may not get everything right, and they might even make colossal blunders from time to time, one thing they get right—and the thing you'll never get to judge for yourself—is the multitude of toys they secretly develop to spy on people.

Cameras? Long before a new design reaches the market, it's employed to get a glimpse at the bad guys. Were they used *only* on the bad guys? Well, I can't swear to something I don't know for sure.

Let's just say you'd be stunned at the images on my screen, sent from a drone flying 90 feet above the street on a moonless night. If I held a playing card out the car window, not only would you be able to tell it was the seven of hearts, you'd be able to tell if my nails were properly trimmed. And it would look as clear and bright as if it were a sunny afternoon.

Shit like that will shake you up if you're not used to it.

On my laptop, I pulled up a picture-in-picture. This was a map of the neighborhood, with a yellow dot representing our flying spy. Leachman's compound was highlighted as well, so it was no problem for Parnell to steer the drone right to it. Once there, she set it to hover again while we talked.

I pointed to the house on the screen. "I expect everything about this place to be upgraded to the highest levels of tech imaginable. Leachman seemed to be very proud of his upgrades. We'll have to do an eyeball exam ourselves for ground sensors, but let's have our little friend here scout out the cameras first."

Parnell nodded and maneuvered the drone downward until it was over the center of the house, about eight feet above the roof. She leaned over to look at the image on the laptop, then pointed to a setting. "That one. Switch it on."

When I did, the left side of the screen changed to a series of LED meters, six of them, each registering zero at the moment. If Ceti's castle had the kind of cameras we expected, they'd have their own unique electronic signal. We could technically hijack them using the drone, but that might also trigger an alarm. For now, we just wanted to catalog them.

Parnell moved the drone, taking it on an aerial tour around the perimeter of the roof, the infrared camera showing every detail.

"Wait, back up," I said. "There."

It was small and relatively camouflaged against the home, but definitely a surveillance device. Parnell adjusted one of the drone's extensions, aiming it at the camera. I looked at the meters on my screen. The second one from the top lit up.

"Camera and motion detector," Parnell said. "Probably set to ignore anything under a certain size. Mark that one."

We sat there another 15 minutes, sending the drone around the house. We marked nine devices, and another two that were only security lights by the garage. Next, we studied the guest house, the smaller building that currently held the bodies of Katrina Yu and my old shell. It, too, had motion detectors only hooked up to security lights. But Parnell pointed at something on the video screen.

"He went cheap with these. I can disable those without setting off an alarm."

I watched her make an adjustment with the control unit, which had more buttons than the TV remote in my condo. "You can do that with the drone? Or will you do that in person?"

"It's done," she said.

"Oh. Great. Well, do me a favor and take it back to the main house. I want to scan the roof itself."

When we had a good view, it was my turn to point. "There. That's our way in."

We were looking at an attic vent. It was perched on one side of the highest point of the house, which meant all we had to do was figure out how to get up there without being detected. Not easy, but surely not the hardest part of the night.

The last assignment for our flying spy was to check for camera signals covering the grounds. There was one by the entrance to the driveway, easily bypassed, and two more randomly covering the back side of the property.

"Okay," Parnell said. "Let's bring the bird home and we'll go check out the grounds in person."

It took ten minutes to land the drone and stow it in the trunk, then another five minutes to reach Ceti's home base. We made the walk in silence, each carrying a large backpack. I had a pair of night vision goggles tipped up on my head, like sunglasses. Even though the homes had significant space between them, it was still a residential neighborhood. We couldn't afford to look like commandos on a moonlit raid. A phone call to the Burlington police could be disastrous.

Once at the edge of his property, we slowed to a casual stroll. Using a small tablet, I engaged an app and pointed it toward the edge of the lawn. We stopped and Parnell knelt, pretending to tie a shoe while I swept the tablet back and forth. That's all it took. She got back to her feet and we continued down the street. The tablet spewed its findings.

"Ground sensors," I said. "Level three. No, four. Good stuff. But not impenetrable."

"The house is 244 feet from the street," Parnell said. "The garage, 280. Guest house, 292."

"That's where we'll go," I said. "The guest house. We can get from the roof of the guest house to the main building and bypass the cameras entirely. Give me a minute and I'll take care of the sensors."

We crossed to the other side of the street and reversed course, then stopped behind a car parked against the curb. It took me all of 30 seconds to scramble the ground sensors, essentially confusing them. It wouldn't sound an alarm, but would temporarily render them useless while they rebooted. The makers of this particular security system would be amazed to know how vulnerable they were. Or maybe they wouldn't.

I flipped down the night vision goggles and scanned the property. The sensors were good enough that they likely induced a feeling of safety and security, and I doubted there would be anyone patrolling the grounds. I was right. Besides, Tanner Leachman had no reason to think anyone would be stalking him. In his mind, he'd eliminated the two people he considered a threat.

"It's all clear," I said. "I see no reason to go back and plan anything. Do you?"

"How about we make a side bet?" she answered. "Whoever gets killed buys a round the next time we connect."

"Throw in a steak dinner and you're on."

"I don't eat red meat."

"Lobster?"

"Done."

"I'll keep mine a steak. Make a note. Medium well, with garlic mashed."

She shook her head. "I got shot last time, ya wanker. It's your turn. Let's go."

I keyed the radio on my headset and let the FBI team know we were on our way in and to stand by. "If you don't hear back from us in 30 minutes, join the party."

Then, after another glance around, we crossed the street, walked to the edge of the property, and made our way across the lawn to a large tree. We waited there a moment, taking the temperature of the situation. Everything remained quiet. If we'd moved toward the main house, the security cameras would've nailed us. But Parnell had put the motion detectors on the guest house into nap mode. We veered left and made our way over to its far side.

It took less than a minute to secure a line to the small building's roof and pull ourselves up. From there, we took advantage of the moonless night to scramble across to the far side, which also benefited from the shield of another large tree. We collected ourselves and studied the roof of the main house, about 60 feet away.

I pointed to one of the chimneys. "There, yes?"

"Yes." She shrugged off her backpack and removed a small but stout crossbow that had been collapsed for transport. After assembling it, she attached the end of a thin cable curled into the bottom of the pack. Without another word, she took aim and fired. With a *pfft* sound, the specialized hook rocketed across the empty space, trailing the cable behind it, and impacted with the chimney. It took no time to secure our end and pull the cable taut.

I won't lie. So much of spy craft is boring as hell. Lots of time driving or sitting in a hotel room or following a suspect. It's not what Parnell and I were really hired to do. We were trained in combat and a bunch of sneaky shit like this. My pulse picked up a few beats. Not out of fear or apprehension, but out of excitement. *This* was the kind of stuff I couldn't get enough of. Hollywood makes it seem like spies do this all the time. We don't. But when we do, we eat it up.

Parnell went first. Shouldering her backpack again, she gripped the cable and began shimmying across. She was good, and she was quick, which put a bit of pressure on me. I couldn't let the Brit show me up, especially on my home turf. When she reached the other side, I began to follow. I was only about a third of the way across when I heard a short, soft whistle from Parnell.

I froze. A door slammed, and I picked up the unmistakable sound of someone on a phone call. If there's a way of making yourself invisible while gripping a cable in mid-air with your hands and feet, I was doing my best. I took slow, quiet breaths and kept my face turned away from the ground. I imagined Parnell lying flat on the roof, her weapon aimed at the heart of our guest.

The voice grew louder as he approached. Then, surprisingly, it moved directly beneath me, where the guy stopped and kept up his animated conversation. Something about a bookie and how some guy named Trevor was an asshole. Then he fell silent while listening to the other person, probably acknowledging that Trevor was indeed a supreme asshole.

Pulling myself along a cable like this was child's play. But hanging there for a few minutes, completely immobile, can be hell on your muscles, especially when it's one of your first days to ever use those muscles. I felt a bead of sweat roll from my hairline toward my ear and hoped it wouldn't fall on the dickhead standing 18 feet beneath me.

Come on, I thought. *Let's all agree that Trevor sucks and get on with our lives.*

After another minute of talk and laughter, the guy made his way back toward the door. He wrapped up the call and went inside.

With a heavy exhale and my muscles screaming, I continued my journey. Reaching the far side, Parnell helped me to my feet and laughed.

"You're lucky he was so focused on his call and his feet."

I took in lungfuls of air and flexed my arm muscles to fight off the fatigue. "It doesn't really matter. By not shooting him now you saved him at most a half hour of life."

"You expecting a massacre?"

"I'm expecting one or two seasoned pros and a handful of total amateurs. Trevor's phony friend falls into the latter category and he won't see the sunrise." I stood up. "Let's go tour the Ceti mansion."

The roof's slope was severe but we had the right soles on our shoes for traction. We reached the attic vent, ran a quick scan for an alarm—which came up negative—and quickly had it removed. The interior was dark and quiet.

"Ladies first," I said.

She muttered something that probably included a bit of

profane British slang, pushed her backpack through the opening, then ducked inside. I followed the same procedure, folding my large frame in two to squeeze through. I waited for my eyes to adjust, but it wasn't happening. The attic was completely dark on multiple levels: no light whatsoever, overlaid with a heavy feeling of despair. I'm no empath, but I got a distinct sense of negative energy. Maybe I was projecting, based on the few minutes I'd spent with the vile wretch who owned the place. In my experience, though, mass murderers were a conflicted cesspool of inner hatred, and that almost always bled into their surroundings. Both the buildings and the people.

Yes, there are times I'm so deep I make myself sick.

I leaned back outside, grabbed the vent, and pulled it into place. We moved a few feet away before chancing the light from a phone. When we did, it revealed . . . nothing. The attic was completely empty: no boxes, no old furniture, nothing. I was actually impressed; my parents had been borderline pack rats, and I respected anyone who could live in a space and still have *space*.

We spied the only door to the room and stepped gently over to it, consciously reducing the chance of our footsteps arousing suspicion somewhere below. Out of habit, I tapped the Glock in the holster at my side. I knew damned well it would sing soon enough.

At the door, I looked up at Parnell's face, barely illuminated from the glow of her phone. Her eyes were half-lidded, a somewhat creepy look, but one that told me she was dialed in. Parnell was damned good at this job. I gave her a mischievous grin, because that was how I rolled. She replied with a shake of her head.

"I can already taste the lobster," she said.

"Dream on, Limey. Let's go clean house."

CHAPTER THIRTY

The attic door opened with a small whine, a pitiful cry for WD-40. A dark carpeted staircase emptied onto the second floor landing, where a table lamp finally offered a glimpse into the gloom. I moved against the wall to take the stairs. Parnell followed without a sound, about four steps behind me. We now both had our weapons out, prepared for the inevitable company. At the base of the stairs, I glanced left, then right, then back to the left. We'd need to clear each room.

I turned and nodded at Parnell, who holstered the gun and lifted her phone. She'd dialed in the application that detected the presence of motion detectors. After two quick sweeps, she gave me a thumbs-up, pocketed the phone, and withdrew her gun again.

I nodded to the right. Without a response, she slipped past me and headed that way. I went to the left.

There were three doors at this short end of the hall. The first one was open and revealed a small bathroom. Of the other two doors, one was open to a dark—and empty—bedroom. The knob to the other turned easily in my hand. Once it was unlatched, I pulled a second gun from a zippered pocket of my backpack. This one packed a punch of tranquilizers that would put someone out for at least two or three hours.

I pushed the door open slowly and gazed at a figure stretched out beneath a comforter. The faint light from the hall illuminated a box fan chugging away near the foot of the bed, probably used for white noise. After making sure it was just this lone occupant in the room, I tiptoed over, both barrels trained on the lump. They must've been a light sleeper, because as soon as I sidled up next to them, they sat up with a start.

It was Ceti's robotic food helper. Jan, if I recalled correctly. Now her hair was down and the look on her face showed she was indeed capable of emotion. In this case, astonishment. Before she could cry out, I pointed the Glock at her forehead.

"Sshh," I whispered.

She kept her voice low. "Who are you? What do you want?"

"I wanted to see if you had anything besides haddock, because I lied. I really don't care for it."

Her expression changed to bewilderment, which was replaced yet again with surprise when the tranquilizer dart hit her square in the chest. She fell back onto her pillow and tried to make a sound, but what seeped out sounded mostly like a balloon losing air. I watched as her eyes fluttered then closed.

I pulled the comforter back up to her chin. "Sweet dreams, Julia Child."

Parnell waited for me back at the staircase.

"Anything?" I asked in a low voice.

She shook her head. "A master suite and two guest rooms, all empty. You?"

"House staff. That means all the nasty types must be on the first floor or in the basement. Night owls."

"Makes sense he would do most of his work after hours. Less likely to be caught prowling around a company's site?"

"Maybe. Or the shithead could've left. Which would *really* piss me off."

I pulled out my phone and composed a quick text to our FBI friends waiting a few blocks away. But the message would not send. I tried again. Same response. I held the screen up to my partner.

She studied it, then nodded. "He's put a signal blanket around the house. It probably takes a particular frequency to cut through. Or it's only clear in certain rooms." Then her eyes narrowed. "It might also alert him that we're here."

"Shit," I said and pocketed the phone. Not only could I not reach our backup, but I might've tripped a digital alarm. I cursed myself for not thinking of that.

This time, Parnell took the lead down the stairs. I stayed a few steps back and cast an occasional glance back up the stairs in case someone came out of nowhere. When she was still four steps from the first floor, Parnell checked again for motion sensors. With the house still awake, it wasn't likely. Without a sound or signal, she raised her gun and finished the descent. At the base of the stairs, there was considerably more light.

A door opened around the corner and we both pushed against the wall, waiting. A solitary man strolled into view right next to Parnell, who waited until he passed, then put her Krav Maga training into action. A chop to his windpipe put him on his knees and I put him to sleep with another tranquilizer. Together, we dragged him into an empty room and stashed him behind a couch. I put away the tranquilizer gun; my instinct told me the rest of the night would not involve much stealth.

That came true a minute later.

We must've tripped some sort of alarm, either through a motion detector, or perhaps with my failed effort to contact the FBI. As we returned to the hall, another man burst out from a door 15 feet away. He had a gun in his hand and raised it the moment he saw us. Parnell and I each dropped to a knee and our combined gunfire blew him backward.

And just like that, the covert portion of our incursion was over.

From the same door, a head peered out, then pulled back. A moment later, his hand reached around and fired shots our way. Parnell leapt into the room we'd just vacated, and I dropped to the floor as rounds whizzed over my head. I took aim at the hand sticking out down the hall, but before I could fire, it disappeared again. I began a military crawl down the hall, expecting to see the hand or a head poke out again.

I wasn't disappointed. When he took a chance of leaning out, I put a shot between his eyes and he slumped down, blocking the doorway. Back on my feet, I hustled down to look into the room. There was one other person in there.

Jared Hicks.

It took me a moment to process the scene. He stood against a far wall, leaning over a desk, furiously banging out something on a computer keyboard. But there was a bizarre darkened gap in the wall behind him, and eventually I realized I was looking at an old-fashioned secret passage, the kind I always dreamed about when I was a kid. Leachman had told me that he'd fulfilled some of his childhood fantasies in the home's remodel, so it seemed we had at least a few things in common. Perhaps he had that indoor water slide somewhere, too.

Hicks looked up. He wouldn't recognize me in my latest body, but he must've registered that I was on the opposing team.

I threw a glance back down the hall, but there was no sign of Parnell, which was odd. But she was a pro; if she wasn't here, something must've captured her attention.

I walked toward Hicks, my Glock extended toward his chest. His eyes behind the rectangular glasses grew wide and I saw him throw a quick glance at the panel opening behind him, perhaps gauging whether he could make it through the gap before I shot him.

"Nope," I said, letting him know I'd read his mind. "You can't outrun a bullet, Jared."

He squinted, wondering how I knew his name.

When I reached him, I placed the Glock up under his chin. The barrel got lost in the thick clump of beard and I saw a massive jolt of fear flash into his eyes. No matter how many times you see it on television or in the movies, you can never, ever prepare yourself for the feel of that cold steel against your head. I imagined him pissing his pants a little, which brought me a fair amount of joy.

"Katrina sent me," I said, and he visibly shook. "Yeah, she reached out from the other side. I asked her if she forgave you for putting a bullet in her gut, but she said '*Hell no.*' I mean, I can't blame her. You gotta admit, Jared, that was a chickenshit thing to do, ya goddamned coward. Oh, and then she told me to blow your brains out." I pushed the gun harder against his chin, tilting his head back. He let out a child's whimper. "But I think I'll let you live for now, Jared. As long as you tell me where I can find that skinny boss of yours. Do we have a deal?"

He opened his mouth to speak, but the fear prevented him from forming intelligible words.

"You can do it," I said. "String a couple of syllables together. Where's the boss? Come on, I don't have all night. There are too many other dickheads walking around this place."

As if on cue, the sound of gunfire erupted from down the hall. No doubt Parnell had found herself more action. The sound made Hicks jump, and this time I was convinced we'd find a big urine stain on his pants.

"See what I mean?" I said. "Bad people everywhere. And

when a bunch of people start shooting like that, who knows where a stray bullet will land? So how about it? Where is Tanner?"

Jared managed a large gulp, even with the Glock pressed to his chin. "He's—"

Before he could squeeze out another word, I caught a glimpse of Tough Guy in the doorway I'd come through. Within a second he had his gun raised and pointed right at me. I had no choice but to pull the Glock away from Jared and dive behind the desk. Shots rang out. One slug sent splinters flying from the desk while others slammed into the wall behind me. Jared wasted no time, bolting through the dark opening in the wall. I cursed that the shithead had gotten away, but at the moment I had a more pressing issue to handle.

"Hey," I yelled from behind the desk. "Stop shooting. I'm hit. I—I need help. Don't shoot."

To augment my story, I raised my left hand up in the air.

"Both of 'em," Tough Guy said, and I heard him advancing into the room. "Both hands. Up."

"I can't," I said with a grunt. "That's where I'm hit. It's—it's shattered."

He was now only about 10 or 12 feet away. "All right. Stand up."

Keeping my left hand in the air, I made it look like I was staggering to my feet. He watched me warily, but I could swear there was a half smile on his face. The smile of victory.

It was my pleasure to wipe it right off that ugly mug. In one deft motion, I raised my perfectly fine right hand—the one holding the Glock—and placed a round through his left eye.

I shook my head. "Moron."

I turned to the secret passage behind me, where a dim stairwell faded into inky blackness. This was my priority, but I couldn't just leave my partner behind. I hustled back to the door to the hallway. Without sticking my head through, I called out. "Hey, Limey." There was no sound. I shouted it again, a little louder.

Now I got a response, but it sounded oddly far away.

"Are you hit?" I yelled, still wary of sticking my neck out the door.

It was Parnell's voice answering, but it still sounded too distant for me to make out the words. But she was alive. I mumbled a few choice words about the risk, then spun out the door, my gun raised.

There were two bodies crumpled on the floor, one partly draped over the other. One was the second gunman who'd stood behind Leachman at our impromptu dinner party. Parnell had scored a two-fer. But at what cost?

I chanced calling out to her again. This time I heard her more clearly. I eased down the hallway, hugging one wall, peering through the dim light, both hands around the Glock. I was approaching the room where she'd originally disappeared when I saw the hole.

It was just like the secret panel I'd left behind, only it was in the floor. It was a goddamned trapdoor. After checking each direction for movement, I knelt down.

I could just make her out, a good 12 feet below me, lying on her side. "What the hell, Parnell?"

She looked up. "It's like a carnival funhouse in this place. Although not so much fun for me. This is concrete down here."

"How bad is it?"

"Fractured an ankle for sure. Maybe a cracked elbow. Hurts like hell."

I looked back at the two bodies. "At least you took out the trash before dropping out."

"Yeah." She grimaced. "I think it's remote controlled. There have to be cameras on us right now. Probably mics, too. Watch yourself."

"All right. You okay for now."

She waved me away. "Clean up the mess and then get me some help. Don't leave me down here, wanker."

"Do I still get the steak dinner?"

"Do I look like I've been shot?"

I grinned and got back on my feet. "Hang tight, Limey. I'll be back with help."

Instead of just rushing back into the den with the sliding panel, I slowed and peered around the corner, in case someone had come up the hidden stairwell.

They had. A familiar shape knelt over the body of Tough Guy.

It was Arlo. He'd apparently come up through the secret passage to investigate.

I shook my head. Occasionally I came across people on the wrong side who I genuinely liked. Killing them wasn't something I relished. Parnell had been one of those people, caught up in a bad situation, working for lunatics. Arlo fell into that category, and I regretted what I knew had to happen next. Parnell never worshiped the people she worked for in the first place, which meant she was salvageable; Arlo would fight to the death, and I instinctively knew it.

Before he could get back to his feet, I spun around and aimed the Glock at him. "Hello, Arlo," I said.

He looked up, stunned that Tough Guy's killer had come back so soon. But he didn't try to stand, and he didn't let go of the weapon in his hand.

After recovering from the surprise, he said, "We've met?"

"Sort of. In another life."

A little smile crept across his face. "Another life? I'm afraid I don't believe in that stuff." He still didn't let go of his weapon.

"I didn't either until I tried it a few times." I pointed my gun at his. "I'm gonna need you to set that down. Save us a lot of pain and anguish. Pain for you, anguish for me."

He worked his jaw a little, probably still fighting through a lot of pain. "You do seem familiar. But I never forget a face, and yours is coming up blank."

I returned the smile. "I wasn't kidding about that past life. But I've got work to do, so why don't you carefully set that down and you can ride out the rest of tonight's action in the safety of some handcuffs. Deal?"

He raised an eyebrow. "Then ride out the next 20 years in a cell. Not much of a deal, would you agree?"

"Well, we could have a long talk about consequences, but I'm sure this isn't the time. What I know for a fact is that I need to go down that staircase behind you. I'm assuming your boss is hiding in that rathole, correct?"

"What's your name?" he asked.

"Arlo, if I told you my name, you wouldn't believe me." I paused. "You're going to make this difficult, aren't you?"

He gave a slight shrug and opened his mouth to answer. But at that moment he quickly raised his gun hand. I'd been expecting it the whole time.

I put him down.

"Dammit," I muttered under my breath. "Stupid son of a bitch."

After pausing for a moment, I stepped around the two corpses and the copious volume of blood. I tried my best to not look down at what I'd done.

Tried and failed. At the open panel, I stopped and looked back at the body of Arlo Benn. His eyes were open, which bothered me for some reason. They'd been a warm brown, with a softness that didn't seem to fit someone who killed for a living. Now, they simply wore a look of surprise, staring at nothing and yet every-thing. At any other time, and probably with any other victim, I wouldn't have cared. This was different, and the difference alone disturbed me. Guilt is not a trait that serves an assassin well.

I stepped back, knelt down, looking at those eyes. "Stupid son of a bitch," I whispered again, not entirely sure I was speaking to Arlo. Then, with a quick movement, I pulled his eyelids down and turned back to the passageway.

CHAPTER THIRTY-ONE

After loading a fresh magazine into the Glock, I took a centering breath and shone my phone's flashlight into the murky stairwell. It had all the makings of a trap. If there were sliding panels and trap doors up here, what awaited in the dungeon below?

But then, this narrow passageway was never meant to be found. This was a refuge, not a defensive bunker. I had to remember that Ceti's specialty was digital warfare—the quiet war Katrina had mentioned. He naively relied upon hired guns, never really believing that *he'd* be the target of an incursion. Enemies of the state who fought with traditional weapons had the presence of mind to fortify their positions because that was their background. Ceti wouldn't think that way.

Of course, I was betting my life on this. But I bet my life on a regular basis, and right now I just didn't have time to poke along.

Reaching into my backpack, I retrieved the night-vision goggles again. These, too, had been improved in the last few years, providing a sharp, crystal clear image. Holding the Glock up by my ear, I picked my way down the curving steps, each of my senses on high alert. I realized I appreciated the well-tuned condition of this new body. After every few steps, I'd stop and listen for even the slightest sound, peering ahead, wondering what might lie just around the curve. I even sniffed the air like a dog, alert for any change.

Don't laugh. Sniffing the air actually saved one of my lives. Here's a pro tip for wannabe villains: Lay off the cologne.

A sound made me freeze. It could've been a footstep, but it didn't repeat. Whoever was down here knew I was coming. Hicks would've been nearly hysterical when he burst in, so there certainly was no element of surprise. That had evaporated once the first gunshots rang out.

I edged ahead until I noticed a soft light. Pulling the goggles down around my neck, I crouched and leaned cautiously around the bend. I saw an open door with a short hallway beyond, then a closed door at the far end. Hicks would be in there. I assumed Leachman was, too. But what dangers lurked in that seemingly innocent corridor? I pulled back out of sight, and, leaning against the wall, considered my options.

There weren't many. And every second I spent contemplating them, Leachman was punching keys.

I pulled off the goggles and stashed them in the backpack. Then, taking a deep breath, I pushed off the wall and took a few steps into the hallway. The moment I entered, the lights brightened considerably. Part of Leachman's fancy design: the high-tech home.

My guess had been correct. I reached the far end without being assaulted. This was Ceti's private work space; Arlo and his henchmen had been deemed sufficient protection. Unless another gunman awaited inside, they all were now either unconscious or dead.

I placed a hand on the doorknob. It was locked. There was only one remedy.

With a powerful kick, the door flew open and splintered off

the top hinge. I'd dropped to a crouch, gun extended, only to find a solitary figure seated in the middle of a horseshoe-shaped workstation. He was frozen, gaping at me, both hands resting on a keyboard.

It was Tanner Leachman. Four supersized monitors played a symphony around him. The rest of the room was nondescript. The walls were bare, slathered with your typical eggshell white, the carpet perfunctory. There were no other pieces of furniture in the room other than the workstations and a single armchair, which seemed more of an afterthought. This was Ceti's nerve center, the nucleus of his war machine, and required no frills.

Pulling off a small computer headset, Leachman studied me. He wore an amused expression now. It was an odd reaction—but everything about the man and his fun house seemed odd.

"I have no idea who you are," he finally said. "But you're too late."

With that, he went back to work, tapping a few keys, unfazed by the interruption. I had to give him credit for courage. As my grandmother would say, he had '*starch*.'

But I had the gun.

"Please take your hands away, Mr. Leachman. I could just shoot the monitor in front of you, but that would be a waste, and overly dramatic for my taste. Besides, if I'm too late, there shouldn't be anything left for you to do. Except gloat, I guess. I can tolerate that."

He paused, and from the side I saw the crooked smile. "Nothing you do now will stop what I've begun. Besides—" He hit one key with a flourish, then turned back to face me. "—neither of you will shoot."

As he said this, I felt the presence of someone else in the room. Looking to my left, I saw Jared Hicks. He'd slipped in from an adjoining room. The house had gone from being delightfully eccentric to just plain irritating. The only thing for certain was that while I had a gun trained on Leachman, Hicks had a gun pointed at me. It wouldn't have surprised me if it was the same one he'd used to kill Katrina.

I kept my eyes on Hicks while talking to Leachman. "What makes you say that?"

"You're probably with the FBI, and you have rules. Can't just storm in and shoot an unarmed man." He threw a glance at his employee. "And Jared is one of the weakest men I've ever known. All brash and beard. But no balls."

Jared winced at this, and his lips moved beneath the hair.

"Just drop it," I said to Jared. "You can still walk out of here. But if you kill a federal agent, there's no guarantee what the others parked outside the house will do when they come crashing in."

Leachman chuckled. "See? Those are the balls I wish Jared had. Bluffing in the face of death."

"No bluff," I said. "Once you guys killed Katrina and left Swan for dead—which was a monumental mistake—you pretty much sealed the deal. Now, both of you, let's take a walk upstairs. You'll have to step over some pretty gruesome carnage, but that just shows you that you're not playing with amateurs here."

Leachman's smile remained on his face, but his eyes narrowed. "I'm impressed." Then, with a sigh, he turned his attention to Hicks. "Jared, if you're not going to use the gun, just put it down before you shoot yourself by accident." He looked back at me. "I should've kept Samantha around instead. At least she had the proper nerve, and it pained me to have her killed. But I liked the idea of Jared working so closely with the federal government. He was just inept enough to make you suspicious, but not skilled enough to know exactly what I was doing. So if he was caught, there wouldn't be much he could do to hurt me. He didn't even know about this house until yesterday."

Then Leachman laughed. "If I could've turned Katrina? Well,

that would've been a coup. She was always the brain of their business." He looked again at Hicks. "And now she's dead."

Hicks was visibly shaking, and I knew something bad was about to happen. But I'd gambled on the fact that shooting Katrina had produced the same effect in him I'd seen countless times. Shooting someone in cold blood seems easy enough when you watch it in a movie. And yes, in rare cases it sometimes whets an appetite that leads to more killing; we call those people psychopaths and serial killers. But for everyone else, the taking of an innocent life isn't glamorous, not the way it's portrayed in fiction. It changes a person. Murder, in a way, kills both people: one physically, the other emotionally.

Hicks hadn't known that when he'd pulled the trigger in the guest house. But I'd seen his face just before he walked out of the room, while his girlfriend—fake girlfriend or not—had crumpled to the floor. I read him immediately and knew that the shot, which had seemed so easy to do in the moment, would echo through his skull for the rest of his life.

And I had a feeling, even as frightened as he was right now, that he'd be loath to pull the trigger a second time, especially against a federal agent, and most especially at the behest of a man who was emasculating him.

I decided to press my advantage. Staring at Leachman, I said, "Tell me about your landmines."

This time, his face registered real shock. The smile disappeared and his mouth drooped open. After a moment, he composed himself. "Well. If I hadn't cloaked this house in every electronic piece of security you could find, I'd say I've been bugged. Where did you hear about these '*landmines*?'"

I glanced from him to Jared and back again. "If we're going to have a friendly chat, how about we all lower our weapons? Agreed?"

Leachman chewed his lip, then nodded at Hicks, who slowly

lowered his gun to his side. As much as he trembled, I was thankful. A wobbly trigger finger tends to distract me from my business.

"Your problem," I said to Leachman, "is that you stay cocooned in this digital fortress of yours, spinning your little web of terror. You make grandiose proclamations about '*saving for a rainy year*,' which is rather corny. You see the results on a screen, and you bask in the online worship of a few sycophants and other misguided losers, people who always equate contrarian behavior with courage. Which is bullshit.

"But while you see these reactions spilling across your screen, you *don't* see the faces of the people you're terrorizing. And when you don't see that? When you can't look into the eyes of the people you hurt? Well, you develop a false sense of dominance, Tanner. You watch the damage scroll across in ones and zeroes and you read the text of mouth-breathing morons who see you as a hero. And all of that pushes you further and further away from reality."

I nodded toward Hicks. "Now Jared, here. He's looked into the face of someone as he gunned them down. He didn't do it with a computer mouse. He wasn't playing a video game. He pointed that gun and pulled the trigger, and *witnessed* the damage in real time. You think he's weak?" I grunted a laugh. "The only reason he may be reluctant to kill again is because he's seen firsthand what it's like. Just like I've seen it, time and time again. Jared's a coward because he killed an innocent, unarmed woman. But you, Tanner? You're a pathetic scumbag who hides behind a computer monitor and an alias, causing unspeakable pain for millions of people. Who faked his death while he was busy killing others. Worse than a coward."

I let that linger before adding, "So, no, asshole; I don't think I'll share any more information with you." I took a step toward him. "I want you to tell me about your landmines. And if you don't, we'll see just how much pain *you* can stand."

He didn't move, but his right eye twitched. With my peripheral vision, I noticed Hicks shifting uncomfortably from one foot to another. Again, I got the feeling shit was about to go down.

Finally, Leachman spoke, his voice a beastly growl. "You can't manipulate me. You've killed people face-to-face? And you think that somehow makes you a *nobler* killer than I am?" He pointed a finger at me. "You talk about that worm over there, Jared, and how killing someone has made him reluctant to do it again. Well, what does that say about you? You've experienced it, just like he has, but *you* don't shy away from it. You rush back in. You might justify it by saying it's your job, or that you've built up some kind of emotional callousness. Is that what you do? Is that how you live with yourself? Is that how you walk through the *carnage* you say you left upstairs?"

He looked at Hicks for a moment with utter disdain before turning his gaze back to me. "The difference between us is that you kill simply because someone tells you to. They point and snap their fingers and you jump to serve them. I, at least, have a mission, something I believe in. I don't care whether or not you find it justified or honorable. I'm doing what I think is right; you only do what you're told to do. You're a pawn. A deadly pawn. And one that probably doesn't even understand what it's doing half the time. So you can stop with the sanctimonious performance. We have different motivations, but we're no different. All three of us in this room have killed. Jared will never pull the trigger again because he's spineless. You and I most certainly will."

I stared at him, unwilling to flinch, to show him just how close to the mark his words hit. For a full half minute, the room was quiet, the three of us locked into some dark, disgusting showdown.

And then, behind me and up the stairs, I heard shouting. The FBI must've finally busted in.

Leachman heard it, too. He spun around in his chair and began furiously typing something, perhaps priming the fuse for whatever landmines he'd placed. All I could think to do was to follow through with my earlier threat. I raised the Glock and fired a shot into the monitor, which erupted in splintered glass and sparks. Leachman threw his hands up to protect his face.

At the same time, Hicks finally broke free from his paralysis. He raised his own gun, perhaps out of panic, but it left me no choice. I whipped around, dropping to a knee, and put a shot into his chest. It threw him back against the wall behind him, his eyes wide.

But I realized those eyes weren't trained on me. He stared at Tanner Leachman. And, as he began to slump toward the floor, he quickly raised his arm again. I fired a second time, but it was simultaneous with the shot Jared Hicks squeezed off. My round struck Hicks directly in the heart and he toppled to the floor.

I turned to see what had become of the shot he'd fired.

Tanner Leachman sprawled backward in his chair, his chin resting on his chest. A string of blood oozed from a neat bullet hole in his forehead.

CHAPTER THIRTY-TWO

Parnell's hospital bed was cranked so that she sat almost upright, holding a carton of juice with her good arm and sucking it down through a straw. A cast stretched from her foot to just below her right knee while another wrapped most of her right arm.

"Kind of pointless to do surgery on your ankle, don't you think?" I asked, sitting in one of those uncomfortable chairs that hospitals make sure to place in each room. "Shouldn't they just have put you into a new body?"

She set down the carton on the tray before her. "They're not meant to be disposable just for convenience's sake, Swan. Besides, I like this one. It won't take me that long to heal. Have a little respect for the merchandise."

"Whatever you say. Does it hurt?"

"Like bloody hell without the meds. You met with Quanta yet?"

I shook my head. "I'm flying back to DC as soon as I leave here. Unless you need me to stay in Vermont and babysit you."

"If you want to know the truth, I'm actually looking forward to the down time. Not that I don't enjoy your company, but I intend to read, watch horrible telly, and sleep."

"Sounds good."

"Liar."

I laughed. "Yeah, all right. Sounds horrible to me. But whatever brings you joy, Parnell."

She paused for a moment, then said, "You doing okay? I mean, the way it eventually came down?"

My smile faded away. "Oh. Sure." I looked out the window of her hospital room in the direction of the sunset over Lake Champlain. While I'd waited to see Parnell, one of the nurses had told me it was really the sixth Great Lake but just never got any respect.

Parnell let me off with my lame response, probably because she knew my debriefing with Quanta would open up plenty. And whatever the boss failed to get out of me, my upcoming meeting with Miller would likely dig it out.

The British agent took another swig of juice, then said, "You probably told me this when they pulled me out of that concrete bunker, but I was in too much pain to fully comprehend. Did you terminate Leachman?"

"No. I wanted him alive. He had way too much information we could use. Not just the shit he's done the last few years, but his association with the Arcetri. I have no proof, but I'm sure they're just getting up to speed. You and I will bump into them down the road, I know it."

"So if it wasn't you—"

"Hicks. The last thing he did was to prove to Leachman he had the balls to kill again."

But I knew that wasn't really the full story. In my mind, Jared Hicks had been a tortured soul for a long, long time. Unsure of his role in Ceti's world, uncomfortable in his role as a lover and partner with Katrina Yu, he'd stumbled along. I think the decision to eliminate Katrina blew his final fuse. His assassination of Tanner Leachman might have somehow been a last ditch effort to right all the wrongs he'd accumulated through the years. A final lunge to balance the universe's books.

We'll never know, but it felt like the right answer to me.

Neither Parnell nor I could think of what else to say, so I wished her well and made my exit.

But not before grabbing a black marker and drawing the image of a swan on her arm cast.

WE PASSED on the usual workout in Quanta's garden and instead sipped cucumber water at the round table in her kitchen nook. A cocktail sounded better, but that would have to wait until I got home.

She looked tired. The last few weeks had put a strain on everyone, but I think Quanta's trans-Atlantic trips played a big part in her weariness, and not just because of the air travel or jet lag. She'd been under enormous pressure from multiple government agencies this time, and she was forced to not only direct an investigation through her own department, but to also play diplomat with our allies.

It was at times like this I remembered Quanta was no longer a young woman. Perhaps the years had begun wearing her down. She was an icon in the international intelligence world, proclaimed by many of the greatest field agents of the last half century, but now reduced to the role of administrator. It was like the world-champion athlete who, after so many years at the top of her game, suddenly stood on the sidelines, coaching. I guess that would make anyone go gray, mostly out of heartbreak.

She finished a sip of the water and eyed me. "This turned out to be a rather bloody affair. Bloodier than I think anyone expected."

I couldn't tell if this was a simple observation or an indictment.

"I don't see it getting any better," I said. "It's a world of escalation. *Everything* escalates. No one is content anymore to unleash chaos unless they somehow raise the bar on the misery they produce. It's the dark, mirror image of people fretting over how many followers they get on social media, or how many 'likes' they get. Evil keeps its own scorecard. Why should we expect it any other way?"

"What a cynical view of the world."

"Cynical? Detached emotionally, maybe. But not cynical. Just realistic. It keeps me from becoming depressed."

I looked out the window into her garden. It was a sunny day, which, after days of cool, rainy weather, called to me. It was the tonic I needed at the moment.

"What's the update on Leachman's plan?" I asked. "His '*land-mines*,' as he put it."

She locked her fingers together in front of her. "Still unknown. Once he knew his time was up, it gave him the opportunity to destroy any way of tracing his work. Everything was wiped in a way that's making it difficult for the people on the second floor."

"But they *can* get in and find these triggers, right?"

"We hope so."

I sat back in my chair. *Hope* was never a good strategy when it came to intelligence work and national security. For a few moments, I imagined Ceti's landmines being more like ticking time bombs, set to go off and unleash their payload of destruction when no one suspected it. Perhaps after we'd all forgotten about it. That would be something I could see Tanner Leachman doing: striking back from beyond the grave.

It gave me a shiver knowing the ax might still be hanging over our heads.

"You know," I said, "Two other things for us to consider. When I mentioned the people he'd had killed, Leachman said, 'Oh, they're not all dead.' Which made it sound like some of his disciples might still be around to continue his work."

Quanta nodded. "And the other thing to consider?"

"Katrina had an idea that Ceti would sell his services to some foreign power. She thought everything he was constructing would someday be auctioned to the highest bidder. Of course, we don't know if he ever got that far. For all I know, that furious typing he was doing at the end might've been part of some wicked arrangement. But if Katrina was right, his little landmines might be in someone else's control as we speak."

Quanta fell silent, considering this. I knew she'd make it a priority as soon as I left her house. The CIA, I imagined, would be looped in, since Q2 rarely did work overseas. I wondered if that might change in the near future.

After a while, she looked at me and her tone softened a little. "And how did this assignment affect you?"

"As long as it took for us to make headway, I'd like to say it taught me patience. But I'm not sure that's in my nature."

She shook her head. "You know that's not what I mean."

I stared at her for a long time, but she never broke eye contact. These types of discussions were becoming more frequent with my boss.

"Don't worry," I said. "I'm going to chat with Miller after I leave here."

"That's good. But you can still answer the question."

"How did it affect me? Well . . . I don't think anyone should live a life of fear, but we're starting to paint ourselves into that corner. As more and more of these incursions take place, as more people are victimized by identity theft and attacked with ransomware, we'll all get to the point where the villains will essentially hack our minds."

Quanta pursed her lips. "That's an interesting way of phrasing it."

"It's true. The definition of hacking is '*gaining unauthorized access*.' Well, isn't that what they're accomplishing by terrorizing us? It's not just unauthorized access to our data; we're letting them hack our peace of mind." I paused. "And, really, who would know more about getting their mind hacked than me?"

She didn't comment.

"But the other way this case affected me? It pissed me off. Tanner Leachman was another insecure, vulnerable person who was an easy recruit for the Arcetri. Someone they could lure in because he had a sob story. Then they fanned those flames until he not only felt that he *could* strike back at the world, but that he *should* strike back. This group has now established a track record of inciting troubled people into becoming dangerous ones. Murderous ones. And that, too, is only going to escalate, Quanta. They won't stop until the world as we know it is in flames."

She took another drink. "What's the solution?"

It was a good question, and I told her so. "We can't keep waiting and reacting every time another one of their disciples ventures out to punish the big, mean world. Maybe—" I stopped to put my thoughts into order. "Maybe we could go on the offensive with the Arcetri."

"Infiltrate," she said.

I nodded. "Although that might not be the proper term. The ones we've spoken to make it clear there are no official meetings. I get the impression the rank and file members don't even know how many other people are associated with them. Which is actually a brilliant way of running things. They're about the most disorganized organization you'll find, and that serves them. Makes it damned near impossible to sneak inside."

She paused. "Damned *near*. But not actually impossible."

After a moment, I gave in to the smile forcing itself upon me.

"Oh, Quanta. You'll always find some new way to get me killed, won't you?"

I KEPT MY WORD. Leaving Quanta's suburban retreat, I made my way toward Q2 headquarters, an unremarkable, characterless building in DC. It would take a while, time I used to call Christina.

"How's the hitchhiker?"

She laughed. "Kicking, as usual. Tired of the ride, I think."

"Yeah, what about you? You ready for the big show?"

"Hey, whenever it happens. I want this cake to be perfectly baked before it comes out."

I grinned. "Then this child is in the right hands. The world's best chef will prepare a masterpiece."

"You're very sweet. I take it you're back in Washington?"

"How can you tell?"

"Your tone is different when a case is over. Well, your voice is different now, too, which means I should expect a new face walking in, I suppose. They must've sent you right back out when you picked up the new host."

"It's true. You'll like this one, I think. But if not, too bad."

We caught up for a few minutes without me going into detail about Vermont. She wouldn't want to know, anyway. Instead, she gave me the lowdown on life at the restaurant and how two nice gentlemen had changed a tire for her on the side of the road.

It was a little thing, something you'd usually just acknowledge and then move on. But I knew this brief story would be another one of those incidents that stayed with me for some time. Another case of my wife needing to turn to others because her husband was away. Again. It gnawed at me, but I kept the despair to myself.

Of course, Christina is totally capable of looking after herself.

But she's also nearly to term with a pregnancy and I'd kinda like to be the knight every once in a while. Based on the way my conversation with Quanta had ended, I didn't see me galloping to Christina's rescue anytime soon. The country's maybe, but not my wife's.

I grew silent for a moment and she clearly picked up on my feelings. "How about we go out tonight?"

"Really?" I said. "You don't have to work?"

"I don't want to work tonight. I want to take my superhero husband out to dinner."

I laughed. "It's good to be the boss, I guess."

"You damned right."

It was the same chair I sat in every time, but I liked the view it provided to the outside world. I'm sure Miller was aware of that and he happily obliged. Anything to keep me comfortable and to keep me talking.

Which wasn't that much of a struggle anymore. I was no longer a word miser.

"I'm sorry about what happened with Katrina," Miller said. "After working together for a while, you must've grown close."

I thought about that. "You know, for a few days, I was convinced she was the mole. It didn't make sense to me that the guy I pegged from the start would actually be the asshole. Seemed too . . . predictable."

"He wasn't as good of an actor as you."

"I am pretty good, aren't I?" Then I lapsed into silence for a bit. Miller let me swim in the memory of those last few minutes with Katrina. He didn't need to know particulars, and I wasn't likely to ever share those with anyone.

"Anyway," I finally said, "sometimes we're actors because we want to fool ourselves as much as we want to fool others."

He gave a nod. "I agree. I know some of the ways you admit you're trying to fool yourself. What about this mission? Anything you want to say about your suicide? Did it bring anything else bubbling to the surface that you'd like to gloss over?"

"That's a helluva way to put it, Doc."

"I'm in blunt mode today. So answer the question."

He gave me time to sit there and ponder. I studied the scene outside his window, catching sight of an aircraft's vapor trail. The condensation held its form for a few seconds before gradually drifting apart, disintegrating before my eyes, eventually leaving no sign that the jet had been there.

I kept my eyes on the sky when I finally answered him.

"When I was a kid, I had a favorite mystery series I liked to read. Three kids, getting into tough scrapes while they solved mysteries. But that's not important. Years later, when I was an adult, I came across some piece the author of those books had written about nature and second chances. I never forgot it. His name was Robert Arthur, and he said something along the lines of, '*Nature is inflexible and remorseless.*'"

I could hear Miller scribbling something on his pad again, which normally irked me. This time I was glad he did.

"He was trying to get across this notion that giving second chances is a purely human concept. We're famous for giving second chances, really. Someone does something horrible, they go on national TV and shed some tears, and we tend to give them a break. Or if your kid does something wrong, you lecture them and give them a second chance to make it right.

"But Arthur was saying that nature doesn't give life a second chance. When an animal makes a mistake, it almost always pays for it with its life. Entire species, too, for that matter. No second chances."

I turned to look at Miller. "After Jared Hicks killed Ceti, I did two things. I went back upstairs and helped the FBI get Parnell out of that concrete trap she'd fallen into. And then I walked over to the guest house and broke into its basement room."

Miller remained quiet, studying my face.

"I found Katrina on the couch where I'd left her. I spent a few moments just looking into her face. I even told her I was sorry I hadn't kept her from . . . from getting killed. And then I—"

I never cried during sessions with Miller. This time I felt the tears coming on. I let them fall without wiping them away.

"I walked into the bathroom and found what I'd left behind. Found my old body, slumped in a . . . in a disgusting pool of blood. And I just knelt down, Miller. Knelt down and stared at that pale white face. Thought about the decision to throw that life away in order to come back and try to make things right."

When I grew silent, Miller spoke in a soft voice. "And you know it was the right decision for that specific situation. It was all you could do."

"Yeah. All I could do. Because I knew I'd get that next chance. I could continue to be the freak that I am, the freak that defies nature's rule of no second chances. I get chance after chance after chance."

Another pause. Then Miller said, "We defy nature in a lot of ways, Swan."

"Not like this."

"No, but—"

"I've spent years taking advantage of these chances. One, to serve my country, and I don't regret that at all. But two, for my own raging curiosity. My own search for meaning, or whatever the hell you wanna call it. I've often thought of myself as that freak. But when I knelt in that bathroom, looking at the person I'd been, the goddamned human being I'd discarded for *a job* . . . well, it made me wonder if I'm not just a freak, but a criminal in my own way. Breaking nature's law, the ultimate law, really."

He didn't answer, and I didn't expect him to. The whole idea of these sessions was for me to expunge the dark, ugly remnants left over from my transitions between one body to the next. I'd ignored those toxic remains for a long time; lately they'd forced their way to the surface, and I was no longer shy about voicing them, even at the risk of being removed from the program. I'm sure it only added to Miller's earlier suspicion about my so-called death wish, but that was out of my control.

There was more here. Miller knew it. I knew it. There were other layers waiting to be exposed, and I had a grim feeling they'd get bleaker the further down I went. But the journey was inevitable.

I looked outside again and finally wiped the back of a hand across my eyes.

* * *

Need more Swan? Stand by, the thrilling sixth adventure, *Arms Race*, is coming soon.
To be alerted as soon as it's ready, just turn the page and join the Swaniverse.

Reviews are crucial for indie authors. If you enjoyed this book, please take a few seconds to leave a review. And thank you.

Join the Swaniverse.
Get cool stuff.

How did Quanta ever find Swan in the first place?

Learn how it happened, and follow Swan on his very first caper for Q2. It doesn't exactly go as planned.

Join the Swaniverse and you'll get Swan's *Origin* story as my gift to you. Plus, you'll be the first to learn of each new adventure *before* they're published. Just let me know where to find you.

Two ways to make it happen. Scan this QR code with your phone's camera and it'll take you to the Swaniverse page to sign up.

Or log on to EricSwan.com.

Thanks, and happy reading.
Dom Testa

More Eric Swan from Dom Testa

Power Trip: Eric Swan Thriller #1

Swan takes on diabolical twins determined to bring down the power grid. If he fails, the country will slip into a dark age of chaos and anarchy.

Poison Control: Eric Swan Thriller #2

A treacherous madman is intent on poisoning the water supply. Swan must outsmart this rogue scholar before he can release his apocalyptic toxin.

God Maker: Eric Swan Thriller #3

Agent One has resurfaced, and he's kidnapped the mother of Q2's investment technology. Swan must not only battle this psychotic killer, but come to grips with his own fears.

Field Agent: Eric Swan Thriller #4

Swan's on the hunt for a tech billionaire who's out to control the world's food supply. But there's a sinister element to the plan with terrifying consequences.

Reviews matter.
They really do.

Reviews are critical for independent authors like me.

We don't have mega-publishers in New York or London pumping millions of dollars into promoting our work.

What we do have . . . is you. And you're very important to us.

One honest review from you can do so much to help an indie author. People *do* read them, and they *do* make decisions based on them.

So please, let other thriller fans know what you thought of Eric Swan. It's very appreciated.

Dom Testa

www.ingramcontent.com/pod-product-compliance
Lightning Source LLC
Chambersburg PA
CBHW050745190726
48285CB00005B/1529